# 美国缪斯:诗与诗论

# American Muses: Poetry and Poetics

耿纪永 编著

同济大学出版社
TONGJI UNIVERSITY PRESS

## 内容提要

本书选取美国文学中在理论上最具创新意识、实践中开一代诗风的代表诗人 25 家，诗作 100 余首，诗论 12 篇，集作品与诗学批评于一体，可供高年级本科生、研究生英诗选读和美国诗歌与诗论等课程选做教材，亦是一部美国诗歌研究的重要参考书。

**图书在版编目(CIP)数据**

美国缪斯：诗与诗论：汉、英/耿纪永编著. --上海：同济大学出版社，2016.7

ISBN 978-7-5608-6347-4

Ⅰ.①美… Ⅱ.①耿… Ⅲ.①诗歌研究—美国—汉、英 Ⅳ.①I712.072

中国版本图书馆 CIP 数据核字(2016)第 123110 号

**美国缪斯：诗与诗论**

耿纪永 **编著**

**责任编辑** 吴凤萍 **助理编辑** 戴如月 **责任校对** 徐春莲 **封面设计** 张 微

出版发行 同济大学出版社 www.tongjipress.com.cn

(地址：上海市四平路 1239 号 邮编：200092 电话：021-65985622)

经 销 全国各地新华书店

印 刷 同济大学印刷厂

开 本 787mm×1 092mm 1/16

印 张 21.75

字 数 543 000

版 次 2016 年 7 月第 1 版 2016 年 7 月第 1 次印刷

书 号 ISBN 978-7-5608-6347-4

定 价 48.00 元

# 前　言

美国诗歌的历史，如果从安妮·布拉德斯特里特（Anne Bradstreet，1612—1672）1650年出版的《近来北美出现的第十位缪斯》算起，只有300多年，然而却涌现出了惠特曼、狄金森、庞德、艾略特、威廉斯及金斯堡等众多举世公认的一流诗人，在诗歌大国——中国也拥有众多的读者。因此，国内大多数高校也都开设了诸如“美国诗歌”或“英美诗歌”的研究生或本科生相关课程。

目前，关于美国诗歌的教材基本上沿用了过去国内英美文学教材编写的路子，主要是提供了诗歌文本和一些注释或简评，往往缺少诗人创作理论和诗歌批评的内容。本书编者根据为研究生和本科生开设“美国诗歌”和“英语诗歌”课程的实际需要出发，选取了25家代表诗人的100余首诗作，除了通常教材所包含的内容（如诗人简介、诗歌文本、注释及题解等）外，特别增加了两个部分：一是选取了12位独具创新意识的诗人的12篇诗论；二是为每个单元设计了“研究指南”，选介国内外最具代表性的评论观点，以期加深对诗歌的理解，同时也为进一步研究提供指引。

本书作为一本教材，虽算不上科研成果，但囿于编者的学识、资料等限制，如果没有一些师友的鼓励和帮助恐难完成。本书在成书前以讲义的形式曾在我院研究生和本科生教学中试用。2012年10月在同济大学主办的全国美国文学年会上，南京大学的张子清教授建议编者将讲义整理出版。2013年加州大学伯克利分校的著名诗人、学者罗伯特·哈斯教授，欣然邀请本人到该校作为访问学者从事美国诗歌研究，本人得以利用伯克利丰富的藏书，充实和修订了部分内容。在本书编写过程中，我的研究生张洁、刘恒、朱龙梅及姜建建等，在题解撰写、文字录用等方面也协助做了不少工作，在此一并表示感谢。最后还要感谢上海市教委科研创新项目（13ZS022）和同济大学研究生院为本书的编写和出版提供了及时的资助，感谢同济大学出版社编辑老师的辛勤付出。

由于本人学识有限，该书的错误与不足在所难免，欢迎读者批评指正，以期今后改正和完善。

编　者

2016年6月

# Contents

# 1. Anne Bradstreet (1612–1672)

## Introduction

Anne Bradstreet was born in Northampton, England, daughter of a gentlewoman named Dorothy Yorke and of Thomas Dudley, a nonconformist minister who managed the business interests of the earl of Lincoln. Educated by private tutors in the earl's households, she married Simon Bradstreet, a future governor of the Massachusetts Bay Colony, in 1628. In 1630, Bradstreet immigrated to America with her husband and parents. When she first came to the colonies, she "found a new world and new manners," as she later remembered. "But after I was convinced it was the way of God I submitted to it and joined to the church of Boston." While caring for her growing family (she had eight children), she continued to write. A volume of poems was published in London in 1650. Entitled *The Tenth Muse Lately Sprung Up in America*, the book was published by Bradstreet's brother-in-law without her knowledge (or so he claimed). It sold very well; a second edition, containing numerous corrections and additions, appeared six years after her death.

Anne Bradstreet was considered by many to be the first American poet. Her poetry was mostly based on her life experience, and her love for her husband and family. Her style is deceptively simple, yet speaks of a woman of high intelligence and ideals who was very much in love, and had unconditional faith. While it was difficult for women to air their views in the 17th Century, Anne Bradstreet did so with ease, as her rich vocabulary and polyvalent knowledge brought a lyrical, yet logical quality to her work which made it pleasant for anyone to read.

# Selected Reading A

## The Author to Her Book

Thou[1] ill-formed offspring[2] of my feeble brain,
Who after birth didst[3] by my side remain,
Till snatched from thence by friends, less wise than true,
Who thee[4] abroad, exposed to public view,
Made thee in rags, halting to th'[5] press to trudge,
Where errors were not lessened (all may judge).
At thy[6] return my blushing was not small,
My rambling brat[7](in print) should mother call,
I cast thee by as one unfit for light,
Thy visage[8] was so irksome[9] in my sight;
Yet being mine own, at length affection would
Thy blemishes amend, if so I could.
I washed thy face, but more defects I saw,
And rubbing off a spot still made a flaw.
I stretched thy joints to make thee even feet[10],
Yet still thou run'st[11] more hobbling than is meet;
In better dress to trim thee was my mind,
But nought[12] save home-spun cloth, i'[13] th'[14] house I find.

---

① thou: you.

② Note that she considers her poetry to be her child, a metaphor which runs throughout the poem which perhaps only a fond mother would have used. Certainly no male writer at the time would have developed such a metaphor.

③ didst: did.

④ thee: you.

⑤ th': the.

⑥ thy: your.

⑦ brat: child; specifically an ill-mannered annoying child.

⑧ visage: face, appearance. This extended metaphor of washing the face of her poems is a marvelous example of the tedious process of revision.

⑨ irksome: wearisome.

⑩ feet: pun on metrical feet, meaning that she wanted to make the meter more regular.

⑪ run'st: run.

⑫ nought: nothing.

⑬ i': in.

⑭ th': the.

In this array 'mongst① vulgars② mayst③ thou roam.
In critic's hands, beware thou dost④ not come,
And take thy way where yet thou art⑤ not known;
If for thy father asked, say, thou hadst⑥ none;
And for thy mother, she alas is poor,
Which caused her thus to send thee out of door.

## About the Selection

《作者致自己的诗集》写于作者第一本书发表之后,叙述了作者因作品未经同意而出版,而产生不安的情感。通过拟人和隐喻的修辞方法,作者把这本书喻为一个孩子,便于读者对这首诗的复杂情感有一个完整的理解。对这本书了解和指导的需要,好似一个父母必须照顾和抚养一个孩子。有时羞愧和爱会伴随着一个不完美的孩子,但这一切最终会在作品产生之后烟消云散。随着诗歌的发展,作者也由不安、懊悔转向骄傲,但最后还是以悔恨收尾。

## Research Guide

1. In "The Author to her Book," a poem about the book published in 1650 as *The Tenth Muse, Lately Sprung up in American*, Bradstreet identifies her book as her child. In so doing, she recognizes the authority Puritan mothers exercised in criticizing their children, while demonstrating her power as a writer by criticizing her book as if it were a child. In conformity with the Puritan ideal of female humility, Bradstreet apologizes for the imperfections of her own that are manifest in her child — "Thou ill-form'd offspring of my feeble brain" — and in conformity with the Puritan mode of harshly affectionate mothering, she recalls how hard she worked to improve her child — "I stretcht thy joynts to make thee even feet." (Porterfield 1992: 114)

2. In "The Author to Her Book" the sexualized language is evident from the beginning, as Bradstreet evokes the common convention among Renaissance writers — the metaphor of reproduction. [...] Bradstreet extends the metaphor of the poem as her child by using language to personify the poem as a body, but the image of "joynts" and "feet" also refers to the technical features of lyrical poetry, a poetic form often written in iambic pentameter, with rhyming stanza patterns where "feet" measure the accented and unaccented syllables in a single line. [...] By claiming and flaunting responsibility for

---

① 'mongst: amongst, among.
② vulgar: common people; average readers.
③ mayst: may.
④ dost: do.
⑤ art: are.
⑥ hadst: had.

the text as a single mother who alone produced the offspring, Bradstreet takes full responsibility as author, undermining the claim she establishes in the beginning of the poem that it was her friends who "exposed" the text to public view. Bradstreet becomes the fallen woman who has succumbed to seduction, producing a child out of wedlock. Yet, it is not the image of a fallen woman that the reader sees. Controlling the image, Bradstreet quickly forces the reader to see her instead as a good mother who warns her child about the "vulgar" world and as a poor victim forced by society, since she has no husband, to provide for herself by entering into the forbidden marketplace. Self-authorizing herself in such a way, Bradstreet justifies her "home-spun art" and daringly challenges her critics' sentiments about female authorship. (Engberg 2010: 11-12)

3. The poem serves as an apt and witty introduction to this new book because domestic imagery is a strong component of many of the new poems, which are much more personal than the stiffer, more formal and academic works of the first edition. Further, these references to the domestic are ironic because they both embody "feminine" discourse and serve as a vehicle to transcend that limited discursive field. (Elliot 1994: 241)

## Selected Reading B

### To My Dear and Loving Husband

If ever two were one, then surely we.
If ever man were loved by wife, then thee;
If ever wife was happy in a man,
Compare with me, ye① women, if you can.
I prize thy love more than whole mines② of gold,
Or all the riches that the East doth hold.
My love is such that rivers cannot quench③,
Nor ought④ but love from thee give recompense⑤.
Thy love is such I can no way repay;
The heavens reward thee manifold⑥, I pray.

---

① ye: the second-person, plural, personal pronoun (nominative).

② mines: In the original versions, "mines" is capitalized. It may simply emphasize vast wealth. Until almost the early nineteenth century, rules for capitalization were not standardized, and writers often capitalized nouns for emphasis.

③ quench: to put out, as a fire; to satisfy a thirst; to suppress, inhibit.

④ ought: anything.

⑤ recompense: compensate, pay for, return in kind, repay.

⑥ manifold: many times, a great deal; marked by diversity or variety.

Then while we live, in love let's so persever[①],
That when we live no more, we may live ever.

## About the Selection

《致我亲爱的丈夫》写于 1641 年至 1643 年之间。这首诗给读者展现了清教徒对待爱情、婚姻和上帝的态度。诗中作者宣示了她与丈夫之间伟大的爱情。比起任何人间财富,作者更重视他们之间的爱情。诗的第一节多次使用 if 从句,逻辑论证了作者发自内心的情绪。第二节通过隐喻和一些宗教意象来抒发自己的内心。最后一节,回到理性的本质。他们的爱是如此长久,即使在死后也将一直存在。这是一个悖论,符合清教徒神学和伟大的爱情诗。

## Research Guide

1. Anne Bradstreet had small patience with the Petrarchan convention in which a poet adores his lady from afar. [...] For Anne Bradstreet, the ideal love finds its consummation and continuation in marriage. The importance of marriage for her as for all Puritans, was increased by the belief in the family as the basic unit of government in both the state and the congregation. Especially in New England the state was considered to be made up of families, who were expected to exercise control over their members. Thus marriage was important to the state, but essential to marriage was love. God had commanded man and wife to love one another; hence the duty to love was a part of the marriage contract. Though marriages were usually arranged by Puritan families on the basis of social rank, young people were not forced to marry where they felt love would be impossible. (Stanford, 1974: 19)

2. Her work is influenced, first of all, by the ideas circulated generally among all educated people of the late sixteenth and early seventeenth centuries, ideas of the nature of man and the universe and of politics that differ markedly from those we hold today. Beyond these, her work reflects the Puritan religious concepts with which she was thoroughly indoctrinated; it shows, too, a remarkable sensitivity to the forms and genres which she inherited from the Elizabethans and which were being developed by other seventeenth-century writers. But above all, Anne Bradstreet's entire canon represents the struggle between the visible and the invisible worlds. Earth and the things of earth had on her a solid grasp. (Stanford, 1974: i)

3. 女诗人在这首题为《献给我的亲爱的丈夫》[②]的诗中,感情完全超越了宗教信仰和天规戒

① The archaic verb "persever" imports the idea of abiding continuity transcending death. In addition it repeats the key term "ever," used in each of the poem's thee opening lines as well as the concluding line.

② 此处为引文,诗名译法与编者不同。

律,像一只出笼的鸟,在自由的宇宙中快活地翱翔。无论受社会和传统所制约的生活环境如何,人们总能在自己的感情世界里保留一块私有的天地,以使自己倍受羁束的想象能有自由伸张的余地,自己近乎僵固的感情能有迸发的处所。作为艺术家的安妮·布雷兹特里特,尤其珍惜自己所保留的私有艺术角落,以使自己的艺术自我能够成长和得以表达。于是我们发现,安妮·布雷兹特里特并非只用一种声音讲话。(常耀信,1998:31)

## Supplementary Reading

### Verses upon the Burning of our House July 10th, 1666

In silent night when rest I took
For sorrow near I did not look
I wakened was with thund'ring[①] noise
And piteous[②] shrieks of dreadful voice.
That fearful sound of "Fire!" and "Fire!"
Let no man know is my desire.
I, starting up, the light did spy[③],
And to my God my heart did cry
To straighten me in my distress
And not to leave me succourless[④].
Then, coming out, behold a space
The flame consume my dwelling place.
And when I could no longer look,
I blest His name that gave and took,
That laid my goods now in the dust.
Yea, so it was, and so 'twas[⑤] just.
It was His own, it was not mine,
Far be it that I should repine[⑥];
He might of all justly bereft[⑦]
But yet sufficient for us left.

---

① thund'ring: thundering.
② piteous: pitiful.
③ spy: see.
④ succourless: helpless.
⑤ 'twas: it was.
⑥ repine: complain.
⑦ bereft: (past tense and past participle of bereave) completely without.

When by the ruins oft[1] I past
My sorrowing eyes aside did cast,
And here and there the places spy
Where oft I sate and long did lie:
Here stood that trunk, and there that chest,
There lay that store I counted best.
My pleasant things in ashes lie,
And them behold no more shall I.
Under thy roof no guest shall sit,
Nor at thy table eat a bit.
No pleasant talk shall e're be told,
Nor things recounted done of old.
No candle e'er[2] shall shine in thee,
Nor bridegroom's voice e'er heard shall be.
In silence ever shalt[3] thou lie,
Adieu[4], Adieu, all's vanity.
Then straight I 'gin my heart to chide[5],
And did thy wealth on earth abide?
Didst fix thy hope on mold'ring[6] dust?
The arm of flesh didst make thy trust?
Raise up thy thoughts above the sky
That dunghill[7] mists away may fly.
Thou hast[8] a house on high erect,
Framed by that mighty Architect[9],
With glory richly furnished,
Stands permanent though this be fled.
It's purchased and paid for too
By Him who hath[10] enough to do.
A price so vast as is unknown

① oft: often.
② e'er: ever.
③ shalt: shall.
④ Adieu: Goodbye.
⑤ I 'gin my heart to chide: I begin to scold my heart.
⑥ mold'ring: mouldering.
⑦ dunghill: a heap of dung.
⑧ hast: have.
⑨ Architect: it refers to God here.
⑩ hath: has.

Yet by His gift is made thine[1] own;
There's wealth enough, I need no more,
Farewell, my pelf[2], farewell my store.
The world no longer let me love,
My hope and treasure lies above.

## References and Further Reading


1. Bremer, Francis J. *The Puritan Experiment: New England Society from Bradford to Edwards*. New York: St. Martin's Press, 1976.
2. Douglas, Emily Taft. *Remember the Ladies: The Story of Great Women Who Helped Shape America*. New York: Putnam, 1966.
3. Elliot, Emory. "New England Puritan Literature." *The Cambridge History of American Literature: 1590 - 1820*. Eds. Sacvan Bercovitch, Cyrus R. K. Patell. Cambridge: Cambridge University Press, 1997. 169-306.
4. Engberg, Kathrynn Seidler. *The Right to Write: The Literary Politics of Anne Bradstreet and Phillis Wheatley*. Lanham, MD: University Press of America, 2010.
5. Hammond, Jeffrey. *Sinful Self, Saintly Self: The Puritan Experience of Poetry*. Athens: University of Georgia Press, 1993.
6. Hensley, Jeannine. *The Works of Anne Bradstreet*. Cambridge: Harvard University Press, 1967.
7. Parini, Jay and Brett C. Miller. *The Columbia History of American Poetry*. Columbia: Columbia University Press, 1993.
8. Piercy, Josephine K. *Anne Bradstreet*. New York: Twayne Publishers, 1965.
9. Porterfield, Amanda. *Female Piety in Puritan New England: The Emergence of Religious Humanism*. New York: Oxford University Press, 1992.
10. Stanford, Ann. *Anne Bradstreet: The Worldly Puritan*. New York: Burt Franklin & Co., 1974.
11. 常耀信.美国文学史(上).天津:南开大学出版社,1998.


---

[1] thine: your.
[2] pelf: possessions or wealth.

# 2. William Cullen Bryant (1794–1878)

## Introduction

William Cullen Bryant was born on November 3, 1794, in Cummington, Massachusetts, son of Dr. Peter Bryant and Sarah Snell Bryant. His family circumstances in Cummington exerted great influence on the shaping of Bryant's mind and personality, whose father encouraged the early literary efforts of his son. Bryant entered William College in Massachusetts at 16. His first verse was published at 14. With his poem "Thanatopsis", published on *North American Review* at 16, he brought the Romantic Movement into American literature. After 1821, he was succeeded in his poems, both as a lecturer and as a lawyer. Several years later, Bryant decided to enter journalism and still continued to publish poetry. His friends' death caused by typhus promotes his theme of death in his poems. William Cullen Bryant stood among the most celebrated figures in the nineteenth century America. The fame he won as a poet while in his youth remained with him as he entered his eighties. At his death, all New York City went into mourning for its most respected citizen, the first American national poet and one of American's earliest nature poets.

## Selected Reading A

### Thanatopsis[①]

To him who in the love of Nature holds

---

① Thanatopsis: a meditation over death. (It is a compound Greek word made by *thanatos* meaning death while *opsos* meaning think or look at)

Communion with her visible forms, she speaks
A various language; for his gayer hours[①]
She has a voice of gladness, and a smile
And eloquence of beauty, and she glides
Into his darker musings, with a mild
And healing sympathy that steals away
Their sharpness[②] ere he is aware. When thoughts
Of the last bitter hour come like a blight
Over thy spirit, and sad images
Of the stern agony, and shroud, and pall,
And breathless darkness, and the narrow house[③],
Make thee to shudder, and grow sick at heart; —
Go forth, under the open sky, and list
To Nature's teachings, while from all around —
Earth and her waters, and the depths of air, —
Comes a still voice — Yet a few days, and thee
The all-beholding sun shall see no more
In all his course; nor yet in the cold ground,
Where thy pale form was laid, with many tears.
Nor in the embrace of ocean, shall exist
Thy image. Earth, that nourished thee, shall claim
Thy growth, to be resolved to earth again,
And, lost each human trace, surrendering up
Thine individual being, shalt thou go
To mix for ever with the elements,
To be a brother to the insensible rock
And to the sluggish clod[④], which the rude swain[⑤]
Turns with his share[⑥], and treads upon. The oak
Shall send his roots abroad, and pierce thy mold.

Yet not to thine eternal resting-place
Shalt thou retire alone, — nor couldst thou wish

---

① gayer hours: happy time.

② sharpness: the piecing painfulness caused by their meditation.

③ the narrow house: the grave.

④ clod: soil.

⑤ swain: farmer.

⑥ share: plowshare.

Couch[①] more magnificent. Thou shalt lie down
With patriarchs of the infant[②] world — with kings,
The powerful of the earth — the wise, the good,
Fair forms, and hoary seers of ages past,
All in one mighty sepulchre. The hills
Rock-ribbed and ancient as the sun; the vales[③]
Stretching in pensive quietness between;
The venerable woods; rivers that move
In majesty, and the complaining brooks
That make the meadows green; and, poured round all
Old Ocean's gray and melancholy waste, —
Are but the solemn decorations all
Of the great tomb of man. The golden sun,
The planets, all the infinite host of heaven,
Are shining on the sad abodes of death,
Through the still lapse of ages. All that tread
The globe are but a handful to the tribes
That slumber in its bosom. — Take the wings
Of morning[④], traverse the Barca's[⑤] desert sands,
Or lose thyself in the continuous woods
Where rolls the Oregan[⑥], and hears no sound,
Save his own dashings — yet — the dead are there:
And millions in those solitudes, since first
The flight of years began, have laid them down
In their last sleep — the dead reign there alone.
So shalt thou rest, and what if thou withdraw
In silence from the living, and no friend
Take note of thy departure? All that breathe
Will share thy destiny. The gay will laugh
When thou art gone, the solemn brood of care
Plod on, and each one as before will chase
His favorite phantom; yet all these shall leave

---

① couch: bed.

② infant: early.

③ vales: valleys.

④ Cf. Psalm 139. 9-10: "If I take the wings of morning, and dwell in the uttermost parts of the sea; even there shall thy hand lead me..."

⑤ Barca: Desert in northeast Libya.

⑥ Oregan: Initial name of the Columbia River in Oregon.

Their mirth and their employments, and shall come,
And make their bed with thee. As the long train
Of ages glide away, the sons of men,
The youth in life's green spring, and he who goes
In the full strength of years, matron and maid,
And the sweet babe, and the gray-headed man, —
Shall one by one be gathered to thy side,
By those, who in their turn shall follow them.

So live, that when thy summons comes to join
The innumerable caravan, which moves
To that mysterious realm, where each shall take
His chamber in the silent halls of death,
Thou go not, like the quarry-slave at night,
Scourged to his dungeon, but, sustained and soothed
By an unflattering trust, approach thy grave
Like one who wraps the drapery of his couch[①]
About him, and lies down to pleasant dreams.

## About the Selection

《死亡随想》这首无韵诗以自然和死亡为主题，诗人间接地描述了他对死亡的观点：人人最终都会死，但人生在这个自然界中，自然会治愈人的痛苦。在诗人眼中，死亡并不可怕，因为自然会引导人们更好地了解生活、死亡与重生。这首诗广受人们喜欢的原因之一也是它帮助人们对生命与死亡有了一个全新的认识，从而战胜对死亡的恐惧。

## Research Guide

1. While "THANATOPSIS" has received appreciative glances from literary historians, who view it as a convenient transitional piece between deism and romanticism, and from moralists, who consider it a "broad and noble consolation for death," there is hardly a whisper to indicate that this poem stands within an indigenous literary and intellectual tradition. Too often we have concentrated upon William Cullen Bryant's extreme youth when he composed the poem and thus have lapsed into an assumption that "Thanatopsis" is merely a superior imitation of Wordsworth and the graveyard poets. A somewhat broader perspective, however, reveals that Bryant drew heavily upon his New England environment for both the form of his work and its basic rationality. His debt to the Puritan plain style puts "Thanatopsis" in a new light that offers much to both historians and moralists. (McLean, 1960: 474)

---

① wraps the drapery of his couch: wraps his bedclothes.

2. In "Thanatopsis" trust wins over fear through aesthetic experience and artistic control. Eventual calm builds legitimately out of craft and vision. Here, in the demonstrated prowess of the poet, is Bryant's highest moment. No American poet, with the possible exception of Edgar Allan Poe, would reach any higher for a generation to come. (Ferguson, 1980: 463)

3. 这首歌颂死亡的诗表现出明显的"墓地诗人"的影响。死在这里变成为宇宙运行之必然,不像基督教所宣扬的死后入天国那样快乐,或下地狱那样可怕。……布莱恩特笔下的死很有异教的风貌,对死的态度很有自然崇拜的意味:人最终要同大自然的形体相融合。(常耀信,1998:381-382)

## Selected Reading B

### To a Waterfowl[1]

Whither, 'midst[2] falling dew,
While glow the heavens with the last steps of day,
Far, through their rosy depths[3], dost thou pursue
Thy solitary way?

Vainly the fowler's[4] eye
Might mark[5] thy distant flight to do thee wrong,
As, darkly seen against the crimson sky,
Thy figure floats along.

Seek'st thou the plashy[6] brink
Of weedy lake, or marge[7] of river wide,
Or where the rocking billows rise and sink
On the chafed[8] ocean side?

There is a Power whose care

① waterfowl: A rather large American bird, probably a Canada goose. It often flies steadily and quietly.
② 'midst: amidst.
③ depths: the far, distant reach of the rosy sky.
④ fowler: hunter.
⑤ mark: aim at.
⑥ plashy: marshy, swampy.
⑦ marge: margin, edge.
⑧ chafed: become irritated or impatient.

Teaches thy way along that pathless coast, —
The desert[1] and illimitable[2] air,
Lone wandering, but not lost,

All day thy wings have fanned,
At that far height, the cold, thin atmosphere;
Yet stoop not, weary, to the welcome land,
Though the dark night is near.

And soon that toil shall end,
Soon shalt thou find a summer home, and rest,
And scream among thy fellows; reeds shall bend,
Soon, o'er thy sheltered nest.

Thou'rt[3] gone, the abyss of heaven
Hath swallowed up thy form, yet, on my heart
Deeply has sunk the lesson thou hast given,
And shall not soon depart.

He, who, from zone to zone,
Guides through the boundless sky thy certain flight,
In the long way that I must trace alone,
Will lead my steps aright.

## About the Selection

《致水鸟》以美国北方常见的水鸟为抒情对象，是一首托物言志之作。诗人的困惑与迷惘没有人能够化解，因此诗人试图从水鸟的身上寻找解决困惑的启示。当水鸟在天空中的飞行变得坚定有力时，对于未来，诗人也不再感到迷茫了，他坚信神会给他以指引。

## Research Guide

1. Arguably the finest of Bryant's early poems, "To a Waterfowl" reveals a careful reading of Lyrical Ballads and an understanding of Wordsworth's concept of the association of ideas. The poem also reflects Bryant's knowledge of the Scottish Common Sense philosophers, whom he had read while preparing for admission to William College. Common Sense philosophy claims that nature stimulates moral feelings in men and

① desert: deserted.
② illimitable: limitless.
③ thou'rt: you are.

women. Bryant popularized this influential idea in early nineteenth-century American literature, criticism, and art. In "To a Waterfowl," he transplanted the analogies and correspondences between nature and the human condition into native soil. (Muller, 2008: 21)

2. Matthew Arnold and Hartley Coleridge claimed that "To a Waterfowl" was the best short poem in English. A contemporary poet and critic, Richard Wilber, concurs: "I suppose, if there must be ranking and priorities, that 'To a Waterfowl' may be America's first flawless poem." (Muller, 2008: 22)

3. 布赖恩特深受苏格兰的联想说哲学影响,认为大自然的物质世界是灵感的来源,昭示了造物主的圣意,可以起到净化人的灵魂的作用。布赖恩特的创作标志着由清教徒的传统观念向超验主义思想的过渡。在超验主义经典之作《自然》中,超验主义最杰出的代表人物爱默生阐述了超验主义哲学的基本观点,表达了他对大自然深挚的爱,认为来自天体世界的光芒会使人脱离低级趣味,置身于无边无际的空间,狭隘的自我会消失得不见踪影。《自然》发表于 1836 年,那时该是布赖恩特创作比较活跃的时期,而《自然》中的不少观点又与布赖恩特在其自然诗歌中流露出来的观点极其相似。(史志康, 1996:29)

## Supplementary Reading

### The Yellow Violet

When beechen buds begin to swell,
    And woods the blue-bird's warble know[①],
The yellow violet's modest bell[②]
    Peeps from the last year's leaves below.

Ere[③] russet[④] fields their green resume,
    Sweet flower, I love, in forest bare,
To meet thee, when thy faint perfume
    Alone is in the virgin air.

Of all her train, the hands of Spring

① woods the blue-bird's warble know: woods know the blue bird's warble.
② bell: the corolla of a flower.
③ ere: before.
④ russet: reddish brown.

First plant thee in the watery mould,
And I have seen thee blossoming
Beside the snow-bank's edges cold.

Thy parent sun, who bade thee view
Pale skies, and chilling moisture sip,
Has bathed thee in his own bright hue,
And streaked with jet thy glowing lip.

Yet slight thy form, and low thy seat,
And earthward bent thy gentle eye,
Unapt the passing view to meet
When loftier flowers are flaunting① nigh②.

Oft, in the sunless April day,
Thy early smile has stayed my walk;
But midst the gorgeous blooms of May,
I passed thee on thy humble stalk.

So they, who climb to wealth, forget
The friends in darker fortunes tried.
I copied them — but I regret
That I should ape the ways of pride.

And when again the genial hour
Awakes the painted tribes of light,
I'll not o'erlook the modest flower
That made the woods of April bright.

## References and Further Reading


1. Ferguson, Robert A. "William Cullen Bryant: The Creative Context of the Poet." *New England Quarterly* 53. 4(1980): 431 - 463.
2. Gado, Frank. *William Cullen Bryant: An American Voice*. White River Junction, VT: Antoca Press, 2006.


① flaunt: display proudly; act ostentatiously or pretentiously.
② nigh: near.

3. Krapf, Norbert. *Under Open Sky: Poets on William Cullen Bryant*. New York: Fordham University Press, 1986.
4. McLean, Albert F. Jr., "Bryant's 'Thanatopsis': A Sermon in Stone." *American Literature* 31. 4(1960): 474-479.
5. Muller, Gilbert H. *William Cullen Bryant: Author of America*. New York: State University of New York Press, 2008.
6. 常耀信.美国文学史(上).天津:南开大学出版社,1998.
7. 史志康."道"在天地间——威廉·卡伦·布赖恩特自然诗歌初探.外国语,1996(3): 26-29.

# 3. Ralph Waldo Emerson (1803–1882)

## Introduction

No one has a better claim than Ralph Waldo Emerson to being the central figure in the whole history of American literature. His nineteenth-century reformation of such seventeenth-century motives was decisively influential on poets such as Walt Whitman, Emily Dickinson, Robert Frost, and Wallace Stevens. His presence and example were deeply felt in American philosophy, religion, music, and education, both during his lifetime and into the twentieth century. He is more remembered as an essayist for his great inspiration in lecturing. In his essays, we see his wisdom in advocating transcendentalism. His essay even marks the dependence of American literature.

Though Emerson earned his central place in American culture as an essayist and philosopher, since his death his reputation as a poet has grown as well. His poems speak to his most passionately held belief: that external authority should be disregarded in favor of one's own experience. From the embattled farmers who "fired the shot heard round the world" in the stirring "Concord Hymn," to the flower in "The Rhodora," whose existence demonstrates "that if eyes were made for seeing, / Then Beauty is its own excuse for being," Emerson celebrates the existence of the sublime in the human and in nature. Combining intensity of feeling with his famous idealism, Emerson's poems reveal a moving, more intimate side of the man revered as the Sage of Concord.

## Selected Reading A

### The Rhodora

*On Being Asked, Whence Is the Flower?*

In May, when sea-winds pierced our solitudes,
I found the fresh Rhodora in the woods,
Spreading its leafless blooms in a damp nook[①],
To please the desert and the sluggish brook.
The purple petals, fallen in the pool,
Made the black water with their beauty gay;
Here might the red-bird come his plumes to cool[②],
And court the flower that cheapens his array[③].
Rhodora! if the sages ask thee why
This charm is wasted on the earth and sky,
Tell them, dear, that if eyes were made for seeing,
Then Beauty is its own excuse for being:
Why thou wert there, O rival of the rose!
I never thought to ask, I never knew;
But, in my simple ignorance, suppose
The self-same Power that brought me there brought you.

## About the Selection

《杜鹃花》作于 1847 年,全诗围绕着第一句中的问题“这花从何而来?”展开,描画了一朵普普通通的杜鹃花,不争奇斗艳,却有着清新淡雅的美。诗人赞美杜鹃花,也表达了对大自然无处不在的美的赞美和陶醉。

## Research Guide

1. Emerson's poems do not often achieve immediacy. This is so in great part because of the a priori nature of many of them or because of their “panoramic” quality. As a result their impact is frequently vague and general as, for example, in “The Rhodora”. (Ryan, 1959: 10)

2. Poems containing a marked preponderance of perfect rhymes... “The Rhodora,” sixteen lines (two couplets plus four lines of alternate rhyme, repeated), with solitudes, woods constituting the only imperfect rhymes although there is a shift from masculine to feminine rhyme in seeing, being. (McEuen, 1948: 35)

3. Different poets have used the subject and the themes of nature in their poetry, but the treatment of Emerson in his poems is typical towards Nature. “The Rhodora” unfolds his

① nook: a sheltered and secluded place.
② come his plumes to cool: come to cool his plumes.
③ array: clothing, especially for fine or decorative clothing.

concept of beauty, where the poet left popular flowers of the British origin and gave an American shape to it, by selecting this flower of the American forest which blooms in the month of May. (Kaintura, 2005: 2)

4. 爱默森的诗名一向为文名所掩，但是他的诗也独创一格，造诣极高。……爱默森的种种观念时常在他的诗里重新出现——除非他的诗是那些观念的发源地，那就不应当说“重新出现”——但是那些诗不仅只是观念。(张爱玲, 1989:5-6)

## Selected Reading B

### Days

Daughters of Time, the hypocritic[1] Days,
Muffled and dumb like barefoot dervishes[2],
And marching single in an endless file,
Bring diadems[3] and fagots[4] in their hands.
To each they offer gifts after his will,
Bread, kingdoms, stars, and sky that holds them all.
I, in my pleached garden, watched the pomp[5],
Forgot my morning wishes, hastily
Took a few herbs and apples, and the Day
Turned and departed silent. I, too late,
Under her solemn fillet[6] saw the scorn.

### About the Selection

《日子》一诗发表于1851年，被认为是爱默生写得最好的一首诗。该诗就如一则关于时间问题的寓言。诗人眼中的“日子”是伪善而狡黠的，她们表面慷慨公正地按照人们的心愿分配礼物，却使人们忘掉了“早晨的愿望”，在满足人们简单的物质需求的同时却使人忽略了精神上的缺失。

### Research Guide

1. “Days” was first printed in *Atlantic Monthly* in November, 1857. When the verses

① hypocritic: professing feelings or virtues that one does not have.
② dervish: an ascetic Muslim monk.
③ diadems: headdresses signifying sovereignty.
④ fagots: bundles of sticks bound together for burning.
⑤ pomp: elegance, splendor.
⑥ fillet: a narrow strip of ribbon worn as a headband.

were collected in *May-Day and Other Pieces* (1867), Emerson was shocked to discover that some fastidious editor had altered "Daughter" to "Damsels." In writing to Cabot, Emerson succinctly observed, "'Daughters' was right & shall be."(Adkins, 1948: 271)

2. Thus the famous opening line of Emerson's poem, "Daughters of Time, the hypocritic Days," derives clearly from young. Yet except for this single striking parallel, Emerson's reliance on Young was slight. To Young the days are indeed hypocritic, flattering confiding man only in the end to deceive him. To the more optimistic Emerson the days are also clothed in deceit. Yet Man's fate then, lies in his choice, and the irony of existence comes from the discoverer that our choice all too often has been paltry and inadequate. (Adkins, 1948: 270)

3. The subject, as I have said, is obviously a very big one. Emerson is talking about basic values, about perception, about nothing less than "how to live." Incidentally, he points out that the march of time is endless, but not for the individual, who has made his good, bad, and indifferent choices within a restricted time. There is an astonishing thematic richness packed into the eleven lines... No one, I think, has ever expressed better in a few words the sad fact that most men are blind to opportunities for genuinely high achievement, not the vulgar concept of success, but accomplishment of another and transcendent order. (Clark, 1962: 60)

4. The figure of the poem, the image, is simple; yet it is appealing to the imagination. It is suitable to carry the basic thought of the poem, and at the same time it yields itself admirably to Emerson's quality of unpretentious decoration. (Oliver, 1946: 518)

5. 爱默生的诗歌乃是他的思想的引申。虽然他一直以诗人自诩,而且在诗歌创作形式上,如在诗行和声调方面也有革新,但总的说来,他的诗歌成就不算出类拔萃。……有的评论者由于偏爱而说此诗(指《日子》——引者注)像希腊警句一样清晰而完美;其实,这首诗的主要意义在于它的自由体形式:它摆脱了五步抑扬格的羁束,为挣扎中的美国独立诗歌指出了一条可行之路。(常耀信,1998:179-180)

## Supplementary Reading

### Brahma①

If the red slayer② think he slays,

① Brahma: one of the three major deities in the later Hindu pantheon, the Creator.
② slayer: Death.

Or if the slain think he is slain,
They know not well the subtle ways
I keep, and pass, and turn again.

Far or forgot to me is near;
Shadow and sunlight are the same;
The vanished gods to me appear;
And one to me are shame and fame.

They reckon ill who leave me out;
When me they fly, I am the wings;
I am the doubter and the doubt,
And I the hymn the Brahmin① sings.

The strong gods pine for my abode,
And pine in vain the sacred Seven,
But thou, meek lover of the good!
Find me, and turn thy back on heaven.

## Two Rivers

Thy summer voice, Musketaquit②,
Repeats the music of the rain;
But sweeter rivers pulsing flit
Through thee, as thou through the Concord Plain.

Thou in thy narrow banks art pent:
The stream I love unbounded goes
Through flood and sea and firmament;
Through light, through life, it forward flows.

I see the inundation sweet,
I hear the spending of the steam
Through years, through men, through Nature fleet,
Through love and thought, through power and dream.

Musketaquit, a goblin strong,

---

① Brahmin: name of the caste (social class) to which Hindu priests belong; a priest himself.

② Musketaquit: an Indian name for the Concord river.

Of shard and flint makes jewels gay;
They lose their grief who hear his song,
And where he winds is the day of day.

So forth and brighter fares my stream, —
Who drink it shall not thirst again;
No darkness taints its equal gleam,
And ages drop in it like rain.

## Song of Nature

Mine are the night and morning,
The pits of air, the gulf of space,
The sportive sun, the gibbous moon①,
The innumerable days.

I hid in the solar glory,
I am dumb in the pealing song,
I rest on the pitch of the torrent,
In slumber I am strong.

No numbers have counted my tallies,
No tribes my house can fill,
I sit by the shining Fount of Life,
And pour the deluge still;

And ever by delicate powers
Gathering along the centuries
From race on race the rarest flowers,
My wreath shall nothing miss.

And many a thousand summers
My apples ripened well,
And light from meliorating stars
With firmer glory fell.

I wrote the past in characters
Of rock and fire the scroll,

① gibbous moon: a moon more than half full.

The building in the coral sea,
The planting of the coal.

And thefts from satellites and rings
And broken stars I drew,
And out of spent and aged things
I formed the world anew;

What time the gods kept carnival,
Tricked out in star and flower,
And in cramp elf and saurian forms
They swathed their too much power.

Time and Thought were my surveyors,
They laid their courses well,
They boiled the sea, and baked the layers
Or granite, marl, and shell.

But he, the man-child glorious, —
Where tarries he the while?
The rainbow shines his harbinger,
The sunset gleams his smile.

My boreal lights leap upward,
Forthright my planets roll,
And still the man-child is not born,
The summit of the whole.

Must time and tide forever run?
Will never my winds go sleep in the west?
Will never my wheels which whirl the sun
And satellites have rest?

Too much of donning and doffing,
Too slow the rainbow fades,
I weary of my robe of snow,
My leaves and my cascades;

I tire of globes and races,

Too long the game is played;
What without him is summer's pomp,
Or winter's frozen shade?

I travail in pain for him,
My creatures travail and wait;
His couriers come by squadrons,
He comes not to the gate.

Twice I have moulded an image,
And thrice outstretched my hand,
Made one of day, and one of night,
And one of the salt sea-sand.

One in a Judaean① manger,
And one by Avon② stream,
One over against the mouths of Nile③,
And one in the Academe.

I moulded kings and saviours,
And bards o'er kings to rule; —
But fell the starry influence short,
The cup was never full.

Yet whirl the glowing wheels once more,
And mix the bowl again;
Seethe, fate! the ancient elements,
Heat, cold, wet, dry, and peace, and pain.

Let war and trade and creeds and song
Blend, ripen race on race,
The sunburnt world a man shall breed
Of all the zones, and countless days.

No ray is dimmed, no atom worn,

---

① Judaean: the southern part of ancient Palestine.

② Avon: a river in southwestern England.

③ Nile: the world's longest river flows northward through eastern Africa.

My oldest force is good as new,
And the fresh rose on yonder thorn
Gives back the bending heavens in dew.

## Each and All

Little thinks, in the field, yon red-cloaked clown[1]
Of thee from the hill-top looking down;
The heifer[2] that lows in the upland farm,
Far-heard, lows not thine ear to charm;
The sexton[3], tolling his bell at noon,
Deems not that great Napoleon
Stops his horse, and lists with delight,
Whilst his files sweep round yon Alpine height;
Nor knowest thou what argument
Thy life to thy neighbor's creed has lent.
All are needed by each one;
Nothing is fair or good alone.
I thought the sparrow's note from heaven,
Singing at dawn on the alder bough;
I brought him home, in his nest, at even;
He sings the song, but it pleases not now,
For I did not bring home the river and sky;—
He sang to my ear, — they sang to my eye.
The delicate shells lay on the shore;
The bubbles of the latest wave
Fresh pearls to their enamel gave,
And the bellowing of the savage sea
Greeted their safe escape to me.
I wiped away the weeds and foam,
I fetched my sea-born treasures home;
But the poor, unsightly, noisome things
Had left their beauty on the shore
With the sun and the sand, and the wild uproar.
The lover watched his graceful maid,
As 'mid the virgin train she stayed,

① red-cloaked clown: referring to the heifer.
② heifer: young cow.
③ sexton: an officer of the church.

Nor knew her beauty's best attire
Was woven still by the snow-white choir,
At last she came to his hermitage,
Like the bird from the woodlands to the cage; —
The gay enchantment was undone,
A gentle wife, but fairy none.
Then I said, "I covet truth;
Beauty is unripe childhood's cheat;
I leave it behind with the games of youth:" —
As I spoke, beneath my feet
The ground-pine curled its pretty wreath,
Running over the club-moss burrs;
I inhaled the violet's breath;
Around me stood the oaks and firs;
Pine-cones and acorns lay on the ground;
Over me soared the eternal sky,
Full of light and of deity;
Again I saw, again I heard,
The rolling river, the morning bird; —
Beauty through my senses stole;
I yielded myself to the perfect whole.

## References and Further Reading

1. Adkins, Nelson F. "Emerson's 'Days' and Edward Young." *Modern Language Notes* 63.4 (1948): 269-271.
2. Bussey, Jennifer. "Critical Essay on 'The Rhodora'." *Poetry for Students*. Detroit: The Gale Group, 2003.
3. Clark, William Ross. "Poems for Study." *The Clearing House* 37.1 (1962): 59-60.
4. Kaintura, D. S. "Delineation of Nature in Emerson's Poetry." *Critical Perspectives in American Literature*. Ed. Meenakshi Raman. New Delhi: Atlantic Publishers and Distributors, 2005. 1-10.
5. McEuen, Kathryn Anderson. "Emerson's Rhymes." *American Literature* 20.1(1948): 31-42.
6. Oliver, Egbert S. "Emerson's 'Days'." *The New England Quarterly* 19.4 (1946): 518-524.
7. Ryan, Alvan S. "Frost and Emerson: Voice and Vision." *The Massachusetts Review*

1.1 (1959): 5-23.
8. 常耀信.美国文学史(上).天津:南开大学出版社,1998.
9. 张爱玲.爱默森的生平和著作.美国诗选,林以亮编选.北京:三联书店,1989.

# 4. Edgar Allan Poe (1809–1849)

## Introduction

Poe was born in Boston, Massachusetts, in 1809, the son of an actress. Orphaned in 1811, he moved to Richmond, Virginia, to live with his adoptive family. He briefly attended the University of Virginia before leaving to join the Army and attend West Point Military Academy; he was expelled from West Point after a year. Poe worked as a journalist and editor in New York, Baltimore, and Richmond. Despite his success as a writer, he lived in poverty. He suffered from alcoholism, depression, and possibly diabetes. In 1836 Poe married his cousin Virginia Clemm, and they remained together until her death from tuberculosis in 1847. After giving lectures in Norfolk and Richmond, Poe died in a Baltimore hospital in 1849; the cause of his death is not known.

Poe's work as an editor, a poet, and a critic had a profound impact on American and international literature. His stories mark him as one of the originators of both horror and detective fiction. Many anthologies credit him as the "architect" of the modern short story. He was also one of the first critics to focus primarily on the effect of the style and of the structure in a literary work; as such, he has been seen as a forerunner to the "art for art's sake" movement. French Symbolists such as Mallarmé and Rimbaud claimed him as a literary precursor. Baudelaire spent nearly fourteen years translating Poe into French. Today, Poe is remembered as one of the first American writers to become a major figure in world literature.

## Selected Reading A

### Annabel Lee

It was many and many a year ago,
In a kingdom by the sea,
That a maiden there lived whom you may know
By the name of Annabel Lee;
And this maiden she lived with no other thought
Than to love and be loved by me.

*She* was a child and *I* was a child,
In this kingdom by the sea,
But we loved with a love that was more than love —
I and my Annabel Lee —
With a love that the winged seraphs① of Heaven
Coveted② her and me.

And this was the reason that, long ago,
In this kingdom by the sea,
A wind blew out of a cloud by night
Chilling my Annabel Lee;
So that her highborn③ kinsmen came
And bore her away from me,
To shut her up in a sepulchre④
In this kingdom by the sea.

The angels, not half so happy in Heaven,
Went envying her and me;
Yes! that was the reason (as all men know,
In this kingdom by the sea)
That the wind came out of the cloud, chilling

① seraphs: angels of the highest order.
② coveted: envied, resented.
③ highborn: of noble or aristocratic birth.
④ sepulchre: grave.

And killing my Annabel Lee.

But our love it was stronger by far than the love
Of those who were older than we —
Of many far wiser than we —
And neither the angels in Heaven above,
Nor the demons down under the sea,
Can ever dissever[①] my soul from the soul
Of the beautiful Annabel Lee:

For the moon never beams without bringing me dreams
Of the beautiful Annabel Lee;
And the stars never rise but I see the bright eyes
Of the beautiful Annabel Lee;
And so, all the night-tide[②], I lie down by the side
Of my darling, my darling, my life and my bride,
In the sepulchre there by the sea —
In her tomb by the sounding sea.

## About the Selection

《安娜贝尔·李》被许多评论家认为是诗人为悼念亡妻而作，全诗情景交融，既生动形象地演绎了一个爱情传奇，又委婉感人地抒发了诗人缠绵悲伤的心情。美人之死正是爱伦·坡诗歌作品的一贯主题，诗人对音韵技巧的强调也值得关注。另外，该诗与我国宋代诗人苏东坡的《江城子——乙卯正月二十日夜记》在意境上颇为相似。

## Research Guide

1. I know nothing that can beat, if I know anything that can equal, "Annabel Lee." It begins quite quietly but with a motion of gathering speed and a sort of flicker of light and glow of heat: and these things quicken and brighten and grow till they finish in the last stanza, that incomparable explosion of rapturous regret that towers to the stars and sinks to the sea. (Saintsbury, 1933: 323)

2. "Annabel Lee" exemplifies several traits of Poe's feminine ideal, especially that of being wholly subsumed by the male. Her unnaturally young age for marriage (she and the narrator are each described as "a child") is, of course, evocative of Poe's own child-bride, his thirteen-year-old cousin Virginia. (Weekes, 2004:152)

---

① dissever: separate.

② night-tide: night time.

3. The repetition of Annabel's name throughout the poem contributes another strong linking of sound with sense. The name literally means "beautiful Anna," and Anna means "gracious" and "merciful." "Gracious" derives from "agreeable," which quality is evident in our information regarding the love of Annabel and the speaker. "Merciful" may also mean "loving," and that state, too, obtains in this poem. To paraphrase, the speaker has lost beauty, grace and love, all those qualities suggesting balance. No wonder, then, that the grief-stricken lover uses song to convey the intensity of his lament. (Fisher, 2008: 46-47)

4. 他的诗的背景几乎全是黑夜，我们不可能在他的诗中看见阳光或是活人。他的诗中充满了对于另一世界的向往；那气氛和他的故事中的气氛是完全一样的。一切都是虚幻，都是梦，诗中即使有人物出现，这些人物也无非是"寄居于一已死之肉体的灵魂"而已，他们只不过维持不死(remain undead)，并不在活。他的世界不是一个道德的世界，甚至不是一个感官的世界；一切都出没于浸着阴湿湿的月光的潜意识里。过去并无历史，未来仅余死亡，现在只有忧郁，绝望，回忆与幻觉。(余光中，1989:23)

## Selected Reading B

### The Raven

Once upon a midnight dreary, while I pondered, weak and weary,
Over many a quaint① and curious volume of forgotten lore—
While I nodded, nearly napping, suddenly there came a tapping,
As of some one gently rapping, rapping at my chamber② door.
"'Tis③ some visitor," I muttered, "tapping at my chamber door —
Only this, and nothing more."

Ah, distinctly I remember it was in the bleak December;
And each separate dying ember④ wrought its ghost⑤ upon the floor.
Eagerly I wished the morrow⑥; — vainly I had sought to borrow
From my books surcease⑦ of sorrow — sorrow for the lost Lenore —

① quaint: odd, strange.
② chamber: bedroom or study.
③ 'Tis: It is.
④ ember: a hot fragment of wood or coal that is left from a fire and is glowing or smoldering.
⑤ wrought its ghost: formed ash.
⑥ morrow: the next day or tomorrow.
⑦ surcease: stop.

For the rare and radiant maiden whom the angels name Lenore —
Nameless *here* for evermore.

And the silken, sad, uncertain rustling of each purple curtain
Thrilled me — filled me with fantastic terrors never felt before;
So that now, to still the beating of my heart, I stood repeating
"'Tis some visitor entreating entrance at my chamber door —
Some late visitor entreating entrance at my chamber door; —
This it is, and nothing more."

Presently my soul grew stronger; hesitating then no longer,
"Sir," said I, "or Madam, truly your forgiveness I implore;
But the fact is I was napping, and so gently you came rapping,
And so faintly you came tapping, tapping at my chamber door,
That I scarce was sure I heard you" — here I opened wide the door; —
Darkness there and nothing more.

Deep into that darkness peering, long I stood there wondering, fearing,
Doubting, dreaming dreams no mortals ever dared to dream before;
But the silence was unbroken, and the stillness gave no token,
And the only word there spoken was the whispered word, "Lenore?"
This I whispered, and an echo murmured back the word, "Lenore!"
Merely this and nothing more.

Back into the chamber turning, all my soul within me burning,
Soon again I heard a tapping somewhat louder than before.
"Surely," said I, "surely that is something at my window lattice:
Let me see, then, what thereat① is, and this mystery explore —
Let my heart be still② a moment and this mystery explore; —
'Tis the wind and nothing more!"

Open here I flung the shutter, when, with many a flirt and flutter,
In there stepped a stately Raven of the saintly days of yore③;
Not the least obeisance made he; not a minute stopped or stayed he;

① thereat: there, at that place.
② still: an adjective here, meaning "unmoved and quiet."
③ of yore: refer to a period of time in the past.

But, with mien[①] of lord or lady, perched above my chamber door —
Perched upon a bust of Pallas[②] just above my chamber door —
Perched, and sat, and nothing more.

Then this ebony bird beguiling[③] my sad fancy into smiling,
By the grave and stern decorum[④] of the countenance it wore.
"Though thy crest be shorn and shaven, thou," I said, "art sure no craven[⑤],
Ghastly grim and ancient Raven wandering from the Nightly shore —
Tell me what thy lordly name is on the Night's Plutonian shore[⑥]!"
Quoth the Raven "Nevermore."

Much I marvelled this ungainly fowl to hear discourse so plainly,
Though its answer little meaning — little relevancy bore;
For we cannot help agreeing that no living human being
Ever yet was blest with seeing bird above his chamber door —
Bird or beast upon the sculptured bust above his chamber door,
With such name as"Nevermore."

But the Raven, sitting lonely on the placid[⑦] bust, spoke only
That one word, as if his soul in that one word he did outpour.
Nothing farther then he uttered — not a feather then he fluttered —
Till I scarcely more than muttered,"Other friends have flown before —
On the morrow *he* will leave me, as my Hopes have flown before."
Then the bird said "Nevermore."

Startled at the stillness broken by reply so aptly spoken,
"Doubtless," said I, "what it utters is its only stock and store
Caught from some unhappy master whom unmerciful Disaster
Followed fast and followed faster till his songs one burden bore —
Till the dirges[⑧] of his Hope that melancholy burden bore
Of'Never — nevermore.'"

---

① mien: manner.

② Pallas: Athena, Greek goddess of wisdom and the arts.

③ beguiling: charming, coaxing.

④ decorum: polite behavior.

⑤ craven: very cowardly.

⑥ the Night's Plutonian shore: the infernal regions which are ruled by Pluto. Pluto was the Greek god of the underworld.

⑦ placid: calm, quiet, peaceful.

⑧ dirge: a song or hymn of mourning composed or performed as a memorial to a dead person.

But the Raven still beguiling all my fancy into smiling,
Straight I wheeled a cushioned seat in front of bird, and bust and door;
Then, upon the velvet sinking, I betook myself to linking
Fancy unto fancy, thinking what this ominous bird of yore —
What this grim, ungainly, ghastly, gaunt and ominous bird of yore
Meant in croaking "Nevermore."

This I sat engaged in guessing, but no syllable expressing
To the fowl whose fiery eyes now burned into my bosom's core;
This and more I sat divining, with my head at ease reclining
On the cushion's velvet lining that the lamp-light gloated o'er,
But whose velvet violet lining with the lamp-light gloating o'er,
*She* shall press, ah, nevermore!

Then, methought, the air grew denser, perfumed from an unseen censer
Swung by seraphim whose foot-falls tinkled on the tufted floor.
"Wretch," I cried, "thy God hath lent thee — by these angels he hath sent thee
Respite — respite and nepenthe① from thy memories of Lenore;
Quaff, oh quaff this kind nepenthe and forget this lost Lenore!"
Quoth the Raven "Nevermore."

"Prophet!" said I, "thing of evil! — prophet still, if bird or devil! —
Whether Tempter sent, or whether tempest tossed thee here ashore,
Desolate yet all undaunted, on this desert land enchanted —
On this home by Horror haunted — tell me truly, I implore —
Is there — *is* there balm in Gilead?②— tell me — tell me, I implore!"
Quoth the Raven, "Nevermore."

"Prophet!" said I, "thing of evil! — prophet still, if bird or devil!
By that Heaven that bends above us — by that God we both adore —
Tell this soul with sorrow laden if, within the distant Aidenn③,
It shall clasp a sainted maiden whom the angels name Lenore —

① nepenthe: oblivion-inducing drug.

② As in Jeremiah 8.22: "Is there no balm in Gilead; is there no physician there?" Evergreens growing in Gilead, a mountainous area east of the Jordan River, were tapped for medicinal resins.

③ Aidenn: invented place-name, suggestive of Eden.

Clasp a rare and radiant maiden whom the angels name Lenore."
Quoth the Raven "Nevermore."

"Be that word our sign of parting, bird or fiend!" I shrieked, upstarting —
"Get thee back into the tempest and the Night's Plutonian shore!
Leave no black plume as a token of that lie thy soul hath spoken!
Leave my loneliness unbroken! — quit the bust above my door!
Take thy beak from out my heart, and take thy form from off my door!"
Quoth the Raven "Nevermore."

And the Raven, never flitting, still is sitting, *still* is sitting
On the pallid① bust of Pallas just above my chamber door;
And his eyes have all the seeming of a demon's that is dreaming,
And the lamp-light o'er him streaming throws his shadow on the floor;
And my soul from out that shadow that lies floating on the floor
Shall be lifted — nevermore!

## About the Selection

《乌鸦》是爱伦·坡创作于1844年的一首叙事诗,1845年1月甫一发表,即引起轰动,至今仍是各教材和选本的必刊之作,成为美国诗歌的典范。它讲述了一只会说话的乌鸦对一名因失去恋人而极度悲伤的学者的神秘拜访。它坐在帕拉斯胸像上,不断重复着那句"永不复焉",一步步煽动着"我"的忧伤,令"我"不能自已,几近疯狂。该诗大量使用头韵、行内韵和谐韵,节奏上采用扬抑格,由八音步与七音步相结合,长短轻重错落有致。无论是出自乌鸦之口的"nevermore"一词,还是长元音/ɔː/的反复出现都加强了叙述者低沉哀婉的语气,读来如一步三叹,声音与意义完美结合,很好地实现了坡所主张的诗歌创作的"效果"。

## Research Guide

1. "The Raven" has taken rank over the whole world of literature, as the very first poem yet produced on the American continent. [...] The worth of "The Raven" is not in any "Moral", nor is its charm in the construction of its story. Its great and wonderful merits consist in the strange, beautiful and fantastic imagery and colours with which the simple subject is clothed — the grave and supernatural tone with which it rolls on the ear — the extraordinary vividness of the word painting, — and the powerful but altogether indefinable appeal which is made throughout to the organs of ideality and marvelousness. Added to these is a versification indescribably sweet and wonderfully difficult — winding and convoluted about like the mazes of some complicated overture by Beethoven. To all

① pallid: pale.

who have a strong perception of tune, there is a music in it which haunts the ear long after reading. These are great merits, and "The Raven" is a gem of art. It is stamped with the image of true genius — and genius in its happiest hour. It is one of those things an author never does but once. (Daniel, 1845: 145-147)

2. "The Raven" is the drama of nightmare awakening in the American poetic consciousness where there is no history which is not dispossession, little reality to the American promise, and nothing of consequence to place trust in except the song, the ode of celebration... "The Raven" is the croaking and anguished nightmare ode of allegiance, and we have been finding ourselves in it ever since Poe began hearing "Nevermore." (Smith, 1995: 10)

3.《乌鸦》可谓爱伦·坡诗歌理论乃至文学理念最全面的体现,其主题是他认为最富诗意的"美女之夭亡和失美之哀伤"。为了效果的统一性,他只写了108行;为了格律的独创性,他配置了一种前人未尝试过的诗节;为了情节的复杂性,他故意让主人公一开始把乌鸦翅膀拍窗的声音误认为是敲门声;为了艺术作品的暗示性,他设计了一个其字词不变,但其寓意却不断变化的叠句——永不复焉。(曹明伦, 2013)

4. 在气质上,美国十九世纪的三位最富创造力的诗人之中,惠特曼是一个平民,狄瑾荪是一个隐士,而爱伦·坡则是一个贵族;惠特曼属于人,狄瑾荪属于神,而爱伦·坡属于鬼。(余光中,1989:24)

## Supplementary Reading

### To Helen

Helen[1], thy beauty is to me
    Like those Nicean barks[2] of yore[3],
That gently, o'er a perfumed sea,
    The weary, way-worn[4] wanderer bore
    To his own native shore.

On desperate seas long wont[5] to roam,

① Helen: Helen of Troy, whose beauty was renowned and whose abduction led to the Trojan War.
② Nicean barks: boats, perhaps from some Mediterranean location; variously interpreted by Poe scholars.
③ yore: formerly; of long ago.
④ way-worn: wearied by traveling.
⑤ wont: accustomed.

Thy hyacinth① hair, thy classic face,
Thy Naiad② airs have brought me home
To the glory that was Greece
And the grandeur that was Rome.

Lo③! in yon brilliant window-niche
How statue-like I see thee stand,
The agate lamp within thy hand!
Ah! Psyche④, from the regions which
Are Holy Land!

## Israfel⑤

In Heaven a spirit doth dwell
"Whose heart-strings are a lute⑥";
None sing so wildly well
As the angel Israfel,
And the giddy stars (so legends tell),
Ceasing their hymns, attend the spell⑦
Of his voice, all mute.

Tottering above
In her highest noon,
The enamored⑧ moon
Blushes with love,
While, to listen, the red levin⑨

---

① hyacinth: In Greek mythology, the blood of the slain youth Hyacinthus, whom the god Apollo loved, was changed into a purple flower.

② Naiad: nymphlike.

③ Lo: look.

④ In classical mythology, a beautiful princess, whose name means "soul" in Greek. Having lost her lover, Cupid, (Roman) god of erotic love, because she disobeyed his order not to look at him (he awakened when a drop of hot oil from her lamp fell on him), Psyche appealed for help to his mother, Venus, goddess of love and beauty. One punitive task set by Venus was that Psyche bring her a portion of the beauty of Proserpina, queen of the underworld.

⑤ Israfel: Poe derived the title from the name of an angel in Islamic literature. According to Islam, an archangel named Israfel, also spelled Israfil, will blow a trumpet to awaken the dead for final judgment on the Day of Resurrection at the end of the world.

⑥ Line 2 expresses Poe's view of what constitutes good poetry: musicality and genuine emotion. "Whose heart-strings are a lute" is a metaphor saying, in effect, "whose emotions are music."

⑦ spell: magic power.

⑧ enamored: variant spelling of enamored, meaning captivated or filled with love.

⑨ levin: lightning.

(With the rapid Pleiads①, even,
Which were seven,)
Pauses in Heaven.

And they say (the starry choir
And the other listening things)
That Israfeli's fire
Is owing to that lyre
By which he sits and sings —
The trembling living wire
Of those unusual strings.

But the skies that angel trod,
Where deep thoughts are a duty,
Where Love's a grown-up God —
Where the Houri② glances are
Imbued with all the beauty
Which we worship in a star.

Therefore, thou art not wrong,
Israfeli, who despisest
An unimpassioned song;
To thee the laurels③ belong,
Best bard, because the wisest!
Merrily live, and long!

The ecstasies above
With thy burning measures④ suit —
Thy grief, thy joy, thy hate, thy love,
With the fervor of thy lute —
Well may the stars be mute!

---

① rapid Pleiads: In Greek mythology, the seven daughters of Atlas, the Titan god who carried the heavens on his shoulders. Zeus, the king of the gods, changed the Pleiades into stars to put them beyond the reach of Orion, a giant hunter of Boeotia who was pursuing them. The names of the Pleiades are Alcyone, Celaeno, Electra, Maia, Merope, Sterope, and Taygete. The word "rapid" suggests that the Pleiades are still running from Orion. After his death, he was also changed into a star. In astronomy, the Pleiades are a star group in the constellation of Taurus.

② Houri: Arabic word, meaning "a black-eyed damsel".

③ laurels: wreath of laurel with which ancient Greeks and Romans crowned high achievers in poetry, oratory, athletics, war, and other activities.

④ measures: short passages in music or poetry.

Yes, Heaven is thine; but this
Is a world of sweets and sours;
Our flowers are merely — flowers,
And the shadow of thy perfect bliss
Is the sunshine of ours.

If I could dwell
Where Israfel
Hath dwelt, and he where I,
He might not sing so wildly well
A mortal melody,
While a bolder note than this might swell
From my lyre within the sky.

## Eldorado[①]

Gaily bedight[②],
A gallant knight,
In sunshine and in shadow,
Had journeyed long,
Singing a song,
In search of Eldorado.

But he grew old —
This knight so bold —
And o'er his heart a shadow
Fell as he found
No spot of ground
That looked like Eldorado.

And, as his strength
Failed him at length,
He met a pilgrim shadow[③]—
"Shadow," said he,

---

① Eldorado: The gilded one (Spanish). The name of a mythical South American land of gold and vast wealth, sought by European explorers beginning in the sixteenth century; more generally, any such place.

② bedight: arrayed; dressed.

③ pilgrim shadow: shadow of a traveler.

"Where can it be —
This land of Eldorado?"

"Over the Mountains
Of the Moon,
Down the Valley of the Shadow,
Ride, boldly ride,"
The shade① replied —
"If you seek for Eldorado!"

## References and Further Reading


1. Auden, W. H. "Edgar Allan Poe." *Forewords and Afterwords*. Ed. Edward Mendelson. New York: Random House, 1973. 209-220.
2. Daniel, John Moncure. "Introduction to 'The Raven'." *Richmond Examiner*. September 25, 1849. Reprinted in *Edgar Allan Poe: The Critical Heritage*. Ed. I. M. Walker. London: Routledge & Kegan Paul, 1986. 145-147.
3. Fisher, Benjamin F. *The Cambridge Introduction to Edgar Allan Poe*. Cambridge: Cambridge University Press, 2008.
4. Griswold, Rufus Wilmot. "Memoir of the Author." *Critical Essays on Edgar Allan Poe*. Ed. Eric W. Carlson. Boston: G. K. Hall and Company, 1987. 52-58.
5. Saintsbury, George. "Edgar Allan Poe." *Prefaces and Essays*. Ed. Oliver Elton. Macmillan & Co., 1933. 314-323.
6. Weekes, Karen. "Poe's Feminine Ideal." *The Cambridge Companion to Edgar Allan Poe*. Ed. Kevin J. Hayes. Cambridge: Cambridge University Press, 2004. 148-162.
7. 爱伦·坡.爱伦·坡诗集(诗苑译林).曹明伦译.长沙:湖南文艺出版社,2012.
8. 曹明伦.诗人爱伦·坡和他的诗.中华读书报,2013 年 7 月 24 日.
9. 余光中.爱伦·坡的生平和作品.美国诗选,林以亮编选.北京:三联书店,1989.


① the shade: reference to the pilgrim shadow.

# 5. Walt Whitman (1819–1892)

## Introduction

Walt Whitman was born in 1819, into a working-class family. At the age of eleven, Whitman concluded formal schooling. He worked as an office boy, a teacher, a journalist, etc, and he didn't become a professional writer until he took up journalism. In 1855, Whitman published his first edition of Leaves of Grass, with his own money and not well received by the public. This book, however, is later regarded as the mark of birth of truly American poetry. During the Civil War, Whitman worked as a volunteer nurse, fought for freedom and democracy. Whitman died on March 26, 1892.

Whitman owns different titles. He is a democrat, an individualist, a nationalist, a pantheist, and often labeled as the father of free verse, though he did not invent it. Whitman believed that there was a symbiotic relationship between the poet and society. In his poems, he revealed an optimistic expectation and enthusiasm about new things and future. He showed his concern for the hardworking labors and attacked the slavery system. He advocated the pursuit of love, happiness, and individual value. He sang of nature, American nation, common people, human dignity, equality, freedom, democracy, and the bright future of human beings.

## Selected Reading A

### *From* Song of Myself

1

I celebrate myself, and sing myself,

And what I assume you shall assume,
For every atom belonging to me as good belongs to you.

I loafe[①] and invite my soul,
I lean and loafe at my ease observing a spear of summer grass.

My tongue, every atom of my blood, form'd from this soil, this air,
Born here of parents born here from parents the same, and their parents the same,
I, now thirty-seven years old in perfect health begin,
Hoping to cease not till death.

Creeds and schools in abeyance[②],
Retiring back a while sufficed at what they are, but never forgotten,
I harbor for good or bad, I permit to speak at every hazard,
Nature without check with original energy.

5

I believe in you my soul, the other I am must not abase itself to you,
And you must not be abased to the other.

Loafe with me on the grass, loose the stop from your throat,
Not words, not music or rhyme I want, not custom or lecture, not even the best,
Only the lull I like, the hum of your valvèd voice.

I mind how once we lay such a transparent summer morning,
How you settled your head athwart my hips and gently turn'd over upon me,
And parted the shirt from my bosom-bone, and plunged your tongue to my bare-stript heart,
And reach'd till you felt my beard, and reach'd till you held my feet.

Swiftly arose and spread around me the peace and knowledge that pass all the argument of the earth,
And I know that the hand of God is the promise of my own,
And I know that the spirit of God is the brother of my own,
And that all the men ever born are also my brothers, and the women my sisters

① loafe: loaf.

② in abeyance: a state of disuse or suspension; in the air.

and lovers,
And that a kelson[1] of the creation is love,
And limitless are leaves stiff or drooping in the fields,
And brown ants in the little wells beneath them,
And mossy scabs of the worm fence, heap'd stones, elder, mullein and poke-weed.

6
A child said *What is the grass*? fetching it to me with full hands;
How could I answer the child? I do not know what it is any more than he.

I guess it must be the flag of my disposition, out of hopeful green stuff woven.

Or I guess it is the handkerchief of the Lord,
A scented gift and remembrancer designedly dropt,
Bearing the owner's name someway in the corners, that we may see and remark, and say Whose?

Or I guess the grass is itself a child, the produced babe of the vegetation.

Or I guess it is a uniform hieroglyphic,
And it means, Sprouting alike in broad zones and narrow zones,
Growing among black folks as among white,
Kanuck[2], Tuckahoe[3], Congressman, Cuff[4], I give them the same, I receive them the same.

And now it seems to me the beautiful uncut hair of graves.

Tenderly will I use you curling grass,
It may be you transpire from the breasts of young men,
It may be if I had known them I would have loved them,
It may be you are from old people, or from offspring taken soon out of their mothers' laps,
And here you are the mothers' laps.

---

[1] kelson: keelson, a longitudinal beam connected to the keel of ship.
[2] Kanuck: Canuck, namely French Canadian.
[3] Tuckahoe: tidewater Virginian.
[4] Cuff: African American.

This grass is very dark to be from the white heads of old mothers,
Darker than the colorless beards of old men,
Dark to come from under the faint red roofs of mouths.

O I perceive after all so many uttering tongues,
And I perceive they do not come from the roofs of mouths for nothing.

I wish I could translate the hints about the dead young men and women,
And the hints about old men and mothers, and the offspring taken soon out of their laps.

What do you think has become of the young and old men?
And what do you think has become of the women and children?

They are alive and well somewhere,
The smallest sprout shows there is really no death,
And if ever there was it led forward life, and does not wait at the end to arrest it,
And ceas'd the moment life appear'd.

All goes onward and outward, nothing collapses,
And to die is different from what any one supposed, and luckier.

11
Twenty-eight young men bathe by the shore,
Twenty-eight young men and all so friendly;
Twenty-eight years of womanly life and all so lonesome.

She owns the fine house by the rise of the bank,
She hides handsome and richly drest aft the blinds of the window.

Which of the young men does she like the best?
Ah the homeliest of them is beautiful to her.

Where are you off to, lady? for I see you,
You splash in the water there, yet stay stock still in your room.

Dancing and laughing along the beach came the twenty-ninth bather,
The rest did not see her, but she saw them and loved them.

The beards of the young men glisten'd with wet, it ran from their long hair,
Little streams pass'd all over their bodies.

An unseen hand also pass'd over their bodies,
It descended tremblingly from their temples and ribs.

The young men float on their backs, their white bellies bulge to the sun, they do not ask who seizes fast to them,
They do not know who puffs and declines with pendant and bending arch,
They do not think whom they souse with spray.

13

The negro holds firmly the reins of his four horses, the block swags underneath on its tied-over chain,
The negro that drives the long dray of the stone-yard, steady and tall he stands pois'd on one leg on the string-piece,
His blue shirt exposes his ample neck and breast and loosens over his hip-band,
His glance is calm and commanding, he tosses the slouch of his hat away from his forehead,
The sun falls on his crispy hair and mustache, falls on the black of his polish'd and perfect limbs.

I behold the picturesque giant and love him, and I do not stop there,
I go with the team also.

In me the caresser of life wherever moving, backward as well as forward sluing,
To niches aside and junior bending, not a person or object missing,
Absorbing all to myself and for this song.

Oxen that rattle the yoke and chain or halt in the leafy shade, what is that you express in your eyes?
It seems to me more than all the print I have read in my life.

My tread scares the wood-drake and wood-duck on my distant and day-long ramble,
They rise together, they slowly circle around.

I believe in those wing'd purposes,
And acknowledge red, yellow, white, playing within me,

And consider green and violet and the tufted crown intentional,
And do not call the tortoise unworthy because she is not something else,
And the jay in the woods never studied the gamut, yet trills pretty well to me,
And the look of the bay mare shames silliness out of me.

24

Walt Whitman, a kosmos, of Manhattan the son,
Turbulent, fleshy, sensual, eating, drinking and breeding,
No sentimentalist, no stander above men and women or apart from them,
No more modest than immodest.

Unscrew the locks from the doors!
Unscrew the doors themselves from their jambs!

Whoever degrades another degrades me,
And whatever is done or said returns at last to me.

Through me the afflatus surging and surging, through me the current and index.

I speak the pass-word primeval, I give the sign of democracy,
By God! I will accept nothing which all cannot have their counterpart of on the same terms.

Through me many long dumb voices,
Voices of the interminable generations of prisoners and slaves,
Voices of the diseas'd and despairing and of thieves and dwarfs,
Voices of cycles of preparation and accretion,
And of the threads that connect the stars, and of wombs and of the father-stuff,
And of the rights of them the others are down upon,
Of the deform'd, trivial, flat, foolish, despised,
Fog in the air, beetles rolling balls of dung.

Through me forbidden voices,
Voices of sexes and lusts, voices veil'd and I remove the veil,
Voices indecent by me clarified and transfigur'd.

I do not press my fingers across my mouth,
I keep as delicate around the bowels as around the head and heart,
Copulation is no more rank to me than death is.

I believe in the flesh and the appetites,
Seeing, hearing, feeling, are miracles, and each part and tag of me is a miracle.

Divine am I inside and out, and I make holy whatever I touch or am touch'd from,
The scent of these arm-pits aroma finer than prayer,
This head more than churches, bibles, and all the creeds.

If I worship one thing more than another it shall be the spread of my own body, or any part of it,
Translucent mould of me it shall be you!
Shaded ledges and rests it shall be you!
Firm masculine colter it shall be you!
Whatever goes to the tilth of me it shall be you!
You my rich blood! your milky stream pale strippings of my life!
Breast that presses against other breasts it shall be you!
My brain it shall be your occult convolutions!
Root of wash'd sweet-flag! timorous pond-snipe! nest of guarded duplicate eggs! it shall be you!
Mix'd tussled hay of head, beard, brawn, it shall be you!
Trickling sap of maple, fibre of manly wheat, it shall be you!
Sun so generous it shall be you!
Vapors lighting and shading my face it shall be you!
You sweaty brooks and dews it shall be you!
Winds whose soft-tickling genitals rub against me it shall be you!
Broad muscular fields, branches of live oak, loving lounger in my winding paths, it shall be you!
Hands I have taken, face I have kiss'd, mortal I have ever touch'd, it shall be you.

I dote on myself, there is that lot of me and all so luscious,
Each moment and whatever happens thrills me with joy,
I cannot tell how my ankles bend, nor whence the cause of my faintest wish,
Nor the cause of the friendship I emit, nor the cause of the friendship I take again.

That I walk up my stoop, I pause to consider if it really be,
A morning-glory at my window satisfies me more than the metaphysics of books.

To behold the day-break!
The little light fades the immense and diaphanous shadows,
The air tastes good to my palate.

Hefts of the moving world at innocent gambols silently rising freshly exuding,
Scooting obliquely high and low.

Something I cannot see puts upward libidinous prongs,
Seas of bright juice suffuse heaven.

The earth by the sky staid with, the daily close of their junction,
The heav'd challenge from the east that moment over my head,
The mocking taunt, See then whether you shall be master!

52

The spotted hawk swoops by and accuses me, he complains of my gab and my loitering.

I too am not a bit tamed, I too am untranslatable,
I sound my barbaric yawp over the roofs of the world.

The last scud① of day holds back for me,
It flings my likeness after the rest and true as any on the shadow'd wilds,
It coaxes me to the vapor and the dusk.

I depart as air, I shake my white locks at the runaway sun,
I effuse my flesh in eddies, and drift it in lacy jags.

I bequeath myself to the dirt to grow from the grass I love,
If you want me again look for me under your boot-soles.

You will hardly know who I am or what I mean,
But I shall be good health to you nevertheless,
And filter and fibre your blood.

Failing to fetch me at first keep encouraged,
Missing me one place search another,

① scud: the swiftly moving cloud.

I stop somewhere waiting for you.

## About the Selection

《我自己的歌》是《草叶集》中最有名，也是诗集中最长的一首。该诗版本几经修改，最初题为"Poem of Walt Whitman, an American"，直到第七版才更名为大家所熟知的"Song of Myself"。该诗展现了惠特曼非凡的艺术构思和深邃的思想火花，对自我的描绘与歌颂也是对美国的描述和歌颂，将自我意识与民族意识合二为一，自我之歌因而也是民族之歌，民主之歌，平等自由之歌。诗中折射出的民族主义和民主主义光芒使之具有了史诗的性质。

## Research Guide

1. Walt Whitman's solution to the problem of a democratic American epic can be seen in miniature in *Song of Myself*, the initial poem in the first version *of Leaves of Grass*. Despite his admiration for older epic narratives, he found the aristocratic heroes of the Greeks, Romans, and north Europeans clearly unsuitable for a democratic work ... Whitman needed to invent a modem, democratic hero, and Jorges Luis Borges, for one, was struck by the poet's boldness. (Trecker, 2011: 11)

2. Whitman's response was an amazing one: he himself would be the hero of the poem — first, as common circumstances had made him, as an American of his time; second, as magnified by hope, by joy, by exultation, and by the proud, full sail of his great verse. (Miller, 1979: 38-39)

3. Whitman drew heavily on religious oratory and biblical language in the construction of his poems... Whitman most frequently presented himself as a competitor or successor to traditional religious views and his writings were frequently censored as obscene and impious. Whitman's emphasis on the divinity of the individual put him within the Transcendentalist tradition initiated by Ralph Waldo Emerson. (Corley, 2006:1)

---

# Selected Reading B

---

## O Captain! My Captain!

O Captain! my Captain! our fearful trip is done,
The ship has weather'd① every rack, the prize we sought is won,
The port is near, the bells I hear, the people all exulting②,

---

① weather'd: endure, get through.

② exulting: cheering.

While follow eyes the steady keel, the vessel grim and daring;
But O heart! heart! heart!
O the bleeding drops of red,
Where on the deck my Captain lies,
Fallen cold and dead.

O Captain! my Captain! rise up and hear the bells;
Rise up — for you the flag is flung — for you the bugle trills,
For you bouquets and ribbon'd wreaths — for you the shores a-crowding,
For you they call, the swaying mass, their eager faces turning;
Here Captain! dear father!
This arm beneath your head!
It is some dream that on the deck,
You've fallen cold and dead.

My Captain does not answer, his lips are pale and still,
My father does not feel my arm, he has no pulse nor will,
The ship is anchor'd safe and sound, its voyage closed and done,
From fearful trip the victor ship comes in with object won;
Exult O shores, and ring O bells!
But I with mournful tread①,
Walk the deck my Captain lies,
Fallen cold and dead.

## About the Selection

《船长,我的船长》发表于1865年,是为悼念刚被刺杀的林肯总统而作。1861年,美国内战爆发,林肯总统领导联邦军队,平息了叛乱,维护了美国的统一,废除了奴隶制度,为美国历史建立了卓著的功勋。然而,在内战胜利的时刻,林肯总统却遭暗杀身亡。惠特曼极度悲痛,写下了这首悲壮的诗。诗人将美国比作船,将林肯比作船长,将废奴运动和统一国家比作惊涛骇浪的航程。在诗行的安排上,惠特曼更是匠心独运地将其书写成了一艘艘航船的外形。林肯总统带领这艘航船乘风破浪,抵达安全的港湾,而自己却在举国欢腾之时死去。

## Research Guide

1. Speaking of the voice of the civil servant, the poet refuses really to engage the feeling unleashed by Lincoln's violent death... Through the rigid deployment of rhyme, meter, refrain and regularly patterned stanzas, Whitman keeps Lincoln's death distant, contained, and safe, as he memorializes the president in his more public and legendary

① tread: step.

dimension as the martyr of the cause of national union. (Erkkila 1989: 238)

2. With a mostly regular rhyme scheme (aabbcded), iambic rhythm of unaccented and accented syllables, and regular stanzaic shape, "O Captain! My Captain!" was a departure into tradition for Whitman, whose verse was mainly free verse devoid of regular meter, rhyme, and stanzas. This deviation would cause the poet problems because "O Captain! My Captain!" became one of his most popular poems: "If Walt Whitman had written a volume of My Captains," wrote a contemporary critic, "instead of filling a scrapbasket with waste and calling it a book the world would be better off today and Walt Whitman would have some excuse for living." (Hochman, 1997: 153)

3. There is a paradoxical character about Whitman's poems which it is important to note, and which makes it difficult even to criticize them in adequate terms without some appearance of paradox. He applies his mind's eye to so many things, sees them so intensely as wholes, and so clearly on all sides, and uses such decisive terms in speaking of them that he tends continually to overstate each aspect of the facts and to leave the several aspects, however conflicting they may be or appear, to harmonize themselves as best they may without his aid... The explanation of this is that Whitman is both an absolute realist and an absolute optimist. (Rossetti, 1949: 980)

## Supplementary Reading

### When I Heard the Learn'd Astronomer

When I heard the learn'd astronomer,
When the proofs, the figures, were ranged in columns before me,
When I was shown the charts and the diagrams, to add, divide, and measure them;
When I sitting heard the astronomer where he lectured with much applause in the lecture-room,
How soon unaccountable I became tired and sick,
Till rising and gliding out I wander'd off by myself,
In the mystical moist night-air, and from time to time,
Look'd up in perfect silence at the stars.

### A Noiseless Patient Spider

Anoiseless patient spider,

I mark'd where, on a little promontory① it stood, isolated,
Mark'd how to explore the vacant vast surrounding,
It launch'd forth filament②, filament, filament, out of itself,
Ever unreeling③ them, ever tirelessly speeding them.

And you O my soul where you stand,
Surrounded, detached, in measureless oceans of space,
Ceaselessly musing, venturing, throwing, seeking the spheres, to connect them;
Till the bridge you will need, be form'd, till the ductile anchor hold,
Till the gossamer④ thread you fling catch somewhere, O my Soul.

## References and Further Reading


1. Corley, Liam. "Literary Contexts in Poetry: Walt Whitman's 'Song of Myself'." *Understanding Literature — Literary Contexts in Poetry & Short Stories*, 2006.
2. Erkkila, Betsy. *Whitman the Political Poet*. Oxford: Oxford University Press, 1989.
3. Hochman, Jhan. "An Overview of 'O Captain! My Captain!'." *Poetry for Students* Vol. 2. Detroit: Gale, 1997. 153-156.
4. Miller, James E. *The American Quest for a Supreme Fiction*, *Whitman's Legacy in the Personal Epic*. Chicago: University of Chicago Press, 1979.
5. Rossetti, William Michael. "Walt Whitman's Poems." *The Poetry and Prose of Walt Whitman*. Ed. Louise Untermeyer. New York: Simon and Schuster, 1949. 977-982.
6. Trecker, Janice Law. "The Ecstatic Epistemology of Song of Myself." *Midwest Quarterly*, 53.1 (2011): 11-25.
7. 惠特曼.草叶集.赵萝蕤译.上海:上海译文出版社, 1991.


① promontory: a cliff that juts out into the sea.
② filament: a very slender fiber.
③ unreeling: unwind from a reel.
④ gossamer: spider's thread.

# 6. Emily Dickinson (1830–1886)

## Introduction

Emily Elizabeth Dickinson (1830 – 1886) was born in Amherst, Massachusetts, to a successful family with strong community ties. Dickinson spent seven years at the Amherst Academy, taking classes in English, history, classical literature, "mental philosophy," arithmetic, etc. Dickinson was known for her penchant for white clothing and reluctance to greet guests. After 1858, she seldom left her house, and after 70s, even her room. She lived a contemplative life, a somehow monastic life, and thus was even nicknamed "the nun of Amherst." Dickinson composed 1 775 poems, among which only about seven was published during her lifetime. Dickinson's cache of poems was not discovered until her death in 1886 by her sister Lavinia, and her first collection of poetry was published and heavily edited in 1890 by her personal acquaintances Thomas Wentworth Higginson and Mabel Loomis Todd. *The Poems of Emily Dickinson*, a complete and mostly unaltered collection of Dickinson's poetry was published by Thomas H. Johnson in 1955.

Dickinson's poems can be divided into three different periods. Before 1861, her poems are more conventional and sentimental. From 1861 to 1865 is the most creative period of Dickinson, and a lot of poems created in this period share the theme of immortality and death. The third period begins from 1866, almost 2/3 of her poems are written before this year. Dickinson's poems are unique for her era considering the choice of diction, image, grammar and rhyme. Her poems are usually rich in images, contain short lines, lack titles, recurrently use dashes, and often adopt slant rhyme, etc. Her poems are usually interpreted by readers into multiple meanings. The inner world, religious views, ideas on love, nature, and death are recurrent themes of her poems.

## Selected Reading A

### Because I could not stop for Death

Because I could not stop for Death —
He kindly stopped for me —
The Carriage held but just Ourselves —
And Immortality.

We slowly drove — He knew no haste
And I had put away
My labor and my leisure too,
For His Civility①—

We passed the School, where Children strove②
At Recess — in the Ring —
We passed the Fields of Gazing Grain — ③
We passed the Setting Sun —④

Or rather — He passed Us —
The Dews drew quivering and Chill —
For only Gossamer, my Gown⑤—
My Tippet — only Tulle⑥—

We paused before a House⑦ that seemed
A Swelling of the Ground —
The Roof was scarcely visible —
The Cornice⑧— in the Ground —

---

① civility: politeness.
② Represents the childhood.
③ Represents the middle age.
④ Represents the old age, dying.
⑤ The wedding dress for her marriage to Death.
⑥ tulle: netting.
⑦ house: tomb of the speaker.
⑧ cornice: A molding at the corner between the ceiling and the top of a wall.

Since then — 'tis Centuries — and yet
Feels shorter than the Day
I first surmised the Horses' Heads
Were toward Eternity —

## About the Selection

《因为我不能停下来等待死亡》是一首关于死亡的诗。狄金森将死亡比作一位驾着马车风度翩翩的绅士，带着女主人公驶向坟墓，随行的还有"永生"。马车载着她走过孩子们的校园，走过成熟的庄稼地，告别西沉的斜阳，隐喻人生所经历的童年、中年、晚年三个阶段。诗中的死亡一反常人眼中狰狞的面目，变成了女主人公的未婚夫，载着身披婚纱的她驶向坟墓。因而这首诗被普遍认为是表达了诗人对死亡的从容。她从一个全新的角度来阐释死亡与永生，告诉人们死亡并不可怕，而是通往永生的大门。

## Research Guide

1. ["Because I could not stop for Death" is] one of the perfect poems in English... and it exemplifies better than anything else [Emily Dickinson] wrote the special quality of her mind... If the word great means anything in poetry, this poem is one of the greatest in the English language; it is flawless to the last detail. (Tate, 1936: 13-14)

2. Allen Tate is on the right track in referring to death as her "general symbol of Nature." It is the logical culmination of nature, and the greatest example of the change which is constantly moving through nature... Emily Dickinson's wild nights are bound and her fears assuaged with the images of her immediate reality. But this immediate reality is made up of her personal terms, and has come from her own heart, not from the tenets of her church. (Larrabee, 1943: 117)

3. A comment by Richard Chase on Emily Dickinson's "Because I Could not stop for Death," reads in part as follows:

*The only pressing technical objection to this poem is the remark that "Immortality" in the first stanza is a meretricious and unnecessary personification and that the common sense of the situation demands that Immortality ought to be the destination of the coach and not one of the passengers. The personification of death, however, is unassailable. In the literal meaning of the poem, he is apparently a successful citizen who has amorous but genteel intentions. He is also God...*

The trouble with this remark is that it does not present the common sense of the situation... The horses' heads are toward eternity, but not toward immortality. (Hoepfner, 1957: 96)

4. The central theme [of"Because I could not stop for Death"] is the interpretation of mortal experience from the standpoint of immortality. A theme stemming from that is the defining of eternity as timelessness. The poet uses these abstractions — mortality, immortality, and eternity — in terms of images. (Glenn, 1943: 585)

5. Although the poem"Because I could not stop for Death —" (no. 712) may seem to have been picked clean by extensive and repeated dissections, that jewel in the crown of Emily Dickinson's poetic oeuvre can still surprise us with some facets which have eluded scrutiny... Analyzing the poem sequentially, line by line, has tended to obscure some structural patterns. From a satellite view, however, two significant features stand out: verbs of uncertainty and phrases of reversal. (Frank, 2000: 82)

## Selected Reading B

### The Soul selects her own Society

The Soul selects her own Society —
Then — shuts the Door —
To her divine Majority —
Present no more —

Unmoved — she notes the Chariots — pausing —
At her low Gate —
Unmoved — an Emperor be kneeling
Upon her Mat —

I've known her — from an ample nation —
Choose One —
Then — close the Valves of her attention —
Like Stone —

### About the Selection

该诗写于1862年狄金森创作的鼎盛时期。人们对它有多种不同的解释。有人认为这首诗表达了狄金森对 Charles Wadsworth 的情有独钟,也有人认为狄金森这首诗中的社会指的是她的诗歌创作事业,表达自己选择了终身的事业,决定远离社交场合,不再与人交往。还有人把该诗当作是一首关于狄金森宗教信仰的诗。当然,也有人认为这首诗与作者本身的经历无关,诗是自主体,是人类经验的共性。

## Research Guide

1. This poem is not usually conceived of as a riddle, but rather as a description of those instinctive preferences and choices, those defiantly nonrational elections and allegiances... To the degree that the poem has been construed as a private and guarded revelation of the poet's emotional life, and to some circumstantial events in it, there is a dispute about whether the choice of "one" means someone else or the poet herself; whether she is electing the solitude of a society of one, or committing herself to another. And it is not out of place, I think, to construe the poem as being about love. (Hecht, 1986: 108)

2. Poem 303 is a strong statement about the power of the self alone. The soul is shown living within a space defined by door, gate, and mat. The external world, with its nations and their rulers, is kept outside... Traditional ideas about power are reversed here. Not control over vast populations but the ability to construct a world for oneself comprises the greatest power, a god-like achievement, announces the opening stanza. Not only is the soul alone "divine," but it is also identified as "Society" and "Majority": the poem also challenges our ideas about what constitutes a social group. (Juhasz, 1983: 15)

## Supplementary Reading

### Success

Success is counted sweetest
By those who ne'er succeed.
To comprehend a nectar[1]
Requires sorest need.

Not one of all the purple Host[2]
Who took the Flag today
Can tell the definition,
So clear of Victory,

① nectar: a sweet liquid secretion that is attractive to pollinators, usually referring the food and drink of the gods; mortals who ate it became immortal.

② the purple Host: referring to the army.

As he defeated — dying —
On whose forbidden ear
The distant strains of triumph
Break, agonized and clear.

## Wild Nights! — Wild Nights!

Wild Nights — Wild Nights!
Were I with thee
Wild nights should be
Our luxury!

Futile — the winds —
To a Heart in port —
Done with the Compass —
Done with the Chart!

Rowing in Eden —
Ah — the Sea!
Might I but moor — tonight —
In thee!

## "Hope" is the thing with feathers

"Hope" is the thing with feathers —
That perches in the soul —
And sings the tune without the words —
And never stops — at all —

And sweetest — in the Gale — is heard —
And sore must be the storm —
That could abash the little Bird
That kept so many warm —

I've heard it in the chillest land —
And on the strangest Sea —
Yet — never — in Extremity,
It asked a crumb — of me.

## Much Madness is divinest Sense

Much Madness is divinest Sense —

To a discerning Eye —
Much Sense — the starkest Madness —
'Tis the Majority
In this, as all, prevail —
Assent — and you are sane —
Demur — you're straightway dangerous —
And handled with a Chain —

## I died for Beauty — but was scarce

I died for Beauty — but was scarce
Adjusted in the Tomb
When One who died for Truth, was lain
In an adjoining Room —

He questioned softly "Why I failed?"
"For Beauty", I replied —
"And I — for Truth — Themself are One —
We Brethren, are", He said —

And so, as Kinsmen, met a Night —
We talked between the Rooms —
Until the Moss had reached our lips —
And covered up — our names —

## I heard a Fly buzz — when I died —

I heard a Fly buzz — when I died —
The Stillness in the Room
Was like the Stillness in the Air —
Between the Heaves of Storm —

The Eyes around — had wrung them dry —
And Breaths were gathering firm
For that last Onset — when the King
Be witnessed — in the Room —

I willed my Keepsakes — Signed away
What portion of me be
Assignable — and then it was

There interposed a Fly —

With Blue — uncertain stumbling Buzz —
Between the light — and me —
And then the Windows failed — and then
I could not see to see —

## The Brain — is wider than the Sky —

The Brain — is wider than the Sky —
  For — put them side by side —
The one the other will contain
  With ease — and You — beside.

The Brain is deeper than the sea —
  For — hold them — Blue to Blue —
The one the other will absorb —
  As Sponges — Buckets — do —

The Brain is just the weight of God —
  For — Heft them — Pound for Pound —
And they will differ, if they do,
  As Syllable from Sound —

## A narrow Fellow in the Grass

A narrow Fellow in the Grass
Occasionally rides—
You may have met Him — did you not
His notice sudden is —

The Grass divides as with a Comb —
A spotted shaft is seen —
And then it closes at your feet
And opens further on —

He likes a Boggy Acre —
A Floor too cool for Corn —
But when a Boy and Barefoot —
I more than once at Noon

Have passed, I thought, a Whip lash
Unbraiding in the Sun
When stooping to secure it
It wrinkled, and was gone —

Several of Nature's People
I know, and they know me —
I feel for them a transport
Of cordiality —

But never met this Fellow
Attended, or alone
Without a tighter breathing
And Zero at the Bone —

## Tell all the Truth but tell it slant

Tell all the Truth but tell it slant —
Success in Circuit lies
Too bright for our infirm Delight
The Truth's superb surprise
As Lightning to the Children eased
With explanation kind
The Truth must dazzle gradually
Or every man be blind —

## To make a prairie

To make a prairie it takes a clover and one bee, —
One clover, and a bee,
And revery.
The revery alone will do,
If bees are few.

## References and Further Reading

1. Chase, Richard. *Modern Poetry and the Tradition*. Chapel Hill: The University of North Carolina Press, 1939.
2. Frank, Bernhard. "Dickinson's 'Because I Could Not Stop for Death —'." *The Explicator* 58.2 (2000): 82-84.

3. Glenn, Eunice. "Emily Dickinson's Poetry: A Revaluation." *The Sewanee Review*, 51 (1943): 574-588.

4. Hecht, Anthony. "The Riddles of Emily Dickinson." *Obbligati: Essays on Criticism*. New York: Atheneum, 1986. 85-117.

5. Hoepfner, Theodore C. "'Because I Could Not Stop for Death'." *American Literature*, 29.1 (1957): 96.

6. Juhasz, Suzanne. *The Undiscovered Continent: Emily Dickinson and the Space of the Mind*. Bloomington: Indiana University Press, 1983.

7. Larrabee, Ankey. "Three Studies in Modern Poetry." *Accent*, 3 (1943): 115-121.

8. Tate, Allen. *Reactionary Essays on Poetry and Ideas*. New York: Charles Scribner's Sons, 1936.

9. 狄金森.艾米莉・狄金森全集.蒲隆译.上海:上海译文出版社,2013.

10. 刘守兰.狄金森研究.上海:上海外语教育出版社,2006.

# 7. Edwin Arlington Robinson (1869–1935)

## Introduction

Edwin Arlington Robinson was born on December 22, 1869, in Head Tide, Maine. He is the descendant of Anne Bradstreet. Robinson's family had many alcohol problems, and his brother died of alcohol poisoning. His childhood was described as "stark and unhappy." When he was 21, he entered Harvard. His first book was published in 1896. During his life, Robinson won the Pulitzer Prize for poetry three times: 1922, 1925 and 1928. Robison maintained a solitary life and never married. He died in New York in April, 1935.

Robinson's writing was shaped by the conflicts and problems of his life and the lives of those around him. He is an important poet in the transition from American traditional poetry to modern poetry. His poetry is stylistically simple and neat, and rhymes with basic rhyme schemes. It has simple feet and meter, and lyrical construction. Robinson's poems are usually psychological, typified, and are famous for his use of the dramatic monologue. His tone is ironic and aloof, which combines seriousness and humor. Most frequented themes in his poetry include: failure of the American dream, Arthurian legends, anti-materialism, failure of individual relationship, etc.

## Selected Reading A

### Miniver Cheevy

Miniver Cheevy, child of scorn,
  Grew lean while he assailed the seasons;
He wept that he was ever born,
  And he had reasons.

Miniver loved the days of old
  When swords were bright and steeds were prancing;
The vision of a warrior bold
  Would set him dancing.

Miniver sighed for what was not,
  And dreamed, and rested from his labors;
He dreamed of Thebes and Camelot①,
  And Priam's② neighbors.

Miniver mourned the ripe renown
  That made so many a name so fragrant;
He mourned Romance, now on the town,
  And Art, a vagrant.

Miniver loved the Medici③,
  Albeit he had never seen one;
He would have sinned incessantly
  Could he have been one.

Miniver cursed the commonplace
  And eyed a khaki suit④ with loathing;

---

① Thebes: Greek city on the Nile. Camelot: the mythical city of King Arthur's court.

② Priam: king of Troy, father of Aeneus (founder of Rome) and killed in the seven years' war with the Greek at Troy.

③ Medici: rulers of Renaissance Florence known for both a love of scholarship and art, and a penchant for a pitiless use of power.

④ a khaki suit: a military uniform, colored yellow-brown.

He missed the medieval grace
Of iron clothing.

Miniver scorned the gold he sought,
But sore annoyed was he without it;
Miniver thought, and thought, and thought,
And thought about it.

Miniver Cheevy, born too late,
Scratched his head and kept on thinking;
Miniver coughed, and called it fate,
And kept on drinking.

## About the Selection

这首诗发表于1921年,是一首戏剧抒情诗。诗中的主人公米尼弗·契维生活在20世纪却渴望过去的英雄式生活。他以怀念旧时光及喝酒来逃避现实的重压。他将自己生活的失败归罪于命运,归罪于生不逢时的悲剧。这是一首充满讽刺色彩的诗,诗人借契维来讽刺那些活在幻想的旧时光里不能自拔而不愿面对现实的人。但从另一个角度来看,诗人同时也讽刺了契维时代那些经济富足却过分贬低过去的人。

## Research Guide

1. In no poem in *The Town Down The River* was the problem of the artist more sharply etched than in the popular "Miniver Cheevy." Miniver Cheevy was drawn to the past as he dreamed of Thebes and Camelot. He disliked the present, cursing the commonplace. But the crux of his difficulty was that he "scorned the gold he sought/ But sore annoyed was he without it." This was a succinct rendering of the dynamic which motivated much of Robinson's commentary on mankind's search for happiness. (Burton, 1987: 54)

2. "Miniver Cheevy" is usually described as a mocking self-portrait, but such an observation tells us little about the poem itself. Indeed, such phrases as "mocking self-portrait" are usually a means of dodging a poem. I suggest that one must ask why Miniver Cheevy (not Edwin Arlington Robinson) prefers an earlier, more "romantic" era than his own, what it is that he loses, if anything, by being out of phase with his time, and, finally, if his anachronistic attachment is virtuous or vicious. These questions burden an admittedly middle-weight poem and I shall not burden it further with specific answers. Still, does not the sum of reasonable answers amount to an impression that Miniver's escapism is really an effort to establish an individuality which a world of "progress" denies? (Squires, 1969: 181-182)

3. In "Miniver Cheevy" three aspects of nineteenth-and early twentieth-century American culture, as analyzed by T. J. Jackson Lears, resonate: materialism, which with its components of work, action, and acquisition formed the ethos of the age and the measure of progress; militarism, a manifestation of the effort to overcome the ennui of the age and what was perceived as the feminization of American culture in the latter nineteenth century; and antimodernism, an expression of the desire to escape the material-spiritual dilemmas that persisted and an effort to retrieve, if only in the imagination, the glories and principles of an earlier time. Clearly, the three are interrelated and all find satirical rendering in Robinson's poem. (Sullivan, 1986: 186)

4. In "Miniver Cheevy," without question a self-portrait, Robinson could laugh at the contradictions in his own life; but, while laughing, he could see that Miniver was a character to be projected into the universal... But Robinson was acutely aware of the complex and highly structured nature of poetry; and he was, moreover, too skillful a craftsman not to insist upon excellence in poetic form. Further still, he was especially conscious of the quality of language; the variable responses that words can and do elicit. In Cheevy, juxtaposed contrasts of past and present, of ideality and reality, of contempt for money and a recognized need for it, of Art and Romance on the one hand and vagrancy on the other: these are the elements that lift the poem onto a high plane of artistic achievement. (Franchere, 1968: 79)

## Selected Reading B

### Richard Cory

Whenever Richard Cory went down town,
We people on the pavement looked at him:
He was a gentleman from sole to crown,
Clean favored, and imperially slim.

And he was always quietly arrayed,
And he was always human when he talked;
But still he fluttered pulses when he said,
"Good-morning," and he glittered when he walked.

And he was rich — yes, richer than a king —
And admirably schooled in every grace:
In fine, we thought that he was everything

To make us wish that we were in his place.

So on we worked, and waited for the light,
And went without the meat, and cursed the bread;
And Richard Cory, one calm summer night,
Went home and put a bullet through his head.

## About the Selection

这首小诗将克利的一生凝聚于短短十六行诗句中。他拥有常人眼中代表成功的一切:光彩的外表,高贵的举止,无尽的财富,过人的才智。所有人都认为他是幸福和成功的,然而他却出人意料地自杀了。最后一行中的这颗子弹结束的是克利的生命和人们对成功的偏见。常人眼中的成功却是某些人眼中的虚无,没有任何意义。物质的富足也无法弥补精神的空虚与内心的孤独和黑暗。这首诗经常被认为传达出了现代人内心的孤寂与创伤,因而克利也被普遍认为是"心理困惑"的一个代名词。当然,这首诗也可以从其他角度进行解读。例如,常人看到的光鲜往往只在表面,外表往往是具有欺骗性的;或是美国梦的破灭;也有人认为这首诗是关于他死于 1901 年的兄弟。

## Research Guide

1. Here we have a man's life-story distilled into sixteen lines. A dramatist would have been under the necessity of justifying the suicide by some train of events in which Richard Cory's character would have inevitably betrayed him. A novelist would have dissected the psychological effects of these events upon Richard Cory. The poet, with a more profound grasp of life than either, shows us only what life itself *would* show us; we know Richard Cory only through the effect of his personality upon those who were familiar with him, and we take both the character and the motive for granted as equally inevitable. Therein lies the ironic touch, which is intensified by the simplicity of the poetic form in which this tragedy is given expression. (Morris, 1969: 22)

2. The suicide of Richard Cory is not, or ought not to be, a surprise. It is an inevitability, predetermined by the subjugation of selfhood. Even more significantly, however, the subjugated self reclaims itself in the act of suicide. Not that the poem recommends suicide as a way of asserting individuality. Rather, it observes an extreme gesture in an extreme case. To see the poem in this way is to see it as neither bitter nor negative, at least not entirely so. We read ill if we cannot see that Richard Cory is granted an oblique triumph at the end, for he has refused to suppose himself made happy by what "everyone" supposes will make him everyone happy. In short, Richard Cory's self emerges neurotically perhaps; still it emerges triumphant over the imposed role of "success". (Squires, 1969: 181)

3. "Richard Cory" is wry, grim, laconic: it is a typical Robinsonian perception of the bleak comedy of the human condition, and this perception features in much of his best — and worst — work. In addition, the poem has that first-rate anecdotal quality which Robinson shares with Hardy... (Lucas, 1985: 32)

4. Was it his conspicuous wealth, his lonely existence without family or kin, or perhaps some secret crime he committed that led him to take his own life? We never know; what we are left with is the darkness inside his soul, which only grows more impenetrable as one reflects on it. Robinson keeps himself out of the poem, letting it be told by the people of the town, the "we" who are left to puzzle it out at the end. Despite having a name symbolic of a noble family — *Richard Cory* rhymes with *glory* and evokes the name of Richard Coeur de Lion — Cory's death leaves behind no other "king" in Tilbury Town. (Pratt, 1996: 116)

## Supplementary Reading

### Credo

I cannot find my way: there is no star
In all the shrouded heavens anywhere;
And there is not a whisper in the air
Of any living voice but one so far
That I can hear it only as a bar
Of lost, imperial music, played when fair
And angel fingers wove, and unaware,
Dead leaves to garlands where no roses are.

No, there is not a glimmer, nor a call,
For one that welcomes, welcomes when he fears,
The black and awful chaos of the night;
For through it all — above, beyond it all —
I know the far-sent message of the years,
I feel the coming glory of the Light.

### The Sheaves

Where long the shadows of the wind had rolled,
Green wheat was yielding to the change assigned;
And as by some vast magic undivined

The world was turning slowly into gold.
Like nothing that was ever bought or sold
It waited there, the body and the mind;
And with a mighty meaning of a kind
That tells the more the more it is not told.

So in a land where all days are not fair,
Fair days went on till on another day
A thousand golden sheaves were lying there,
Shining and still, but not for long to stay —
As if a thousand girls with golden hair
Might rise from where they slept and go away.

## Mr. Flood's Party

Old Eben Flood, climbing alone one night
Over the hill between the town below
And the forsaken upland hermitage
That held as much as he should ever know
On earth again of home, paused warily.
The road was his with not a native near;
And Eben, having leisure, said aloud,
For no man else in Tilbury Town to hear:

"Well, Mr. Flood, we have the harvest moon
Again, and we may not have many more;
The bird is on the wing, the poet says,
And you and I have said it here before.
Drink to the bird." He raised up to the light
The jug that he had gone so far to fill,
And answered huskily: "Well, Mr. Flood,
Since you propose it, I believe I will."

Alone, as if enduring to the end
A valiant armor of scarred hopes outworn,
He stood there in the middle of the road
Like Roland's ghost winding a silent horn.
Below him, in the town among the trees,
Where friends of other days had honored him,
A phantom salutation of the dead

Rang thinly till old Eben's eyes were dim.

Then, as a mother lays her sleeping child
Down tenderly, fearing it may awake,
He set the jug down slowly at his feet
With trembling care, knowing that most things break;
And only when assured that on firm earth
It stood, as the uncertain lives of men
Assuredly did not, he paced away,
And with his hand extended paused again:

"Well, Mr. Flood, we have not met like this
In a long time; and many a change has come
To both of us, I fear, since last it was
We had a drop together. Welcome home!"
Convivially returning with himself,
Again he raised the jug up to the light;
And with an acquiescent quaver said:
"Well, Mr. Flood, if you insist, I might.

"Only a very little, Mr. Flood —
For auld lang syne. No more, sir; that will do."
So, for the time, apparently it did,
And Eben evidently thought so too;
For soon amid the silver loneliness
Of night he lifted up his voice and sang,
Secure, with only two moons listening,
Until the whole harmonious landscape rang —

"For auld lang syne." The weary throat gave out,
The last word wavered; and the song being done,
He raised again the jug regretfully
And shook his head, and was again alone.
There was not much that was ahead of him,
And there was nothing in the town below —
Where strangers would have shut the many doors
That many friends had opened long ago.

## The House on the Hill

They are all gone away,
  The House is shut and still,
There is nothing more to say.

Through broken walls and gray
  The winds blow bleak and shrill;
They are all gone away.

Nor is there one to-day
  To speak them good or ill:
There is nothing more to say.

Why is it then we stray
  Around that sunken sill?
They are all gone away.

And our poor fancy-play
  For them is wasted skill:
There is nothing more to say.

There is ruin and decay
  In the House on the Hill:
They are all gone away,
There is nothing more to say.

## References and Further Reading


1. Burton, David H. *Edwin Arlington Robinson: Stages in a New England Poet's Search*. Lewiston: Edwin Mellen Press, 1987.
2. Franchere, Hoyt C. *Edwin Arlington Robinson*. New York: Twayne Publishers, 1968.
3. Lucas, John. *Moderns and Contemporaries*. Brighton, Sussex : Harvester Press, 1985.
4. Morris, Lloyd. *The Poetry of Edwin Arlington Robinson: An Essay in Appreciation*. Port Washington: Kennikat Press, 1969.
5. Pratt, William. *Singing the Chaos: Madness and Wisdom in Modern Poetry*. Kansas City: Curators of the University of Missouri, 1996.
6. Squires, Radcliffe. "Tilbury Town Today." *Edwin Arlington Robinson: Centenary Essays*.

Ed. Ellsworth Barnard. Athens: University of Georgia Press, 1969. 175-184.

7. Sullivan, Winifred H. "The Double-Edged Irony of E. A. Robinson's 'Miniver Cheevy'." *Colby Library Quarterly* 22.3 (1986): 185-191.

# 8. Robert Frost (1874–1963)

## Introduction

Robert Lee Frost is highly regarded for his realistic depictions of rural life and his command of American colloquial speech. His work frequently employed settings from rural life in New England in the early twentieth century. He won the Pulitzer Prize for four times and received honorary degrees. In 1961, when he was 87, he was honored to read one of his poems at the inauguration of President John F. Kennedy.

Frost began his writing of his poems very early and got a good reputation for it. After school, he had to run a farm left by his grandfather to support the family. He was a sincere lover of nature and country life. However, most of his poetic works were refused by publishing houses in the United States. Therefore, he decided to go to England. It was Ezra Pound who brought him to the attention of influential critics and introduced him to British publishers. Later he was forced to return to the United States because of the First World War. To his surprise, Frost was welcomed by American people and American publishers. Anyway Frost still considered the farm his home and its activities remained the focus of his poetic works.

Frost was a serious poet. He wrote many poems investigating the basic themes of human life. Frost learned from tradition and made the colloquial New England speech into a poetic expression. Compared with his contemporaries, his poems are filled with more energy and loaded with more pleasure. He combined the traditional sonnet, rhyming couplets and blank verse with American local speech rhythm. With a simple form, his poems presented profound ideas.

## Selected Reading A

### Mending Wall

Something there is that doesn't love a wall,
That sends[①] the frozen-ground-swell under it,
And spills the upper boulders[②] in the sun;
And makes gaps even two can pass abreast.
The work of hunters is another thing[③]:
I have come after them[④] and made repair
Where they have left not one stone on a stone[⑤],
But they would have the rabbit out of hiding,
To please the yelping dogs. The gaps I mean,
No one has seen them made or heard them made,
But at spring mending-time we find them there.
I let my neighbor know beyond the hill;
And on a day we meet to walk the line[⑥]
And set the wall between us once again.
We keep the wall between us as we go.
To each the boulders that have fallen to each.
And some are loaves[⑦] and some so nearly balls
We have to use a spell to make them balance:
"Stay where you are until our backs are turned!"
We wear our fingers rough with handling them.
Oh, just another kind of out-door game,
One on a side. It comes to little more:
There where it is we do not need the wall:
He is all pine and I am apple orchard.
My apple trees will never getacross
And eat the cones under his pines, I tell him.

---

① sends: cause to become.
② boulders: large round stones.
③ is another thing: maybe the other possible reason.
④ them: the hunters.
⑤ have left not one stone on a stone: have turned over every piece of stone.
⑥ to walk the line: to measure, to walk along the fence together.
⑦ loaves: boulders in a long, round shape.

He only says, "Good fences make good neighbors."
Spring is the mischief in me, and I wonder
If I could put a notion in his head:
"*Why* do they make good neighbors? Isn't it
Where there are cows? But here there are no cows.
Before I built a wall I'd ask to know
What I was walling in or walling out①,
And to whom I was like to give offense.
Something there is that doesn't love a wall,
That wants it down." I could say "Elves" to him,
But it's not elves exactly, and I'd rather
He said it for himself. I see him there
Bringing a stone grasped firmly by the top
In each hand, like an old-stone savage armed②.
He moves in darkness as it seems to me,
Not of woods only and the shade of trees.
He will not go behind③ his father's saying,
And he likes having thought of it so well
He says again, "Good fences make good neighbors."

## About the selection

《修墙》是弗罗斯特的一首名诗,诗中描写的是一件既平凡又简单的小事——修墙。然而,在修墙这件事的后面却蕴含着极其深刻的人生哲理:人与人之间的相互沟通。从字面上看,诗人讲的是一堵石墙,而实际上他讲的是人与人之间相互沟通的障碍——一堵堵有形或无形的隔墙。人世间有许多毫无存在理由或存在必要的有形或无形的墙、障碍,墙倒塌了是因为有很多人不喜欢它,不需要它。人们应该解放思想,共同拆除这些人为的障碍。令人遗憾的是,他终未能使他的邻居觉醒而停止修墙或开始拆墙,因为他的那位邻居深信:"有好的围墙才能有好的邻居。"

## Research Guide

1. In sum, the speaker of the poem exhibits, both in his manner and in his actions, a certain flexibility. He unsettles walls that he also always repairs; he is at once Apollonian and Dionysian. Once again — as in the introduction to *King Jasper* and "The Future of Man" — Frost's conservative and rebellious tendencies are perfectly balanced, just as the "intransigent" and "accommodating" tendencies of the speaker of "Good Hours" are

① walking in: enclose with a wall  walking out: defend against; get rid of.

② an old-stone savage armed: like an armed uncivilized man of the Old Stone Age.

③ go behind: have a profound thinking about.

metrically and thematically balanced. (Richardson, 1997: 143-144)

2. At the conscious level (if we adopt Northrop Frye's centering theme) the poem plays off two human attitudes, one wintry, one spring-like. The warm spring-like (but dangerous) walls-down feeling corresponds to a poet's wish for a cozy but risky return to some original oneness. The neighbor's wintry, New England stand offishness, his walls-up sense of privacy and separateness, corresponds to the cold, hard, more grownup reality of individuation. In a theme Richard Poirier develops, the walls-down feeling corresponds to the poet's wayward imaginings, the walls-up to the control of that imagination. (Holland, 1988: 31)

3. 诗歌的浓郁的艺术魅力有时可以是双重的,甚至是三重的。《修墙》不仅洋溢着不可抑制的幽默感,更好的是,它还蕴藏着耐人寻味的哲理性。既有内心的微笑,又有内心的思考,这正是弗罗斯特诗歌艺术的了不起的成就。《修墙》长期受到读者的欢迎,被公认为弗罗斯特的代表作之一,不是偶然的,它充分展现了诗人的这种成熟的艺术风格。(方平,1988:13)

## Selected Reading B

### Fire and Ice

Some say the world will end in fire,
Some say in ice.
From what I've tasted of desire[1]
I hold with those who favor fire.
But if it had to perish twice,
I think I know enough of hate
To say that for destruction ice
Is also great
And would suffice[2].

### About the selection

《冰与火》是罗伯特·弗罗斯特颇受欢迎的一首抒情诗。诗歌以小言大,短小精悍,充满无限的寓意。作者比较分析了火与冰这两种极具毁灭性的力量,在开头两句道出世界毁灭于火或者冰的可能,并用火象征激情与欲望,用冰象征冷酷和仇恨。

[1] tasted of desire: understanding or knowledge about "desire."

[2] suffice: be enough; be adequate (to destroy the world).

## Research Guide

1. Like ice shrieking across a red-hot griddle, his poetry does, indeed, ride on its own melting. One cannot, and Frost has ensured this absolutely with his unstable irony, make a validated choice between the fire and the ice, or between the language, so insistently mundane, and the potent oversound. Fire and ice are, after all, the inextricable complementarities of one apocalyptic vision: that endlessly regenerative cycle of desire and (self) hatred that necessarily brings the productive poet to scourge his own voice as he mocks both the poetic vocation and the state to which poetry-and if poetry then all language-has come. Frost anticipates modernism's lament and, it may be said, prefigures in his dualism its dubious palliative of self-referential irony. The lyric birds and the weary speakers tell us the genuine Frostian wisdom of achieving a commonsensical accommodation with the fallen world, while inciting at another, and ineffable, level a profound disquiet. (Kearns, 1994: 159)

2. For a poet, Robert Frost was a pretty good scientist, say astrophysicists Fred Adams and Greg Laughlin. Frost's fire-or-ice scenario neatly sums up two outcomes from their new study of possible future encounters between our solar system and passing stars. (Pobojewski, 1999: 28)

# Supplementary Reading

## Design

I found a dimpled spider, fat and white,
On a white heal-all①, holding up a moth
Like a white piece of rigid satin② cloth —
Assorted characters of death and blight
Mixed ready to begin the morning right③,
Like the ingredients④ of a witches' broth —
A snow-drop spider, a flower like a froth,
And dead wings carried like a paper kite.

① heal-all: plant that is believed to cure every disease.
② stain: silk material that is shiny and smooth on one side.
③ Mixed ready to begin the morning right: wake up right in the morning.
④ ingredients: the characters of death and blight which had been mixed ready to cook the broth.

What had that flower to do with being white,
The wayside blue and innocent heal-all?
What brought the kindred spider to that height,
Then steered the white moth thither in the night?
What but design of darkness to appall? —
If design govern in a thing so small.

## The Pasture

I'll only stop to rake the leaves away
(And wait to watch the water clear, I may):
I shan't be gone long. — You come too.

I'm going out to fetch the little calf
That's standing by the mother. It's so young,
It totters when she licks it with her tongue.
I shan't be gone long. — You come too.

## My November Guest

My Sorrow, when she's here with me,
    Thinks these dark days of autumn rain
Are beautiful as days can be;
She loves the bare, the withered tree;
    She walks the sodden pasture lane.

Her pleasure will not let me stay.
    She talks and I am fain to list:
She's glad the birds are gone away,
She's glad her simple worsted grey
    Is silver now with clinging mist.

The desolate, deserted trees,
    The faded earth, the heavy sky,
The beauties she so truly sees,
She thinks I have no eye for these,
    And vexes me for reason why.

Not yesterday I learned to know
    The love of bare November days
Before the coming of the snow,

But it were vain to tell her so,
　　And they are better for her praise.

## Mowing

There was never a sound beside the wood but one,
And that was my long scythe whispering to the ground.
What was it it whispered? I know not well myself;
Perhaps it was something about the heat of the sun,
Something perhaps, about the lack of sound —
And that was why it whispered and did not speak.
It was not dream of the gift of idle hours,
Or easy gold at the hand of fay or elf:
Anything more than the truth would have seemed too weak
To the earnest love that laid the swale in rows,
Not without feeble-pointed spikes of flowers
(Pale orchises), and scared a bright green snake.
The fact is the sweetest dream that labor knows.
My long scythe whispered and left the hay to make.

## Nothing Gold Can Stay

Nature's first green① is gold,
Her hardest hue to hold.
Her early leaf's② a flower;
But only so an hour.
Then leaf subsides to leaf.
So Eden sank to grief③,
So dawn goes down to day,
Nothing gold can stay.

# References and Further Reading

1. Faggen, Robert. *The Cambridge Companion to Robert Frost*. Cambridge: Cambridge University Press, 2001.

① green: In old English, "green" signified "growth" as well as a color.

② her early leaf: the youth of human beings.

③ Eden sank to grief: the merriest garden as Eden may be turned into a sorrowful place. The Hebrew word "Eden" means "delight", and it is here contrasted with "grief."

2. Holland, Norman. *The Brain of Robert Frost*: *A Cognitive Approach to Literature*. London: Routledge, 1988.

3. Kearns, Katherine. *Robert Frost and a Poetics of Appetite*. London: Cambridge University Press, 1994.

4. Newman, Lea. *Robert Frost*: *The People*, *and Stories Behind His New England Poetry*. Shelburne: The New England Press, 2000.

5. Pobojewski, Sally. "This Is the Way the World Ends." *LSA Magazine* 23.1 (1999): 28-29.

6. Raab, Lawrence. *Touchstone*: *American Poets on a Favorite Poem*. Hanover: University Press of New England, 1996.

7. Richardson, Mark. *The Ordeal of Robert Frost*: *The Poet and His Poetics*. Chicago: the Board of Trustees of the University of Illinois, 1997.

8. 方平.一条未走的路.上海:上海译文出版社,1988.

9. 弗罗斯特.弗罗斯特集:诗全集、散文和戏剧作品(上下册).理查德·普瓦里耶,马克·理查森编,曹明伦译.沈阳:辽宁教育出版社,2002.

10. 黄宗英.弗罗斯特研究.上海:上海外语教育出版社,2011.

# 9. Wallace Stevens (1879–1955)

## Introduction

Wallace Stevens (1879–1955) was an American Modernist poet, whose father contributed substantially to his early education by providing their home with an extensive library and by encouraging reading. He won the Pulitzer Prize for Poetry for his *Collected Poems* in 1955. Stevens' early years with the insurance firm brought great personal change. By 1913 Stevens was enjoying great success in the field of insurance law. After he began publishing his poems Stevens changed jobs again, becoming resident vice-president in New York City. He left that position in 1916 to work for the Hartford Accident and Indemnity Company, where he remained employed for the rest of his life, becoming vice-president in 1934. Stevens largely ignored the literary world. For most of his adult life, Stevens pursued contrasting careers as an insurance executive and a poet. Wallace Stevens, whose work was meditative and philosophical, is a poet of ideas. More than any other modern poet, Stevens was concerned with the transformative power of the imagination. Stevens contended that the poet's purpose was to interpret the external world of thought and feeling through the imagination. He was a master stylist, employing an extraordinary vocabulary and a rigorous precision in composing his poems. Because of the extreme technical and thematic complexity of his work, Stevens was sometimes considered a difficult poet. But he was also acknowledged as an eminent abstractionist and a provocative thinker, and that reputation has continued since his death.

Though now considered one of the major American poets of the $20^{th}$ century, he did not receive widespread recognition until the publication of his *Collected Poems*, just a year before his death. Stevens died in Hartford in 1955.

# Selected Reading A

## The Snow Man

One must have a mind of winter
To regard the frost and the boughs
Of the pine-trees crusted with snow;

And have been cold a long time
To behold the junipers shagged with ice①,
The spruces② rough in the distant glitter

Of the January sun; and not to think
Of any misery in the sound of the wind,
In the sound of a few leaves,

Which is the sound of the land
Full of the same wind
That is blowing in the same bare place

For the listener, who listens in the snow,
And, nothing himself③, beholds
Nothing that is not there and the nothing that is.

## About the Selection

《雪人》出自于华莱士·史蒂文斯的第一本诗集《簧风琴》。诗歌运用象征主义的写作技巧又表现出了意象派的创作手法,同时体现了现代派诗人对纷繁复杂的现实哲理性的思考。通过诗歌语言,使诗人和读者的思维经历了抽象—具体—抽象,诗歌中采用不同的意象,使诗人和读者的感观由视觉逐步转化为听觉。通过简单直白的语言勾勒出几个冬之意象,由此营造出丰富的想象空间。"人必须怀有冬日的心境,才能去看雪。"人应该发挥主观能动性,真正地与自然融合在一起,做到自我与自然的和谐。

## Research Guide

1. Still dwelling on "The Snow Man", we may note that the poem posits two types of

① junipers shagged with ice: trees roughly covered with ice.
② spruce: a type of evergreen tree with dense foliage.
③ nothing himself: forget everything of himself.

listener. One would hear a "misery in the sound of the wind."... The other listener would hear nothing more than the sound of the wind. He would exert none of this spontaneous and almost inevitable creativity. The poem embodies Stevens' central theme, the relation between imagination and reality. Endless permutations of this theme were possible. Was reality the world seen without imagination? If so, was imagination the world seen without reality? That was a bitter truth, if it was the truth. But perhaps the snowman, who heard no "misery" in the wind, was projecting himself into the scene just as much as the other listener. Perhaps the snowman beheld nothing only because he was "nothing himself," since, to cite a later poem, whoever "puts a pineapple together" always sees it "in the tangent of himself." (Perkins, 1976: 543-544)

2. Finally and most pointedly, what the listener actually "beholds" in the last line is "Nothing that is not there and the nothing that is." In other words, the snowman beholds two phenomena: (a) "nothing that is not there" and (b) "the nothing that is" there. The overt repetition of "nothing" lures us into construing an entirely barren scene, but rephrasing the line according to its parallel structure actually creates a choice: Either the listener beholds the something that is there as well as the nothing that is not there, or, if we suspend the article "the" in the second clause, he beholds *nothing* that is not there and (yet) *some thing* that is not there. To say he beholds "nothing that is not there" implies that he beholds *only that which is there* and nothing else: such a listener perceives only what is before him. On the other hand, to say he beholds "the nothing that is" (or some thing that is not there) can only mean that he beholds *that which is not there*, namely, nothingness — an absence which, for Stevens, is an imaginary, not a real, state of being. [...] The poem does, in fact, insinuate that death to the individual imagination would have to occur for one's mind to become the snowman's. But it does not take into consideration the erasure of the imagination beyond individual death. The point here is not to fault the poem or to detract from its light touch; rather, it is to draw attention to how Stevens concerns himself with an erasure of the imagination without feeling compelled also to consider that state of unimaginable nothingness beyond good and evil we call annihilation. (Gery, 1996: 153-155)

3. "The Snow Man" is an ice-sketched landscape, like Frost's "Desert Places," but its lyrically graced, barren chill leads to more than personal despair. Only the snow man knows himself, the poem knows of itself. Anthropomorphic sentiment, creating a human effigy of snow, must be balanced with the objective knowledge that "misery" plays a false part in this scene... Imposing summer's loss on the image, a human sense of misery, or worse, the listener feeling "nothing himself," could melt the snow man in elegiac sentiment. Here is where the other, outside our perceiving self, must be respected as a projection that both is, and is not: ourselves perceiving, Adam on time's

seesaw, and a native *it* as *nothing that is*. *Is* it *was*, time's fall dictates, just *as* we perceive it... So the snow man is our wintry opposite, here, out there. This anti-man translates culturally as the natural or primitive self artifacted, the wild or savage native, disowned, driven down under the veneer of civilization. This distorting sublimation is an autumnal tug on the modern mind, fall eulogist to spring lyricist, especially in Adamic America, where "the poverty of dirt" haunts a "World without Peculiarity." (Lincoln, 2000: 206-207)

## Selected Reading B

### The Emperor of Ice-Cream

Call the roller of big cigars①,
The muscular one, and bid him whip
In kitchen cups concupiscent curds②.
Let the wenches dawdle in such dress
As they are used to wear, and let the boys
Bring flowers in last month's newspapers.
Let be be finale of seem.
The only emperor is the emperor of ice-cream.

Take from the dresser of deal.
Lacking the three glass knobs, that sheet
On which she embroidered fantails once
And spread it so as to cover her face.
If her horny feet protrude, they come
To show how cold she is, and dumb.
Let the lamp affix its beam.
The only emperor is the emperor of ice-cream.

### About the Selection

《冰激凌皇帝》一诗结构精致、构思巧妙，共分两节，每节八行。在这首诗中，守灵夜却成了一个喧嚣的享受冰激凌的晚会，青年男女们对死亡、守灵无所谓的态度，突出了生之快乐和死之寒冷的对比。诗中最令人费解的两句诗句是："Let be be the finale of seem, the only emperor is the emperor of ice-cream"。自问世以来，这首诗引起了文学评论界的极大

① the roller of big cigars: the one who rolls big cigars.
② concupiscent curds: lustful or sensual curds.

关注,人们对该诗要表达的主题也是众说纷纭:生命与死亡、享乐主义与及时行乐、私欲与责任。冰激凌这一意象构成了诗歌的主体,不断地强化了史蒂文斯这首诗中的主题:生存和死亡之间的对立关系。

## Research Guide

1. We cannot know what personal events prompted this 1922 poem, apparently set in Key West (so the poet Elizabeth Bishop conjectured, who knew Key West, where Cubans worked at the machines in cigar factories, where blacks always had ice cream at funerals), but it derives resonance from Stevens's mother's death ten years earlier. What is certain is that it represents symbolically, with the Procrustean bed of its two rooms, the bitter moment of choosing life over death, at a time when life seems particularly lonely, self-serving, lustful, and sordid. Art is exposed as too scanty in its powers to cover up death; the embroidered sheet (a figure for the embellished page), if it is pulled up to cover the dead woman's face, reveals her "horny feet," which show "how cold she is, and dumb." In choosing to "let the lamp affix its beam," as in a morgue, and in acquiescing to the command, "Let be be finale of seem," Stevens makes his momentous choice for reality over appearance. (Vendler, 1993: 383)

2. Not that "The Emperor of Ice-Cream" is an unimaginative poem. Though Stevens spoke of its "deliberately commonplace costume" when he chose it as his favorite in 1933, he also said that it seemed to him to contain something of the "essential gaudiness" of poetry. These remarks seem contradictory until one remembers that Stevens, in keeping with a fundamental precept of pure poetry, typically inverted the usual hierarchy of subject and style. Since poetry is the true subject of a pure poem, the ostensible subject is, relatively speaking, mere "costume." Such costume is not dispensable, however. "Poetry is like anything else," Stevens told Latimer; "it cannot be made suddenly to drop all its rags and stand out naked, fully disclosed." Consequently, though the "essential gaudiness" of "The Emperor of Ice-Cream" lies in its expressive diction and oratorical flair, "The Emperor" does have clothes: the woman's wake. Because its costume is so prosaic — as compared, for example, with "Domination of Black" — the poem is a triumph of attitude over reference. Ostensibly an endorsement of "be", it testifies still more eloquently to the power of "seem." One is not surprised to learn that Stevens, when he tried to recall the inception of the poem years later, could remember the "state of mind" which gave rise to it but not the external occasion. (Bates, 1985: 144)

3. Dreaming *jouissance* is critical. The imagination, Stevens said in his *Letters*, is "like light, it adds nothing, except itself." The "supreme fiction," lighting us to the end, is to believe in our world, "my green, my fluent mundo," as one lives and faces death in others (no less than Emily Dickinson a-wake or Sitting Bull the sash-wearer). Poetry is to

imagine well what must be. "The final belief is to believe in a fiction," Stevens wrote in *Adagia*, "which you know to be a fiction, there being nothing else. The exquisite truth is to know that it is a fiction and that you believe in it willingly" (reflective chronotope turned precept).

With rhyming comic finality (come/dumb/beam/cream), the refrain rides on a boisterous iambic pentameter, "The *on*ly *em*peror *is* the *em*peror of *ice-cream*." The fourteen syllables curdle in a spondee (as with the twelve-syllable, shaggy last line of "The Snow Man"). There's a youthful break in the pace, a jump-rope skip completing the Falstaffian form. From bunioned foot to embroidered fantail, earthly base to fanciful end, this elegy resists loss by making art of what seems to be, seeing what is, delightfully. It is an act of the imagination at a wake; the final test, to return to childhood joy in "cream" made of "ice" (Carolina "aspic nipples" sweetened). A concupiscent summer is whipped up from winter's absence, the snow man's "nothing" curdled by sweet belief. (Lincoln, 2000: 209-210)

## Supplementary Reading

### The Idea of Order at Key West

She sang beyond the genius of the sea.
The water never formed to mind or voice,
Like a body wholly body, fluttering
Its empty sleeves; and yet its mimic motion
Made constant cry, caused constantly a cry,
That was not ours although we understood,
Inhuman, of the veritable ocean.
The sea was not a mask. No more was she.
The song and water were not medleyed sound
Even if what she sang was what she heard,
Since what she sang was uttered word by word.
It may be that in all her phrases stirred
The grinding water and the gasping wind;
But it was she and not the sea we heard.
For she was the maker of the song she sang.
The ever-hooded, tragic-gestured sea
Was merely a place by which she walked to sing.
Whose spirit is this? we said, because we knew
It was the spirit that we sought and knew

That we should ask this often as she sang.

If it was only the dark voice of the sea
That rose, or even colored by many waves;
If it was only the outer voice of the sky
And cloud, of the sunken coral water-walled,
However clear, it would have been deep air,
The heaving speech of air, a summer sound
Repeated in a summer without end
And sound alone. But it was more than that,
More even than her voice, and ours, among
The meaningless plungings of water and the wind,
Theatrical distances, bronze shadows heaped
On high horizons, mountainous atmospheres
Of sky and sea.
It was her voice that made
The sky acutest at its vanishing.
She measured to the hour its solitude.
She was the single artificer of the world
In which she sang. And when she sang, the sea,
Whatever self it had, became the self
That was her song, for she was the maker. Then we,
As we beheld her striding there alone,
Knew that there never was a world for her
Except the one she sang and, singing, made.

Ramon Fernandez, tell me, if you know,
Why, when the singing ended and we turned
Toward the town, tell why the glassy lights,
The lights in the fishing boats at anchor there,
As the night descended, tilting in the air,
Mastered the night and portioned out the sea,
Fixing emblazoned zones and firey poles,
Arranging, deepening, enchanting night.

Oh! Blessed rage for order, pale Ramon,
The maker's rage to order words of the sea,
Words of the fragrant portals, dimly-starred,
And of ourselves and of our origins,

In ghostlier demarcations, keener sounds.

## Of Modern Poetry

The poem of the mind in the act of finding
What will suffice. It has not always had
To find: the scene was set; it repeated what
Was in the script.
Then the theatre was changed

To something else. Its past was a souvenir.
It has to be living, to learn the speech of the place.
It has to face the men of the time and to meet
The women of the time. It has to think about war
And it has to find what will suffice. It has
To construct a new stage. It has to be on that stage,
And, like an insatiable actor, slowly and
With meditation, speak words that in the ear,
In the delicatest ear of the mind, repeat,
Exactly, that which it wants to hear, at the sound
Of which, an invisible audience listens,
Not to the play, but to itself, expressed
In an emotion as of two people, as of two
Emotions becoming one. The actor is
A metaphysician in the dark, twanging
An instrument, twanging a wiry string that gives
Sounds passing through sudden rightnesses, wholly
Containing the mind, below which it cannot descend,
Beyond which it has no will to rise.
It must
Be the finding of a satisfaction, and may
Be of a man skating, a woman dancing, a woman
Combing. The poem of the act of the mind.

## Sunday Morning

I

Complacencies of the peignoir[①], and late
Coffee and oranges in a sunny chair,

① peignoir: loose dressing gown of a woman.

And the green freedom of a cockatoo[1]
Upon a rug mingle to dissipate
The holy hush of ancient sacrifice[2].
She dreams a little, and she feels the dark
Encroachment of that old catastrophe,
As a calm darkens among water-lights.
The pungent oranges and bright, green wings
Seem things in some procession of the dead,
Winding across wide water, without sound.
The day is like wide water, without sound,
Stilled for the passing of her dreaming feet
Over the seas, to silent Palestine,
Dominion of the blood and sepulchre[3].

Ⅱ

Why should she give her bounty to the dead?
What is divinity if it can come
Only in silent shadows and in dreams?
Shall she not find in comforts of the sun,
In pungent fruit and bright, green wings, or else
In any balm or beauty of the earth,
Things to be cherished like the thought of heaven?
Divinity must live within herself:
Passions of rain, or moods in falling snow;
Grievings in loneliness, or unsubdued
Elations when the forest blooms; gusty
Emotions on wet roads on autumn nights;
All pleasures and all pains, remembering
The bough of summer and the winter branch.
These are the measures destined for her soul.

Ⅲ

Jove[4] in the clouds had his inhuman birth.

---

① cockatoo: colorful and noisy parrot.

② The Christian mass remembers Christ's crucifixion by sharing his body and blood as bread and wine with the faithful.

③ sepulchre: the Church of the Holy Sepulchre shelters the tomb in which Jesus' body was laid on Good Friday and discovered missing on the Sunday afterward.

④ Jove: Jupiter.

No mother suckled him, no sweet land gave
Large-mannered motions to his mythy mind.
He moved among us, as a muttering king,
Magnificent, would move among his hinds①,
Until our blood, commingling, virginal,
With heaven, brought such requital to desire
The very hinds discerned it, in a star②.
Shall our blood fail? Or shall it come to be
The blood of paradise? And shall the earth
Seem all of paradise that we shall know?
The sky will be much friendlier then than now,
A part of labor and a part of pain,
And next in glory to enduring love,
Not this dividing and indifferent blue.

Ⅳ

She says, "I am content when wakened birds,
Before they fly, test the reality
Of misty fields, by their sweet questionings;
But when the birds are gone, and their warm fields
Return no more, where, then, is paradise?"
There is not any haunt of prophesy,
Nor any old chimera③ of the grave,
Neither the golden underground, nor isle
Melodious, where spirits gat④ them home,
Nor visionary south, nor cloudy palm
Remote on heaven's hill, that has endured
As April's green endures; or will endure
Like her remembrance of awakened birds,
Or her desire for June and evening, tipped
By the consummation of the swallow's wings.

Ⅴ

She says, "But in contentment I still feel

① hinds: farm workers, here shepherds.

② star: pointer to the birthplace of the Christ-child, as seen by the shepherds and the three kings.

③ chimera: bad dream, literally a she-monster whose body, in Greek myth, consists of a goat's torso, a lion's head, and a snake's tail.

④ gat: betook themselves.

The need of some imperishable bliss."
Death is the mother of beauty; hence from her,
Alone, shall come fulfilment to our dreams
And our desires. Although she strews the leaves
Of sure obliteration on our paths,
The path sick sorrow took, the many paths
Where triumph rang its brassy phrase, or love
Whispered a little out of tenderness,
She makes the willow shiver in the sun
For maidens who were wont to sit and gaze
Upon the grass, relinquished to their feet.
She causes boys to pile new plums and pears
On disregarded plate①. The maidens taste
And stray impassioned in the littering leaves.

Ⅵ

Is there no change of death in paradise?
Does ripe fruit never fall? Or do the boughs
Hang always heavy in that perfect sky,
Unchanging, yet so like our perishing earth,
With rivers like our own that seek for seas
They never find, the same receding shores
That never touch with inarticulate pang?
Why set the pear upon those river-banks
Or spice the shores with odors of the plum?
Alas, that they should wear our colors there,
The silken weavings of our afternoons,
And pick the strings of our insipid lutes!
Death is the mother of beauty, mystical,
Within whose burning bosom we devise
Our earthly mothers waiting, sleeplessly.

Ⅶ

Supple and turbulent, a ring of men
Shall chant in orgy on a summer morn
Their boisterous devotion to the sun,

① disregarded plate: Stevens had to explain to Harriet Monroe, editor of *Poetry*, that he meant, by this, family silverware that was no longer used (*Letters*, 183-84).

Not as a god, but as a god might be,
Naked among them, like a savage source.
Their chant shall be a chant of paradise,
Out of their blood, returning to the sky;
And in their chant shall enter, voice by voice,
The windy lake wherein their lord delights,
The trees, like serafin[①], and echoing hills,
That choir among themselves long afterward.
They shall know well the heavenly fellowship
Of men that perish and of summer morn.
And whence they came and whither they shall go
The dew upon their feet shall manifest.

Ⅷ

She hears, upon that water without sound,
A voice that cries, "The tomb in Palestine
Is not the porch of spirits lingering.
It is the grave of Jesus, where he lay."
We live in an old chaos of the sun,
Or old dependency of day and night,
Or island solitude, unsponsored, free,
Of that wide water, inescapable.
Deer walk upon our mountains, and the quail
Whistle about us their spontaneous cries;
Sweet berries ripen in the wilderness;
And, in the isolation of the sky,
At evening, casual flocks of pigeons make
Ambiguous undulations[②] as they sink,
Downward to darkness, on extended wings.

## Anecdote of the Jar

I placed a jar in Tennessee,
And round it was, upon a hill.
It made the slovenly wilderness
Surround that hill.

---

① serafin: seraphim, angels.
② undulations: wave-like rise-and-falls.

The wilderness rose up to it,
And sprawled around, no longer wild.
The jar was round upon the ground
And tall and of a port in air.

It took dominion everywhere.
The jar was gray and bare.
It did not give of bird or bush,
Like nothing else in Tennessee.

## References and Further Reading

1. Bates, J. Milton. *Wallace Stevens: A Mythology of Self*. Berkeley: University of California Press, 1985.
2. Brazeau, Peter. *Parts of a World: Wallace Stevens Remembered*. San Francisco: North Point Press, 1985.
3. Gery, John. *Ways of Nothingness: Nuclear Annihilation and Contemporary American Poetry*. Gainesville: University Press of Florida, 1996.
4. Lincoln, Kenneth. *Sing with the Heart of a Bear: Fusions of Native and American Poetry 1890-1999*. Berkeley: University of California Press, 2000.
5. MacLeod, Glen. *Wallace Stevens and Modern Art: From the Armory Show to Abstract Expressionism*. New Haven: Yale University Press, 1993.
6. Perkins, David. *A History of Modern Poetry: From the 1890s to the High Modernist Mode*. Cambridge: Harvard University Press, 1976.
7. Righelato, Pat. *American Poetry: The Modernist Ideal*. New York: St. Martin's Press, 1995.
8. Vendler, Helen. "Wallace Stevens." *The Columbia History of American Poetry*. New York: Columbia University Press, 1993. 370-394.
9. Walker, David. *The Transparent Lyric*. Princeton: Princeton University Press, 1984.
10. 华莱士·史蒂文斯.最高虚构笔记:史蒂文斯诗文集.陈东飚,张枣译.上海:华东师范大学出版社,2009.

# 10. William Carlos Williams (1883–1963)

## Introduction

Born in Rutherford, New Jersey, William Carlos Williams (1883–1963) had a prolific career as a poet, novelist, essayist, and playwright. He began writing poetry while a student at Horace Mann High School, and received his Medical Degree in 1906 from the University of Pennsylvania, where he met and befriended Ezra Pound. Throughout his life, Williams sustained his medical practice and worked hard at being a writer. His major works include *Kora in Hell* (1920), *Spring and All* (1923), *Pictures from Brueghel and Other Poems* (1962), the five-volume epic *Paterson* (1963), and *Imaginations* (1970).

Early in his career, Williams was greatly influenced by Ezra Pound who in 1913 arranged for a London press to publish William's second collection of poetry, *The Tempers*. Following Pound, Williams was one of the principal poets of the Imagist movement. However, as time went on, he began to develop opinions that differed from those of his fellow imagists. Critical of Eliot's highly intellectual style with its frequent use of foreign languages and allusions to classical and European literature, Williams preferred colloquial language that grew out of American society and invented an entirely fresh and unique American form of poetry whose subject matter was centered on everyday circumstances of life and the lives of common people. He also examined the role of the poet in American society and famously summarized his poetic method in the phrase "No ideas but things" (found in his poem "A Sort of Song" and repeated again and again in *Paterson*).

His influence as a poet spread slowly during the 1920s and 1930s, overshadowed, he felt, by the immense popularity of Eliot's "The Waste Land"; however, his work received increasing attention in the 1950s and 1960s and had significant influence on many of American literary movement, including the Beat movement, the San Francisco Renaissance, the Black Mountain school, and the New York School. William's health began to decline after a heart attack in 1948 and a series of strokes, but he continued writing up until his death in New Jersey in 1963. For his prominent achievements in literature, he won the first National Book Award for Poetry in 1950, and was posthumously awarded the Pulitzer Prize in May 1963 for *Pictures from Brueghel and Other Poems* (1962). He was inducted into the New Jersey Hall of Fame in 2009.

## Selected Reading A

### The Red Wheelbarrow

so much depends
upon

a red wheel
barrow

glazed with rain
water

beside the white
chickens.

### About the Selection

《红色手推车》是威廉斯意象主义诗歌的经典作品,充分体现了诗人的诗歌创作理论。威廉斯反对庞德主张的艺术的"国际性",而努力建立美国本土的诗歌。他坚持使用口语,用简单明晰的意象和松散的短句自由组诗,反对晦涩费解、旁征博引和文人味十足的诗歌,《红色手推车》在这方面的努力很明显。诗的开头显得突兀,但是这种单刀直入的方法却很能引人注目,接下来的意象(红色手推车、雨水和几只白色的鸡)只是片刻的观察,没有解释,也没有任何暗示,不禁激起读者诸多思考,是什么使这辆车吸引着诗人?车与鸡是怎样的关系?几个单纯的意象之间又有什么样的联系?这也许就是这首小诗的诸多魅力之一。

### Research Guide

1. The metaphor "glazed" captures time in the poem. In a moment, the wheelbarrow will be dry, its sheen gone; yet the hardness suggested by the metaphor is not irrelevant.

This moment is like others in life (of the chickens, the speaker, the reader). Periods of danger, terror, stress do not last. The glaze, like the rainbow, signals a return to normality or restoration. The poem creates a memorable picture of this recurring process; reflections upon its meaning may provide the reassurance that makes us more durable. (Archer, 1976: 37)

2. The wheelbarrow is one of the simplest machines, combining in its form the wheel and the inclined plane... Just as civilization depends on number, civilization depends on simple machines-both in themselves and in their increasingly complex combinations. "So much depends upon" the wheelbarrow in its service not only through the centuries, but as a form whose components are indispensable to the functioning of a highly industrialized civilization. We can identify two contrasts in the poem. One is between the latest advances in machine technology and the continuing but overlooked importance of elementary machines. The other is between the universal and age-old scene depicted in the poem and the radically new free verse form in which it exist. (Ahearn, 1994: 4-5)

3. 这是一首短小的、具有典型的"反诗歌"特色的诗,是直接表现事物的大胆尝试……此诗的四个双行由四个观察组成,从而形成了诗的发展。……每一个双行是一个类别,从抽象(修辞)到静止的物(手推车),再到活动的物(雨水),最后到活生生的动物(白鸡),这一运动暗示了从抽象到活力的发展,从另一个角度也暗示了一种逆向的发展:对可能发生的事物的渴望被现实中平凡的美悄悄地遏止。(彭予,1995: 44)

4. 这样的意象派小品也许并无深意可挖,重要之点在于它为我们观察极其普遍的事物提供了一个新的角度,把红色车子、晶亮雨水、白色鸡群并置对衬,构成一幅有颜色,有亮度,有实物的画面(这是平日我们容易忽略的),而且出之于一种惊喜的口吻(那么多东西/依仗……),好像发现了什么奇迹。其实是他无意中觉察到二种常人视而不见的美。看起来,上述三者都是极常见的景象,但显然经过作者的细心观察,否则不可能写得这么干净、清新、可喜。(袁可嘉,1993: 218)

## Selected Reading B

### Spring and All

By the road to the contagious hospital
under the surge of the blue
mottled clouds driven from the
northeast — a cold wind. Beyond, the
waste of broad, muddy fields

brown with dried weeds, standing and fallen

patches of standing water
the scattering of tall trees

All along the road the reddish
purplish, forked, upstanding, twiggy
stuff of bushes and small trees
with dead, brown leaves under them
leafless vines —

Lifeless in appearance, sluggish
dazed spring approaches —

They enter the new world naked,
cold, uncertain of all
save that they enter. All about them
the cold, familiar wind —

Now the grass, tomorrow
the stiff curl of wildcarrot leaf
One by one objects are defined —
It quickens: clarity, outline of leaf

But now the stark dignity of
entrance — Still, the profound change
has come upon them: rooted, they
grip down and begin to awaken

## About the Selection

《春天及一切》创作于20世纪20年代初,以其简单明晰的视觉印象而著称。本诗前十三行描写诗人在去传染病医院的路上所看到的一派死气沉沉的景象,这不禁让人想到艾略特所著《荒原》的某些意象,然而之后的诗节并没有延续这一给人悲观主义情绪的色调,却为读者带来生的景象,植物开始萌芽、大自然开始苏醒,春天正在迈进。短短的27行诗,威廉斯却细腻地为读者再现了冬春交替时的自然现象,一方面表现了诗人敏锐的观察力和丰富的想象力,另一方面体现了诗人的创作思想,威廉斯认为诗人的任务之一就是去发现"物",然后由此细心地加以观察,通过想象力去了解事物的关联性。读完本诗,细心的读者可能会发现诗节末尾处没有句号,这也许正是诗人想要表达的正如四季交替一样,生命也是循环和延续的主题。

## Research Guide

1. "Spring and All," a related but much more serious poem, expresses tones of awe, respect, and wonder before the process of life taking on form... The inclusive indefiniteness of the pronoun in "They enter the new world naked" allows the process of birth in the vegetative realm to be associated with that of human birth as well. Furthermore, the prose context of the poem in *Spring and All*, a book devoted to the renewal of the imagination, strongly suggests that Williams had in mind the birth of new forms of poetry as well as of plant life (although this idea is not explicit in the poem). The same creative force operating biologically in nature functions at a higher level in human consciousness to create art... The new sprouts "grip down" and "begin to awaken"— to act with a kind of intelligence, to realize "subjective aim," the accomplishment of an inner design. "Spring and All" is not about an entirely alien, inhuman process; the process is mysterious, but it manifests something akin to human creative intelligence. (Markos, 1994: 160-161)

2. The closing imagery of "Spring and All" articulates the doctor's and the poet's "sense of constant discovery" in the figure of birth as rebirth. The newborn are "rooted," as they "grip down" through their roots and "begin to awaken." From the decay of winter arises the rebirth of spring growth; from the poverty of northern New Jersey arises the will to survive. Although death and decay are ever-present, the promise of new life and rebirth never disappears. There are no sentimental notions about spring here, only a belief in the indomitable will to be born, to survive. (Lowney, 1997: 64)

3. As the poem begins "By the road to the contagious hospital," Williams has difficulty seeing any outline or order: "mottled," "patches," "waste," and "scattering" are some of the words he uses. His problems culminate in the third stanza, where inexact adjectives, often afflicted with the suffixes "-ish" or "-y," glut an entire line before a noun can be found. And even then the noun is imprecise: "All along the road the reddish /purplish, forked, upstanding, twiggy /stuff..." Like the contagious diseases in the hospital Williams drives toward, imprecision is a contagion of the mind, potentially fatal. As "one by one objects are defined" by the advancing season, however, Williams' language is also reborn, and he can identify the wild carrot, the only named species in the poem. His battle to see and to name has a "stark dignity" equal to spring's battle with winter... Like the plants, the poet's mind must "grip down," struggling to wrest a name from anonymity. The right name is a strong root; new poetry, and a new world, will grow from it as invincibly as the wild carrot leaf uncurls. (Schmidt, 1980: 403)

## Supplementary Reading

### This Is Just to Say①

I have eaten
the plums
that were in
the icebox

and which
you were probably
saving
for breakfast

Forgive me
they were delicious
so sweet
and so cold

### Landscape with the Fall of Icarus②

According to Brueghel③
when Icarus fell
it was spring

a farmer was ploughing
his field
the whole pageantry

of the year was

---

① This is a famous imagist poem published in 1934 by Williams. In a 1950 interview, John W. Gerber asked Williams what it is that makes "This is Just to Say" a poem, he replied, "in the first place, it's metrically absolutely regular... so, dogmatically speaking, it has to be a poem because it goes that way, don't you see!"

② This poem touches upon the Greek myth of the tragedy of Icarus, son of Daedalus. Icarus took flight from imprisonment wearing the fragile wings his father had fashioned for him. Heedless of his father's warning to keep a middle course over the sea and avoid closeness to the sun, he exultantly flew too close to the burning sun, which melted his wings so that Icarus hurtled to the sea and drowned.

③ Pieter Brueghel, a Dutch Renaissance painter, drew the picture "the fall of Icarus". Williams wrote poem "Landscape with the Fall of Icarus" on this painting. Also W. H. Auden wrote a poem on the same painting.

awake tingling
near

the edge of the sea
concerned
with itself

sweating in the sun
that melted
the wings' wax

unsignificantly
off the coast
there was

a splash quite unnoticed
this was
Icarus drowning

## References and Further Reading


1. Ahearn, Barry. *William Carlos Williams and Alterity: The Early Poetry*. Cambridge: Cambridge University Press, 1994.
2. Archer, Stanley. "Glazed in William's 'The Red Wheelbarrow'." *Concerning Poetry* 9.2 (1976): 34-41.
3. Lowney, John. *The American Avant-Garde Tradition: William Carlos Williams, Postmodern Poetry, and the Politics of Cultural Memory*. Lewisburg: Bucknell University Press, 1997.
4. Markos, Donald W. *Ideas in Things: The Poems of William Carlos Williams*. Teaneck: Fairleigh Dickinson University Press, 1994.
5. Schmidt, Peter. "Some Versions of Modernist Pastoral: Williams and the Precisionists." *Contemporary Literature* 21.3 (1980): 383-406.
6. 彭予.二十世纪美国诗歌——庞德到罗伯特·布莱.开封:河南大学出版社,1995.
7. 袁可嘉.欧美现代派文学概论.上海:上海文艺出版社,1993.

# 11. Ezra Pound (1885–1972)

## Introduction

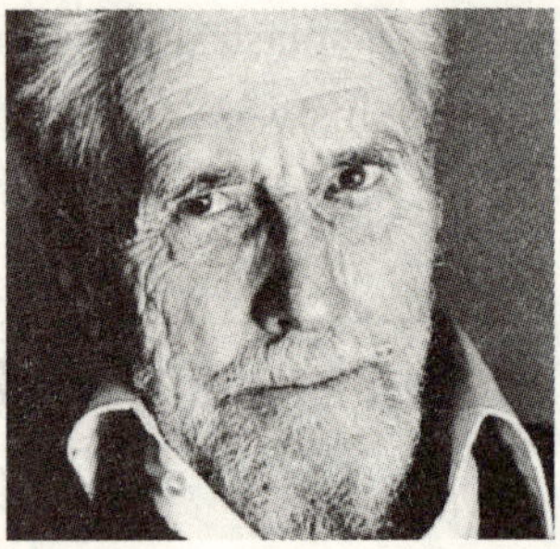

In many ways, Ezra Pound epitomizes the avant-garde modernist poet: out-spoken, experimental, and fiercely iconoclastic.

Pound was undoubtedly a genius. Before he graduated from university, he had mastered 9 languages. He became a professor at the age of 22. Pound's restless energy led him to London in 1908, to Paris in 1920, and then to Italy in 1924, where he would remain until the end of WWII.

In London, he became the leader of the Imagist movement. In Paris, he helped T. S. Eliot and Ernest Hemingway by editing their early writings. In Italy, during the Great Depression of the 1930s, he studied history and economics, and became a supporter of Mussolini. When the Second World War broke out, he made hundreds of pro-Fascist, anti-Jewish propaganda broadcasts to the U. S.

In 1945, the Allied armies invaded Italy and Pound was arrested and charged of treason. While he awaited his trial, he translated Confucius and continued to write his best poetry *The Cantos*. In 1946, an American court judged him insane. Pound was confined for 12 years in St. Elizabeth's Hospital in Washington, a hospital for the criminally insane. There he finished the *Pisan Cantos*, which won him the Bollingen Prize in Poetry in 1949. With the joint effort of such eminent figures as Robert Frost, T. S. Eliot, and Hemingway, Pound was released at the age of 73. He returned to Italy where he continued to write and make translations until he died at the age of 87.

## Selected Reading A

### In a Station of the Metro[①]

The apparition[②] of these faces in the crowd;
Petals on a wet, black bough.

### About the Selection

这首仅有两行的《地铁车站》被公认为意象派的经典之作。两行诗中并置着两个无关、然而又是同构的审美意象：在第一行诗中，有几点明亮的色彩（美丽的脸）在暗的人群中闪现；在第二行诗中，有几点花瓣在湿漉漉的黑树枝上显现。第二个意象强化了前一个意象中的明与暗、优美与粗糙、清新与潮闷的对比感，或许还激起了现代城市生活中的心灵对自然美的依恋、对东方美的向往。

### Research Guide

1. Three years ago in Paris I got out of a "metro" train at La Concorde, and saw suddenly a beautiful face, and then another and another, and then a beautiful child's face, and then another beautiful woman, and I tried all that day to find words for what this had meant to me, and I could not find any words that seemed to me worthy, or as lovely as that sudden emotion. And that evening, as I went home along the Rue Raynouard, I was still trying, and I found suddenly, the expression. I do not mean that I found words, but there came an equation... not in speech, but in little splotches of colour. It was just that — a "pattern", or hardly a pattern, if by "pattern" you mean something with a "repeat" in it. But it was a word, the beginning, for me, of a language in colour. I do not mean that I was unfamiliar with the kindergarten stories about colours being like tones in music. I think that sort of thing is nonsense. If you try to make notes permanently correspond with particular colour, it is like tying narrow meanings to symbols. That evening, in the Rue Raynouard, I realized quite vividly that if I were like a painter, or if I had, often, that kind of emotion, or even if I were a painter, or if I

---

① Pound provided an account of the formation of the genesis and development of this poem: Three years ago in Paris I got out of a "metro" train at La Concorde, and saw suddenly a beautifully face, and then another beautiful woman, and I tried all that day to find words for what this had meant to me, and I could not find any words that seemed to me worthy, or as lovely as that sudden emotion.... I wrote a thirty-line poem, and destroyed it because it was what we call work "of second intensity." Six months later I made a poem half that length; a year later I made the following hokku-like sentence which constitutes the poem. (Brooks, 1973)

② apparition: The word "apparition", with its double meaning, binds the two aspects of the observation together: it means "appearance", in the sense of something which appears, or show up, while it also means something which seems real but perhaps is not real.

had the energy to get paints and brushes and keep at it, I might found a new school of painting, of "non-representative" painting, a painting that would speak only by arrangements in colour... The "one image poem" is a form of super-position, that is to say, it is one idea set on top of another. (Pound, 1960: 86-89)

2. The poem is a significant step in the development of modernist poetry. First of all, its compression was unprecedented: no English poem had been expected to carry so much meaning in so few words. Secondly, by simply juxtaposing two complex images without comment and leaving the reader to establish a relation between them, the poem allows for an extremely open-ended set of possible meanings. As Kenner suggests, the crowd of passengers in the Paris underground can be related to the mythic underworld visited by Odysseus, and the word "apparition" in the first line can suggest phantoms as well as living people. (Beach, 2006: 27)

3. 这首被称为"俳句"式的小诗对当时的庞德意义非凡,因为他认为这首诗体现了他的意象诗的要旨:"纪录某外在的客观事物改变形态,或者说一下冲进主体那一确实的瞬间。"……这首诗实质上是以类比建构的,若"脸"为A,"人群"为B,"花瓣"为C,"树枝"为D,其比喻模式就是A∶C=B∶C。"The apparition"就指内在视觉(the mind's eye)纪录主客体会通顿悟的那一瞬间。这种类比方法和具象并置在中国诗歌传统中太多、太平凡,以致我们习以为常,视而不见。然而对于以逻辑思维为主,受英语句法结构、语法关联约束的庞德,这却是他诗学上的一个突破。(陶乃侃,2006:55)

## Selected Reading B

### A Pact

I make a pact with you, Walt Whitman —
I have detested you long enough.
I come to you as a grown child
Who has had a pig-headed father;
I am old enough now to make friends.
It was you that broke the new wood,
Now is a time for carving.
We have one sap and one root —
Let there be commerce between us.

### About the Selection

《合同》一诗描述了诗人从厌恶惠特曼到愿与他订立合同结交朋友的转变过程,显示出庞德对于传统文化客观的态度和对惠特曼经典诗人身份的认同。

## Research Guide

1. Pound's attitude toward Whitman was highly ambivalent. The ambivalence is reflected in "A Pact," which registers Pound's reconciliation with Whitman in 1913, but adds an important qualification:... the demand for greater conscious technique implied by "carving." Whitman broke the "new wood" of free verse, and Pound seeks to carve a finer product (with the chisel of absolute rhythm). Whitmanism is thus tempered with the ideal of "poetry-as-sculpture" which Pound took over from Gautier. (Witemeyer, 1969: 135)

2. The ambivalence of Pound's response to his poetic forefather Walt Whitman reflects his complex sense of his American literary heritage. As he was well aware, whatever he might say in explanation of Whitman would also in some measure define himself. While Pound recognized the authentic American eloquence of Whitman's "barbaric yawp," the self-conscious craftsman in him winced at the "exceeding great stench" of Whitman's "crudity," "an exceedingly nauseating pill" which he parodically exemplified as "Lo! Behold, I eat watermelons."

In his 1909 essay "What I Feel About Walt Whitman," his distaste for Whitman's expansive self-singing struggles with an even more powerful conviction that Whitman "is America... . He does 'chant the crucial stage' and he is the 'voice triumphant.'" In the end, Pound subordinates the superficial quarrel with Whitman's poetic means to the profound bond of their common origin and message. Whitman is to America "what Dante is to Italy"; "the vital part of my message, taken from the sap and fibre of America, is the same as his"; "It is a great thing, reading a man to know, not 'His Tricks are not as yet my Tricks, but I can easily make them mine' but 'His message is my message. We will see that men hear it.'" (Froula, 1983: 47)

3. 这是一篇诗的革新宣言书,再现了革新的愿望、革新的气概、革新的魄力。……此诗微带调侃,好似一个顽皮的小男孩正在和他老迈的父亲藏猫猫。父亲老眼昏花、步履蹒跚,怎么找得见手脚灵活、欢蹦乱跳的孩子。孩子忽左忽右、忽前忽后地蹦进蹦出,直把父亲累得气喘吁吁,汗流满面。最后一个"买卖"更具现代人气息、美国人特色、商业社会特点。"买卖"极具商业气味,然而,"买卖"不更意味着公开的挑战、公平的竞争、公正的结局吗?(袁若娟,2006:175)

## Supplementary Reading

### Hugh Selwyn Mauberley (Part I)

*E. P. Ode pour l'élection de Son Sépulchre*[①]

For three years, out of key with his time,
He strove to resuscitate the dead art
Of poetry; to maintain "the sublime"
In the old sense. Wrong from the start —

No, hardly, but, seeing he had been born
In a half savage country[②], out of date;
Bent resolutely on wringing lilies from the acorn;
Capaneus; trout for factitious[③] bait:

"*Idmen gar toi panth, os eni Troie*[④]
Caught in the unstopped ear;
Giving the rocks small lee-way
The chopped seas held him, therefore, that year.

His true Penelope was Flaubert[⑤],
He fished by obstinate isles;
Observed the elegance of Circe's[⑥] hair
Rather than the mottoes on sundials.

Unaffected by "the march of events",
He passed from men's memory in *l'an trentiesme*

---

① Cf. Pierre de Ronsard (1524—1585), Odes 4. 5, "De l'election de son sepulchre" [French, "Concerning the choice of his tomb"], in which the poet describes the kind of burial place and the kind of fame he would like to have.

② a half savage country: it refers to the United States here.

③ factitious: false, artificial.

④ The Sirens in Homer's Odyssey (XII, 189) sing, "because we know all things [suffered] in Troy": a line heard by Odysseus (the "him" at l. 12) but not his companions, whose ears were plugged with wax to protect them from the Sirens' words (cf. l. 10).

⑤ Gustave Flaubert (1821—1880), French realist novelist and meticulous craftsman. Penelope, the paradigmatic faithful wife, fended off suitors while Odysseus spent ten years at the siege of Troy and another ten years returning home.

⑥ Circe: Beautiful enchantress who seduced Odysseus; he stayed on her island for over a year.

*De son eage*[1]; the case presents
No adjunct to the Muses' diadem[2].

Ⅱ.

The age demanded an image
Of its accelerated grimace,
Something for the modern stage,
Not, at any rate, an Attic[3] grace;

Not, not certainly, the obscure reveries
Of the inward gaze;
Better mendacities
Than the classics in paraphrase!

The "age demanded" chiefly a mold in plaster,
Made with no loss of time,
A prose kinema[4], not, not assuredly, alabaster
Or the "sculpture" of rhyme.

Ⅲ.

The tea-rose, tea-gown, etc.
Supplants the mousseline of Cos[5],
The pianola "replaces"
Sappho's barbitos.

Christ follows Dionysus[6],
Phallic and ambrosial
Made way for macerations;
Caliban casts out Ariel[7].

All things are a flowing,

---

① In the thirty-first year of his age (French); Pound's age when his book *Lustra* was published.

② diadem: crown3.

③ Attic: Athenian; i. e., simple, pure, classical.

④ kinema: motion (Greek); and an early spelling of "cinema" (motion pictures).

⑤ Cos: Greek island. Mousseline: fine cloth (muslin).

⑥ Dionysus: Greek god of fertility, wine, and poetic inspiration, whose worship included ecstatic frenzies, sexual rites, and dramatic festivals.

⑦ In Shakespeare's *Tempest*, Caliban is earthbound and coarse, Ariel a beautiful and imaginative spirit.

Sage Heracleitus[①] says;
But a tawdry cheapness
Shall reign throughout our days.

Even the Christian beauty
Defects — after Samothrace;
We see *to kalon*[②]
Decreed in the market place.

Faun's flesh is not to us,
Nor the saint's vision.
We have the press for wafer;
Franchise for circumcision.

All men, in law, are equals.
Free of Pisistratus[③],
We choose a knave or an eunuch
To rule over us.

O bright Apollo,
*tin andra, tin eroa, tina theon*[④],
What god, man, or hero
Shall I place a tin wreath upon!

Ⅳ.

These fought, in any case,
and some believing,
pro domo[⑤], in any case ...

Some quick to arm,
some for adventure,
some from fear of weakness,

① Heracleitus: Greek philosopher (ca. 540-ca. 480 B. C. E. ), whose teaching emphasized flux ("all things flow").

② The beautiful (Greek).

③ Pisistratus: Three times the absolute ruler of Athens (d. 527 B. C. E. ), he made the city the foremost power in Ionia and supported the arts.

④ What man, what hero, what god (Greek); cf. the Greek poet Pindar's Olympian Ode 2. 2: "What god, what hero, what man shall we loudly praise?"

⑤ For home (Latin).

some from fear of censure,
some for love of slaughter, in imagination,
learning later ...
some in fear, learning love of slaughter;

Died some pro patria,
non "dulce" non "et décor"... ①
walked eye-deep in hell
believing in old men's lies, then unbelieving
came home, home to a lie,
home to many deceits,
home to old lies and new infamy;
usury age-old and age-thick
and liars in public places.

Daring as never before, wastage as never before.
Young blood and high blood,
Fair cheeks, and fine bodies;
fortitude as never before

frankness as never before,
disillusions as never told in the old days,
hysterias, trench confessions,
laughter out of dead bellies.

V.

There died a myriad,
And of the best, among them,
For an old bitch gone in the teeth,
For a botched civilization.

Charm, smiling at the good mouth,
Quick eyes gone under earth's lid,

For two gross of broken statues,
For a few thousand battered books.

① For one's native land, not sweetly, not gloriously (Latin); cf. the Roman poet Horace's Odes 3. 2. 13: "Sweet and fitting it is to die for one's country."

## Canto XLIX: For the Seven Lakes

For the seven lakes, and by no man these verses:
Rain; empty river; a voyage,
Fire from frozen cloud, heavy rain in the twilight
Under the cabin roof was one lantern.
The reeds are heavy; bent;
and the bamboos speak as if weeping.

Autumn moon; hills rise about lakes
against sunset
Evening is like a curtain of cloud,
a blurr above ripples; and through it
sharp long spikes of the cinnamon,
a cold tune amid reeds.
Behind hill the monk's bell
borne on the wind.
Sail passed here in April; may return in October
Boat fades in silver; slowly;
Sun blaze alone on the river.

Where wine flag catches the sunset
Sparse chimneys smoke in the cross light

Comes then snow scur on the river
And a world is covered with jade
Small boat floats like a lanthorn,
The flowing water closts as with cold. And at San Yin
they are a people of leisure.

Wild geese swoop to the sand-bar,
Clouds gather about the hole of the window
Broad water; geese line out with the autumn
Rooks clatter over the fishermen's lanthorns,

A light moves on the north sky line;
where the young boys prod stones for shrimp.
In seventeen hundred came Tsing to these hill lakes.
A light moves on the South sky line.

State by creating riches shd. thereby get into debt?
This is infamy; this is Geryon.
This canal goes still to TenShi
Though the old king built it for pleasure

K E I M E N R A N K E I
K I U M A N M A N K E I
JITSU GETSU K O K W A
T A N FUKU T A N K A I

Sun up; work
sundown; to rest
dig well and drink of the water
dig field; eat of the grain
Imperial power is? and to us what is it?

The fourth; the dimension of stillness.
And the power over wild beasts.

## References and Further Reading


1. Beach, Christopher. *The Cambridge Introduction to Twentieth-Century American Poetry*. Cambridge: Cambridge University Press, 2003.
2. Brooker, Peter. *A Student's Guide to the Selected Poems of Ezra Pound*. London: Faber and Faber, 1979.
3. Froula, Christine. *A Guide to Ezra Pound's* Selected Poems. New York: New Directions, 1983.
4. Kenner, Hugh. *The Pound Era*. Berkeley: University of California Press, 1971.
5. Perkins, David. *A History of Modern Poetry: Modernism and After*. Cambridge, MA: Harvard University Press, 1987.
6. Pound, Ezra. *Gaudier-Brzeska: A Memoir*. London: New Directions, 1960.
7. Pound, Ezra. *Selected Prose* 1909—1965. London: Faber and Faber, 1973.
8. Qian, Zhaoming. *Orientalism and Modernism: The Legacy of China in Pound and Williams*. Durham and London: Duke University Press, 1995.
9. Witemeyer, Hugh. *The Poetry of Ezra Pound: Forms and Renewal*, 1908—1920. Berkeley: University of California Press, 1969.
10. 陶乃侃.庞德与中国文化.北京:首都师范大学出版社,2006.
11. 叶维廉.庞德与潇湘八景.台北:台湾大学出版中心,2008.
12. 袁若娟.美国现代诗歌精选评析.开封:河南大学出版社,2006.

# 12. T. S. Eliot (1888–1965)

## Introduction

Thomas Stearns Eliot was born in a wealthy American family in 1988, and received good education. In 1914, he moved to the United Kingdom and he became a British citizen in 1927. Eliot was a publisher, playwright, literary and social critic and more importantly, he was "arguably the most important English-language poet of the 20th century". In 1948, Eliot received the Nobel Prize for Literature.

Eliot's poetry is noted for its fresh visual imagery, flexible tone, highly expressive rhythm, dramatic monologue, difficult symbols and allusions, elliptical structures, etc. He also has special views on modern life and poetry. For Eliot, the modern life is chaotic and futile, and poets can create order out of chaos by comparing the past to the present. And in Eliot's aesthetic views, poetry should reflect the fragmentary nature of life without analysis; a poem should be a made object and once finished, the poet has no control of it; also, Eliot believes that the poet should always keep tradition in mind, and use the past to serve the present.

## Selected Reading A

### The Love Song of J. Alfred Prufrock

*S'io credesse che mia risposta fosse*
*A persona che mai tornasse al mondo,*

*Questa fiamma staria senza piu scosse.*
*Ma perciocche giammai di questo fondo*
*Non torno vivo alcun, s'i'odo il vero,*
*Senza tema d'infamia ti rispondo.* ①

Let us go then, you and I,
When the evening is spread out against the sky
Like a patient etherised② upon a table;
Let us go, through certain half-deserted streets,
The muttering retreats③
Of restless nights in one-night cheap hotels
And sawdust restaurants with oyster-shells:
Streets that follow like a tedious argument
Of insidious intent
To lead you to an overwhelming question ...
Oh, do not ask, "What is it?"
Let us go and make our visit.

In the room the women come and go
Talking of Michelangelo.

The yellow fog that rubs its back upon the window-panes,
The yellow smoke that rubs its muzzle on the window-panes
Licked its tongue into the corners of the evening,
Lingered upon the pools that stand in drains,
Let fall upon its back the soot that falls from chimneys,
Slipped by the terrace, made a sudden leap,
And seeing that it was a soft October night,
Curled once about the house, and fell asleep.

And indeed there will be time
For the yellow smoke that slides along the street,
Rubbing its back upon the window-panes;

---

① From Dante's *Divine Comedy*, chapter 27. These words are spoken by Count Guido da Montefeltro, who is a lost soul. The quotation means: "If I thought my answer were to one who could ever return to the world, this flame would move no more; but since no one has ever returned alive from this depth, if what I hear be true, without fear of infamy I answer you."

② etherise: anesthetize with ether, indicated a sense of helpless.

③ retreats: places where secrete conversations are taken.

There will be time, there will be time
To prepare a face to meet the faces that you meet;
There will be time to murder and create,
And time for all the works and days[①] of hands
That lift and drop a question on your plate;
Time for you and time for me,
And time yet for a hundred indecisions,
And for a hundred visions and revisions,
Before the taking of a toast and tea.

In the room the women come and go
Talking of Michelangelo.

And indeed there will be time
To wonder, "Do I dare?" and, "Do I dare?"
Time to turn back and descend the stair,
With a bald spot in the middle of my hair —
[They will say: "How his hair is growing thin!"]
My morning coat, my collar mounting firmly to the chin,
My necktie rich and modest, but asserted by a simple pin —
[They will say: "But how his arms and legs are thin!"]
Do I dare
Disturb the universe?
In a minute there is time
For decisions and revisions which a minute will reverse.

For I have known them all already, known them all —
Have known the evenings, mornings, afternoons,
I have measured out my life with coffee spoons;
I know the voices dying with a dying fall
Beneath the music from a farther room.
So how should I presume?

And I have known the eyes already, known them all —
The eyes that fix you in a formulated phrase,
And when I am formulated, sprawling on a pin,
When I am pinned and wriggling on the wall,

① "Works and days" is the title of a long poem by Hesiod, an early Greek poet.

Then how should I begin
To spit out all the butt-ends of my days and ways?
    And how should I presume?

    And I have known the arms already, known them all —
Arms that are braceleted and white and bare
[But in the lamplight, downed with light brown hair!]
It is perfume from a dress
That makes me so digress?
Arms that lie along a table, or wrap about a shawl.
    And should I then presume?
    And how should I begin?

Shall I say, I have gone at dusk through narrow streets
And watched the smoke that rises from the pipes
Of lonely men in shirt-sleeves, leaning out of windows? ...

    I should have been a pair of ragged claws
Scuttling across the floors of silent seas.

And the afternoon, the evening, sleeps so peacefully!
Smoothed by long fingers,
Asleep ... tired ... or it malingers,
Stretched on the floor, here beside you and me.
Should I, after tea and cakes and ices,
Have the strength to force the moment to its crisis?
But though I have wept and fasted, wept and prayed,
Though I have seen my head [grown slightly bald] brought in upon a platter①,
I am no prophet—and here's no great matter;
I have seen the moment of my greatness flicker,
And I have seen the eternal Footman hold my coat, and snicker,
And in short, I was afraid.

    And would it have been worth it, after all,
After the cups, the marmalade, the tea,
Among the porcelain, among some talk of you and me,

① Echoes the story from Matthew, Herod delivered the head of John the Baptist to Salome as a reward for her dancing.

Would it have been worth while,
To have bitten off the matter with a smile,
To have squeezed the universe into a ball①
To roll it toward some overwhelming question,
To say:"I am Lazarus, come from the dead,
Come back to tell you all, I shall tell you all" —
If one, settling a pillow by her head,
  Should say:"That is not what I meant at all.
  That is not it, at all."

  And would it have been worth it, after all,
Would it have been worth while,
After the sunsets and the dooryards and the sprinkled streets,
After the novels, after the teacups, after the skirts that trail along the floor—
And this, and so much more? —
It is impossible to say just what I mean!
But as if a magic lantern threw the nerves in patterns on a screen:
Would it have been worth while
If one, settling a pillow or throwing off a shawl,
And turning toward the window, should say:
  "That is not it at all,
  That is not what I meant, at all."

. . . . .

No! I am not Prince Hamlet, nor was meant to be;
Am an attendant lord, one that will do
To swell a progress, start a scene or two,
Advise the prince; no doubt, an easy tool,
Deferential, glad to be of use,
Politic, cautious, and meticulous;
Full of high sentence, but a bit obtuse;
At times, indeed, almost ridiculous —
Almost, at times, the Fool.

  I grow old . . . I grow old . . .
I shall wear the bottoms of my trousers rolled.

  Shall I part my hair behind? Do I dare to eat a peach?

① Echoes Marvell's "To His Coy Mistress".

I shall wear white flannel trousers, and walk upon the beach.
I have heard the mermaids singing, each to each.

I do not think that they will sing to me.

I have seen them riding seaward on the waves
Combing the white hair of the waves blown back
When the wind blows the water white and black.

We have lingered in the chambers of the sea
By sea-girls wreathed with seaweed red and brown
Till human voices wake us, and we drown.

## About the Selection

《情歌》是艾略特的代表作之一，现代主义诗歌经典。该诗写于1910—1911年间，其时艾略特23岁，正处于思想的转变时期。这首诗也被普遍认为是艾略特现代主义诗歌转型的标志性作品。该诗名为情歌，实是主人公普鲁弗洛克对冷漠的社会感到不满，却又无力挣脱，内心彷徨挣扎的写照。

## Research Guide

1. If other consciousnesses exist only as opaque objects for Prufrock, he has an equally unhappy relation to time and space. One of the puzzles of the poem is the question as to whether Prufrock ever leaves his room. It appears that he does not, so infirm is his will, so ready "for a hundred indecisions, /And for a hundred visions and revisions, /Before the taking of a toast and tea" (CP, 4). In another sense Prufrock would be unable to go anywhere, however hard he tried. If all space has been assimilated into his mind, then spatial movement would really be movement in the same place, like a man running in a dream. There is no way to distinguish between actual movement and imaginary movement. [...] Time disappears in the same way. (Miller, 1965: 139)

2. In the same essay where Eliot locates the beginnings of a poem in an unknown, dark "psychic material" that is put into form by the conscious mind, he allows for a secondary resurgence of the unconscious that arises from the very process of poetic composition. [...] The mental forces at work in Eliot's description of the poetic process serve as an analogy to the conflicts besetting the speaker in Prufrock. The speaker is a failed poet in terms of his inability to "murder" existing structures in order to "create" anew; he finds it impossible to say what he wants to say. (Spurr, 1984: 10)

3. Eliot's particular transformation of the dramatic monologue in "Prufrock" depends on

the character of the pronouns "you" and "I," which linguists call "shifters" because they are mutually defining and depend for their meanings on the pragmatic context of the discourses in which they occur. Instead of naming something unchanging, these pronouns indicate positions that can be variously occupied. (Riquelme, 1991: 159)

4. J. Alfred Prufrock is not just the speaker of one of Eliot's poems. He is the Representative Man of early Modernism. Shy, cultivated, oversensitive, sexually retarded (many have said impotent), ruminative, isolated, self-aware to the point of solipsism, as he says, "Am an attendant lord, one that will do / To swell a progress, start a scene or two." Nothing revealed the Victorian upper classes in Western society more accurately, unless it was a novel by Henry James, and nothing better exposed the dreamy, insubstantial center of that consciousness than a half-dozen poems in Eliot's first book. (Mitchell, 1991: 43)

## Selected Reading B

### The Waste Land

"Nam Sibyllam quidem Cumis ego ipse oculis meis vidi
in ampulla pendere, et cum illi pueri dicerent: **Σιβυλλα
τι θελει ς**; respondebatilla: **αποθανειν θελω**."[①]

For Ezra Pound
*il miglior fabbro*.

### Ⅰ. The Burial of the Dead

April is the cruellest month, breeding
Lilacs out of the dead land, mixing
Memory and desire, stirring
Dull roots with spring rain.
Winter kept us warm, covering
Earth in forgetful snow, feeding
A little life with dried tubers.
Summer surprised us, coming over the Starnbergersee
With a shower of rain; we stopped in the colonnade,

① Epigraph: meaning: I have seen with my own eyes the Sibyl hanging in a jar, and when the boys asked her "What do you want?" She answered, "I want to die."

And went on in sunlight, into the Hofgarten,
And drank coffee, and talked for an hour.
Bin gar kine Russin, stamm' aus Litauen, echt deutsch.①
And when we were children, staying at the arch-duke's,
My cousin's, he took me out on a sled,

And I was frightened. He said, Marie,
Marie, hold on tight. And down we went.
In the mountains, there you feel free.
I read, much of the night, and go south in the winter.

What are the roots that clutch, what branches grow
Out of this stony rubbish? Son of man,
You cannot say, or guess, for you know only
A heap of broken images, where the sun beats,
And the dead tree gives no shelter, the cricket no relief,
And the dry stone no sound of water. Only
There is shadow under this red rock,
(Come in under the shadow of this red rock),
And I will show you something different from either
Your shadow at morning striding behind you
Or your shadow at evening rising to meet you;
I will show you fear in a handful of dust②.

*Frisch weht der Wind*
*Der Heimat zu,*
*Mein Irisch Kind,*
*Wo weilest du?*③

"You gave me hyacinths first a year ago;
"They called me the hyacinth girl."
– Yet when we came back, late, from the Hyacinth garden,
Your arms full, and your hair wet, I could not
Speak, and my eyes failed, I was neither

① Bin gar kine Russin, stamm' aus Litauen, echt deutsch: I am not Russian at all; I come from Lithuania, I am a real German.

② a handful of dust: the title of Evelyn Waugh's novel: *A Handful of Dust*.

③ (German): The wind blows fresh
To the Homeland
My Irish Girl
Where are you lingering?

Living nor dead, and I knew nothing,
Looking into the heart of light, the silence.
*Oed' und leer das Meer*[①].

Madame Sosostris, famous clairvoyante,
Had a bad cold, nevertheless
Is known to be the wisest woman in Europe,
With a wicked pack of cards. Here, said she,
Is your card, the drowned Phoenician Sailor,
(Those are pearls that were his eyes. Look!)
Here is Belladonna, the Lady of the Rocks,
The lady of situations.
Here is the man with three staves, and here the Wheel,
And here is the one-eyed merchant, and this card
Which is blank, is something he carries on his back,
Which I am forbidden to see. I do not find
The Hanged Man. Fear death by water.
I see crowds of people, walking round in a ring.
Thank you. If you see dear Mrs. Equitone,
Tell her I bring the horoscope myself:
One must be so careful these days.

Unreal City,
Under the brown fog of a winter dawn,
A crowd flowed over London Bridge, so many,
I had not thought death had undone so many.
Sighs, short and infrequent, were exhaled,
And each man fixed his eyes before his feet.
Flowed up the hill and down King William Street,
To where Saint Mary Woolnoth kept the hours
With a dead sound on the final stroke of nine.
There I saw one I knew, and stopped him, crying: "Stetson!
"You who were with me in the ships at Mylae!
"That corpse you planted last year in your garden,
"Has it begun to sprout? Will it bloom this year?
"Or has the sudden frost disturbed its bed?
"Oh keep the Dog far hence, that's friend to men,

---

① Oed'und leer das meer: Desolate and empty the sea.

"Or with his nails he'll dig it up again!
"You! hypocrite lecteur! — mon semblable, — mon frère!"①

## About the Selection

《荒原》一诗作于1922年,是艾略特的代表作。原诗800多行,在庞德的删改下,现剩下433行。该诗被誉为西方现代诗歌的一个里程碑,也是20世纪最重要的诗歌之一。《荒原》描绘了西方人的精神荒原,一战之后整个一代人的迷惘,信仰的缺失和精神的空虚。诗中引用了几十位作家作品,运用了德语,法语等6种语言。全诗共分五个部分:"死者的葬仪","对弈","火诫","水里的死亡"和"雷霆的话",选文摘录自《荒原》第一部分:"死者的葬仪"。

## Research Guide

1. The poem would undoubtedly be"clearer" if every symbol had a single, unequivocal meaning; but the poem would be thinner, and less honest. For the poet has not been content to develop a didactic allegory in which the symbols are two-dimensional items adding up directly to the sum of the general scheme. They represent dramatized instances of the theme, embodying in their own nature the fundamental paradox of the theme. (Brooks 1937: 135)

2. *The Waste Land* summarizes the Grail legend, not precisely in the usual order, but retaining the principal incidents and adapting them to a modern setting. Eliot's indebtedness both to Sir James Frazer and to Jessie L. [...] The Grail legend corresponds to the great hero epics, it dramatizes initiation into maturity, and it bespeaks a quest for sexual, cultural, and spiritual healing. Through all these attributed functions, it influenced Eliot's symbolism. (Smith, 1956: 70)

3. *The Waste Land*, Eliot's first long philosophical poem, can now be read simply as it was written, as a poem of radical doubt and negation, urging that every human desire be stilled except the desire for self-surrender, for restraint, and for peace. Compared with the longing expressed in later poems for the "eyes" and the "birth," the "coming" and "the Lady" (in "The Hollow Men," the Ariel poems, and "Ash-Wednesday"), the hope held out in *The Waste Land* is a negative one. Following Hugh Kenner's recommendation, we should lay to rest the persistent error of reading *The Waste Land* as a poem in which five motifs predominate: the nightmare journey, the Chapel, the Quester, the Grail Legend, and the Fisher King. (Hay, 1982: 48)

4. *The Waste Land* does not merely reflect the breakdown of an historical, social, and cultural order battered by violent forces operating under the name of modernity. For

---

① Hypocrite reader! — my doppelganger — my brother!

Eliot the disaster that characterized modernity was not an overturning, but the unavoidable, and ironic, culmination of that very order so lovingly celebrated in Victoria's last decade on the throne. Unlike the older generation, who saw in events like the Great War the passing of a golden age, Eliot saw only that the golden age was itself a heap of absurd sociopolitical axioms and perverse misreadings of the cultural past that had proved in the last instance to be made of the meanest alloy. (Cooper 1987: 85)

## Supplementary Reading

### Rhapsody on a Windy Night

Twelve o'clock.
Along the reaches of the street
Held in a lunar synthesis,
Whispering lunar incantations
Dissolve the floors of memory
And all its clear relations,
Its divisions and precisions.
Every street lamp that I pass
Beats like a fatalistic drum,
And through the spaces of the dark
Midnight shakes the memory
As a madman shakes a dead geranium.

Half-past one,
The street-lamp sputtered,
The street-lamp muttered,
The street-lamp said, "Regard that woman
Who hesitates toward you in the light of the door
Which opens on her like a grin.
You see the border of her dress
Is torn and stained with sand,
And you see the corner of her eye
Twists like a crooked pin."

The memory throws up high and dry
A crowd of twisted things;
A twisted branch upon the beach

Eaten smooth, and polished
As if the world gave up
The secret of its skeleton,
Stiff and white.
A broken spring in a factory yard,
Rust that clings to the form that the strength has left
Hard and curled and ready to snap.

Half-past two,
The street-lamp said,
"Remark the cat which flattens itself in the gutter,
Slips out its tongue
And devours a morsel of rancid butter."
So the hand of the child, automatic,
Slipped out and pocketed a toy that was running along the quay.
I could see nothing behind that child's eye.
I have seen eyes in the street
Trying to peer through lighted shutters,
And a crab one afternoon in a pool,
An old crab with barnacles on his back,
Gripped the end of a stick which I held him.

Half-past three,
The lamp sputtered,
The lamp muttered in the dark.
The lamp hummed:
"Regard the moon,
La lune ne garde aucune rancune①,
She winks a feeble eye,
She smiles into corners.
She smooths the hair of the grass.
The moon has lost her memory.
A washed-out smallpox cracks her face,
Her hand twists a paper rose,
That smells of dust and eau de Cologne,
She is alone
With all the old nocturnal smells

① The moon holds no grudges. From Jules Laforgue's "Complainte de cette Bonne Lune".

That cross and cross across her brain."
The reminiscence comes
Of sunless dry geraniums
And dust in crevices,
Smells of chestnuts in the streets,
And female smells in shuttered rooms,
And cigarettes in corridors
And cocktail smells in bars.

The lamp said,
"Four o'clock,
Here is the number on the door.
Memory!
You have the key,
The little lamp spreads a ring on the stair,
Mount.
The bed is open; the tooth-brush hangs on the wall,
Put your shoes at the door[①], sleep, prepare for life."

The last twist of the knife.

### Morning at the Window

They are rattling breakfast plates in basement kitchens,
And along the trampled edges of the street
I am aware of the damp souls of housemaids
Sprouting despondently at area gates.

The brown waves of fog toss up to me
Twisted faces from the bottom of the street,
And tear from a passer-by with muddy skirts
An aimless smile that hovers in the air
And vanishes along the level of the roofs.

## References and Further Reading

1. Brooks, Cleanth. "The Waste Land: Critique of the Myth." *Southern Review* 3

① Put your shoes at the door: for staff to clean.

(1937): 106-136.

2. Cooper, John Xiros. *T. S. Eliot and the Politics of Voice: The Argument of "The Waste Land."* Ann Arbor: UMI Research Press, 1987.
3. Hay, Eloise Knapp. *T. S. Eliot's Negative Way*. Cambridge, MA: Harvard UP, 1982.
4. Miller, J. Hillis. *Poets of Reality: Six Twentieth-Century Writers*. Cambridge, MA: The Belknap Press of Harvard UP, 1965.
5. Mitchell, Roger. "Modernism Comes to American Poetry: 1908—1920." *A Profile of Twentieth-Century American Poetry*. Ed. Jack Myers and David Wojahan. Carbondale: Southern Illinois UP, 1991.
6. Riquelme, John Paul. *Harmony of Dissonances: T. S. Eliot, Romanticism, and Imagination*. Baltimore : The Johns Hopkins University Press, 1991.
7. Smith, Grover. *T. S. Eliot's Poetry and Plays: A Study in Sources and Meaning*. Chicago: The University of Chicago Press, 1956.
8. Spurr, David. *Conflicts in Consciousness: T. S. Eliot's Poetry and Criticism*. Urbana: University of Illinois Press, 1984.
9. 艾略特.荒原.赵萝蕤、张子清译.北京:人民日报出版社,2000.
10. 董洪川."荒原"之风:T. S. 艾略特在中国.北京:北京大学出版社,2004.
11. 黄宗英编.赵萝蕤汉译〈荒原〉手稿.北京:高等教育出版社,2013.

# 13. E. E. Cummings (1894–1962)

## Introduction

Edward Estlin Cummings (1894-1962), born in Cambridge, Massachusetts in a middle class family, was an innovative American poet. He had his name legally written in lowercase form "e. e. cummings". Cummings received his B. A. in 1915 and M. A. the following year in Harvard University. 1917 saw his first poems published in the anthology *Eight Harvard Poets*, the same year, Cummings volunteered for French-based Norton-Harjes Ambulance Service during World War I. However, because of his disregard of regulations, he was interned four months in Normandy, which he recounted in his novel, *The Enormous Room*. During the 1920s and 1930s, Cummings travelled widely in Europe, meeting poets and artists, including Pablo Picasso, a great influence on his early art forms as well as on his writing.

His major poetry collections included*Tulips and Chimneys* (1923), *&* (1925), *XLI Poems* (1925), *Ninety-five Poems* (1958) and so on, besides poetry, he wrote two autobiographical novels, four plays and several essays. As an innovative poet, Cummings experimented radically with the arrangement of words, punctuation, capitalization, dislocated syntax, and misuse of parts of speech and traditional techniques to create a new means of poetic expression. Moreover, as a painter, Cummings was very conscious of the visual effects of poetry, and this training had its noticeable effect on typographical and visual appearance of his poems on page. At the time of his death, he was the second most widely read poet in the United States, after Robert Frost.

## Selected Reading A

### l(a

l(a

le
af
fa

ll

s)
one
l

iness

### About the Selection

"l(a"是卡明斯诗集1958年出版的诗集 *95 poems* 中的第一首，这首诗共有四个词(loneliness, a, leaf, falls)组成，分为5节，每节分别有1-3-1-3-1行。整首诗的句法杂乱而无序，在阅读中，读者会受到这种奇特句法影响而减慢阅读速度，视线的移动仿佛就是在看一片飘落的树叶。作为一个实验派诗人，卡明斯所接受的视觉艺术的教育使他非常重视诗歌的视觉效果，这首诗在页面上的排版就是很好的证明。对于诗作主题的解析，有的评论家认为它是讲死亡的，树叶飘落让人想到随时面临死亡的迟暮之年，而死亡本身又是很孤独的，就像看到一片树叶飘落的感觉。也有人从后结构主义的角度解析本诗，得出本诗是讲"one/singular/alone"的。

### Research Guide

1. Without even reading the words and using fields of representation perhaps unusual in poetry (the visual in this case), the reader is drawn toward one of the main themes of the poem — that of "one." It is no surprise that this poem was the first poem in Cummings' book *95 Poems* and was numbered "I", further impressing the main theme upon the reader. Furthermore, in the original printing of *95 Poems* (1958), "l(a" appeared opposite a blank page — thus at once suggesting the loneliness explicit in the poem-whilst all other poems except the last appeared in twos. The twenty-three characters (including the title) seemed lost, overwhelmed by the white space and one's eyes are automatically

drawn to the fragile construction. Metaphorically, then, the poem enacts the vastness of space and the smallness of man within that space. This has existential undertones and implicitly suggests another theme of the poem-that of death (autumn). (Landles, 2001: 39)

2. Meaning is thus enhanced by the overlapping fields of representation, promoting a kind of unification of meaning-a "one-ness." Yet the closer we examine the poem the more the concept / numeral "one" is shown to be both fragmented and multiple. Thus, the themes of "one / singular / alone" are only perceptible, paradoxically, through the splintered, diverse, and shattered syntax. The "I / l" is, literally, seen to be many "l's" at the same time. Metaphorically, then, the poem enacts the same "dismantling" of man that has occurred with the rise of post-structuralism. However, leaving this point for future investigation, this analysis shall turn to the theories of Derrida in order to examine the syntax of this poem further. (Landles, 2001: 39)

3. The first poem [l(a] in the book is the most delicately beautiful literary constructthat Cummings ever created. It consists of the phrase "a leaf falls" and the word "loneliness": that is all, although the two are intertwined. After the first line, "l(a," the rest of the letters of the parenthetical intrusion, "a leaf falls)," are scattered down the page, five move lines in a pattern of alternating consonants and vowels, as if to demonstrate how the leaf drifts to and fro in falling. Then comes the word "one," which continues the spelling of "loneliness." Then an "l" by itself, reminding us that an "l" and a numeral one are the same key on a typewriter. The rest of the word "loneliness" (which also contains "oneliness") is completed. (Kennedy, 1994: 463)

## Selected Reading B

### [in Just-]

in Just-
spring          when the world is mud-
luscious the little
lame balloonman

whistles          far          and wee
and eddieandbill[①] come

① eddieandbill: Eddie and Bill, two boys' names.

running from marbles and
piracies and it's
spring

when the world is puddle-wonderful
the queer
old balloonman whistles
far      and      wee
and bettyandisbel[1] come dancing

from hop-scotch and jump-rope and

it's
spring
and

      the

      goat-footed

balloonMan      whistles
far
and
wee

## About the Selection

这首诗是《郁金香和烟囱》诗集中"天真之歌"部分里的第一首。从表面上看，诗中描述了在万物复苏的春天里，一群玩耍的孩子看到一位卖气球的跛足老者，便欢心雀跃地跑过去，将孩童的天真无邪展现得淋漓尽致。然而诗中的两处大写，其一是诗首对"Just-"的大写，其二是诗尾对"balloonMan"中"Man"的大写，以及本诗大量运用的跨行手法，诗人对词间距的不同寻常的排列等，这些都会激起读者的反复思考：这首诗仅仅如其表面看起来表达的那么简单、普通吗？这些形式与本诗要表达的主题有没有关系？有何关系？此外，"goat-footed"中"goat"有象征"lust"的意义，因此读者在品味此诗时，很容易把 goat-footed（半人半羊的）卖球者跟"satyr"或者"god Pan"意象联系起来，这为本诗的解读提供了又一个视角。

## Research Guide

1. It is time to address this issue and attempt to interpret Cummings from a post-

① bettyandisbel：Betty and Isabel，two girls' names.

structuralist perspective since it is only with post-structuralist theory that these connections can be made.

In their search for a"truth" or "meaning" for "in Just-," the critics have interpreted parts of the poem which seem at odds with the general theme of innocence / childhood. Furthermore, given Cummings' reputation for syntactical oddities, the critics seem to ignore, or gloss over these very issues in the poem. [...] Thus, Kidder states that the poem's innocent surface also contains "an underlying presence inimical to that very innocence." [...] In other words, that the children, at this moment, are moving from an innocent state to a state of knowledge-a "growing up" of sorts. However, the conclusion that the poem shows this move from childhood to adulthood is flawed in that the children are still children at the end of the poem. What has changed is the "Man" in "balloonman." This suggests that Cummings wished to emphasise the "man" part of the "balloonman." The children are unaffected by this change, for nowhere in the poem do we glimpse either the children interacting with one another (sexually), or "growing up" for any particular reason. Instead, much is left out. (Landles, 2001: 34-35)

2. These alternating patterns of momentum and stasis undermine the simple surface meanings of the words and complicate the presentation of innocence and renewal symbolized by the children and springtime. Instead, the rhythms create an aura of mystery and ambiguity, of tension and disquiet, that results in the poem becoming a complex embodiment of irony and dissonance... Long vowels, such as those in "lameballoonman," "far and wee," and "marbles and piracies" slow the tempo, create a smooth rhythm, and impart melodiousness and resonance, as well as a keening quality, a tone of regret, that contradicts the idea of joyous renewal with which spring is typically associated. Thus, an aura of mystery and ambiguity permeates the poem and belies its words, and this ambiguity invites and enables composers to emphasize what they wish—the surface meaning of the words of the poem, or the shadowy, darker undercurrents. (Pollack, 1995: 123-124)

3. By its emphasis on mud and water, growth and vitality, sexuality and propagation, the poem may be read as a displacement and adaptation of the creation myth or the account of primal creation in Genesis. The loam from which Adam was created, the inspiriting that ensued, the creation of Eve, her introduction to and relationship with Adam in the verdant Garden of Eden, and the procreative function of their relationship mandated by God are all elements in the paradigm adumbrated in Scripture. Against the foregoing context, the balloonman appears. His classical analogue is Pan, not only the lecherous goat-man, the prototype in physical appearance of the Christian conception of the devil, but also the Good Shepherd who oversees the well-being of his flock and encourages their propagation. By awakening in the children the impulses or instincts of

sexuality, the balloonman, in effect, creates new beings, promotes other relationships, and imparts the potential for consequences—evil, goodness, and variations or interactions thereof—that may result from the pairings of male and female in adolescence and eventually adulthood. One surmises that the unusual spelling of "balloonMan" in its third appearance in the poem looks toward adulthood. (Labriola, 1992: 42)

## Supplementary Reading

### When God Decided to Invent

when god decided to invent
everything he took one
breath bigger than a circustent
and everything began

when man determined to destroy
himself he picked the was
of shall and finding only why
smashed it into because

### Who Sharpens Every Dull

who sharpens every dull
here comes the only man
reminding with his bell
to disappear a sun

and out of houses pour
maids mothers widows wives
bringing this visitor
their very oldest lives

one pays him with a smile
another with a tear
some cannot pay at all
he never seems to care

he sharpens is to am
he sharpens say to sing

you'd almost cut your thumb
so right he sharpens wrong

and when their lives are keen
he throws the world a kiss
and slings his wheel upon
his back and off he goes

but we can hear him still
if now our sun is gone
reminding with his bell
to reappear a moon

## A Like a

a like a
grey
rock wandrin

g
through
pasture
wom

an creature whom
than
earth hers

elf
could
silent more no
be

## r-p-o-p-h-e-s-s-a-g-r

r-p-o-p-h-e-s-s-a-g-r
                        who
a)s w(e loo)k
upnowgath
            PPEGORHRASS
                                    eringint(o-

aThe):l
eA
! p:
S
a
(r
rIvInG .gRrEaPsPhOs)
to
rea(be)rran(com)gi(e)ngly
,grasshopper;

## References and Further Reading


1. Friedman, Norman, ed. *E. E. Cummings: A Collection of Critical Essays*. Englewood Cliffs: Prentice-Hall, 1972.
2. Kennedy, Richard S. *Dreams in the Mirror: A Biography of E. E. Cummings*. New York: Norton, 1994.
3. Labriola, Albert C. "Reader-Response Criticism and the Poetry of E. E. Cummings: 'Buffalo Bill's defunct' and 'in Just-.'" *Cithara* 31.2 (1992): 40-42.
4. Landles, Iain. "An Analysis of Two Poems by E. E. Cummings." *Spring: The Journal of the E. E. Cummings Society* 10 (2001): 31-43.
5. Pollack, Norma. "Poems of Cummings Set to Music." *Spring: The Journal of the E. E. Cummings Society* 4 (1995): 123-24.
6. Rotella, Guy, ed. *Critical Essays on E. E. Cummings*. Boston: G.K. Hall, 1984.
7. 史志康."奇语天下惊——试谈 e.e.肯明斯怪异的诗歌语言",解放军外国语学院学报. 1996(1):59-63.

# 14. Langston Hughes (1902–1967)

## Introduction

Langston Hughes was born on February 1, 1902, in Joplin, Missouri. He was raised mainly by his grandmother when he was a child. He began to show his talent in poetry writing when he was in 8$^{th}$ grade and was called "class poet" by his peer. By the time Hughes enrolled in Columbia University, he had already begun his literary career. After leaving Columbia, Hughes spent some years doing menial jobs and traveled abroad. He never got married and died in New York in 1967 during surgery.

Hughes is a productive writer and his works cover many fields, including poetry, novels, operas, television scripts, musicals, children's book, etc. Hughes was one of the earliest innovators of the then-new literary art form jazz poetry. His life and work made great contribution to the Harlem Renaissance in 1920s. His works can be divided mainly into three categories: racial, political and children literature. He brought the race and political problem to the surface through his works and called for democracy, freedom and equality. Many of Hughes' poems are written in a rhythmical way and were set to music. It is said that his poems were meant to be "read aloud, crooned, shouted and sung."

## Selected Reading A

### The Negro Speaks of Rivers

I've known rivers:

I've known rivers ancient as the world and older than the flow of human blood
in human veins.
My soul has grown deep like the rivers.

I bathed in the Euphrates[①] when dawns were young.
I built my hut near the Congo and it lulled me to sleep.
I looked upon the Nile and raised the pyramids above it.
I heard the singing of the Mississippi when Abe Lincoln[②] went down to New Orleans,
and I've seen its muddy bosom turn all golden in the sunset.

I've known rivers:
Ancient, dusky rivers[③].

My soul has grown deep like the rivers.

## About the Selection

《黑人谈河》是休斯发表的第一首也是其最有名的诗作之一。创作该诗的时候,休斯还是一个学生,坐在火车上,经过密西西比河,想起了自己的种族,于是在十分钟之内就创作完成了这首诗。休斯在诗题中使用了第三人称的视角,而在诗歌中却用了第一人称。在这首诗里,"河流"是一个高度凝练的意象,可以被理解为是历史的象征。一个黑人对河流的追溯,就是其对自身历史、文化、故土的追溯和寻根。诗中第一人称的"我"并非特指某一个黑人,而是指整个黑人种族。整首诗表达了诗人对黑人历史的自豪感,也表现出诗人对黑人所受深重苦难的感伤。在诗人生活的年代,该诗具有强大的感召力。

## Research Guide

1. "The Negro Speaks of Rivers" is perhaps the most profound of these poems of heritage and strength. Composed when Hughes was a mere 17 years old, and dedicated to W. E. B. DuBois, it is a sonorous evocation of transcendent essences so ancient as to appear timeless, predating human existence, longer than human memory. The rivers are part of God's body, and participate in his immortality. They are the earthly analogues of eternity: deep, continuous, mysterious. They are named in the order of their association with black history... In a time and place where black life is held cheap and the days of black men appear to be numbered, the poem is a majestic reminder of the strength and fullness of history, of the source of that life which transcends even ceaseless labor and

① Euphrates, Congo, Nile, and Mississippi: Hughes named all these rivers that represent the history of western culture.

② When Lincoln was the president of America, he abolished slavery and librated the black slaves.

③ Dusky rivers could be indicating the black history.

burning crosses. (Jemie, 1976: 103-104)

2. With its allusions to deep dusky rivers, the setting sun, sleep, and the soul, "The Negro Speaks of Rivers" is suffused with the image of death and, simultaneously, the idea of deathlessness. As in Whitman's philosophy, only the knowledge of death can bring the primal spark of poetry and life. Here Langston Hughes became "the outsetting bard," in Whitman's phrase, the poet who sings of life because at last he has known death. Balanced between the knowledge of love and of death, the poetic will gathers force. (Rampersad, 2002: 40)

3. Readers rarely notice that if the soul of the Negro in this poem goes back to the Euphrates, it goes back to a pre-"racial" dawn and a geography far from Africa that is identified with neither blackness nor whiteness—a geography at the time of Hughes's writing considered the cradle of all the world's civilizations and possibly the location of the Garden of Eden. Thus, even in this poem about the depth of the Negro's soul Hughes avoids racial essentialism while nonetheless stressing the existential, racialized conditions of black and modern identity. (Hutchinson, 1995: 415)

4. This poem was written as an internal dialogue with his father whose "strange dislike of his own people" baffled and disturbed Hughes, and, of course, implicated his son as object of that dislike. In this poem, Hughes joins affirmative blackness to a universal human quest, by putting into a global context the racial stresses and demands of the United States. The poem (as is well known) lists four key rivers, all "ancient as the world. Three of the four flow through regions of colored peoples; they are "rivers in our past". The word "our" is marked. (Duplessis, 2001: 95)

## Selected Reading B

### The Weary Blues①

Droning a drowsy syncopated② tune,
Rocking back and forth to a mellow croon,
    I heard a Negro play.

---

① Blues: a type of folksong that originated among Black Americans at the beginning of the 20th century; It has a melancholy sound from repeated use of blue notes.

② syncopated: In syncopated music, the weak beats in the bar are stressed instead of the strong beats. Syncopation in music is similar to situational irony in literature when something unexpected or illogical happens.

Down on Lenox Avenue① the other night
By the pale dull pallor of an old gas light
He did a lazy sway... .
He did a lazy sway... .
To the tune o' those Weary Blues.
With his ebony hands on each ivory key
He made that poor piano moan with melody.
O Blues!
Swaying to and fro on his rickety stool
He played that sad raggy tune like a musical fool.
Sweet Blues!
Coming from a black man's soul.
O Blues!
In a deep song voice with a melancholy tone
I heard that Negro sing, that old piano moan —
"Ain't got nobody in all this world,
Ain't got nobody but ma self.
I's gwine to quit ma frownin'
And put ma troubles on the shelf."
Thump, thump, thump, went his foot on the floor.
He played a few chords then he sang some more —

"I got the Weary Blues
And I can't be satisfied.
Got the Weary Blues
And can't be satisfied —
I ain't happy no mo'
And I wish that I had died."
And far into the night he crooned that tune.
The stars went out and so did the moon.
The singer stopped playing and went to bed
While the Weary Blues echoed through his head.
He slept like a rock or a man that's dead.

## About the Selection

《疲惫的布鲁斯》是休斯同名诗集中的开篇作。该诗创作于哈莱姆区一个演奏布鲁斯音乐的俱乐部,休斯经常一边听爵士和布鲁斯音乐一边作诗。这首"疲惫的布鲁斯"就是用演

---

① Lenox Avenue: a main street in Harlem, which is seen as the uptown of New York.

奏的乐器所创作的。该诗的语言，诗行的重复和诗中包含的布鲁斯歌词以及布鲁斯音乐特有的忧伤曲调，让读者能够感受到诗中布鲁斯演奏者的心声，同时也表达了休斯把黑人音乐与语言融入其创作的诗歌中的想法。

## Research Guide

1. The poem is a fitting opening not only to this volume, but to all of Hughes's volumes. It combines traditional blues stanzas that emphasize the roots of African-American experience, touches of vaudeville blues as the roots were being "refined," pride in African-American creativity and forms of expression, and a sense of the weariness that ties together generations of African-Americans. With the words "Sweet Blues," Hughes strikes upon the central paradox with which the poem attempts to come to terms. It is one of his central themes. (Tracy, 1988: 223)

2. Steven Tracy's compelling argument asserts that the piano player and speaker are united by the performance. I would like to argue to the contrary however. In my view, the poem works out Hughes's apprehension, his feeling that his ability to understand the emotions that generated this form of artistic expression was not on a par with the expression itself This is indicated by the last line of the poem, where the speaker notes that the piano player "slept like a rock or a man that's dead." The key word here is "or," for it denotes the imprecision of the speaker's understanding. What the blues articulates is the simultaneous presence of the "tragic and comic aspects of the human conditions." Thus, the blues in the poem is not the conventional "either/or" condition configured within the Cartesian construct. Rather, the piano player, by metaphorizing loneliness has already chosen self-recovery. The poem's last line, then, ignores the blues performer's ability to articulate pain and likewise to subsume it. That the speaker and the piano player never meet, or as Tracy asserts, "strike up a conversation, share a drink, or anything else," suggests that the experience does not rupture the speaker's externality. He never enters that space whereby the piano player is speaking for him, giving utterance to his loneliness. Finally, at no point in time does the speaker in the poem insert himself into the lyrics. (Beavers, 1992: 3-4)

3. The poem contains a complex reversal. The blues singer's apparent self-exhaustion (for his state is a product of his will, his soul) is counterbalanced by the fact that he has played himself into the heart and mind of the speaker in "The Weary Blues". This effect is less obvious here than in Wordsworth's "The Solitary Reaper", a strangely analogous poem, but the speaker's attachment comes out in two ways. First, more than the coming of daylight is indicated in the line "The stars went out and so did the moon"; we may understand also that the speaker is possessed by the singer's woe, and his art, and so loses a sense of the world beyond And second, the speaker is telling as much about himself as

about the singer when he says: "The singer stopped playing and went to bed / While The Weary Blues echoed through his head. / He slept like a rock or a man that's dead." Has the speaker followed the singer home in fascination, in obsession? And in whose head does the echo of the weary blues play? The singer's, yes, but not his alone. The speaker is also bearing "that music", as Wordsworth says, in his heart. Not even the speaker's empathy with the blues singer, though, can enable us to penetrate the latter's veil of sleep, a veil as opaque as rock and as deep as death. It is an accident that offsets the singer's repetitious self-veilings. Clearly he goes through his routine, his ritual, every night, and as clearly a Langston Hughes does not often happen by. (Cooke, 1984: 63-64)

4. His performance clearly implies several dramatic actions. While one sets the dynamic playing—the Black self-affirmation against what fades — a second presents a vital remaking of the Black self-image. A third shows the transcendence through racial stereotype into lyrical style. From the dramatic situation of the player, both musical as well as performed, the poem imposes isolation and loneliness yet the refusal to accept them. The song marks a metonym for the human imagination. In a deftness often overlooked, Hughes uses anaphora to narrate an imperial self so as to sustain the blues stanza as countermelody and ironic understatement: "Ain't got nobody in all this world, / Ain't got nobody but ma self." What most complements the lyric skill is the dramatic movement of feeling. In narrative distancing his speakers achieve a double identification. (Miller, 1989: 55)

## Supplementary Reading

### Harlem

What happens to a dream deferred?

Does it dry up
like a raisin in the sun?
Or fester like a sore —
And then run?
Does it stink like rotten meat?
Or crust and sugar over —
like a syrupy sweet?

Maybe it just sags

like a heavy load.

*Or does it explode?*

## I, Too, Sing America

I, too, sing America.

I am the darker brother.
They send me to eat in the kitchen
When company comes,
But I laugh,
And eat well,
And grow strong.
Tomorrow,
I'll be at the table
When company comes.
Nobody'll dare
Say to me,
"Eat in the kitchen,"
Then.

Besides,
They'll see how beautiful I am
And be ashamed —
I, too, am America.

## Theme for English B

The instructor said,

*Go home and write*
*a page tonight.*
*And let that page come out of you —*
*Then, it will be true.*

I wonder if it's that simple?
I am twenty-two, colored, born in Winston-Salem.
I went to school there, then Durham, then here
to this college on the hill above Harlem.
I am the only colored student in my class.

The steps from the hill lead down into Harlem,
through a park, then I cross St. Nicholas,
Eighth Avenue, Seventh, and I come to the Y,
the Harlem Branch Y, where I take the elevator
up to my room, sit down, and write this page:

It's not easy to know what is true for you or me
at twenty-two, my age. But I guess I'm what
I feel and see and hear, Harlem, I hear you:
hear you, hear me — we two — you, me, talk on this page.
(I hear New York, too.) Me — who?
Well, I like to eat, sleep, drink, and be in love.
I like to work, read, learn, and understand life.
I like a pipe for a Christmas present,
or records — Bessie, bop, or Bach.
I guess being colored doesn't make me *not* like
the same things other folks like who are other races.
So will my page be colored that I write?
Being me, it will not be white.

But it will be
a part of you, instructor.
You are white —
yet a part of me, as I am a part of you.
That's American.
Sometimes perhaps you don't want to be a part of me.
Nor do I often want to be a part of you.
But we are, that's true!
I guess you learn from me —
although you're older — and white —
and somewhat more free.

This is my page for English B.

## References and Further Reading

1. Beavers, Herman. "Dead Rocks and Sleeping Men: Aurality in the Aesthetic of Langston Hughes." *Langston Hughes Review* 11(1992): 1-5.
2. Cooke, Michael G. *Afro-American Literature in the Twentieth Century: The Achievement of Intimacy*. New Haven: Yale University Press, 1984.
3. Duplessis, Rachel Blau. *Genders, Races, and Religious Cultures in Modern American Poetry, 1908—1934*. London: Cambridge University Press, 2001.
4. Hutchinson, George. *The Harlem Renaissance in Black and White*. Cambridge: Harvard UP, 1995.
5. Jemie, Onwuchekwa. *Langston Hughes: An Introduction to the Poetry*. New York: Columbia University Press, 1976.
6. Miller, R. Baxter. *The Art and Imagination of Langston Hughes*. Lexington: The University Press of Kentucky, 1989.
7. Rampersad, Arnold. *The Life of Langston Hughes, Vol*. 1. London: Oxford University Press, 2002.
8. Tracy, Steven C. *Langston Hughes and the Blues*. Urbana: University of Illinois Press, 1988.
9. 罗良功.艺术与政治的互动:论兰斯顿·休斯的诗歌.上海:上海外语教育出版社,2010.

# 15. Charles Olson (1910–1970)

## Introduction

Charles Olson was an innovative poet and essayist whose works influenced numerous other writers during the 1950s and 1960s. In 1910, Charles Olson was born in Worcester, Massachusetts. He received his BA and MA from Wesleyan University. Olson taught English for two years at Clark University then entered Harvard University in 1936, where he completed coursework for a PhD in American civilization. He published his influential essay "Projective Verse" in 1950, in which he claimed "a poem is energy transferred from where the poet got it... by way of the poem itself to, all the way over to, the reader..." In 1951, Olson was hired as a visiting professor at Black Mountain College in North Carolina. Poets and artists including John Cage and Robert Creeley studied or taught at the College, which was a home for experimental and socially-progressive thought. Olson's ideas of verse had a profound influence on a whole generation of poets, including writers such as Denise Levertov, Paul Blackburn, and Robert Duncan. After the school closed in 1956, Olson moved to Gloucester, Massachusetts. He served as a visiting professor at the State University of New York at Buffalo (1963—1965) and at the University of Connecticut (1969). Charles Olson died from cancer in 1970.

## Selected Reading A

### *from* The Kingfishers

1

What does not change / is the will to change

He woke, fully clothed, in his bed. He
remembered only one thing, the birds, how
when he came in, he had gone around the rooms
and got them back in their cage, the green one first,
she with the bad leg, and then the blue,
the one they had hoped was a male

Otherwise? Yes, Fernand, who had talked lispingly of Albers & Angkor Vat.
He had left the party without a word. How he got up, got into his coat,
I do not know. When I saw him, he was at the door, but it did not matter,
he was already sliding along the wall of the night, losing himself
in some crack of the ruins. That it should have been he who said, "The kingfishers!

who cares
for their feathers
now?"

His last words had been, "The pool is slime." Suddenly everyone,
ceasing their talk, sat in a row around him, watched
they did not so much hear, or pay attention, they
wondered, looked at each other, smirked, but listened,
he repeated and repeated, could not go beyond his thought
"The pool     the kingfishers' feathers were wealth     why
did the export stop?"

It was then he left

2
I thought of the E on the stone, and of what Mao said
"la lumiere"
        but the kingfisher
"de l'aurore"
        but the kingfisher flew west
est devant nous![1]
        he got the color of his breast
        from the heat of the setting sun!

---

① La lumiere de l'aurore est devant nous: the dawn's light is before us.

The features are, the feebleness of the feet (syndactylism of the 3rd & 4th digit)
the bill, serrated, sometimes a pronounced beak, the wings
where the color is, short and round, the tail
inconspicuous.

But not these things are the factors. Not the birds.
The legends are
legends. Dead, hung up indoors, the kingfisher
will not indicate a favoring wind,
or avert the thunderbolt. Nor, by its nesting,
still the waters, with the new year, for seven days.
It is true, it does nest with the opening year, but not on the waters.
It nests at the end of a tunnel bored by itself in a bank. There,
six or eight white and translucent eggs are laid, on fishbones
not on bare clay, on bones thrown up in pellets by the birds.

On these rejectamenta
(as they accumulate they form a cup-shaped structure) the young are born
And, as they are fed and grow, this nest of excrement and decayed fish becomes
a dripping, fetid mass
Mao concluded:
nous devons
nous lever
et agir![1]

## About the Selection

《翠鸟》发表于1949年,是奥尔森的早期代表作,被认为是二战后最具革新精神的诗作之一。这里选取全诗的第一和第二部分,通过几个话题(翠鸟、毛泽东语录等)的互相交叉渗透来探讨文化的传承、异化、交流等主题。

## Research Guide

1. These verses tell us that Olson opposes all that Fernand represents. They comment ironically on the text, for intellectuals like Fernand lack the will to change. Both Fernand and Olson acknowledge the Heraclitean flux, the lapse in time of the meaning and force of tradition, the decline and fall of civilizations. But Fernand is a dilettante who despairs and loses himself in the past ("night... / some crack of the ruins") where Olson, concerned chiefly with the present use of the past, wishes to meet inevitable

[1] Nous devons/ nous lever/ et agir!: we must get up and act!

change with his own will to change. (Paul, 1978: 14)

2. Olson... engages Mao as an exemplar of activism, of the desire for change itself, never mind change from what to what. Change itself is the goal. This is the controlling focus of "The Kingfishers" and of Olson's first book of poems, In Cold Hell, In Thicket (1953): change itself is the value to be asserted. The particular ideology that insists on change, whether by controlling or by communicating with rival ideologies, is not Olson's concern. (von Hallberg, 1978: 19-20)

3. The thought of the E is accompanied by the recollection of an excerpt from Mao's 1948 Report to his Party, which is straightaway placed in serial opposition with the legend accounting for the kingfisher's red breast... . On the one hand, we have ancient Western myth pleading a return to a pre-Socratic cultural stance; on the other hand, a contemporary Eastern realism calling for assertive, popular power. Not only does one sense in this contrast the will to cohere versus the will to disperse and the man of achievement versus the man of power, but the two options are precisely those Olson saw facing Mexico. (Merrill, 1982: 73-74)

4. Indeed, in the 1950s a whole generation of quasi MacLeishes industriously churned out poems which were deliberately designed for explication by those very New Critics who denounced" the heresy of paraphrase." To escape the trap of meaning, Olson realized, a poem must do something more than "be." It must also act. And a poem that moves, that allows itself to be a kinetic force traveling through space-time, truly does escape the trap of meaning. In "The Kingfishers," I have argued, Olson created such a poem. (Hatlen, 1989: 570)

## Selected Reading B

### I, Maximus of Gloucester, to You

Off-shore, by islands hidden in the blood
jewels & miracles, I, Maximus
a metal hot from boiling water, tell you
what is a lance, who obeys the figures of
the present dance

1

the thing you're after

may lie around the bend
of the nest (second, time slain, the bird! the bird!
And there! (strong) thrust, the mast! flight
(of the bird
o kylix, o
Antony of Padua
sweep low, o bless
the roofs, the old ones, the gentle steep ones
on whose ridge-poles the gulls sit, from which they depart,

And the flake-racks
of my city!

2
love is form, and cannot be without
important substance (the weight
say, 58 carats each one of us, perforce
our goldsmith's scale

feather to feather added
(and what is mineral, what
is curling hair, the string
you carry in your nervous beak, these
make bulk, these, in the end, are
the sum
(o my lady of good voyage
in whose arm, whose left arm rests
no boy but a carefully carved wood, a painted face, a schooner!
a delicate mast, as bow-sprit for

forwarding

3
the underpart is, though stemmed, uncertain
is, as sex is, as moneys are, facts!
facts, to be dealt with, as the sea is, the demand
that they be played by, that they only can be, that they must
be played by, said he, coldly, the
ear!

By ear, he sd.
But that which matters, that which insists, that which will last,
that! o my people, where shall you find it, how, where, where shall you listen
when all is become billboards, when, all, even silence, is spray-gunned?

when even our bird, my roofs,
cannot be heard

when even you, when sound itself is neoned in?

when, on the hill, over the water
where she who used to sing,
when the water glowed,
black, gold, the tide
outward, at evening

when bells came like boats
over the oil-slicks, milkweed
hulls

And a man slumped,
attentionless,
against pink shingles

o sea city)

4
one loves only form,
and form only comes
into existence when
the thing is born

born of yourself, born
of hay and cotton struts,
of street-pickings, wharves, weeds
you carry in, my bird

of a bone of a fish
of a straw, or will

of a color, of a bell
of yourself, torn

5

love is not easy
but how shall you know,
New England, now
that pejorocracy is here, how
that street-cars, o Oregon, twitter
in the afternoon offend
a black-gold loin?

how shall you strike,
o swordsman, the blue-red black
when, last night, your aim
was mu-sick, mu-sick, mu-sick
And not the cribbage game?

(o Gloucester-man,
weave
your birds and fingers
new, your roof-tops,
clean shit upon racks
sunned on
American
braid
with others like you, such
extricable surface
as faun and oral,
satyr lesbos vase

o kill kill kill kill kill
those
who advertise you
out)

6

in! in! the bow-sprit, bird, the beak
in, the bend is, in, goes in, the form

that which you make, what holds, which is
the law of object, strut after strut, what you are, what you must be, what
the force can throw up, can, right now hereinafter erect,
the mast, the mast, the tender
mast!

The nest, I say, to you, I Maximus, say
under the hand, as I see it, over the waters
from this place where I am, where I hear,
can still hear

from where I carry you a feather
as though, sharp, I picked up
in the afternoon delivered you
a jewel,
it flashing more than a wing,
than any old romantic thing,
than memory, than place,
than anything other than that which you carry

than that which is,
call it a nest, around the head of, call it
the next second

than that which you
can do!

## About the Selection

《我,格罗斯特的马克西莫斯对你说》选自奥尔森的长诗《马克西莫斯诗抄》。这首长诗体现了奥尔森所谓"投射诗"的一些重要原则,反对学院派的诗歌传统——规则的韵律、理性的逻辑、封闭的情感。因此,诗行和诗句的长度不受音步的限制,而由诗人在表达情感时呼吸的节奏决定,诗句常突破句法和语法,形成破碎的语片。

## Research Guide

1. From the mid-1940s on, Olson was preoccupied with writing a long poem to be called *The Maximus Poems* on the origins of America and its long cultural background reaching back to Mesopotamia. He chose as his speaker the itinerant mystic and writer Maximus, who had lived on the Phoenician coast in the fourth century A. D. and thus occupied a geographical locus parallel to Olson's on the Gloucester coast of North America. Like

many long works of the twentieth century, Olson's engaged the present and informed it by means of ancient cultural paradigms: myths, cultural morphologies, and the archetypal events underlying the civilizations of the Western descent. (Christensen, 2000)

2. *Maximus* is a big poem, the "sort ... of epic" Olson mentioned in "Projective Verse"—a demonstration, in fact, of his belief that the practice of projective verse might solve the "problem of larger content and of larger forms ..." The numbers indicate the limits of the present volume and promise subsequent poems, and the initial poem addresses us (intimately: Whitman's you whoever you are) at a pitch of high resolve, with unusual verbal force, and with a didactic, moral insistence as reminiscent of Pound, perhaps his most conspicuous teacher, as of Maximus of Tyre, a mediator or model of the self Maximus of Gloucester sometimes assumes and Olson assumed when he introduced himself with this poem in *Origin* 1, the issue featuring him. (Paul, 1975:119)

## Supplementary Reading

### You, Hart Crane

Space—shroud and swaddle—you wore,
transcontinental blood of Indian girl,
beat of your dream. Fledged by the modern,
new Archeopteryx, you Hart Crane
drank the poison as Crockett the cloud,
tall man's thirst

I remember your death, reject all answers.
Noon, tall time, at Orizaba stern you stood.
In ecstasy of wake you who made a bridge leaped

### Love

(down,
to my soul:

assume your nature as yourself,
for the love of God

not even good enough

Stories
only
the possibility
of discrete
men

There is no intelligence
the equal of
the situation

There are only
two ways:
create the situation
  (and this is love)
or avoid it.
This also can be
Love.

## References and Further Reading


1. Christensen, Paul. *Charles Olson: Call Him Ishmael*. Austin: University of Texas Press, 1979.
2. Christensen, Paul. "Olson, Charles John." *American National Biography Online Feb*. 2000. http://www.anb.org/articles/16/16-02171.html.
3. Davenport, Guy. "Olson." *The Geography of the Imagination: Forty Essays*. San Francisco: North Point, 1981. 80-99.
4. Hatlen, Burton. "Kinesis and Meaning: Charles Olson's 'The Kingfishers' and the Critics." *Contemporary Literature*. 30. 4 (1989): 546-572.
5. Merrill, Thomas F. *The Poetry of Charles Olson, a Primer*. Newark, DE: University of Delaware Press, 1982.
6. Paul, Sherman. "In and about the Maximus Poems: The Maximus Poems 1-10." *The Iowa Review*. 6.1 (1975): 118-130.
7. Paul, Sherman. *Olson's Push, "Origin," Black Mountain, and Recent American Poetry*. Baton Rouge: Louisiana State University Press, 1978.
8. Von Hallberg, Robert. *Charles Olson: The Scholar's Art*. Cambridge: Harvard University Press, 1978.

# 16. Robert Lowell (1917–1977)

## Introduction

Born in Boston, Massachusetts in a celebrated family, Robert Lowell (1917—1977) was one of the most outstanding poets in contemporary America. He was appointed the sixth Poet Laureate Consultant in Poetry to the Library of Congress where he served from 1947 until 1948, and won the Pulitzer Prize in both 1947 and 1974, the National Book Award in 1960, and the National Book Critics Circle Award in 1977. Even so, his personal life was not smooth; he married three times. In 1977, he died of a heart attack on his way to see his second wife.

Lowell's literary career could be divided into four periods. The first period was that of formalism poem from 1938 to 1951. Poetry collections included *Land of Unlikeness* (1944), *Lord Weary's Castle* (1946, awarded the Pulitzer Prize in 1947) and *The Mills of the Kavanaughs* (1951). Poetry in this period was greatly influenced by Ransom and Allen Tate, complicated in structure, neat in form, strict in rhyme, concise in language, obscure in images and full of satire, religious symbols, and obscure metaphors with the overt sign of New Criticism.

The second period from 1952 to 1967 witnessed Lowell's transition to free verse. The publication of *Life Studies* (1959) marked both a big turning point in Lowell's career and for American poetry. Because many of the poems documented details from Lowell's family life and personal problems, one critic, M. L. Rosenthal, labeled these poems "confessional". His next book *For the Union Dead* (1964) was widely praised, particularly for its title poem, which was invoked by Allen Tate's "Ode to the Confederate Dead." The subject matter was much broader, expanding to historical and political matter. Another collection in this period was *Near the Ocean* (1967).

The third period was that of sonnet from 1967 to 1973. Poetry collections in this period included *Notebook 1967—1968*. *Notebook* (*1970*), *To Liggie and Harriet*, *History*, and *The Dolphin* (awarded Pulitzer Prize in 1974). In the last period Lowell gave up the sonnet form, and returned to the the second period of free verse. *Day by Day* (1977) was his last book.

Besides, Lowell had his translation work *Imitations* (1961), a volume of loose translations of poems by classical and modern European poets, including Baudelaire, Pasternak, and Rimbaud, for which he received the 1962 Bollingen Poetry Translation Prize. He also wrote one play, titled *The Old Glory* (1965), a trilogy based on works by Herman Melville and Nathaniel Hawthorne.

## Selected Reading A

### Skunk Hour

(For Elizabeth Bishop)①

Nautilus Island's② hermit
heiress still lives through winter in her Spartan cottage;
her sheep still graze above the sea.
Her son's a bishop. Her farmer
is first selectman③ in our village;
she's in her dotage.

Thirsting for
the hierarchic privacy
of Queen Victoria's century,
she buys up all
the eyesores facing her shore,
and lets them fall.

The season's ill —
We've lost our summer millionaire,

---

① Bishop once dedicated the poem "The Armadillo" to Lowell, and Lowell dedicated this poem to Bishop in return.

② Nautilus Island: in Castine, Maine, where Lowell had a summerhouse.

③ selectman: many New England towns are administrated by an elected board of selectmen.

who seemed to leap from an L. L. Bean[①]
catalogue. His nine-knot yawl[②]
was auctioned off to lobstermen.
A red fox stain covers Blue Hill.

And now our fairy[③]
decorator brightens his shop for fall;
his fishnet's filled with orange cork,
orange, his cobbler's bench and awl;
there is no money in his work,
he'd rather marry.

One dark night,
my Tudor Ford climbed the hill's skull;
I watched for love-cars. Lights turned down,
they lay together, hull to hull,
where the graveyard shelves on the town....
My mind's not right.

A car radio bleats,
"Love, O careless Love.... ."[④] I hear
my ill-spirit sob in each blood cell,
as if my hand were at its throat....
I myself am hell[⑤];
Nobody's here —

only skunks, that search
in the moonlight for a bite to eat.
They march on their soles up Main Street:
white stripes, moonstruck eyes' red fire
under the chalk-dry and spar spire
of the Trinitarian Church.

---

① L. L. Bean: a mail-order company in Maine, originally specializing in fishing, hunting and camping gear.

② yawl: a small fishing boat.

③ fairy: here it means "homosexual".

④ From a popular song of the time, "Careless Love," which includes the lines "Now you see what careless lovewill do... / Make you kill yourself and your sweetheart too."

⑤ I myself am hell: Quoted from Satan in Milton's *Paradise Lost*: "Which way I fly is Hell; myself am Hell."

I stand on top
of our back steps and breathe the rich air —
a mother skunk with her column of kittens swills the garbage pail.
She jabs her wedge-head in a cup
of sour cream, drops her ostrich tail,
and will not scare.

## About the Selection

《臭鼬的时光》是罗威尔尤为著名的一首诗,被安排在诗集《生活研究》(*Life Studies*)的最后,作为全书的基石。女诗人伊丽莎白·毕肖普(Elizabeth Bishop)曾将一首题为《犰狳》(*The Armadillo*)的诗献给罗威尔,罗威尔后来仿效《犰狳》写了这首诗作为酬答。《臭鼬的时光》表现的是诗人所处时代的精神和道德风貌。前四节以高密度的语言和凝练的象征展现了隐居的女继承人、破产的百万富翁以及同性恋装饰商的形象,表现了政治、经济、社会、宗教、性和艺术的堕落。第五、第六节中,诗人开始观察自己,把自己的堕落暴露在道德的聚光灯下。第七、第八节描述的是在人们处于堕落与病态之时,令人厌恶的臭鼬却大摇大摆地在大街与教堂出没,宛如世界的主人。罗威尔曾在一篇散文中透露,在开始写作此诗时他只写了关于他自己的那部分,诗的前四节是后来加上去的。这样通过先描述诗人周围的生活环境,罗威尔把自己的遭遇阐释为文化整体堕落的其中一个表现,同时个人生活细节的展现又表现了人类在面对这一现代悲剧时所感到的痛苦与悲哀。

## Research Guide

1. The first four stanzas are meant to give a dawdling more or less amiable picture of a declining Maine sea town. I move from the ocean inland. Sterility howls through the scenery, but I try to give a tone of tolerance, humor, and randomness to the sad prospect. The composition drifts, its direction sinks out of sight into the casual, chancy arrangements of nature and decay. Then all comes alive in stanzas V and VI. This is the dark night. I hoped my readers would remember St. John of the Cross's poem. My night is not gracious, but secular, puritan, and agnostical. An Existentialist night. (Lowell, 1968: 131-132)

2. The poem begins with an eccentric heiress who prefers "Queen Victoria's century" to the present but who is powerless to halt temporal and social disintegration. [...] She at least is "Spartan" and old-fashioned, but the town has lost even its modern, showy millionaire. [...] The final phase of the town's decay is evoked by a decorator who converts real, functional objects of the town's past (a cobbler's bench and awl) into art objects (aimed at the tourist trade) by painting them orange — a way of preserving the past that empties it of its reality. But the next two stanzas turn on and subvert the first four, as "Skunk Hour" abruptly shifts from ironic account of disintegrating town to the "dark night" of a personal ordeal. The disintegration, it now appears, is Lowell's own,

the changing of self into landscape. Instead of observing that "the season's ill," Lowell now speaks of "my ill-spirit" and admits that "my mind's not right." In fact, by presenting himself watching lovers in parked cars, Lowell uncovers his core self — " unseen and all-seeing" — and desperately in want, but while a withdrawn and helpless spectator, he projects himself onto the outside world — a way of preserving self and other that empties both of their reality. The two stanzas thus culminate with a moving and crucial act of self-recognition: "I myself am hell; / nobody's here" — the quotation from Milton's Satan defining the projecting as demonic self. All the sequence's images of sealed enclosures are really representations of the poet's own encapsulated consciousness; Lowell now confronts his own "air / of lost connections," his radical isolation. (Breslin, 1983: 137-139)

3. In "Skunk Hour," the confessional mirroring of public and private is expressed formally in the poem's symmetrical division into four stanzas about the social environment and four about the poet's "dark night" of voyeurism and incipient madness. [...] There is a curious, and as it turns out, crucial slippage of tense in stanza five. The "dark night" is recounted for five lines, in the past tense. Then comes an ellipsis and the declaration, in present tense, that "my mind's not right." The poem continues in present tense, although the events are recollected, all the way to the end, implying that the encounter with the skunks occurred when the speaker returned from his voyeuristic prowl among the "love-cars." It makes a great deal of difference whether the recognitions expressed in "my mind's not right" and "I myself am hell" occur in the narrative past, as realizations already made during the dark night and now recollected, or whether they now strike the poet unexpectedly for the first time in the moment of recollection. For if the speaker of the first four stanzas has already had these insights, one cannot suppose that he catches himself in a self-deception as a new interpretation of the recollected experience suddenly dawns on him. The blurred boundary between recollected experience and the process of recollection makes it impossible to decide whether the analogues in the first four stanzas should be taken as reliable or not. (Breslin, 1987: 68-70)

4. 罗威尔在作品中一直关注这么三个方面:对公众行为和态度的批判;对个体自我的批判;历史、宗教、神话和文学的语境感,它在任何时候都可以提供理解公众和私人生活的各种可能性的视角。《臭鼬的时光》充分地体现了罗威尔的这些关注。此诗共分为八节,前四节写的是非个人的社会环境,其中充满了宗教、政治、经济、社会、性、艺术的堕落和倒错。后四节写的是个人的内部世界,诗人把自己和自己的堕落暴露在道德的聚光灯下。这种形式上的对称划分把公共的方面和私人的方面平行起来,起到了一种自白式的"镜子"反映效果。(彭予,2004:82)

## Selected Reading B

### For the Union Dead

*"Relinquunt Omnia Servare Rem Publicam."*[①]

The old South Boston Aquarium stands
in a Sahara of snow now. Its broken windows are boarded.
The bronze weathervane cod has lost half its scales.
The airy tanks are dry.

Once my nose crawled like a snail on the glass;
my hand tingled
to burst the bubbles
drifting from the noses of the cowed, compliant fish.

My hand draws back. I often sigh still
for the dark downward and vegetating kingdom
of the fish and reptile. One morning last March,
I pressed against the new barbed and galvanized

fence on the Boston Common. Behind their cage,
yellow dinosaur steamshovels were grunting
as they cropped up tons of mush and grass
to gouge their underworld garage.

Parking spaces luxuriate like civic
sandpiles in the heart of Boston.
A girdle of orange, Puritan-pumpkin colored girders
braces the tingling Statehouse,

① During the Civil War, Colonel Robert Gould Shaw (1837—1863) and the men of the Massachusetts 54th Regiment, a regiment entirely composed of Negro soldiers, were killed in the assault on Fort Wagner, South Carolina. The American (Irish born) sculptor Augustus Saint-Gaudens (1848—1907) designed a monument in 1897 in memory of them. The monument stands at the edge of Boston Common, across from the Massachusetts State House. In the upper right it bears the Latin motto of the Society of the Cincinnati, *Omnia relinquitservare rem publicam* ("He gives up everything to serve the republic"). Lowell changed the epitaph from "he gives"to "they give."

shaking over the excavations, as it faces Colonel Shaw
and his bell-cheeked Negro infantry
on St. Gaudens' shaking Civil War relief,
propped by a plank splint against the garage's earthquake.

Two months after marching through Boston,
half the regiment was dead;
at the dedication,
William James① could almost hear the bronze Negroes breathe.

Their monument sticks like a fishbone
in the city's throat.
Its Colonel is as lean
as a compass-needle.

He has an angry wrenlike vigilance,
a greyhound's gentle tautness;
he seems to wince at pleasure,
and suffocate for privacy.

He is out of bounds now. He rejoices in man's lovely,
peculiar power to choose life and die —
when he leads his black soldiers to death,
he cannot bend his back.

On a thousand small town New England greens,
the old white churches hold their air
of sparse, sincere rebellion; frayed flags
quilt the graveyards of the Grand Army of the Republic.

The stone statues of the abstract Union Soldier
grow slimmer and younger each year —
wasp-waisted, they doze over muskets
and muse through their sideburns...

Shaw's father wanted no monument
except the ditch,

① William James: philosopher and psychologist (1842—1910), who taught at Harvard University.

where his son's body was thrown
and lost with his "niggers."

The ditch is nearer.
There are no statues for the last war[1] here;
on Boylston Street[2], a commercial photograph
shows Hiroshima boiling

over a Mosler Safe, the "Rock of Ages"
that survived the blast[3]. Space is nearer.
When I crouch to my television set,
the drained faces of Negro school-children rise like balloons.[4]

Colonel Shaw
is riding on his bubble,
he waits
for the blessèd break.

The Aquarium is gone. Everywhere,
giant finned cars nose forward like fish;
a savage servility
slides by on grease.

## About the Selection

《给联邦死难者》是罗威尔同名诗集中最著名的一首标题诗。此诗作于美苏冷战高潮、人权运动刚刚兴起之时,距离南北战争差不多一百年,模仿的是艾伦·塔特(Allen Tate)的名诗《联邦死难者颂》(*Ode to the Confederate Dead*)。诗的开头描写的是波士顿水族馆的破败景象,眼前如沙漠般的荒凉不禁使诗人回想过去,这曾经是诗人经常玩耍的游乐天地。接下来描写的是位于波士顿市中心正在修建的地下停车库。附近的肖上校和他的黑人兵团纪念浮雕靠木头支撑着,抵挡挖土机制造的"地震"。为了自由,无数的北方战士在战斗中牺牲,然而生活在现在社会的人们不仅没有对这些铁血战士表示出敬意,还恣意践踏着他们用生命打下的这片江山。现代社会下的人正在奴化,非人的机器开始主宰世界。在这首诗中,诗人有意让历史事件和现代社会的景象并存,让童年的回忆同社会现实碰撞。只有反复阅读与思索本诗,才能体会到诗人的命意所在。

---

① the last war: referring to the Second World War.

② Boylston Street: a street in Boston.

③ blast: referring to the U. S. throwing atomic bomb to Japanese city of Hiroshima.

④ The struggles to integrate public schools (first in the South, and later in the North) were frequently featured in television newscasts.

## Research Guide

1. Asked to participate in the Boston Arts Festival in 1960, Lowell delivered "For the Union Dead," a poem about a Civil War hero, Robert Gould Shaw, whose sister Josephine had married one of Lowell's ancestors, Charles Russell Lowell (who, like Robert Gould Shaw, was killed in the war). The poem is thus, though undeclaredly, a family poem. (Vendler, 1995: 13)

2. "For the Union Dead" provisionally completes an arc from the monumental aspirations of *Lord Weary's Castle* and its author to the rather more modest but more powerful expression of a fully human speaker's fully human responses to history. In this way it records and recommends a shift in Lowell's sense of poetry's mission in postwar America, a shift from static inscription to responsive speech. No longer does Lowell attempt to concretize his personal reaction and set it up for others to admire or emulate. Rather, Lowell now offers a delicate web of referents and significances, at once personal and public, that moves with our breath. As Shaw seems so precariously poised as to fall if blown on, so Lowell's speaker in "For the Union Dead," a speaker so closely identified with Lowell as to be indistinguishable from him, provides a point for our idealization. (Thurston, 2000: 103)

3. 在《给联邦死难者》一诗中,罗威尔把个人回忆同文化回忆糅合在一起,把自传素材同历史和政治糅合在一起,通过个人化取得了真正的非个人化,既是一首个人的哀歌,也是一首社会的哀歌。《给联邦死难者》充分体现了罗威尔诗中通常的历史和诗人个人生活相互作用的模式,使用的是类比的技巧:童年回忆与历史时刻、内战与现代世界、说话人与肖上校之相互作用产生了诗的张力。(彭予,2004:86-87)

# Supplementary Reading

## Waking in the Blue

The night attendant, a B. U.[1] sophomore,
rouses from the mare's-nest of his drowsy head
propped on *The Meaning of Meaning*.[2]
He catwalks down our corridor.

① B. U.: Boston University.

② *The Meaning of Meaning*: one book about philosophy and literal criticism, written by I. A. Richards (1893—1979) and C. K. Ogden (1889—1957) in 1923.

Azure day
makes my agonized blue window bleaker.
Crows maunder on the petrified fairway.
Absence! My hearts grows tense
as though a harpoon were sparring for the kill.
(This is the house for the "mentally ill.")

What use is my sense of humour?
I grin at Stanley, now sunk in his sixties,
once a Harvard all-American fullback,
(if such were possible!)
still hoarding the build of a boy in his twenties,
as he soaks, a ramrod
with a muscle of a seal
in his long tub,
vaguely urinous from the Victorian plumbing.
A kingly granite profile in a crimson gold-cap,
worn all day, all night,
he thinks only of his figure,
of slimming on sherbet and ginger ale —
more cut off from words than a seal.

This is the way day breaks in Bowditch Hall at McLean's[①];
the hooded night lights bring out "Bobbie,"
Porcellian'29,[②]
a replica of Louis XVI
without the wig —
redolent and roly-poly as a sperm whale,
as he swashbuckles about in his birthday suit
and horses at chairs.
These victorious figures of bravado ossified young.

In between the limits of day,
hours and hours go by under the crew haircuts
and slightly too little nonsensical bachelor twinkle
of the Roman Catholic attendants.

---

① McLean's: McLean Hospital in Belmont, Massachusetts.

② Porcellian '29: one member of a social club of Harvard University in 1929.

(There are no Mayflower
screwballs in the Catholic Church.)

After a hearty New England breakfast,
I weigh two hundred pounds
this morning. Cock of the walk,
I strut in my turtle-necked French sailor's jersey
before the metal shaving mirrors,
and see the shaky future grow familiar
in the pinched, indigenous faces
of these thoroughbred mental cases,
twice my age and half my weight.
We are all old-timers,
each of us holds a locked razor.

## References and Further Reading


1. Breslin, James E. B. *From Modern to Contemporary: American Poetry 1945—1965*. Chicago: University of Chicago Press, 1983.
2. Breslin, Paul. *The (Psychological) Psycho-Political Muse: American Poetry Since the Fifties*. Chicago: University of Chicago Press, 1987. 68-70.
3. Ferguson, Margaret, Mary Jo Salter, and Jon Stallworthy. *The Norton Anthology of Poetry*. 5th ed. New York: W. W. Norton & Company, 2005.
4. Lowell, Robert. *Robert Lowell: A Collection of Critical Essays*. Ed. Thomas Parkinson. Englewood Cliffs: Prentice Hall, 1968.
5. Thurston, Michael. "Robert Lowell's Monumental Vision: History, Poetic Form, and the Cultural Work of Postwar Lyric." *American Literary History* 12. 1 & 2 (2000): 79-112.
6. Vendler, Helen. *The Given and the Made: Strategies of Poetic Redefinition*. Cambridge, MA: Harvard University Press, 1995. 13-17.
7. 彭予.二十世纪美国诗歌——从庞德到罗伯特·布莱.开封:河南大学出版社,1995.
8. 彭予.美国自白诗探索.北京:社会科学文献出版社,2004.

# 17. Robert Bly (1926– )

## Introduction

Robert Bly was born on December 23, 1926, in Madison, Minnesota. He attended Harvard University and received his M. A. from the University of Iowa in 1956. As a poet, editor, and translator, Bly has had a profound impact on the shape of American poetry.

He is the author of more than thirty books of poetry, including *Stealing Sugar from the Castle*: *Selected Poems* (2013); *Talking into the Ear of a Donkey*: *Poems* (2011); *Reaching Out to the World*: *New and Selected Prose Poems* (2009); *My Sentence Was a Thousand Years of Joy* (2006); *The Night Abraham Called to the Stars* (2001); *Snowbanks North of the House* (1999); *Loving a Woman in Two Worlds* (1987); *This Body is Made of Camphor and Gopherwood* (1977); and *The Light Around the Body* (1967), which won the National Book Award.

As the editor of the magazine *The Sixties* (begun as *The Fifties*), Bly introduced many unknown European and South American poets to an American audience. Bly is also the author of a number of nonfiction books, including *The Sibling Society* (1996); *The Spirit Boy and the Insatiable Soul* (1994); *Iron John*: *A Book about Men* (1990); and *Talking All Morning*: *Collected Conversations and Interviews* (1980).

His honors include Guggenheim, Rockefeller, and National Endowment for the Arts fellowships as well as The Robert Frost Medal from the Poetry Society of America. He lives on a farm in the western part of Minnesota with his wife and three children.

## Selected Reading A

### Driving toward the Lac Qui Parle River

I

I am driving; it is dusk; Minnesota.
The stubble field catches the last growth of sun.
The soybeans are breathing on all sides.
Old men are sitting before their houses on car seats
In the small towns. I am happy,
The moon rising above the turkey sheds.

II

The small world of the car
Plunges through the deep fields of the night,
On the road from Willmar to Milan.
This solitude covered with iron
Moves through the fields of night
Penetrated by the noise of crickets.

III

Nearly to Milan, suddenly a small bridge,
And water kneeling in the moonlight.
In small towns the houses are built right on the ground;
The lamplight falls on all fours on the grass.
When I reach the river, the full moon covers it.
A few people are talking, low, in a boat.

### About the Selection

《驶向言湖河》是勃莱早期诗作的代表,收入1962年出版的《雪野宁静》一书。和诗集里的其他诗歌一样,诗人把我们带入一派田园景象,有玉米地,有月亮,还有小桥流水。诗歌意境如画,语言朴素简洁,体现了勃莱诗歌的美学趣味:闲适、超然、孤寂,大自然与内心的自我融为一体,颇得中国古典诗歌意蕴真谛。同时需要注意,诗人不是以物状物,所有物象都随着诗人的意识在流动在跳跃。诗人刹那间的顿悟,是其挖掘无意识或潜意识的结果。

### Research Guide

1. The poems in Robert Bly's volume *Silence in the Snowy Fields* (1962) felt radically

new to readers of the early 1960s, since they appeared to reject both the religious symbolism of Eliot and the overt Romanticism of Roethke. Bly's most famous poem, "Driving Toward Lac Qui Parle River," contains a notable lack of obvious narrative or psychic drama. The poem is written in an understated language and style, and its intense subjectivity is achieved within the context of a commonplace setting and event. (Beach 2003: 180)

2. As in many of the poems in Snowy Fields, in "Driving Toward the Lac Qui Parle River" things are sinking, drifting down, gravitating to the earth and low places. The houses "are built on the ground"; the moonlight is down upon the water; the people in the boat are there too, and even their talking seems drawn down. In two striking metaphors, beautiful and jarring to reason, water kneels, lamplight "falls on all fours in the grass." They too are involved in the bowing and sinking of things, which is felt before it is consciously noticed or understood. The poem, in its last stanza especially, expresses movements that are fundamental to *Snowy Fields*: movements toward the earth and into what lies beyond the rational, well-lit parts of the mind. (Nelson 1984: 20)

## Selected Reading B

### Counting Small-boned Bodies

Let's count the bodies over again.

If we could only make the bodies smaller
The size of skulls
We could make a whole plain white with skulls in the moonlight!

If we could only make the bodies smaller
Maybe we could get
A whole year's kill in front of us on a desk!

If we could only make the bodies smaller
We could fit
A body into a finger-ring for a keepsake forever.

### About the Selection

《数细骨头尸体》发表于 1967 年的越战期间,收入勃莱的反战题材诗集《身体周围的光》,该集曾于 1968 年获"国家图书诗歌奖",被普遍认为是美国最好的反战诗集。该诗通过战场上的看尸人麻木且变态的内心独白，揭示战争对人类文明的严重破坏。诗歌语言自然质朴、简单通俗，虽只有短短十行，但读来颇具震撼力。

## Research Guide

1. "Counting Small-Boned Bodies" is a short poem of ten lines and, as its title suggests, plays upon official body counts of dead Vietnamese soldiers. The poem's first line, "Let's count the bodies over again," is followed by three tercets, each of which begins with the same line: "If we could only make the bodies smaller." That condition granted, Bly postulates three successive images: a plain of skulls in the moonlight, the bodies "in front of us on a desk," and a body fit into a finger ring which would be, in the poem's last words, "a keepsake forever." One notes in this that Bly uses imagery not unlike that of the pre-Vietnam poems, especially in the image of the moonlit plain. In fact, that very image functions here ironically as the reader perceives that the romantic setting is occupied by the skulls. Bly's method consequently represents an important modification in the use of the Emotive Imagination. The lyricism that attends the natural world has become an ironic lyricism attending horrible reversals of the natural world. The reader, instead of drifting tranquilly inward and toward his own private world, is thrust outward upon the abuses of the public world. The poem does not end in reconciliation or a sense of moral advance; rather, it concludes upon a note of accusation and a sense of moral retrogression. (Lensing and Moran, 1976: 79)

2. One notices first of all how Bly's sense of collective consciousness allows him readily to assume the voice of a whole culture, and his secure sense of values justifies a biting criticism of that culture, not only for its actions (as in Lowell) but for the modes of consciousness that support those actions. Three specific aspects of the public consciousness are dramatized in the poem. First Bly plays on the idea that counting, the manipulation of elements in the outer world, can ever be an adequate measure of events. (The history of body counts provides adequate empirical data to support Bly here.) Counting then leads to a second empty form of public measurement: the poem's tone and grammatical mood express a technological fantasy inspired by the false language of advertising. Finally, the concluding line allies the violence of war with perverted and simplified visions of love. It establishes and casts back over the rest of the poem a purposive role for the irony as intensifying the gap between public desire and the lack of a true inwardness that might define and direct that desire. These distortions then combine to present an inverted version of Bly's typical concentrative movement. The more compressed the bodies become the more the reader approaches the ring, the central unifying symbol of the horror involved in this exercise of perverted love. And the horror is deepened by the fact that advertising's words for this particular union are literally true, though of course in an unexpected sense: those dead bodies will remain intimately

involved with our lives for a terribly long time. (Altieri, 1979: 87)

3. The reference is to one of the peculiarities of the Vietnam period: body counts, reported routinely on the evening news. Again creating a mask, Bly imagines the body-counter himself, who turns out to be a rather cheerful being who sits at a desk and has a taste for scenic vistas, efficiency, technical ingenuity, and expensive trinkets. He is, in short, a citizen of a modern business-dominated, technological, affluent society. The poem manipulates scale and distance with great effectiveness. In his mania for making the bodies smaller — their shrinking suggests their reality receding further and further away — the speaker does not seem to notice or care that all the while they are moving closer to him. The bodies — never regarded as human from the outset — move in three dream-like steps in toward him, from the moon-lit plain to the desk to the ring. The implication is clear, and contained perfectly within the images and their movement: when one succeeds this well in distancing the suffering and death of other human beings, in making them smaller and smaller, one ends up engaged to death itself. The final phrase plays on a well-known advertising slogan, but in this context it takes on a terrible psychological meaning. (Nelson, 1984: 63-64)

## Supplementary Reading

### Waking from Sleep

Inside the veins there are navies setting forth,
Tiny explosions at the waterlines,
And seagulls weaving in the wind of the salty blood.

It is the morning. The country has slept the whole winter.
Window seats were covered with fur skins, the yard was full
Of stiff dogs, and hands that clumsily held heavy books.

Now we wake, and rise from bed, and eat breakfast! —
Shouts rise from the harbor of the blood,
Mist, and masts rising, the knock of wooden tackle in the sunlight.

Now we sing, and do tiny dances on the kitchen floor.
Our whole body is like a harbor at dawn;
We know that our master has left us for the day.

## Talking into the Ear of a Donkey

I have been talking into the ear of a donkey.
I have so much to say! And the donkey can't wait
To feel my breath stirring the immense oats
Of his ears. "What has happened to the spring,"
I cry, "and our legs that were so joyful
In the bobblings of April?" "Oh, never mind
About all that," the donkey
Says. "Just take hold of my mane, so you
Can lift your lips closer to my hairy ears."

## ReferenceS and Further Reading


1. Altieri, Charles. *Enlarging the Temple: New Directions in American Poetry during the* 1960*'s*. Lewisburg: Bucknell University Press, 1979.
2. Beach, Christopher. *The Cambridge Introduction to Twentieth-Century American Poetry*. Cambridge: Cambridge University Press, 2003.
3. Harris, Victoria Frenkel. *The Incorporative Consciousness of Robert Bly*. Carbondale: Southern Illinois University Press, 1992.
4. Lensing, George S. and Ronald Moran. *Four Poets of the Emotive Imagination: Robert Bly, James Wright, Louis Simpson, and William Stafford*. Baton Rouge: Louisiana State University, 1976.
5. Nelson, Howard. *Robert Bly: An Introduction to the Poetry*. New York: Columbia University Press, 1984.
6. 勃莱.罗伯特·勃莱诗选,董继平译.石家庄:河北教育出版社,2002.

# 18. Allen Ginsberg(1926–1997)

## Introduction

Allen Ginsberg was born in Newark, New Jersey in 1926. As an adolescent, Ginsberg savored Walt Whitman and Edgar Allan Poe as his favorite poets. Ginsberg was admitted to Columbia University, and as a student there in the 1940s, he began close friendships with William S. Burroughs, Neal Cassady, and Jack Kerouac, all of whom later became leading figures of the Beat movement. In 1954, Ginsberg moved to San Francisco. His mentor, William Carlos Williams, introduced him to key figures in the San Francisco poetry scene, including Kenneth Rexroth. He also met Michael McClure, who handed off the duties of curating a reading for the newly-established "6" Gallery. The event of "The 6 Gallery Reading" has been hailed as the birth of the Beat Generation, in no small part because it was also the first public reading of Ginsberg's "Howl", a poem which garnered world-wide attention for him and the poets he associated with. In the 1960s and 70s, Ginsberg studied under gurus and Zen masters. As the leading icon of the Beats, Ginsberg was involved in countless political activities, including protests against the Vietnam War. On April 5, 1997, in New York City, he died from complications of hepatitis.

Ginsberg developed an individualistic style which is easily identified. His poems are remembered for the non-traditional feature, free verse poetry. There was a renewed focus on form and structure among academic poets and critics partly inspired by New Criticism. Consequently, Ginsberg often had to defend his choice to employ long, free verse lines, often citing Whitman's free verse used in *Leaves of Grass* as a precursor. Ginsberg believed strongly that traditional formalist considerations were archaic and did not apply to reality. These are his most obvious features in literature. But how would Ginsberg have liked to be remembered? "As someone in the tradition of the old time American transcendentalist individualism," he said, "from that old gnostic tradition... Thoreau, Emerson, Whitman... just carrying it on into the 20th century."

## Selected Reading A

### *From* Howl

I saw the best minds of my generation destroyed by madness, starving hysterical naked,
dragging themselves through the negro streets at dawn looking for an angry fix,
angelheaded hipsters burning for the ancient heavenly connection to the starry dynamo in the machinery of night,
who poverty and tatters and hollow-eyed and high sat up smoking in the supernatural darkness of cold-water flats floating across the tops of cities contemplating jazz,
who bared their brains to Heaven under the El[1] and saw Mohammedan angels staggering on tenement roofs illuminated
who passed through universities with radiant cool eyes hallucinating Arkansas and Blake-light tragedy among the scholars of war,
who were expelled from the academies for crazy & publishing obscene odes on the windows of the skull,
who cowered in unshaven rooms in underwear, burning their money in wastebaskets and listening to the Terror through the wall,
who got busted in their pubic beards returning through Laredo[2] with a belt of marijuana for New York,
who ate fire in paint hotels or drank turpentine in Paradise Alley[3], death, or purgatoried their torsos night after night
with dreams, with drugs, with waking nightmares, alcohol and cock and endless balls,
incomparable blind streets of shuddering cloud and lightning in the mind leaping toward poles of Canada & Paterson,[4] illuminating all the motionless world of Time between,

---

① Elevated railway in New York City; also, Hebrew for God.

② City in Texas, on the Mexican border.

③ Then a tenement courtyard in New York's Lower East Side; the setting of *The Subterraneans*, a 1958 novel by the American writer Jack Kerouac (1922—1969).

④ City in New Jersey where Ginsberg was born.

Peyote solidities of halls, backyard green tree cemetery dawns, wine drunkenness over the rooftops, storefront boroughs of teahead joyride neon blinking traffic light, sun and moon and tree vibrations in the roaring winter dusks of Brooklyn, ashcan rantings and kind king light of mind,
who chained themselves to subways for the endless ride from Battery to holy Bronx① on benzedrine until the noise of wheels and children brought them down shuddering mouth-wracked and battered bleak of brain all drained of brilliance in the drear light of Zoo,
who sank all night in submarine light of Bickford's floated out and sat through the stale beer afternoon in desolate Fugazzi's,② listening to the crack of doom on the hydrogen jukebox,
who talked continuously seventy hours from park to pad to bar to Bellevue③ to museum to the Brooklyn Bridge,
a lost battalion of platonic conversationalists jumping down the stoops off fire escapes off windowsills off Empire State out of the moon,
yacketayakking screaming vomiting whispering facts and memories and anecdotes and eyeball kicks and shocks of hospitals and jails and wars,
whole intellects disgorged in total recall for seven days and nights with brilliant eyes, meat for the Synagogue cast on the pavement,
who vanished into nowhere Zen New Jersey leaving a trail of ambiguous picture postcards of Atlantic City Hall,
suffering Eastern sweats and Tangerian bone-grindings and migraines of China under junk-withdrawal in Newark's bleak furnished Room,
who wandered around and around at midnight in the railroad yard wondering where to go, and went, leaving no broken hearts,
who lit cigarettes in boxcars boxcars boxcars racketing through snow toward lonesome farms in grandfather night,
who studied Plotinus Poe St. John of the Cross④ telepathy and bop kaballa⑤ because the cosmos instinctively vibrated at their feet in Kansas,
who loned it through the streets of Idaho seeking visionary indian angels, who were visionary indian angels,

---

① The south and north extremes of one set of New York subway lines; the zoo is in the Bronx.

② A bar near Greenwich Village, then New York's bohemian center. Bickford's: one of a chain of cafeterias open twenty-four hours a day.

③ A public hospital in New York serving as a receiving center for mental patients.

④ Spanish poet and mystic (1542—1591), who wrote *The Dark Night of the Soul*. Plotinus (205-270), Roman mystic philosopher. Edgar Allan Poe (1809 — 1894), American poet and author of supernatural tales as well as the cosmological *Eureka*.

⑤ A tradition of mystical interpretation of the Hebrew Scriptures. Bop: jazz style especially influential in the 1940s and 1950s.

who thought they were only mad when Baltimore gleamed in supernatural ecstasy,
who jumped in limousines with the Chinaman of Oklahoma on the impulse of winter midnight streetlight smalltown rain,
who lounged hungry and lonesome through Houston seeking jazz or sex or soup, and followed the brilliant Spaniard to converse about America and Eternity, a hopeless task, and so took ship to Africa,
who disappeared into the volcanoes of Mexico leaving behind nothing but the shadow of dungarees and the lava and ash of poetry scattered in fireplace Chicago,
who reappeared on the West Coast investigating the F. E. I, in beards and shorts with big pacifist eyes sexy in their dark skin passing out incomprehensible leaflets,
who burned cigarette holes in their arms protesting the narcotic tobacco haze of Capitalism,
who distributed Supercommunist pamphlets in Union Square weeping and undressing while the sirens of Los Alamos① wailed them down, and wailed down Wall②, and the Staten Island ferry also wailed,
who broke down crying in white gymnasiums naked and trembling before the machinery of other skeletons,
who bit detectives in the neck and shrieked with delight in policecars for committing no crime but their own wild cooking pederasty and intoxication,
who howled on their knees in the subway and were dragged off the roof waving genitals and manuscripts,
who let themselves be fucked in the ass by saintly motorcyclists, and screamed with joy,
who blew and were blown by those human seraphim, the sailors, caresses of Atlantic and Caribbean love,
who balled in the morning in the evenings in rosegardens and the grass of public parks and cemeteries scattering their semen freely to whomever come who may,
who hiccupped endlessly trying to giggle but wound up with a sob behind a partition in a Turkish Bath when the blonde & naked angel came to pierce them with a sword③,

---

① Laboratory in New Mexico where the development of the atomic bomb was completed. Union Square: site of radical demonstrations in New York in the 1930s.

② Wall Street, the center of New York's financial district; but also, Jerusalem's Wailing Wall, a place of prayer and lamentation.

③ An allusion to *The Ecstasy of St. Teresa*, a sculpture by Lorenzo Bernini (1598—1680) based on St. Teresa's (1515—1582) distinctly erotic description of a religious vision.

who lost their loveboys to the three old shrews of fate[①] the one eyed shrew of the heterosexual dollar the one eyed shrew that winks out of the womb and the one eyed shrew that does nothing but sit on her ass and snip the intellectual golden threads of the craftsman's loom,

who copulated ecstatic and insatiate with a bottle of beer a sweetheart a package of cigarettes a candle and fell off the bed, and continued along the floor and down the hall and ended fainting on the wall with a vision of ultimate cunt and come eluding the last gyzym of consciousness,

who sweetened the snatches of a million girls trembling in the sunset, and were red eyed in the morning but prepared to sweeten the snatch of the sunrise, flashing buttocks under barns and naked in the lake,

who went out whoring through Colorado in myriad stolen night-cars, N.C.[②], secret hero of these poems, cocksman and Adonis of Denver—joy to the memory of his innumerable lays of girls in empty lots & diner backyards, moviehouses' rickety rows, on mountaintops in caves or with gaunt waitresses in familiar roadside lonely petticoat upliftings & especially secret gas-station solipsisms of Johns, & hometown alleys too,

who faded out in vast sordid movies, were shifted in dreams, woke on a sudden Manhattan, and picked themselves up out of basements hungover with heartless Tokay and horrors of Third Avenue[③] iron dreams & stumbled to unemployment offices,

who walked all night with their shoes full of blood on the snowbank docks waiting for a door in the East River to open to a room full of steamheat and opium,

who created great suicidal dramas on the apartment cliff-banks of the Hudson under the wartime blue floodlight of the moon & their heads shall be crowned with laurel in oblivion,

who ate the lamb stew of the imagination or digested the crab at the muddy bottom of the rivers of Bowery[④],

who wept at the romance of the streets with their pushcarts full of onions and bad music,

who sat in boxes breathing in the darkness under the bridge, and rose up to build harpsichords in their lofts,

who coughed on the sixth floor of Harlem crowned with flame under the tubercular sky surrounded by orange crates of theology,

---

① In Greek mythology, the three Fates spun, wove, and finally cut the thread of every mortal life.

② Neal Cassady (1926—1968), a friend and lover of Ginsberg. Also a friend of Jack Kerouac, he is the hero of Kerouac's novel *On the Road* (1957).

③ In Manhattan. Tokay: a Hungarian wine.

④ Lower end of Third Avenue; traditional haunt of alcoholics and derelicts.

who scribbled all night rocking and rolling over lofty incantations which in the yellow morning were stanzas of gibberish,
who cooked rotten animals lung heart feet tail borsht & tortillas dreaming of the pure vegetable kingdom,
who plunged themselves under meat trucks looking for an egg,
who threw their watches off the roof to cast their ballot for Eternity outside of Time, & alarm clocks fell on their heads every day for the next decade,
who cut their wrists three times successively unsuccessfully, gave up and were forced to open antique stores where they thought they were growing old and cried,
who were burned alive in their innocent flannel suits on Madison Avenue amid blasts of leaden verse & the tanked-up clatter of the iron regiments of fashion & the nitroglycerine shrieks of the fairies of advertising & the mustard gas of sinister intelligent editors, or were run down by the drunken taxicabs of Absolute Reality,
who jumped off the Brooklyn Bridge this actually happened and walked away unknown and forgotten into the ghostly daze of Chinatown soup alleyways & firetrucks, not even one free beer,
who sang out of their windows in despair, fell out of the subway window, jumped in the filthy Passaic[1], leaped on negroes, cried all over the street, danced on broken wineglasses barefoot smashed phonograph records of nostalgic European 1930's German jazz finished the whiskey and threw up groaning into the bloody toilet, moans in their ears and the blast of colossal steamwhistles,
who barreled down the highways of the past journeying to each other's hotrod-Golgotha jail-solitude watch or Birmingham[2] jazz incarnation,
who drove crosscountry seventytwo hours to find out if I had a vision or you had a vision or he had a vision to find out Eternity,
who journeyed to Denver, who died in Denver, who came back to Denver & waited in vain, who watched over Denver & brooded & loned in Denver and finally went away to find out the Time, & now Denver is lonesome for her heroes,
who fell on their knees in hopeless cathedrals praying for each other's salvation and light and breasts, until the soul illuminated its hair for a second,
who crashed through their minds in jail waiting for impossible criminals with golden heads and the charm of reality in their hearts who sang sweet blues to Alcatraz,
who retired to Mexico to cultivate a habit, or Rocky Mount to tender Buddha or Tangiers to boys or Southern Pacific to the black locomotive or Harvard to

---

① The river that flows through Paterson.
② In Alabama. Golgotha: hill near Jerusalem where Jesus was crucified.

Narcissus to Woodlawn[1] to the daisychain or grave,
who demanded sanity trials accusing the radio of hypnotism & were left with their insanity & their hands & a hung jury,
who threw potato salad at CCNY[2] lecturers on Dadaism and subsequently presented themselves on the granite steps of the madhouse with shaven heads and harlequin speech of suicide, demanding instantaneous lobotomy,
and who were given instead the concrete void of insulin metrasol electricity hydrotherapy psychotherapy occupational therapy pingpong & amnesia,
who in humorless protest overturned only one symbolic pingpong table, resting briefly in catatonia,
returning years later truly bald except for a wig of blood, and tears and fingers, to the visible madman doom of the wards of the madtowns of the East,
Pilgrim State's Rockland's and Greystone's[3] foetid halls, bickering with the echoes of the soul, rocking and rolling in the midnight solitude-bench dolmen-realms[4] of love, dream of life a nightmare, bodies turned to stone as heavy as the moon,
with mother finally * * * * * * ? and the last fantastic book flung out of the tenement window, and the last door closed at 4 AM and the last telephone slammed at the wall in reply and the last furnished room emptied down to the last piece of mental furniture, a yellow paper rose twisted on a wire hanger in the closet, and even that imaginary, nothing but a hopeful little bit of hallucination—
ah, Carl, while you are not safe I am not safe, and now you're really in the total animal soup of time—
and who therefore ran through the icy streets obsessed with a sudden flash of the alchemy of the use of the ellipse the catalog the meter & the vibrating plane,
who dreamt and made incarnate gaps in Time & Space through images juxtaposed, and trapped the archangel of the soul between 2 visual images and joined the elemental verbs and set the noun and dash of consciousness together jumping with sensation of Pater Omnipotens Aeterna Deus[5]

---

① Cemetery in the Bronx. Kerouac was then living in Rocky Mount, North Carolina. Ginsberg and the American writer William Burroughs (1914—1997) had lived in Tangiers. Cassady worked as a brakeman for the Southern Pacific Railroad.

② CCNY: City College of New York.

③ Three mental hospitals near New York. Carl Solomon was an inmate at Pilgrim State and Rockland, and Ginsberg's mother was institutionalized at Greystone.

④ Dolmens are prehistoric monuments of horizontal stone slabs supported by upright stones, found in Britain and France and believed to be tombs.

⑤ All-powerful Father, Eternal God (Latin; "Aeterna" is feminine, the nouns are masculine). Paul Cezanne (1839-1906), the French Impressionist painter, used this phrase to describe the effects of nature on him.

to recreate the syntax and measure of poor human prose and stand before you speechless and intelligent and shaking with shame, rejected yet confessing out the soul to conform to the rhythm of thought in his naked and endless head,
the madman bum and angel beat in Time, unknown, yet putting down here what might be left to say in time come after death,
and rose reincarnate in the ghostly clothes of jazz in the goldhorn shadow of the band and blew the suffering of America's naked mind for love into an eli eli lamma lamma sabacthani[1] saxophone cry that shivered the cities down to the last radio
with the absolute heart of the poem of life butchered out of their own bodies good to eat a thousand years.

## About the Selection

《嚎叫》也许不是金斯堡最好的诗,但无疑是最有名的。该诗在1955年旧金山第六画廊引起注意,并在经历了1957年轰动全国的审判后,成为美国文学史上最为炙手可热的诗歌。该诗共分三部分,这里节选的是第一部分,也是最长最有气势的一节。诗人将自己和朋友(主要是所谓Beat Generation的成员)的故事写入诗中,描写了一群被社会遗弃的垮掉分子,试图用激进的生活方式和思想意识冲破物质主义的枷锁。

## Research Guide

1. "Howl," I have been suggesting, is in many respects a poem that honors the principles of Modernism-le mot juste, the objective correlative, the use of complex semantic and rhetorical figures—even though the critics, put off by its "bad taste," didn't see how fully Ginsberg was working within the tradition. "It is a howl," wrote Richard Eberhart in the New York Times Book Review, "against everything in our mechanistic civilization which kills the spirit, assuming that the louder you shout the more likely you are to be heard". Here Eberhart reinforces Hollander's critique of the poem's "utter lack of decorum." (Shinder, 2006: 39)

2. "Kaddish" is a work of art in the Modernist sense, with characters and a plot; "Howl" is a post-Modernistic, a direct expression of the writer's personality. Moreover, Ginsberg sees himself as a bard and prophet. "All you have to know is what you actually think & feel & every sentence will be a revelation." So that besides expressing Ginsberg's personality, "Howl" reveals eternal truth. (Hyde, 1984: 116)

3. Ginsberg's relation to Whitman is clear in "Howl". Ginsberg learned from Whitman

① My God, my God, why have you forsaken me? (Hebrew). These are Jesus' last words from the cross (Matthew 27.46, Mark 15.34, Psalm 22.1).

the use of the long line, the repetition of the subordinate clause ("who let," "who blew," "who balled," etc.), and the celebration of phallic energy. ... At the same time one can see a great deal of the private mythology of Ginsberg — the search for the sexual encounter as perfect religious experience. While this might seem to originate in Whitman's depiction of the sources of mystic vision as sexual, it should be remembered that Whitman's sexuality is portrayed as both active and passive, and that Whitman devotes as much attention to the image of two lovers simply happy to be together as to actual moments of sexual penetration. In Ginsberg the desire for religious vision is transformed into a desire to be fucked, whereas in Whitman the experience of sexual pleasure leads to a greater understanding of the world. Although Ginsberg calls on Whitman, he transforms an ultimately peaceful vision of human unity into an affirmation of the homosexual's alienation from the "straight" world and a desire to become an object of love rather than a participant in it. Here, as in the later poems, Ginsberg links his passive sexuality to his poetics, as he rejects the "craftsman's loom" for the orgasmic scream. (Martin, 1998: 166)

4. "Howl" was the first poem to bring Ginsberg public attention, and its treatment of homosexuality is characteristic of Ginsberg's position during this time. "Howl" is a lament for "the best minds of my generation," the "angelheaded hipsters" destroyed by the cruelties of American society. The homosexual functions in the world of "Howl" as a figure of angelic innocence, his love a protest against the insensitivity and madness which surrounds him. (Martin, 1998: 165)

## Selected Reading B

### A Supermarket in California

What thoughts I have of you tonight, Walt Whitman, for I walked down the sidestreets under the trees with a headache self-conscious looking at the full moon.

In my hungry fatigue, and shopping for images, I went into the neon fruit supermarket, dreaming of your enumerations!

What peaches and what penumbras! Whole families shopping at night! Aisles full of husbands! Wives in the avocados, babies in the tomatoes! — and you, García Lorca[①], what were you doing down by the watermelons?

I saw you, Walt Whitman, childless, lonely old grubber, poking among the meats

① An Spanish poet and dramatist

in the refrigerator and eyeing the grocery boys.

I heard you asking questions of each: Who killed the pork chops? What price bananas? Are you my Angel?

I wandered in and out of the brilliant stacks of cans following you, and followed in my imagination by the store detective.

We strode down the open corridors together in our solitary fancy tasting artichokes, possessing every frozen delicacy, and never passing the cashier.

Where are we going, Walt Whitman? The doors close in a hour. Which way does your beard point tonight?

(I touch your book and dream of our odyssey in the supermarket and feel absurd.)

Will we walk all night through solitary streets? The trees add shade to shade, lights out in the houses, we'll both be lonely.

Will we stroll dreaming of the lost America of love past blue automobiles in driveways, home to our silent cottage?

Ah, dear father, graybeard, lonely old courage-teacher, what America did you have when Charon quit poling his ferry and you got out on a smoking bank and stood watching the boat disappear on the black waters of Lethe?[1]

## About the Selection

《加州超市》一诗创作于1955年的加州伯克利。诗人似在描述住所附近的一家超市里购物的情景,但他要买的不是水果,却是"意象"。于是,诗中的"超市"、"满月"、"商店的侦探"、"猪排"、"桃子"、"香蕉"等意象都被赋予了独特的象征意义。这些象征一起构成了诗人对1950年代美国社会的批判思考。值得注意的是,诗中三次提到惠特曼。1955年正是惠特曼的《草叶集》出版一百周年。惠特曼是对金斯堡产生重要影响的诗人之一。诗人一方面对惠特曼表示出敬重,同时又流露出摆脱其影响的焦虑。

## Research Guide

1. In its [A Supermarket in California] perspective on American society it measures Ginsberg's distance from Whitman every bit as much as *Howl* does when compared to "Song of the Open Road": "It's the distance of a century — with Civil War and the triumph of the Industrial Revolution and Darwinism and Freud and two world wars, mustard gas, and the hydrogen bomb, the advent of the technological era, Vietnam, and IBM."(Charters, 2001: 354)

2. Ginsberg's poem [A supermarket in California] comes from the same period as Randall Jarrell's laments for the fate of literature in the sad supermarket of

① In Greek mythology, a river of Hades, signifying forgetfulness; Charon ferried the dead across it.

contemporary American culture. But something more suggestive than a deadening, anti-literary supermarket is being activated here, as though this impulse poem could remake the figure of poetic flaneur in the fantasy of a deviant shopper. (Bowlby, 2001: 197)

3. 惠特曼的精神与诗中人自己之间的"断裂"也清晰可见。不过,细读全诗,特别是结合第一行诗句来看,诗中人与惠特曼之间的断裂却在最后一问中得到了一定程度的弥合。从第一行诗句"今夜我怎样来看待你,瓦尔特·惠特曼"到最后一行诗句"啊,亲爱的父亲,你得到了一个什么样的美国"之间过渡的是一个个像是儿子对父亲般的埋怨和诘问,而重叠的是相同的夜晚、树、街道等意象和梦幻、寂寥、孤独等心绪。换句话说,从"今夜我怎样来看待你,瓦尔特·惠特曼"到"啊,亲爱的父亲,灰白的胡须",诗中人在新的语境里完成了对惠特曼的认识,即由原来的质疑和责备转而变为崇敬和喟叹,让我们听出低回在全诗中的基调不是对惠特曼的责怪与怨恨,而是对当下美国社会的愤懑与批判和对未来的惶惑与期盼。(乔国强, 2011: 107)

## Supplementary Reading

### America

America I've given you all and now I'm nothing.
America two dollars and twenty-seven cents[1] January 17, 1956.
I can't stand my own mind.
America when will we end the human war?
Go fuck yourself with your atom bomb
I don't feel good don't bother me.
I won't write my poem till I'm in my right mind.
America when will you be angelic?
When will you take off your clothes?
When will you look at yourself through the grave?
When will you be worthy of your million Trotskyites[2]?
America why are your libraries full of tears?
America when will you send your eggs to India?
I'm sick of your insane demands.
When can I go into the supermarket and buy what I need with my good looks?
America after all it is you and I who are perfect not the next world.
Your machinery is too much for me.

① [I own] two dollars and twenty-seven cents.

② Trotskyites believe in Trotskyism which is the theory of Marxism as advocated by Leon Trotsky.

You made me want to be a saint.
There must be some other way to settle this argument.
Burroughs is in Tangiers I don't think he'll come back it's sinister.
Are you being sinister or is this some form of practical joke?
I'm trying to come to the point.
I refuse to give up my obsession.
America stop pushing I know what I'm doing.
America the plum blossoms are falling.
I haven't read the newspapers for months, everyday somebody goes on trial for murder.
America I feel sentimental about the Wobblies[1].
America I used to be a communist when I was a kid and I'm not sorry.
I smoke marijuana every chance I get.
I sit in my house for days on end and stare at the roses in the closet.
When I go to Chinatown I get drunk and never get laid.
My mind is made up there's going to be trouble.
You should have seen me reading Marx.
My psychoanalyst thinks I'm perfectly right.
I won't say the Lord's Prayer.
I have mystical visions and cosmic vibrations.
America I still haven't told you what you did to Uncle Max after he came over from Russia[2].

I'm addressing you.
Are you going to let our emotional life be run by Time Magazine?
I'm obsessed by Time Magazine.
I read it every week.
Its cover stares at me every time I slink past the corner candystore.
I read it in the basement of the Berkeley Public Library.
It's always telling me about responsibility. Businessmen are serious. Movie producers are serious. Everybody's serious but me.
It occurs to me that I am America.
I am talking to myself again.

Asia is rising against me.
I haven't got a chinaman's chance.
I'd better consider my national resources.

---

① Wobbly is an international worker organization with features of anarchism and Buddhism.
② Ginsberg's uncle was immigrated to U. S. with his parents.

My national resources consist of two joints of marijuana millions of genitals an unpublishable private literature that goes 1400 miles an hour and twentyfive-thousand mental institutions.
I say nothing about my prisons nor the millions of underprivileged who live in my flowerpots under the light of five hundred suns.
I have abolished the whorehouses of France, Tangiers is the next to go.
My ambition is to be President despite the fact that I'm a Catholic.

America how can I write a holy litany in your silly mood?
I will continue like Henry Ford my strophes are as individual as his automobiles more so they're all different sexes
America I will sell you strophes $2500 apiece $500 down on your old strophe
America free Tom Mooney[①]
America save the Spanish Loyalists
America Sacco & Vanzetti[②] must not die
America I am the Scottsboro boys.
America when I was seven momma took me to Communist Cell meetings they sold us garbanzos a handful per ticket a ticket costs a nickel and the speeches were free everybody was angelic and sentimental about the workers it was all so sincere you have no idea what a good thing the party was in 1935 Scott Nearing was a grand old man a real mensch Mother Bloor the Silk-strikers' Ewig-Weibliche made me cry I once saw the Yiddish orator Israel Amter plain. Everybody must have been a spy.
America you don're really want to go to war.
America it's them bad Russians.
Them Russians them Russians and them Chinamen[③]. And them Russians.
The Russia wants to eat us alive. The Russia's power mad. She wants to take our cars from out our garages.
Her wants to grab Chicago. Her needs a Red *Reader's Digest*. Her wants our auto plants in Siberia. Him big bureaucracy running our fillingstations.
That no good. Ugh. Him make Indians learn read. Him need big black niggers.
Hah. Her make us all work sixteen hours a day. Help.

---

① Thomas Mooney was convicted of the crime of planting a bomb in the parade in honor of Preparedness Day. But due to severe mishandling of the trial, he was later pardoned.

② Nicola Sacco and Bartolomeo Vanzetti were two Italian anarchists, who were arrested, tried, and electrocuted in Massachusetts in 1927 on charges of murder of a shoe factory paymaster named Frederick Parmenter and a security guard named Alessandro Berardelli, and of robbery of $15,766.51 from the factory's payroll, although there was much doubt regarding their guilt.

③ An irony of American cold war.

America this is quite serious.
America this is the impression I get from looking in the television set.
America is this correct?
I'd better get right down to the job.
It's true I don't want to join the Army or turn lathes in precision parts factories, I'm nearsighted and psychopathic anyway.
America I'm putting my queer shoulder to the wheel.

## Reading Bai Juyi

I

I'm a traveler in a strange country
China and I've been to many cities
Now I'm back in Shanghai, days
under warm covers in a room with electric heat—
a rare commodity in this country—
hundreds of millions shiver in the north
students rise at dawn and run around the soccerfield
Workmen sing songs in the dark to keep themselves warm
while I sleep late, smoke too much cough,
turn over in bed on my right side
pull the heavy quilt over my nose and go back
to visit the dead my father, mother and immortal
friends in dreams. Supper's served me,
I can go out and banquet, but prefer
this week to stay in my room, recovering
a cough. I don't have to sell persimmons on the streetcurb
in Baoding like the lady with white bandanna'd head
Don't have to push my boat oars around a rocky corner
in the Yangtze gorges, or pole my way downstream
from Yichang through yellow industrial scum, or carry water
buckets on a bamboo pole over my shoulder
to a cabbage field near Wuxi—I'm famous,
my poems have done some men good
and a few women ill, perhaps the good
outweighs the bad, I'll never know.
Still I feel guilty I haven't done more;
True I praised the dharma from nation to nation
But my own practice has been amateur, seedy

—even I dream how bad a student I am—
My teacher's tried to help me, but I seem
to be lazy and have taken advantage of money
and clothes my work's brought me, today
I'll stay in bed again & read old Chinese poets—
I don't believe in an afterworld of god or even
another life separate from this incarnation
Still I worry I'll be punished for my carelessness
after I'm dead—my poems scattered and my name
forgotten and my self reborn a foolish workman
freezing and breaking rocks on a roadside in Hebei.

*Shanghai*, *December* 5, *1984*, 10 A.M

Ⅱ

"Ignorant and contentious" I spent lunch
arguing about boys making love with a student.
Still coughing, reclusive, I went back to bed
with a headache, despite afternoon sun
streaming through the French windows
weakly, to write down these thoughts.
Why've I wanted to appear heroic, why
strain to accomplish what no mortal could—
Heaven on earth, self perfection, household
security, & the accomplishment of changing the World.
A noble ambition, but that of a pathetic dreamer.
Tomorrow if I recover from bronchitis
I'll put on a serious face and go down to the Market.

2:30 P.M.

Ⅲ

Lying head on pillow aching
still reading poems of Tang roads
Something Bai said made me press my finger
to my eyes and weep—maybe his love
for an old poet friend, for I also
have gray on my cheek and bald head
and the Agricultural poet's in the madhouse this week

a telegram told me, more historical
jackanapes maybe tragic maybe comic
I'll know when I come home around the world.
Still with heavy heart and aching head I read on
till suddenly a cry from the garden reminded me
of a chicken, head chopped off running circles spurting blood
from its neck on farm yard dirt, I was eleven years old,
or the raptured scream of a rabbit—I put down my book
and listened carefully to the cry almost drowned
by the metal sound of cars and horns—It was a bird
repeating its ascending whistle, pipe notes burst
into a burble of joyful tones ending wildly
with variable trills in swift succession high and low
and high again. At least it wasn't me, not my song,
a sound outside my mind, nothing to do with my aching brow.

3:30 P.M.

Ⅳ

I lay my cheek on the pillow to nap
and my thoughts floated against the stream
up to Zhong Xian west of the Three Gorges
where Bai Juyi was Governor.
"Two streams float together and meet further on
and mingle their water. Two birds fly upward
beneath the ninth month's cold white cloud.
Two trees stand together bare branched
rooted in the same soil secretly touching.
Two apples hung from the same bough last
month and disappeared into the Market."
So flowed my mind like the river, like the wind.
"Two thoughts have risen together in dream therefore
Two worlds will be one if I wake and write."
So I lifted my head from my pillow and Woke
to find I was a sick guest in a vast poor kingdom
A famous visitor honored with a heated room,
medicines, special foods and learned visitors
inquiring when I'd be well enough to lecture my hosts
on the musics and poetics of the wealthy

Nation I had come from half way round the world

8:15 P.M.

V *China Bronchitis*

I sat up in bed and pondered what I'd learned
while I lay sick almost a month:
That monks who could convert Waste to Treasure
were no longer to be found among the millions
in the province of Hebei. That *The Secret of the Golden Lotus*
has been replaced by the Literature of the Scar, nor's hardly
anybody heard of the *Meditation Cushion of the Flesh*
That smoking Chinese or American cigarettes makes me cough;
Old men had got white haired and bald before
my beard showed the signs of its fifty-eight snows.
That of Three Gorges on the Yangtze the last one downstream
is a hairpin turn between thousand-foot-high rock mountain gates.
I learned that the Great Leap Forward caused millions
of families to starve, that the Anti-Rightist Campaign
against bourgeois "Stinkers" sent revolutionary poets
to shovel shit in Xinjiang Province a decade before
the Cultural Revolution drove countless millions of readers
to cold huts and starvation in the countryside Northwest.
That sensitive poetry girls in Shanghai dream
of aged stars from Los Angeles movies. That down the alley
from the stone bridge at Suzhou where Jiang Ji spent
a sleepless night wakened by the bell of Cold Mountain Temple,
water lapping against his boat a thousand years ago,
a teahouse stands with two-stringed violin and flutes
and wooden stage. That the gold in the Sun setting
at West Lake Hangzhou is manufactured from black Soft Coal.
That roast red-skinned juicy entire dogs with eyes
bulging from their foreheads hang in the market at Canton
That So-Chan meditation's frowned on and martial health
Qi-Gong's approved by Marxist theoreticians. That men in
deep-blue suits might be kind enough to file a report
to your Unit on gossip they've heard about your secret loves.
That "Hang yu hang yu!" song is heard when workmen labor
yodeling on bamboo scaffolds over the street outside all night.

That most people have thought "We're just little men,
what can we count" since the time of Qin Shi Huang.

Ⅵ

Tho the body's heavy meat's sustained
on our impalpable breath, materialists
argue that Means of Production cause History:
once in power, materialists argue what
the right material is, quarrel with each other,
jail each other and exile tens of millions
of people with 10,000 thoughts apiece.
They're worse than Daoists who quibbled about immortality.
Their saving grace this year's that all the peasants are fed.

Ⅶ

Transformation of Bai's "*A Night in Xingyang*"

I grew up in Paterson New Jersey and was
just a virginal kid when I left
forty years ago. Now I'm around the world,
but I did go back recently to visit my stepmother.
Then I was 16 years old, now I'm fifty eight—
All the fears I had in those days—I can still see myself
daydreaming reading N. Y. Times on the Chinese rug on the living room
floor on Graham avenue. My childhood houses are torn down,
none of my old family lives here any more,
mother under the ground in Long Island, father underground
near the border of Newark where he was born.
A highway cuts thru the Fair Street lot where I remember our earliest
apartment, & a little girl's first kiss. New buildings rise on that street,
all the old stores along Broadway have disappeared.
Only the Great Falls and the Passaic river flow
noisy with mist then quietly along the brick factory sides
as they did before.

10:15 P.M.

After Rewi Alley's *Bai Juyi*, 200 *Selected Poems* (Beijing: New World Press, 1983), p. 303.

## References and Further Reading


1. Bowlby, Rachel. *Carried Away*: *The Invention of Modern Shopping*. Columbia: Columbia University Press, 2001.
2. Charters, Ann. *Beat Down to Your Soul*: *What was the Beat Generation*? London: Penguin Books, 2001.
3. Gregory, Stephenson. *The Daybreak Boys*: *Essays on the Literature of the Beat Generation*. Carbondale and Edwardsville: Southern Illinois University press, 1990.
4. Hyde, Lewis, Allen Ginsberg(eds.). *On the Poetry of Allen Ginsberg*. Ann Arbor: University of Michigan Press, 1984.
5. Martin, Robert K. *The Homosexual Tradition in American Poetry*. Iowa: University of Iowa Press, 1998
6. Shinder, Jason(ed.). *The Poem that Changed America*: *Howl Fifty Years Later*. New York: Farrar Straus, 2006.
7. 金斯伯格.金斯伯格诗选,文楚安译.成都:四川文艺出版社,2000.
8. 乔国强."封闭框架中的新文本解析——细读金斯堡的加利福尼亚超市".外语研究 2011(3): 103-107.

# 19. John Ashbery (1927– )

## Introduction

John Ashbery was born in Rochester, New York, on July 28, 1927. He is the author of more than twenty books of poetry, including *Quick Question* (2012); *Planisphere* (2009); *A Worldly Country* (2007); *Where Shall I Wander* (2005); *Chinese Whispers* (2002); *Your Name Here* (2000); *Girls on the Run: A Poem* (1999); *Wakefulness* (1998); *Can You Hear, Bird* (1995); *And the Stars Were Shining* (1994); *Hotel Lautrémont* (1992); *Flow Chart* (1991), and *April Galleons* (1987).

Ashbery has won nearly every major American award for poetry. His collection *A Wave* (1984) won the Lenore Marshall Poetry Prize; *Self-Portrait in a Convex Mirror* (1975) received the Pulitzer Prize for Poetry, the National Book Critics Circle Award, and the National Book Award; and *Some Trees* (1956) was selected by W. H. Auden for the Yale Younger Poets Series.

Ashbery served as the poet laureate of New York State from 2001 to 2003. He was also the first English-language poet to win the Grand Prix de Biennales Internationales de Poésie (Brussels), and has also received the Bollingen Prize, the English Speaking Union Prize, the Feltrinelli Prize, the Ruth Lilly Poetry Prize, two Ingram Merrill Foundation grants, the MLA Common Wealth Award in Literature, the Harriet Monroe Memorial Prize, the Frank O'Hara Prize, the Shelley Memorial Award, and fellowships from the Academy of American Poets, the Fulbright Foundation, the Guggenheim Foundation, and the MacArthur Foundation.

A former Chancellor of the Academy of American Poets, Ashbery is currently the Charles P. Stevenson, Jr., Professor of Languages and Literature at Bard College.

## Selected Reading A

### What Is Poetry

The medieval town, with frieze
Of boy scouts from Nagoya? The snow

That came when we wanted it to snow?
Beautiful images? Trying to avoid

Ideas, as in this poem? But we
Go back to them as to a wife, leaving
The mistress we desire? Now they
Will have to believe it

As we believed it. In school
All the thought got combed out:

What was left was like a field.
Shut your eyes, and you can feel it for miles around.

Now open them on a thin vertical path.
It might give us—what?—some flowers soon?

### About the Selection

《什么是诗歌》选自阿什贝利的一部重要诗集《船屋的日子》(*Houseboat Days*, 1977),集中体现了诗人的诗歌创作思想。该诗以"什么是诗歌"为标题,提出了有关诗歌本质与诗歌创作的一连串重大问题。虽然诗人并没有明确回答这些问题,却能引人深思。

### Research Guide

1. Ashbery's subject matter is similar to that of his favorite poet, Wallace Stevens. Both poets write of the mind forming hypotheses about reality in general, about the ultimate truth or nature of things. Stevens, as I said earlier, took for granted that we cannot know reality in itself. Whether we conceive of it as a colorless, featureless continuum, like gray haze on a winter afternoon, or as a "jostling festival" of concrete, particular identities, like a morning in June full of birdsong, we are in either case forming an imagination of reality. [...]

[...]He[Ashbery] dwells on the impossibility of credibly imagining any reality. Putting it another way, we might say that for both Stevens and Ashbery the imagination creates, destroys and immediately creates another vision of reality, but that in Ashbery the process is enormously speeded up. His envisionings of reality are not merely provisional; they transform themselves and disappear in the very process of being proposed, leaving, as he puts it,"Nothing but a bitter impression of absence." (Perkins, 1987: 619-620)

2. "What Is Poetry", mimicking the sonnet with its seven unrhymed couplets, begins with a singularly unpromising subject matter—"The medieval town, with frieze / Of boy scouts from Nagoya? The snow"—and continues by caricaturing the imagistic exoticism of contemporary poetry, lured away from ever faithful "idea" by "Beautiful images": "But we / Go back to them as to a wife, leaving // The mistress we desire?" Like marriage, the misrepresentations of poetry should be taken, and received, on faith: "Now they / Will have to believe it // As we believe it." Aside from the question mark (unaccountably missing in the title), the most prominent feature of "What Is Poetry" is this mysterious, quasi-religious "it." The poem ends like a field-guide, with fledgling poets, like boy scouts, instructed to look up their answers: "What was left was like a field. / Shut your eyes, and you can feel it for miles around. // Now open them on a thin vertical path. / It might give us—what?—some flowers soon?" This ending came by chance: "In a bookstore I overheard a boy saying to a girl this last line." Beginning with an expletive "It" and harboring two question marks, the boy's remark is ready-made Ashbery. Thus transplanted, the "flowers" are tropes, and "It," the "think vertical path," indicates the vertical axis of metaphorical substitution. The anonymous remark reappears without change under Ashbery's name, yielding its small share of profit in the bookstore where it was overheard. (Shoptaw, 1994: 192-193)

## Selected Reading B

### Paradoxes and Oxymorons

This poem is concerned with language on a very plain level.
Look at it talking to you. You look out a window
Or pretend to fidget. You have it but you don't have it.
You miss it, it misses you. You miss each other.

The poem is sad because it wants to be yours, and cannot.
What's a plain level? It is that and other things,

Bringing a system of them into play. Play?
Well, actually, yes, but I consider play to be

A deeper outside thing, a dreamed role-pattern,
As in the division of grace these long August days
Without proof. Open-ended. And before you know
It gets lost in the steam and chatter of typewriters.

It has been played once more. I think you exist only
To tease me into doing it, on your level, and then you aren't there
Or have adopted a different attitude. And the poem
Has set me softly down beside you. The poem is you.

## About the Selection

《悖论与矛盾修辞》创作于 1979 年，后收入《影子列车》(1981)一书。该诗探讨了诗歌创作与接受中的边界划分问题，涉及诗歌与读者、诗人与语言、诗人与读者、语言与身份等多重复杂关系的悖论，再现了诗歌从写作到阅读的过程中语言、诗人、读者是如何共同参与意义生产的，代表着后现代诗歌的创作理念。

## Research Guide

1. The most popular poem in *Shadow Train* is its tantalizingly simple statement of poetics, "Paradoxes and Oxymorons." ... The poem itself voices Ashbery's populist impulse to reach the common reader, who thinks poems are constructed on many interpretive levels. There is frustration on both sides: [Shoptaw cites the opening 4 lines.]

On the "level plain" of this communications system, the paradoxical pair of poem and reader stands in for two lovers. A few pronominal substitutions bring the romantic discourse to the surface: "Look at me talking to you," "You miss me, I miss you," and so on. This homoerotic subtext connects the poem to the envoy of "Song of Myself": "Failing to fetch me at first keep encouraged, / Missing me one place search another, / I stop somewhere waiting for you." Ashbery gives a more explicit rendition of this romance in his suggestively titled "Or in My Throat" where he recommends poetry as an alternative to oral sex: "It's clean, it's relaxing, it doesn't squirt juice all over" [*Shadow Train* (New York: Penguin, 1981), p. 25].

In the second quatrain of "Paradoxes and Oxymorons" the reader interrupts the poet, as in an interview, with a few questions. [...] Like his paradoxical formulation "on the outside looking out," the oxymoron "A deeper outside thing" is an apt description of Ashbery's poetry, "not / Superficial," as he says in "Self-Portrait [in a Convex Mirror]," "but a visible core." What deepens Ashbery's level playing field are his random [John] Cagean procedures, a hugely varied "division of labor" between the poet and language: "And before you know / It gets lost in the steam and chatter of typewriters." If infinitely many monkeys are set before typewriters, the statistical paradox goes, they will sooner or later produce Shakespeare's plays. Ashbery's poem "has been played" like a record or a trick. But perhaps it is the reader's trick as well. In the communications system, the ideal reader now resembles the Divine Paradox: "I think you exist," the poet asserts, "and then you aren't there." In his final paradox, "the poem is you," varying the dedication "the poem is yours," Ashbery yields himself to the reader, who nevertheless continues to "miss" him. (Shoptaw, 1994: 255-256)

2. "Paradoxes and Oxymorons," while it doesn't express a Barthian or Pynchonian degree of interest in the construction of identity as a function of culture and history , is very much concerned with the poststructural question of the relation between language and identity. The paradox at the heart of "Paradoxes and Oxymorons" is that what is revealed, in a text that represents a subject, is the very representationality of that subject. Phrased as an oxymoron, the subject is true fiction. (Norton, 2000: 42)

## Supplementary Reading

### And *Ut Pictura Poesis* Is Her Name

You can't say it that way any more.
Bothered about beauty you have to
Come out into the open, into a clearing,
And rest. Certainly whatever funny happens to you
Is OK. To demand more than this would be strange
Of you, you who have so many lovers,
People who look up to you and are willing
To do things for you, but you think
It's not right, that if they really knew you . . .
So much for self-analysis. Now,
About what to put in your poem-painting:
Flowers are always nice, particularly delphinium.
Names of boys you once knew and their sleds,
Skyrockets are good—do they still exist?
There are a lot of other things of the same quality
As those I've mentioned. Now one must
Find a few important words, and a lot of low-keyed,

Dull-sounding ones. She approached me
About buying her desk. Suddenly the street was
Bananas and the clangor of Japanese instruments.
Humdrum testaments were scattered around. His head
Locked into mine. We were a seesaw. Something
Ought to be written about how this affects
You when you write poetry:
The extreme austerity of an almost empty mind
Colliding with the lush, Rousseau-like foliage of its desire to communicate
Something between breaths, if only for the sake
Of others and their desire to understand you and desert you
For other centers of communication, so that understanding
May begin, and in doing so be undone.

## References and Further Reading


1. Diggory, Terence. *Encyclopedia of the New York School Poets*. New York: Facts on File Inc., 2009.
2. Norton, Jody. *Narcissus Sous Rature: Male Subjectivity in Contemporary American Literature*. Cranbury: Associated University Presses, Inc., 2000.
3. Perkins, David. *A History of Modern Poetry: Modernism and After*. Cambridge: Harvard University Press, 1987.
4. Shapiro, David. *John Ashbery: An Introduction to the Poetry*. New York: Columbia University Press, 1979.
5. Shoptaw, John. *On the Outside Looking Out: John Ashbery's Poetry*. Cambridge: Harvard University Press, 1994.
6. 约翰·阿什贝利.约翰·阿什贝利诗选,马永波译.石家庄:河北教育出版社,2003.

# 20.W. S. Merwin (1927– )

## Introduction

William Stanley Merwin was born in 1927 in New York. As the son of a Presbyterian minister, Merwin started to write hymns at the age of five, as soon as he "could write with a little pencil". At the age of twenty, Merwin received the bachelor's degree from Princeton University on scholarship. During the college, Merwin studied after famous critic R. P. Blackmur and John Berryman, who had great influence on him. After graduation, Merwin spent another year at Princeton to study Romance language, which laid a solid foundation for his later translating of French, Latin, and Spanish, as well as his traveling around Europe.

In 1952, Merwin's first book *A Mask for Janus* was published and was selected by W. H. Auden for the prestigious Yale Series of Younger Poets award, and thus embarked Merwin's long career as a poet. Until now, Merwin has written nearly 20 books of poetry, plus several collections of prose and translation during 6 decades. He is a distinguished and productive writer, and has made extraordinary achievements as a poet. He has won almost every major award in America poetry circle, including two Pulitzer Prizes, the National Book Award, the Tanning Prize and so on. In 2010, he was honored as the 17th poet laureate of the United States.

Merwin's early subjects were often related to mythological or legendary themes. However, from the volume of *The Drunk in the Furnace* published in 1960s, Merwin began to experiment boldly with metrical irregularity and wrote in a more autobiographical way. In his later volumes, such as *The Compass Rower* (1977), *Opening the Hand* (1983), and *The Rain in the Trees* (1988), Merwin seems to transform his earlier themes in fresh ways, developing a Zen-like indirection. Merwin's latest poems are ecological, dream-like, and full of images.

## Selected Reading A

### The Last One①

Well they'd made up their minds to be everywhere because why not.
Everywhere was theirs because they thought so.
They with two leaves they whom the birds despise.
In the middle of stones they made up their minds.
They started to cut.
Well they cut everything because why not.
Everything was theirs because they thought so.
It fell into its shadows and they took both away.
Some to have some for burning.
Well cutting everything they came to water.
They came to the end of the day there was one left standing.
They would cut it tomorrow they went away.
The night gathered in the last branches.
The shadow of the night gathered in the shadow on the water.
The night and the shadow put on the same head.
And it said Now.
Well in the morning they cut the last one.
Like the others the last one fell into its shadow.
It fell into its shadow on the water.
They took it away its shadow stayed on the water.
Well they shrugged they started trying to get the shadow away.
They cut right to the ground the shadow stayed whole.
They laid boards on it the shadow came out on top.
They shone lights on it the shadow got blacker and clearer.
They exploded the water the shadow rocked.
They built a huge fire on the roots.
They sent up black smoke between the shadow and the sun.
The new shadow flowed without changing the old one.

① Some scholars believe that this poem is inspired in form and spirit by his translation of a South American Indian myth, "The Creation of the Moon".

They shrugged they went away to get stones.
They came back the shadow was growing.
They started setting up stones it was growing.
They looked the other way it went on growing.
They decided they would make a stone out of it.
They took stones to the water they poured them into the shadow.
They poured them in they poured them in the stones vanished.
The shadow was not filled it went on growing.
That was one day.
The next day was just the same it went on growing.
They did all the same things it was just the same.
They decided to take its water from under it.
They took away water they took it away the water went down.
The shadow stayed where it was before.
It went on growing it grew onto the land.
They started to scrape the shadow with machines.
When it touched the machines it stayed on them.
They started to beat the shadow with sticks.
Where it touched the sticks it stayed on them.
They started to beat the shadow with hands.
Where it touched the hands it stayed on them.
That was another day.
Well the next day started about the same it went on growing.
They pushed lights into the shadow.
Where the shadow got onto them they went out.
They began to stomp on the edge it got their feet.
And when it got their feet they fell down.
It got into eyes the eyes went blind.
The ones that fell down it grew over and they vanished.
The ones that went blind and walked into it vanished.
The ones that could see and stood still
It swallowed their shadows.
Then it swallowed them too and they vanished.
Well the others ran.
The ones that were left went away to live if it would let them.
They went as far as they could.

The lucky ones with their shadows①.

## About the Selection

《最后一棵》是默温最为人熟知的诗作之一，全诗笼罩在一种神秘可怖的气氛中，讲述了一个人类疯狂砍伐树木，从而被最后一棵树的阴影所报复的故事。从生态批评的角度看，该诗表现出对人类狂妄自大的极大讽刺和对生态现状的深深忧虑，人类对大自然盲目的摧残最终将导致自身的灭亡。此外，也有研究者从神话批评，心理批评等角度对该诗进行解读。

## Research Guide

1. [Merwin's own answer in an interview about this poem provides a good analysis of it:] My chief doubt about the poem is precisely what you have suggested, that it might be understood as simply saying, from a secure moral vantage point, that those people are doing such dreadful things. That's not the poem, as I see it, and I think the index of what I mean is in the last line—with its suggestion that the relation with what the shadow is in the poem has been ignored, despised, thrown away; that's quite as important to me as the science fiction aspect of the narrative. I'm reminded of the line in the psalm, "Yea they despised the pleasant land." The pleasant land was themselves. [...] When two people stand together and their shadows run together, whose shadow is whose? Who owns the shadow? (Merwin 1982: 55)

2. Human arrogance is the starting point for "The Last One." [...] The poem rejects the American ideal embodied in the idea of "manifest destiny" and given literary formulation in the poetry of Walt Whitman. Merwin sees that ideal not only as destructive of the continent, but also as self-destructive, so he constructs not a creation myth but a de-creation myth. He watches as "they" cut until they come to the water, but then he watches as "the last one" responds. (Hix, 1997: 64-65)

3. And near the beginning of the main "political" sequence [...] stands one of Merwin's most widely admired poems, "The Last One"— his myth of man's uncreation of the natural world, inspired in form and spirit, it would seem, by his translation of a South American India myth, "The Creation of the Moon". (Ramsey, 1987: 30)

---

① The shadow is the key motif in this poem, and can be interpreted in various ways. The last line "The lucky ones with their shadows" pushes the poem into an even deeper meditation, which is called the "index" of the meaning of this poem by Merwin (Merwin, 1982: 55). Their shadows here can be the loggers' shadows, and also the shadows that they hope to escape throughout the poem. There comes the irreducible irony: the shadow that they have been trying so hard to get rid emerges with, or actually is exactly the shadow of theirs. There are even more interpretations made by different researchers, and some examples are offered in the research guide.

4. 在该诗中，阴影成为全诗的核心所在，从生态批评的角度，诗歌流露出默温对当前世界生态现状的深深忧虑，暗示人类的狂妄自大、自以为是引起了大自然的绝地反击，最终导致了他们的自我毁灭。人类生活在末日世界中，其缘由在于人类在这个世界中扮演了刽子手的角色。然而，从心理无意识的角度看，阴影——荣格集体无意识的四大原型之一，作为人类心灵中一切本然的高尚、美好、丑陋与卑劣的源泉，其本身代表了一种原始力量，具有最危险、最具震撼力的能量……或许，诗歌中最后一棵树的阴影本不存在，它仅仅暗示了诗人幻象世界中被抑制的人类丑恶本性最终以灾难的形式爆发。这种无意识幻象世界的原型意象在诗人中期作品中屡屡出现，且大多以灾难、末日等极端事件为背景，成为默温中期诗歌的一大显著特色。（张跃军、邹雯虹，2010：136-137）

## Selected Reading B

### The Asians Dying

When the forests have been destroyed their darkness remains

The ash the great walker follows the possessors
Forever
Nothing they will come to is real
Nor for long
Over the watercourses
Like ducks in the time of the ducks
The ghosts of the villages trail in the sky
Making a new twilight

Rain falls into the open eyes of the dead
Again again with its pointless sound
When the moon finds them they are the color of everything

The nights disappear like bruises but nothing is healed
The dead go away like bruises①
The blood vanishes into the poisoned farmlands
Pain the horizon
Remains
Overhead the seasons rock
They are paper bells

① bruise: an injury that doesn't break the skin but results in some discoloration.

Calling to nothing living

The possessors move everywhere under Death their star
Like columns of smoke they advance into the shadows
Like thin flames with no light
They with no past
And fire their only future

## About the Selection

《消亡中的亚洲人》被普遍认为是一首关于越南战争的诗，全诗以死亡为线索，反映了诗人强烈的反战情绪。该诗选自《虱》，这本诗集赢得了 1971 年的普利策奖。

## Research Guide

1. In the closing group, death is an occurrence that links us with others. This realistic acknowledgment of death can appear with the old abstract concept in the same poem; it is one reason why the ending of "The Asians Dying" is so powerful. (Brunner, 1991: 147)

2. "The Asians Dying" is Merwin's most explicit anti-Vietnam War poem. Though the poem is neither overtly political not anti-American, no American reader who lived through that time would need to have the poem's powerful self-accusing political thrust explained. Though the poem mostly concentrates on effects rather than causes, those responsible are everywhere present and indicted in the poem as the "possessors." The "possessors" will be followed and haunted forever by the ghosts of their victims; "nothing they will come to" will be "real" again; the "possessors" have "Death" as "their star"; they become what they do: they have no past and only fire, or destruction, for their future. ( Rueckert, 1987: 63)

3. The Asians, unlike all of the others in *The Lice* who must find some way of coming to terms with the dichotomy that separates personal and cosmic history, have no past. They carry the bones of dead relatives and the empty accoutrements of their presence. To them, building is synonymous with dwelling. (Gordon, 1972: 135-136)

4. Merwin's "The Asians Dying" is his most famous poem overtly about the Vietnam War; it merits an analysis by infiltration, a criticism surrounded and deadened by the poem's political echoes. I quote the poem's lines, in order, interspersed with my commentary. The poem is a tapestry of recognition and forgetfulness; its lines comment on one another endlessly. Each image (unique in its context) is immediately enfolded by a torpor of historical sameness; in an age whose destiny is past, each name names

everything. The poem is a claustrophobia verbally enhanced by false relief; each new line rediscovers old ground. (Nelson, 1987: 98-99)

## Supplementary Reading

### For A Coming Extinction

Gray whale
Now that we are sending you to The End
That great god
Tell him
That we who follow you invented forgiveness
And forgive nothing

I write as though you could understand
And I could say it
One must always pretend something
Among the dying
When you have left the seas nodding on their stalks
Empty of you
Tell him that we were made
On another day

The bewilderment will diminish like an echo
Winding along your inner mountains
Unheard by us
And find its way out
Leaving behind it the future
Dead
And ours

When you will not see again
The whale calves trying the light
Consider what you will find in the black garden
And its court
The sea cows the Great Auks the gorillas
The irreplaceable hosts ranged countless
And fore-ordaining as stars

Our sacrifices
Join your work to theirs
Tell him
That it is we who are important

## The Animals

All these years behind windows
With blind crosses sweeping the tables

And myself tracking over empty ground
Animals I never saw
I with no voice

Remembering names to invent for them
Will any come back will one

Saying yes

Saying look carefully yes
We will meet again

## References and Further Reading


1. Brunner, J. Edward. *Poetry as Labor and Privilege: The Writings of W. S. Merwin*. Urbana: University of Illinois Press, 1991.
2. Gordon, Ian B. "The Dwelling of Disappearance: W. S. Merwin and *The Lice*." *Modern Poetry Studies* 3.3 (1972): 134-136.
3. Hamilton, Ian. *The Oxford Companion to Twentieth-century Poetry in English*. Oxford: Oxford University Press, 1994.
4. Hix, H. L. *Understanding W. S. Merwin*. Columbia: University of South Carolina Press, 1997.
5. Merwin, W. S. *The Second Four Books of Poems*. Washington: Copper Canyon Press, 1993.
6. Merwin, W. S. "'Fact Has Two Faces': An Interview with W. S. Merwin." Interview by Ed Folsom, Cary Nelson. *The Iowa Review* 13.1(1982): 30-66.
7. Nelson, Cary. "The Resources of Failure: W. S. Merwin's Deconstructive Career." *W. S. Merwin: Essays on the Poetry*. Ed. Cary Nelson and Ed Folsom. Urbana: University of Illinois Press, 1987. 78-121.

8. Ramsey, Jarold. "The Continuities of W. S. Merwin: 'What Has Escaped Us We Bring with Us'." *W. S. Merwin: Essays on the Poetry*. Ed. Cary Nelson and Ed Folsom. Urbana: University of Illinois Press, 1987. 19-44.

9. Rueckert, William H. "Rereading *The Lice*: A Journal." *W. S. Merwin: Essays on the Poetry*. Ed. Cary Nelson and Ed Folsom. Urbana: University of Illinois Press, 1987. 45-64.

10. 耿纪永,张洁."论 W. S. 默温的生态诗与佛禅",外国文学研究,2012(5):109-116.

11. 默温. W.S. 默温诗选(上中下三卷),董继平译.石家庄:河北教育出版社,2003.

12. 张跃军,邹雯虹."论 W.S. 默温中期诗歌风格的变化".江西社会科学,2010(9):133-137.

# 21. Gary Snyder (1930– )

## Introduction

Gary Snyder was born on May 8, 1930, in San Francisco. He has published numerous books of poetry and prose, including *Danger on Peaks* (2005); *The Gary Snyder Reader* (1999); *Mountains and Rivers Without End* (1997); *No Nature: New and Selected Poems* (1993), which was a finalist for the National Book Award; *The Practice of the Wild* (1990); *Left Out in the Rain, New Poems* 1947—1985 (1986); *Axe Handles* (1983), for which he received an American Book Award; *Turtle Island* (1974), which won the Pulitzer Prize for poetry; *Regarding Wave* (1970); and *Myths & Texts* (1960).

He has received an American Academy of Arts and Letters award, the Bollingen Prize, a Guggenheim Foundation fellowship, the Bess Hokin Prize and the Levinson Prize from Poetry, the Robert Kirsch Lifetime Achievement Award from the Los Angeles Times, the Ruth Lilly Poetry Prize, and the Shelley Memorial Award. Snyder was elected a Chancellor of the Academy of American Poets in 2003.

Most recently, he was announced as the recipient of the 2012 Wallace Stevens Award for lifetime achievement by the Academy of American Poets. He is an emeritus professor of English at the University of California, Davis.

## Selected Reading A

### Riprap

Lay down these words
Before your mind like rocks.
placed solid, by hands
In choice of place, set
Before the body of the mind
in space and time:
Solidity of bark, leaf, or wall
riprap of things:
Cobble of milky way,
straying planets,
These poems, people,
lost ponies with
Dragging saddles—
and rocky sure-foot trails.
The worlds like an endless
four-dimensional
Game of *Go*.
ants and pebbles
In the thin loam, each rock a word
a creek-washed stone
Granite: ingrained
with torment of fire and weight
Crystal and sediment linked hot
all change, in thoughts,
As well as things.

### About the Selection

《砌石》选自斯奈德的第一部同名诗集。诗人用自己在山中铺路的经历阐述了自己的诗歌创作。他给诗下了定义,给读者如何欣赏诗作了指导,也为自己今后的诗指出了方向。

### Research Guide

1. He respects workmanship, in this instance the perfect selection and placing of granite rocks in "tight cobble patterns on hard slab." So he instructs himself in a poem that

exemplifies his skill and remains his test of art. [...]

The imperatives of composition are modernist: the unit of composition is the single word, like rock, a solid particular thing of weight and texture that exists in place and time and appeals to the senses ("body of the mind"); and the act of composition is architectural, a building by words, a deliberate handwork—the kind of labor with things that Thoreau said removed the palaver from the scholar's style and that, for Snyder, identifies him with workingmen. Poetry is his craft: "a riprap on the slick rock of metaphysics," as he says later in *Myths & Texts*. The "riprap of things" includes all things, the "cobble of milky way"—the phrase is wonderfully extravagant in Thoreau's sense, like his own metaphor of fishing in the upper air—and "ants and pebbles," the diminutive things that, one recalls in "Song of Myself," were the objects of Whitman's altered perception, the proofs of love. The substance of the poetry, what the art of poetry, the riprap of words, achieves is universal: a footing in the existential world, the granitic result of experience under pressure in a world of time and change that, carefully used, is the foundation of the way. (Paul, 1990: 66-67)

2. If we look at the end of the title poem of *Riprap*, we can see that Snyder does not offer his dense images as only blocks or stones, thrown into the poem with a longed-for palpability in order to combat sensory drift or imprecision. Rather, the density of words and things contains a kind of impacted or solidified energy as well as a merely material dimension. This energized aspect of the "cobble" of rocklike words defines the mind's power to move from one solid place to another, both creating and exploring a field of awareness for itself. Snyder introduces another, ancillary comparison to clarify the mountaineer's "riprap"—one of "worlds like an endless / four-dimensional / Game of Go." This is a Japanese game much like the American child's hopscotch, where a rock or heavy object is thrown to determine the possibility and order of movement. The game utilizes a combination of will and accident, and it tests the limits of both by bringing them into play with one another. Likewise with the mind, or at least the mind as it is structured and reflected in and through the poem, for the mind creates a field of forces, rather than striving for a fixed object or floundering in unobjectified process. (Molesworth, 1983: 19)

3. To speak of laying down words "Before the body of the mind / in space and time" is to infuse English words, operating out of a Western, largely rationalist, philosophico-literary tradition, with a Ch'an sense of the interpenetration of body and mind. From a Ch'an perspective, poems and people are all "lost ponies with / Dragging saddles," caught in a historical round of becoming, the reality of which is sheerly conditional. (Norton, 2000: 95)

## Selected Reading B

### Axe Handles

One afternoon the last week in April
Showing Kai how to throw a hatchet
One-half turn and it sticks in a stump.
He recalls the hatchet-head
Without a handle, in the shop
And go gets it, and wants it for his own.
A broken-off axe handle behind the door
Is long enough for a hatchet,
We cut it to length and take it
With the hatchet head
And working hatchet, to the wood block.
There I begin to shape the old handle
With the hatchet, and the phrase
First learned from Ezra Pound
Rings in my ears!
"When making an axe handle
    the pattern is not far off."
And I say this to Kai
"Look: We'll shape the handle
By checking the handle
Of the axe we cut with—"
And he sees. And I hear it again:
It's in Lu Ji's *Wên Fu*, fourth century
A.D. "Essay on Literature"—in the
Preface: "In making the handle
Of an axe
By cutting wood with an axe
The model is indeed near at hand."
My teacher Shih-hsiang Chen
Translated that and taught it years ago
And I see: Pound was an axe,
Chen was an axe, I am an axe
And my son a handle, soon

To be shaping again，model
And tool，craft of culture，
How we go on.

## About the Selection

《斧柄》是诗人1983年出版的同名诗集中的一首作品。该诗带有一定的自传性，讲述诗人制作斧柄时，先后想到了诗人庞德的话和陆机《文赋》中“至于操斧伐柯，虽取则不远”的说法，并回忆自己在伯克利学习中文时的老师陈世骧。诗人认识到，庞德是造就自已的一把斧头，陈世骧也是，而现在他又作为一把斧子来造就自已的儿子——这就是文明传承的方式。

## Research Guide

1. As Snyder shapes the hatchet handle，he is serving as a handle of knowledge that Kai can grab onto in order to use the hatchet properly when it comes his turn to labor. Snyder makes this point through his own recollection of Pound and the saying that Pound derived from the ancient Chinese，that when making an axe the model is close at hand. Snyder，in his youth，served as a hatchet-head in need of a handle and found the handle and the pattern to become a handle in turn in the poet Ezra Pound，the essayist Lu Ji，and the college professor Shih-hsiang Chen. At the same time，Snyder is shaping Kai so that he will also become a handle，as indicated near the end of the poem. Snyder does not call Pound or Chen either a hatchet-head or a handle but calls each an“axe，” because in their lives they joined together the potential of the head and the knowledge of the handle in poetic and educational practice. Snyder in his fifties has also become an “axe，” complete in both functions as a “model” and as an instrument in the service of the “craft of culture，” and he appears confident that Kai will become an “axe” as well.（Murphy，1992：136）

2. As the first poem in *Axe Handles*，“Axe Handles” begins the first section of the book，Loops，thereby advertising itself as a mode of beginning，a model of starting which always loops back to an earlier beginning. Not only does the opening poem lend the book its title，but it also features on the back of the book-jacket，printed in full，thereby functioning as both beginning and end of the book.（Dean，1991：145）

3. 在中国古典文学理论方面，影响史耐德最深的是陆机的《文赋》，他的老师陈世骧就是研究《文赋》的专家。史耐德仔细研读过陈世骧英译的《文赋》。除了采用《文赋》中“澄心”、“凝思”，即“calm transparency”的观念，以说明山水画画家必要的道家精神境界，还采用《文赋》中“操斧伐柯”的比喻，阐明文艺技术之重要及其传承之重要。（钟玲，2006：122-123）

## Supplementary Reading

### Mid-August at Sourdough Mountain Lookout

Down valley a smoke haze
Three days heat, after five days rain
Pitch glows on the fir-cones
Across rocks and meadows
Swarms of new flies.

I cannot remember things I once read
A few friends, but they are in cities.
Drinking cold snow-water from a tin cup
Looking down for miles
Through high still air.

### Front Lines

The edge of the cancer
Swells against the hill—we feel
        a foul breeze—
And it sinks back down.
The deer winter here
A chainsaw growls in the gorge.

Ten wet days and the log trucks stop,
The trees breathe.
Sunday the 4-wheel jeep of the
Realty Company brings in
Landseekers, lookers, they say
To the land,
Spread your legs.

The jets crack sound overhead, it's OK here;
Every pulse of the rot at the heart
In the sick fat veins of Amerika
Pushes the edge up closer—

A bulldozer grinding and slobbering
Sideslipping and belching on top of
The skinned-up bodies of still-live bushes
In the pay of a man
From town.

Behind is a forest that goes to the Arctic
And a desert that still belongs to the Piute
And here we must draw
Our line.

## For All

Ah to be alive
on a mid-September morn
fording a stream
barefoot, pants rolled up,
holding boots, pack on,
sunshine, ice in the shallows,
northern rockies.

Rustle and shimmer of icy creek waters
stones turn underfoot, small and hard as toes
cold nose dripping
singing inside
creek music, heart music,
smell of sun on gravel.

I pledge allegiance

I pledge allegiance to the soil
of Turtle Island,
and to the beings who thereon dwell
one ecosystem
in diversity
under the sun
With joyful interpenetration for all.

## Ripples on the Surface

"Ripples on the surface of water

were silver salmon passing under—different
from the sorts of ripples caused by breezes"

A scudding plume on the wave—
a humpback whale is
breaking out in air up
gulping herring
—Nature not a book, but a *performance*, a
high old culture.

Ever-fresh events
scraped out, rubbed out, and used, used, again—
the braided channels of the rivers
hidden under fields of grass—

The vast wild
the house, alone.
the little house in the wild,
the wild in the house.
Both forgotten.

*No nature.*

Both together, one big empty house.

## "The Trail Is Not a Trail"

I drove down the Freeway
And turned off at an exit
And went along a highway
Til it came to a sideroad
Drove up the sideroad
Til it turned to a dirt road
Full of bumps, and stopped.
Walked up a trail
But the trail got rough
And it faded away—
Out in the open,
Everywhere to go.

## References and Further Reading

1. Dean, Tim. *Gary Snyder and the American Unconscious: Inhabiting the Ground*. London: Macmillan, 1991.
2. Molesworth, Charles. *Gary Snyder's Vision: Poetry and the Real's Work*. Columbia: University of Missouri Press, 1983.
3. Murphy, Patrick D. *Understanding Gary Snyder*. Columbia: University of South Carolina Press, 1992
4. Murphy, Patrick D. *A Place for Wayfaring: The Poetry and Prose of Gary Snyder*. Corvallis: Oregon State University Press, 2000.
5. Norton, Jody. *Narcissus Sous Rature: Male Subjectivity in Contemporary American Literature*. Cranbury: Associated University Presses, Inc., 2000.
6. Paul, Sherman. "From Lookout to Ashram: The Way of Gary Snyder." *Iowa Review* (1970). Rpt. Murphy, ed. *Critical Essays on Gary Snyder*. Boston: G. K. Hall, 1990. 58-80.
7. 林耀福,梁秉钧编选.山即是心:史耐德诗文选.台北:联合文学出版社,1990.
8. 钟玲.史耐德与中国文化.北京:首都师范大学出版社,2006.

# 22. Sylvia Plath (1932–1963)

## Introduction

Sylvia Plath (1932 —1963), born in Boston, Massachusetts, was an American poet, novelist and short story writer. She married fellow poet Ted Hughes and they lived together first in the United States and then England, having two children together: Frieda and Nicholas. After suffering from depression from the age of 20 and a marital separation, Plath committed suicide in 1963. Plath wrote poetry from the age of eight. By the time she arrived at Smith College she had written over fifty short stories and published in many magazines. She wrote *The Bell Jar*, a semi-autobiographical novel published shortly before her death. In 1960, she published her first collection of poetry *The Colossus* which received positive comment. *Ariel* on which Plath's reputation was rested was published in 1965. Her other collections of poetry include: *Crossing the Water* (1971) and *Winter Trees* (1971). In 1982, she became the first poet to win Pulitzer Prize posthumously for *The Collected Poems* (1981) which contains poetry written from 1956 until her death.

Plath is credited with advancing the genre of confessional poetry and the style of her work compared to other contemporaries, such as Robert Lowell and W. D. Snodgrass. Sylvia Plath's early poems exhibit what became her typical imagery, using personal and nature-based depictions featuring, for example, the moon, blood, hospitals, fetuses, and skulls. They were mostly imitation exercises of poets she admired such as Dylan Thomas, W. B. Yeats and Marianne Moore. After 1960 her work moved into a more surreal landscape darkened by a sense of imprisonment and looming death, overshadowed by her father. *The Colossus* is shot through with themes of death, redemption and resurrection.

Plath's close friend Al Alvarez, who has written about her extensively, said of her later work: "Plath's case is complicated by the fact that, in her mature work, she deliberately used the details of her everyday life as raw material for her art. A casual visitor or unexpected telephone call, a cut, a bruise, a kitchen bowl, a candlestick — everything became usable, charged with meaning, transformed. Her poems are full of references and images that seem impenetrable at this distance, but which could mostly be explained in footnotes by a scholar with full access to the details of her life."

## Selected Reading A

### Lady Lazarus①

I have done it again.
One year in every ten
I manage it —

A sort of walking miracle, my skin
Bright as a Nazi lampshade, ②
My right foot

A paperweight,
My face featureless, fine
Jew linen.

Peel off the napkin③
O my enemy.
Do I terrify? —

The nose, the eye pits, the full set of teeth?
The sour breath
Will vanish in a day.

Soon, soon the flesh

---

① Here is an allusion to Lazarus, who was resurrected from death by Jesus Christ and walked out of tomb. The biblical narrative of The Raising of Lazarus is found in chapter 11 of the Gospel of John.

② Here Plath compared herself to a persecuted Jew, because "Nazi lampshades" were said to be made out of skin from Jews.

③ napkin: here refers to the shroud in which a corpse is wrapped.

The grave cave ate will be
At home on me

And I a smiling woman.
I am only thirty.
And like the cat I have nine times to die.

This is Number Three.
What a trash
To annihilate each decade.

What a million filaments.
The peanut-crunching crowd①
Shoves in to see

Them unwrap me hand and foot —
The big strip tease.②
Gentlemen, ladies,

These are my hands,
My knees.
I may be skin and bone,

Nevertheless, I am the same, identical woman.
The first time it happened I was ten.
It was an accident.

The second time I meant
To last it out and not come back at all.
I rocked shut

As a seashell.
They had to call and call
And pick the worms off me like sticky pearls.

Dying

① peanut-crunching crowd: referring to doctors and nurses who rescue suicides.
② strip tease: a form of erotic entertainment in which a dancer gradually undresses to music.

Is an art, like everything else.
I do it exceptionally well.

I do it so it feels like hell.
I do it so it feels real.
I guess you could say I've a call.

It's easy enough to do it in a cell.
It's easy enough to do it and stay put.
It's the theatrical

Comeback in broad day
To the same place, the same face, the same brute
Amused shout:

"A miracle!"
That knocks me out.
There is a charge

For the eyeing of my scars, there is a charge
For the hearing of my heart —
It really goes.

And there is a charge, a very large charge
For a word or a touch
Or a bit of blood

Or a piece of my hair or my clothes.
So, so, Herr Doktor.[①]
So, Herr Enemy.

I am your opus,
I am your valuable,
The pure gold baby

That melts to a shriek.

---

① Herr Doktor: These words are German, "Herr" used before name as a title equivalent to Mr. in English. Here the utility of German is to compare doctors to Nazi.

I turn and burn.
Do not think I underestimate your great concern.

Ash, ash —
You poke and stir.
Flesh, bone, there is nothing there —

A cake of soap,
A wedding ring,
A gold filling.

Herr god, Herr Lucifer,
Beware
Beware.

Out of the ash
I rise with my red hair①
And I eat men like air.

## About the Selection

死亡是普拉斯诗歌创作中一个重要的主题,《女拉撒路》可谓描写死亡的一个典型。在这首诗中,通篇弥漫着死亡的气息,满眼都是死亡的影子。然而作者并没有滥情自怜,而是利用历史和文化典故,设计了精巧的框架,把自己比作死而复生的拉撒路,外化自己内心中的狂乱情感,更以调侃的口吻向死亡发出了直接的挑战。诗中体现了毁灭、死亡与再生以及女权主义思想。

## Research Guide

1. Plath's late poems are full of speakers whose rigid identities and violent methods not only parody their torment but also permit them to control it. The peculiar nature of the speaker in "Lady Lazarus" defies ordinary notions of the suicide. Suicide is not the joyous act she claims it to be in her triumphant assertion that she has done it again. [...] Her treatment of suicide in such buoyant terms amounts to a parody of her own act. When she compares her suicide to the victimization of the Jews, and when she later claims there is a charge for a piece of her hair or clothes and thus compares her rescued self to the crucified Christ or martyred saint, she is engaging in self-parody. She employs these techniques partly to defy the crowd [...] and partly to taunt her rescuers. [...] She is

① red hair: Phoenix is said to have red hair, so here the speaker compares herself as a resurrected phoenix; maybe the speaker in real life has red hair.

neither a miracle nor an opus, and she fends off those who would regard her in this way. (Dickie, 1979: 161-162)

2. "Lady Lazarus" defines the central aesthetic principles of Plath's late poetry. First, the poem derives its dominant effects from the colloquial language. From the conversational opening ("I have done it again") to the clipped warnings of the ending ("Beware / Beware"), "Lady Lazarus" appears as the monologue of a woman speaking spontaneously out of her pain and psychic disintegration. The Latinate terms ("annihilate," "filaments," "opus," "valuable") are introduced as sudden contrasts to the essentially simple language of the speaker. The obsessive repetition of key words and phrases gives enormous power to the plain style used throughout. (Rosenblatt, 1979: 40)

3. Almost every stanza of "Lady Lazarus" picks up a new possibility for this theatrical voice, from mock movie talk ("So, so, Herr Doktor. /So, Herr Enemy") to bureaucratic politeness, ("Do not think I underestimate your great concern") to witch warnings ("I rise with my red hair/And I eat men like air"). When an author makes a sort of headcheese of style in this way—a piece of gristle, a piece of meat, a piece of gelatin, a piece of rind—the disbelief in style is countered by a competitive faith in it. Style (as something consistent) is meaningless, but styles (as dizzying provisional skepticism) are all. (Vendler, 1982: 124)

4. "Purdah" and "Lady Lazarus"— written within a week of each other during October 1962 — further reveal Plath's conviction that undressing has become for her a powerful poetic gesture, and in these poems it is the female speaker who finally disrobes — and here she attempts to appropriate the power of nakedness for herself. Plath does not simply contemplate from the spectator's point of view the horrors and the vigor of the act of undressing; now her female subject dares to make herself naked, and she does so in an attempt to make herself mighty. (Lant, 1993: 651)

5. 此诗的第一人称说话人是一个歇斯底里的裸露狂，在有窥淫癖的观众面前主动选择"裸露"之苦。……这群人的兴趣是淫荡的，追求的是非法刺激，想着的不是说话人赤裸的肉体，就是她赤裸的心灵。说话人以一种夸张的姿态邀请人们去注意她的自杀。……自杀企图本身是一种裸露，一种自白，一种对内心绝望的公开承认。说话人邀请别人观看她自杀，说明她自暴自弃、自我厌倦、自我毁灭的情绪已达到了顶点。自杀像脱衣舞一样是自我表现和吸引人们注意的有效的富于戏剧性的手段，把自杀同脱衣舞相比虽然带有一定的色情意味，但具有很强的讽刺意义，而且准确有力，充分地表达了自杀性绝望的矛盾心理。（彭予，2004:53-54）

## Selected Reading B

### Daddy

You do not do, you do not do
Any more, black shoe
In which I have lived like a foot
For thirty years, poor and white,
Barely daring to breathe or Achoo.

Daddy, I have had to kill you.
You died before I had time—
Marble-heavy, a bag full of God,
Ghastly statue with one gray toe[1]
Big as a Frisco seal

And a head in the freakish Atlantic
Where it pours bean green over blue
In the waters off the beautiful Nauset.[2]
I used to pray to recover you.
Ach, du.[3]

In the German tongue, in the Polish town[4]
Scraped flat by the roller
Of wars, wars, wars.
But the name of the town is common.
My Polack friend

Says there are a dozen or two.
So I never could tell where you
Put your foot, your root,
I never could talk to you.

---

① one gray toe: Plath father's toe turned black from gangrene, a complication of diabetes.

② Nauset: Massachusetts beach.

③ Ach, du: Ah, you(German). This refers to her father's German origin.

④ in the Polish town: the poet's father, though of German descent, was born in Grabow, Poland.

The tongue stuck in my jaw.

It stuck in a barb wire snare.
Ich, ich, ich, ich,[1]
I could hardly speak.
I thought every German was you.
And the language obscene

An engine, an engine
Chuffing me off like a Jew.
A Jew to Dachau, Auschwitz, Belsen.[2]
I began to talk like a Jew.
I think I may well be a Jew.

The snows of the Tyrol[3], the clear beer of Vienna
Are not very pure or true.
With my gypsy ancestress and my weird luck
And my Taroc pack and my Taroc[4] pack
I may be a bit of a Jew.

I have always been scared of you,
With your Luftwaffe[5], your gobbledygoo.
And your neat mustache
And your Aryan eye, bright blue.
Panzer[6]-man, panzer-man, O You—

Not God but a swastika[7]
So black no sky could squeak through.
Every woman adores a Fascist,
The boot in the face, the brute

---

① ich: I (German).

② Dachau, Auschwitz, Belsen: German concentration camps, where millions of Jews were murdered during World War II.

③ the Tyrol: the Austrian Alpine region.

④ Taroc: variation of Tarot, ancient fortune-telling cards. Gypsies, like Jews, were objects of Nazi genocidalambition, and many died in the concentration camps.

⑤ Luftwaffe: the German air force.

⑥ Panzer: armor(German). It refers to the Nazi tank corps in World War II. Hitler preached the superiority of the Aryans—people of German stock with blond hair and blue eyes.

⑦ Swastika: the official emblem of the Nazi Party and the Third Reich, 卍.

Brute heart of a brute like you.

You stand at the blackboard, daddy,
In the picture I have of you,
A cleft in your chin instead of your foot
But no less a devil for that, no not
Any less the black man who

Bit my pretty red heart in two.
I was ten when they buried you.
At twenty I tried to die
And get back, back, back to you.
I thought even the bones would do.

But they pulled me out of the sack,
And they stuck me together with glue,①
And then I knew what to do.
I made a model of you,
A man in black with a Meinkampf look②

And a love of the rack and the screw.
And I said I do, I do.
So daddy, I'm finally through.

The black telephone's off at the root,
The voices just can't worm through.

If I've killed one man, I've killed two—
The vampire who said he was you
And drank my blood for a year,
Seven years, if you want to know.
Daddy, you can lie back now.

There's a stake in your fat black heart

① This is an allusion to Plath's suicide attempt.

② A man in black with a Meinkampf look: this is a reference to Hitler's autobiography, *Mein Kampf* (*My Struggle*), which was written and published before his rise to power. In this book, Hitler outlined his plans for world conquest.

And the villagers never liked you.
They are dancing and stamping on you.
They always knew it was you.
Daddy, daddy, you bastard, I'm through.

## About the Selection

《爸爸》是普拉斯的重要代表作,创作于1962年,此时她与英国诗人泰德·休斯的婚姻已经出现危机。诗人一方面将父亲比作法西斯、魔鬼等,而自己以犹太人自喻,另一方面又流露出对父亲的爱和依恋,这种爱恨交加的感情,使诗人备受煎熬,最终诗人以死来结束这种精神的折磨。

## Research Guide

1. In the speaker's consciously disturbing over-statement that "Every woman adores a Fascist," Plath asserts that, while the archetypal male figure appearing in the rest of the poem (as father and lover) connotes the escape from freedom through sadism, the female figure's adoration of the Fascist is an extreme result of a stereotypically feminine escape from the feelings of aloneness associated with freedom, through masochistic strivings. Freedom, for the archetypal "feminine" figure in "Daddy," is freedom from the authoritarian father figure. Political realities (in the form of Nazism) and psychological difficulties (in the form of neurosis) are inescapably linked . . . for Plath. Thus Plath's lines in "Daddy" are both psychological and political. They are psychological not because "Daddy" is about Plath's relationship with her father, but in the sense that Plath uses the situation depicted in the poem to explore the dynamics of her attitude toward individualism. (Strangeways, 1996: 372-373)

2. By the time Plath wrote "Daddy," her faith in the inevitability of this violent sexual dynamic apparently remained firm, but her attitude toward her place in this relationship had changed. Tragically, she still cherished the notion that masculine sexuality was the perfect emblem for power ("Every woman adores a Fascist") and that she was doomed to sexual and social victimization ("I think I may well be a Jew" [223]), but in "Daddy," she appropriates that power for herself or for the female voice in that poem, and she does so in sexual terms. She becomes the rapist who terrifies, who imposes himself upon others, who makes his imprint — both poetic and psychological — upon reality. She no longer hides because she no longer has to. She has shed the femininity which threatened to undermine her The existence of the poem itself, addressed to "Daddy," demonstrates that her silence has been broken, that the father who has rendered her speechless has lost his ability to erase her: "I never could talk to you. / The tongue stuck in my jaw" (223). The act of speaking, thus, is her first appropriation of the father/lover's power. (Lant, 1993: 646-647)

3. 普拉斯利用纳粹和犹太人这两种对立的历史形象把自己对专横的父亲的反抗戏剧化。在此诗中父亲不断以各种面目出现：雕像、鞋、纳粹、教师、魔鬼、吸血鬼等，诗人超现实的想象几乎达到一种痴狂程度，此诗的主题是弑父，这一主题非常古老，可以追溯到古希腊和古罗马时代，它在西方文化中似乎有深远的意义，普拉斯在处理这一主题时坦率得令人震惊。这首诗运用了意象主义技巧，解体和错位的意象处处可见，人被降为一堆尸体或一堆货物，对纳粹集中营的恐惧和对破碎的自我的恐惧交织在一起。(彭予，1995：408)

## Supplementary Reading

### Mirror

I am silver① and exact. I have no preconceptions.
Whatever I see I swallow immediately
Just as it is, unmisted② by love or dislike.
I am not cruel, only truthful —
The eye③ of the little god, four-cornered.
Most of the time I meditate on the opposite wall.
It is pink, with speckles. I have looked at it so long
I think it is a part of my heart. But it flickers.
Faces and darkness separate us over and over.

Now I am a lake. A woman bends over me,
Searching my reaches for what she really is.
Then she turns to those liars, the candles or the moon.④
I see her back, and reflect it faithfully.
She rewards me with tears and an agitation of hands.
I am important to her. She comes and goes.
Each morning it is her face that replaces the darkness.
In me she has drowned a young girl, and in me an old woman
Rises toward her day after day, like a terrible fish.

---

① silver: here it refers to the coating on the back of a glass mirror.

② unmisted: not influenced; not prejudiced.

③ eye: the reflecting surface.

④ those liars, the candles or the moon: because candles and moonlight provide only dim illumination, they "lie" about what they see.

## References and Further Reading


1. Britzolakis, Christina. *Sylvia Plath and the Theatre of Mourning*. Oxford: Clarendon Press, 1999.
2. Dickie, Margaret. *Sylvia Plath and Ted Hughes*. Urbana: University of Illinois Press, 1979.
3. Ferguson, M., M. J. Salter, and J. Stallworthy. *The Norton Anthology of Poetry* (5th ed.). New York and London: W. W. Norton & Company, 2005.
4. Lant, Kathleen Margaret. "The Big Strip Tease: Female Bodies and Male Power in the Poetry of Sylvia Plath." *Contemporary Literature* 34. 4 (1993): 620-669.
5. Rosenblatt, Jon. *Sylvia Plath: The Poetry of Initiation*. Chapel Hill: University of North Carolina Press, 1979.
6. Strangeways, Al. "'The Boot in the Face': The Problem of the Holocaust in the Poetry of Sylvia Plath." *Contemporary Literature* 37.3 (1996): 370-390.
7. Vendler, Helen. "An Intractable Metal." *The New Yorker*, Feb. 15(1982): 124.
8. 彭予.二十世纪美国诗歌.开封:河南大学出版社,1995.
9. 彭予.美国自白诗探索.北京:社会科学文献出版社,2004.
10. 张子清.二十世纪美国诗歌史.吉林:吉林教育出版社,1995.
11. 赵毅衡.美国现代诗选(下册).北京:外国文学出版社,1985.

# 23. Robert Hass (1941– )

## Introduction

Robert Hass was born in San Francisco on March 1, 1941. He attended St. Mary's College in Moraga, California and received both an MA and Ph. D. in English from Stanford University.

His books of poetry include *The Apple Trees at Olema: New and Selected Poems* (2010); *Time and Materials* (2007), which won the National Book Award and the Pulitzer Prize; *Sun Under Wood: New Poems* (1996), which won the National Book Critics Circle Award; *Human Wishes* (1989); *Praise* (1979), which won the William Carlos Williams Award; and *Field Guide* (1973), which was selected by Stanley Kunitz for the Yale Younger Poets Series.

About Hass's work, Kunitz wrote, "Reading a poem by Robert Hass is like stepping into the ocean when the temperature of the water is not much different from that of the air. You scarcely know, until you feel the undertow tug at you, that you have entered into another element."

Hass has also co-translated several volumes of poetry with Czesław Miłosz, most recently *Facing the River* (1995), and is author or editor of several other collections of essays and translation, including *What Light Can Do: Essays on Art, Imagination, and the Natural World* (2012); *The Essential Haiku: Versions of Basho, Buson, and Issa* (1994); and *Twentieth Century Pleasures: Prose on Poetry* (1984).

Hass served as Poet Laureate of the United States from 1995 to 1997 and as a Chancellor of The Academy of American Poets from 2001 to 2007. He lives in California with his wife, poet Brenda Hillman, and teaches at the University of California,

Berkeley.

## Selected Reading A

### Ezra Pound's Proposition

Beauty is sexual, and sexuality
Is the fertility of the earth and the fertility
Of the earth is economics. Though he is no recommendation
For poets on the subject of finance,
I thought of him in the thick heat
Of the Bangkok night. Not more than fourteen, she saunters up to you
Outside the Shangri-la Hotel
And says, in plausible English,
"How about a party, big guy?"

Here is more or less how it works:
The World Bank arranges the credit and the dam
Floods three hundred villages, and the villagers find their way
To the city where their daughters melt into the teeming streets,
And the dam's great turbines, beautifully tooled
In Lund or Dresden or Detroit, financed
By Lazard Frères in Paris or the Morgan Bank in New York,
Enabled by judicious gifts from Bechtel of San Francisco
Or Halliburton of Houston to the local political elite,
Spun by the force of rushing water,
Have become hives of shimmering silver
And, down river, they throw that bluish throb of light
Across her cheekbones and her lovely skin.

### About the Selection

在《庞德的命题》中,诗人讲述自己的亲身经历。作为国际河流组织的董事,在曼谷,他遇见一个不超过十四岁的少女,在香格里拉饭店外卖淫。诗人透过这一在发展中国家和地区常见的社会现象,揭示出弯曲缠绕又环环相扣的"运作"程序,隐藏在背后的错综复杂的利益链条。

### Research Guide

1. In "Ezra Pound's Proposition" it's not war but greed that turns sex into violence. The

poem begins in abstraction, working out an equation Pound might well have conceived to express the relationship between desire and money. "Beauty is sexual," Hass writes, "and sexuality / Is the fertility of the earth and the fertility / Of the earth is economics." But the poem turns a corner when life plugs a real face into the variable for beauty and Hass finds himself propositioned by a beautiful young girl on a street in Bangkok. ("Not more than fourteen, she saunters up to you / Outside the Shangri-la Hotel / And says, in plausible English, / 'How about a party, big guy? '") Thinking of Pound, Hass tries to corral the moment in a diagram charting progress, destruction and desire in the abstract: [...] Where Pound might have been able to bury the personal encounter in the dynamics of history, though, Hass can't help circling back to the girl herself and to the actual sensations of desire that seem to pulse even through the light falling across her beautiful face. But the tone of understatement he adopts — from "here's pretty much how it works" to the delicate description of the longing the girl evokes — amplifies the point Pound would have emphasized with rhetoric. In the past Hass found in the world around him models that helped explain, if not assuage, human longing. In *Time and Materials* human desire has become a model for explaining, if not explaining away, what's going wrong in the world. (Davis 2009: 298-299)

2. In *Time and Materials* he continues to search for structures and tropes that allow him to represent 'the horror of the world' in his work. He introduces the haibun, for example—a hybrid form comprising a prose reflection and a haiku—which admirably accommodates the quoted statistics of war deaths. In 'Bush's War', a walk though Berlin in its spring beauty is placed side by side to powerful effect with historical atrocity ('You are never not wondering how / It happened'). And in 'Ezra Pound's Proposition', the connection between the Western-funded building of a dam in Thailand and the subsequent prostitution of children rendered homeless by the project is revealed in a vivid and brutally ironic image: the dam's great turbines... / Spun by the force of rushing water / Have become hives of shimmering silver / And, down river, they throw that bluish throb of light / Across her cheekbones and her lovely skin. (O'Driscoll 2008: 80)

## Selected Reading B

### State of the Planet

*On the occasion of the fiftieth anniversary of the Lamont-Doherty Earth Observatory*

1.
October on the planet at the century's end.

Rain lashing the windshield. Through blurred glass
Gusts of a Pacific storm rocking a huge, shank-needled
Himalayan cedar. Under it a Japanese plum
Throws off a vertical cascade of leaves the color
Of skinned copper, if copper could be skinned.
And under it, her gait as elegant and supple
As the young of any of earth's species, a schoolgirl
Negotiates a crosswalk in the wind, her hair flying,
The red satchel on her quite straight back darkening
Splotch by smoky crimson splotch as the rain pelts it.
One of the six billion of her hungry and curious kind.
Inside the backpack, dog-eared, full of illustrations,
A book with a title like *Getting to Know Your Planet*.

The book will tell her that the earth this month
Has yawed a little distance from the sun,
And that the air, cooling, has begun to move,
As sensitive to temperature as skin is
To a lover's touch. It will also tell her that the air—
It's likely to say "the troposphere"—has trapped
Emissions from millions of cars, idling like mine
As she crosses, and is making a greenhouse
Of the atmosphere. The book will say that climate
Is complicated, that we may be doing this,
And if we are, it may explain that this
Was something we've done quite accidentally,
Which she can understand, not having meant
That morning to have spilled the milk. She's
One of those who's only hungry metaphorically.

2.

Poetry should be able to comprehend the earth,
To set aside from time to time its natural idioms
Of ardor and revulsion, and say, in a style as sober
As the Latin of Lucretius, who reported to Venus
On the state of things two thousand years ago—
"It's your doing that under the wheeling constellations
Of the sky," he wrote, "all nature teems with life—"
Something of the earth beyond our human dramas.

Topsoil: going fast. Rivers: dammed and fouled.
Cod: about fished out. Haddock: about fished out.
Pacific salmon nosing against dams from Yokohama
To Kamchatka to Seattle and Portland, flailing
Up fish ladders, against turbines, in a rage to breed
Much older than human beings and interdicted
By the clever means that humans have devised
To grow more corn and commandeer more lights.
Most of the ancient groves are gone, sacred to Kuan Yin
And Artemis, sacred to the gods and goddesses
In every picture book the child is apt to read.

3.

Lucretius, we have grown so clever that mechanics
In our art of natural philosophy can take the property
Of luminescence from a jellyfish and put it in mice.
In the dark the creatures give off greenish light.
Their bodies must be very strange to them.
An artist in Chicago—think of a great trading city
In Dacia or Thracia—has asked to learn the method
So he can sell people dogs that glow in the dark.

4.

The book will try to give the child the wonder
Of how, in our time, we understand life came to be:
Stuff flung off from the sun, the molten core
Still pouring sometimes rivers of black basalt
Across the earth from the old fountains of its origin.
A hundred million years of clouds, sulfurous rain.
The long cooling. There is no silence in the world
Like the silence of rock from before life was.
You come across it in a Mexican desert,

A palo verde tree nearby, moss-green. Some
Insect-eating bird with wing feathers the color
Of a morning sky perched on a limb of the tree.
That blue, that green, the completely fierce
Alertness of the bird that can't know the amazement
Of its being there , a human mind that somewhat does,

Regarding a black outcrop of rock in the desert
Near a sea, charcoal-black and dense, wave-worn,
And all one thing: there's no life in it at all.

It must be a gift of evolution that humans
Can't sustain wonder. We'd never have gotten up
From our knees if we could. But soon enough
We'd have fashioned sexy little earrings from the feathers,
Highlighted our cheekbones by rubbings from the rock,
And made a spear from the sinewey wood of the tree.

5.

If she lived in Michigan or the Ukraine,
She'd find, washed up on the beach in a storm like this
Limestone fossils of Devonian coral. She could study
The faint white markings: she might have to lick the stone
To see them if the wind was drying the pale surface
Even as she held it, to bring back the picture of what life
Looked like forty millions years ago: a honeycomb with mouths.

6.

Cells that divided and reproduced. From where? Why?
(In our century it was the fashion in philosophy
Not to ask unanswerable questions. That was left
To priests and poets, an attitude you'd probably
Approve.) Then a bacterium grew green pigment.
This was the essential miracle. It somehow unmated
Carbon dioxide to eat the carbon and turn it
Into sugar and spit out, hiss out the molecules
Of oxygen the child on her way to school
Is breathing, and so bred life. Something then
Of DNA, the curled musical ladder of sugars, acids.
From there to eyes, ears, wings, hands, tongues.
Armadillos, piano tuners, gnats, sonnets,
Military interrogation, the coho salmon, the Margaret Truman rose.

7.

The people who live in Tena, on the Napo River,
Say that the black, viscid stuff the pools in the selva

Is the blood of the rainbow boa curled in the earth's core.
The great trees in that forest house ten thousands of kinds
Of beetle, reptiles no human eyes has ever seen changing
Color on the hot, green, hardly changing leaves
Whenever a faint breeze stirs them. In the understory
Bromeliads and orchids whose flecked petals and womb-
Or mouth-like flowers are the shapes of desire
In human dreams. And butterflies, larger than her palm
Held up to catch a ball or ward off fear. Along the river
Wide-leaved banyans where flocks of raucous parrots,
Fruit-eaters and seed-eaters, rise in startled flares
Of red and yellow and bright green. It will seem to be poetry
Forgetting its promise of sobriety to say the rosy shinings
In the thick brown current are small dolphins rising
To the surface where gouts of the oil that burns inside
The engine of the car I'm driving oozes from the banks.

8.

The book will tell her that the gleaming appliance
That kept her milk cold in the night required
Chlorofluorocarbons—Lucretius, your master
Epictetus was right about atoms in a general way.
It turns out they are electricity having sex
In an infinite variety of permutations, Plato's
Yearning halves of a severed being multiplied
In all the ways that all the shapes on earth
Are multiple, complex; the philosopher
Who said that the world was fire was also right—
Chlorofluorocarbons react with ozone, the gas
That makes air tingle on a sparkling day.
Nor were you wrong to describe them as assemblies,
As if evolution were a town meeting or a plebiscite.
(Your theory of wind, and of gases, was also right
And there are more of them than you supposed.)
Ozone, high in the air, makes a kind of filter
Keeping out parts of sunlight damaging to skin.
The device we use to keep our food as cool
As if it sat in snow required this substance,
And it reacts with ozone. Where oxygen breeds it

From ultra-violet light, it burns a hole in the air.

9.

They drained the marshes around Rome. Your people,
You know, were the ones who taught the world to love
Vast fields of grain, the power and the order of the green,
Then golden rows of it, spooled out almost endlessly.
Your poets, those in the generation after you,
Were the ones who praised the packed seed heads
And the vineyards and the olive groves and called them
"Smiling" fields. In the years since, we've gotten
Even better at relentless simplification, but it's taken
Until our time for it to crowd out, savagely, the rest
Of life. No use to rail against our curiosity and greed.
They keep us awake. And are, for all their fury
And their urgency, compatible with intelligent restraint.
In the old paintings of the Italian renaissance,
—In the fresco painters who came after you
(It was the time in which your poems were rediscovered
There was a period when you, and Venus, were lost;
How could she be lost? you may well ask). Anyway
In those years the painters made of our desire
An allegory and a dance in the figure of three graces.
The first, the woman coming toward you, is the appetite
For life; the one who seems to turn away is chaste restraint,
And the one whom you've just glimpsed, her back to you,
Is beauty. The dance resembles wheeling constellations.
They made of it a figure for something elegant or lovely
Forethought gives our species. One would like to think
It makes a dance; that the black-and-white flash
Of a flock of buntings in October wind, headed south
Toward winter habitat, would find that the December fields
Their kind has known and mated in for thirty centuries
Or more, were still intact, that they will not go
The way of the long-billed arctic curlews who flew
From Newfoundland to Patagonia in every weather
And are gone now from the kinds on earth. The last of them
Seen by any human alit in a Texas marsh in 1964.

10.
What is to be done with our species? Because
We know we're going to die, to be submitted
To that tingling dance of atoms once again,
It's easy for us to feel that our lives are a dream—
As this is, in a way, a dream: the flailing rain,
The birds, the soaked red backpack of the child,
Her tendrils of wet hair, the windshield wipers,
This voice trying to speak across the centuries
Between us, even the long story of the earth,
Boreal forests, mangrove swamps, Tiberian wheatfields
In the summer heat on hillsides south of Rome—all of it
A dream, and we alive somewhere, somehow outside it,
Watching. People have been arguing for centuries
About whether or not you thought of Venus as a metaphor.
Because of the rational man they take you for.
Also about why your poem ended with a plague,
The bodies heaped in the temple of the gods.
To disappear. First one, then a few, then hundreds,
Just stopping over here, to vanish in the marsh at dusk.
So easy, in imagination, to tell the story backward,
Because the earth needs a dream of restoration—
She dances and the birds just keep arriving,
Thousands of them, immense arctic flocks, her teeming life.

## About the Selection

《地球现状》是哈斯在 1999 年参加美国哥伦比亚大学拉蒙特—多尔蒂地球观测所 50 周年庆典活动时所作,后收入 2007 年出版的《时间与物质:诗集 1997—2005》一书。在长诗里,诗人思考人类对地球的影响,通过对话古罗马诗人卢克莱修,批评人类采用机械和功利的态度对待其他生物,造成水土流失、物种灭绝、全球变暖等一系列生态灾难。该如何解决这些问题呢?在诗的结尾,诗人给出的答案是梦想——"地球需要恢复的梦想"。诗和诗人虽不能直接指导我们如何切实地做到生态的重建,却能激发我们对重建和修复的向往,令我们对未来心存希望。

## Research Guide

1. While tampering with Horace lets Hass lodge his protest against this seismic shift in the political landscape, he enlists the Roman poet's older contemporary Lucretius to remind us that it's not just global politics that have gone south. "State of the Planet" — a kind of verse *Inconvenient Truth* addressed to the author of *De Rerum Natura* — is in

part a work of environmentalist due diligence, but its description of global warming is less interesting than the way the poem imagines bringing Lucretius up to date. Translating both something of the Earth and something of our human dramas into terms an Epicurian would understand, "State of the Planet" attempts to show how desire elucidates the physical world — "Lucretius," Hass writes, "your master / Epictetus was right about atoms in a general way. / It turns out they are electricity having sex / in an infinite variety of permutations" — and our physical needs help explain our desire: "She's / One of those who's only hungry metaphorically," the poem says of its schoolgirl protagonist. (Hass's mixing of science and ardor reminds me of James Richardson's breathtaking "How Things Are: A Suite for Lucretians," undoubtedly the most beguiling riff on *De Rerum Natura* in contemporary poetry.) What we can take from Lucretius is not, the poem concludes, the sober facts about the nature of things — which Hass concedes are right, when they're right, only "in a general way" — but the artistry that allowed the sober saying of those things to live inside his poem's various dreams. Seamus Heaney once wrote, regarding Robert Frost, that what matters most and lasts longest in poetry is "the counterweight, the oversound, the sweetest dream within the fact — these things are poetically more rewarding than a record, however faithful the data." Or, as Yeats put it, "In dreams begin responsibilities." (Davis, 2009: 295-296)

2. Poetry, for Hass, has increasingly become a conscienced prose, but not necessarily good prose—the syntax is often wobbly; you'd pay a ransom for a few semi-colons; some of the modifiers dangle until hell freezes over; and, when the poet attempts to distinguish between O! and Oh!, he botches it. Hass is too clever and dry a writer for the "poetry of witness," that most deadly of contemporary genres—instead he writes the "poetry of lecture." A long poem called "State of the Planet," commissioned by a famous observatory, starts with one of his gorgeous pastoral set-pieces: "Through blurred glass/ Gusts of a Pacific storm rocking a huge,/shank-needled/Himalayan cedar. Under it a Japanese plum/Throws off a vertical cascade of leaves the color/Of skinned copper." Soon, however, he's droning on about chlorofluorocarbons; by the time he's done preaching about the destruction of the ozone layer, you're counting the tiles on the floor. One poem offers a potted history of aerial bombardment in Vietnam; another, a sandbox account of the Korean War. The facts are numbing, but they're too eager to become parables. Most people learned these things in tenth-grade textbooks, or from Al Gore. Hass's taste for Horatian state-of-the-nation poems too easily becomes moral hectoring—after all the idealism, you long for a little Realpolitik. It's one thing to be nervous about what the lyric ignores, another to blame poetry for the horrors of the world. (Logan, 2007: 68)

3. In "State of the Planet," a long poem written in a series of vignettes, he proposes that

what might have been done to the planet "was something we've done quite accidentally." No matter. There is a price to pay. [...] His style is varied—from short, almost haiku-like couplets to long narrative riffs, conversations (so Whitman-like) with the past, present, and future. (Huston, 2007: 91)

4. 哈斯揭示了我们人类如何无法在自然世界(全世界的一部分)里安身,以及我们如何倾向于退缩,并用一种笛卡尔式的、超越理性的方式高高在上地思考我们与这个世界的关系。……哈斯对"地球国家"的延伸性思考给出一个有希望的结论。他的诗属于我所举的可持续诗,可以容易地被"心中关注";因为其虽有现实评价,却没有陷入悲惨预言的泥淖。不同于《寂静的春天》、《人口炸弹》及其他启示性环境保护作品潜在的、尖锐刺人的道德说教,哈斯的作品就像其他一些可持续诗一样,以充满希望的心理状态为示范,这也是人类面对可持续生存采取任何积极行为的先决条件。(斯洛维克, 2008: 254-255)

## Supplementary Reading

### After the Gentle Poet Kobayashi Issa

New Year's morning—
everything is in blossom!
    I feel about average.

    A huge frog and I
staring at each other,
    neither of us moves.
    This moth saw brightness
in a woman's chamber—
    burned to a crisp.

    Asked how old he was
the boy in the new kimono
    stretched out all five fingers.

    Blossoms at night,
like people
    moved by music

    Napped half the day;
no one

punished me!

Fiftieth birthday:

From now on,
It's all clear profit,
every sky.

Don't worry, spiders,
I keep house
casually.

These sea slugs,
they just don't seem
Japanese.

Hell:

Bright autumn moon;
pond snails crying
in the saucepan.

## Exit Pursued by a Sierra Meadow

That slow, rhythmic flickering of the wings,
As if from the ache of pleasure—
A California tortoiseshell
Fastened to the white umbel of a milkweed stalk.

Smell of water in the dry air,
The almost nutmeg smell of dust.

White fir, Jeffrey pine,
I have no way of knowing whether you prefer
Summer or winter,
Though I think you are more beautiful in winter.

Scarlet fritillary, corn lily,
I don't know which you prefer, either.
So long, horsemint,

Your piebald mix of lavender and soft gray-green under the cottonwoods
On a shelf of lichened granite near a creek
May be the most startling thing in these mountains,
Besides the mountains.
It's good that we stopped just a minute
To look at you and then walked down the trail
Because we had things to do
And because beauty is a little unendurable,
I mean, getting used to it is unendurable,
Because if we can't eat a thing or do something with it,
Human beings get bored by almost everything eventually,
Which is why winter is such an admirable invention.
There's another month of summer here.
August will squeeze the sweetness out of you
And drift it as pollen.

## References and Further Reading


1. Davis, Wes. "Fear and Loathing at Lagunitas". *Parnassus: Poetry in Review*. Vol. 31, Issue 1/2 (2009): 275-306.
2. Fisher-Wirth, Ann and Laura-Gray Street, eds. *The Ecopoetry Anthology*. San Antonio: Trinity University Press, 2013.
3. Hass, Robert. *Time and Materials : Poems 1997—2005*. New York: Harper Collins, 2007.
4. Huston, Karla. "Time and Materials: Poems, 1997—2005." *Library Journal* 132.13 (2007): 91.
5. Logan, William. "The World is Too Much with us." *New Criterion* 26. 4(2007): 61-68.
6. O'Driscoll, Ciaran. "A Kind of Singing." *The Poetry Ireland Review* 94 (2008): 74-81.
7. 斯科特·斯洛维克."生态诗与'可持续诗'",夏光武译.江西社会科学 2008(7):249-256.

# 24.Charles Bernstein (1950-)

## Introduction

Charles Bernstein was born in New York City in 1950. He received his B. A. from Harvard College. Among his more than twenty books of poetry are *Girly Man* (2006), *With Strings* (2001), *Republics of Reality*: *1975—1995* (2000), *Dark City* (1994), *Rough Trades* (1991), *The Nude Formalism* (1989), *Stigma* (1981), and *Parsing* (1976).

He is also the author of three books of essays, *My Way*: *Speeches and Poems* (1999), *A Poetics* (1992), and *Content's Dream*: *Essays 1975 - 1984* (1986). He has edited many anthologies of poetry and poetics including *Close Listening*: *Poetry and the Performed Word* (1998) and *The L = A = N = G = U = A = G = E Book* (1984, with Bruce Andrews).

Bernstein was elected a Fellow of the American Academy of Arts & Sciences in 2006. Other awards and honors include The 1999 Roy Harvy Pearce / Archive for New Poetry Prize of the University of California, San Diego; the University of Pennsylvania Dean's Award for Innovative Teaching; a John Simon Guggenheim Memorial Fellowship; and a National Endowment for the Arts Creative Writing Fellowship. Bernstein is currently Donald T. Regan Professor of English and Comparative Literature at the University of Pennsylvania. He also serves as the Executive Editor, and co-founder, of The Electronic Poetry Center at SUNY-Buffalo.

## Selected Reading

### The Kiwi Bird in the Kiwi Tree

I want no paradise only to be
drenched in the downpour of words, fecund
with tropicality. Fundament be-
yond relation, less'real' than made, as arms
surround a baby's gurgling: encir-
cling mesh pronounces its promise (not bars
that pinion, notes that ply). The tailor tells
of other tolls, the seam that binds, the trim,
the waste. & having spelled these names, move on
to toys or talcums, skates & scores. Only
the imaginary is real—not trumps
beclouding the mind's acrobatic vers-
ions. The first fact is the social body,
one from another, nor needs no other.

### About the Selection

《奇异树上的奇异鸟》是伯恩斯坦的一首有名的语言诗。诗题本身即体现出了语言符号的武断性:奇异树和奇异鸟看似拥有相同的名字——"奇异",实则未必一样。诗题与诗的内容也不相干,也即名不副实。在诗行和句法的处理上也体现出伯恩斯坦所谓的"内爆句法",有些词序杂乱颠倒,一些词甚至被无端地断开,但其中未必有任何深意。

### Research Guide

1. My description of Bernstein's tactics as arbitrary and willful would not strike the poet, I suspect, as a criticism; Bernstein seems deliberately to avoid the belief in the occult rightness of connections established through pun or rhyme that characterizes what we usually take as "poetic" thinking. Indeed, the subject, so far as I'm able to determine it, of this poem is the simultaneous arbitrariness and inescapability of language. (Shetley, 1993: 150)

2. Read from an ideolectical perspective the poem strategically works on establishing relations in the text, and there is a sense that the poem builds its own vocabulary. Bernstein would argue that this interactive process of interpretation presents a possibility of configuring tangible social relationships beyond the terrain of the poem. The opening

of the poem is a surreal visualization of an earth bound paradise, it begins with an expressive speaker and array of syntactical inversions; an adverb becomes a verb "fecund with tropicality", "fundament" is initially associated with the ethereal, but modified to frame a concept "less 'real' than made". In its probing of relations between the everyday and the utopic, the social and the imaginary, the poem opts firstly for a familial tie. Yet, there is only a demarcation of proximity here; the baby may at first seem comforted but we realize that the contact is an embrace of sound "arms surround a baby's gurgling". Any physical contact is certainly encrypted and needs some decoding "encir/cling mesh pronounces its promise", the mesh here could be substituted by "flesh", but this "inscribed" image of cradling requires some lexical excavation. (Williams, 2007: 66-67)

3. For me the poem pulls into directions at the same time, affirming the move of non-identification that Bernstein cherishes in the works of Gertrude Stein while also recalling the "imaginary gardens with real toads in them" that Marianne Moore vividly exposes in her poem "Poetry" (1919). [...] Like Stein's texts and their distinct poetic programs, Bernstein's poem in this way provokes the reader in his or her capacity as meaning-making animal while at the same time frustrating his or her desire to make perfect sense of things, poems, and his or her own position. (Sielke, 2008: 82)

## Supplementary Reading

### Of Time and Line

George Burns[1] likes to insist that he always
takes the straight lines; the cigar in his mouth
is a way of leaving space between the
lines for a laugh. He weaves lines together
by means of a picaresque narrative;
not so Henny Youngman[2], whose lines are strict-
ly paratactic[3]. My father pushed a
line of ladies' dresses—not down the street

① George Burns: masterful comedian born in New York (1896—1996) who often played straight man to his wife and partner, Gracie Allen. He performed while holding a cigar, taking a puff to punctuate the joke.

② Henry Youngman: British-born American comedian (1906—1998), known for his rapid-fire one-liners and his verbal wit.

③ Designating a style in which sentence, or elements within sentence are set down successively with little or no indication of their relationship. Often applied to passages of poetry or prose, the term here suggests Youngman'smethod of telling a succession of brief jokes, each taking only a sentence or two.

in a pushcart but upstairs in a fact'ry
office. My mother has been more concerned
with her hemline. Chairman Mao put forward
Maoist lines, but that's been abandoned (most-
ly) for the East-West line of malarkey
so popular in these parts. The prestige
of the iambic line has recently
suffered decline, since it's no longer so
clear who"I" am, much less who you are. When
making a line, better be double sure
what you're lining in & what you're lining
out & which side of the line you're on; the
world is made up so (Adam didn't so much
name as delineate). Every poem's got
a prosodic lining, some of which will
unzip for summer wear. The lines of an
imaginary are inscribed on the
social flesh by the knifepoint of history.
Nowadays, you can often spot a work
of poetry by whether it's in lines
or no; if it's in prose, there's a good chance
it's a poem. While there is no lesson in
the line more useful than that of the pick-
et line, the line that has caused the most ad-
versity is the bloodline. In Russia
everyone is worried about long lines;
back in the USA, it's strictly soup-
lines. "Take a chisel to write," but for an
actor a line's got to be cued. Or, as
they say in math, it takes two lines to make
an angle but only one lime to make
a Margarita.

## All the Whiskey in Heaven

Not for all the whiskey in heaven
Not for all the flies in Vermont
Not for all the tears in the basement
Not for a million trips to Mars

Not if you paid me in diamonds
Not if you paid me in pearls
Not if you gave me your pinky ring
Not if you gave me your curls

Not for all the fire in hell
Not for all the blue in the sky
Not for an empire of my own
Not even for peace of mind

No, never, I'll never stop loving you
Not till my heart beats its last
And even then in my words and my songs
I will love you all over again

## References and Further Reading

1. Andrews, Bruce and Charles Bernstein, eds. *The L = A = N = G = U = A = G = E Book*. Carbondale: Southern Illinois University Press, 1984.
2. Reinfeld, Linda. *Language Poetry: Writing as Rescue*. Baton Rouge: Louisiana State University Press, 1992.
3. Shetley, Vernon Lionel. *After the Death of Poetry: Poet and Audience in Contemporary America*. Durham: Duke University Press, 1993.
4. Sielke, Sabine. "How Experimental Is It, or: When Did Modernism End?" *Another Language: Poetic Experiments in Britain and North America*. Eds. Kornelia Freitag & Katharina Vester. Münster: Lit, 2008. 77-92.
5. Williams, Nerys. *Reading Error: The Lyric and Contemporary Poetry*. Oxford, Bern, Berlin, Bruxelles, Frankfurt am Main, New York, Wien: Peter Lang, 2007.
6. 查尔斯·伯恩斯坦等.美国语言派诗选,张子清、黄运特编译.成都:四川文艺出版社,1993.
7. 查尔斯·伯恩斯坦.查尔斯·伯恩斯坦诗选,聂珍钊、罗良功编译.武汉:华中师范大学出版社,2011年.
8. 查尔斯·伯恩斯坦.语言派诗学,罗良功等译.上海:上海外语教育出版社,2013年.

# 25. Li-Young Lee (1957– )

## Introduction

Li-Young Lee was born in 1957 in Jakarta, Indonesia, to Chinese parents. His father had been a personal physician to Mao Zedong while in China, and relocated the family to Indonesia, where he helped found Gamaliel University. In 1959, the Lee family fled the country to escape anti-Chinese sentiment and after a five-year trek through Hong Kong, Macau, and Japan, they settled in the United States in 1964.

Lee attended the Universities of Pittsburgh and Arizona, and the State University of New York at Brockport. He has taught at several universities, including Northwestern and the University of Iowa.

His works include *The Winged Seed: A Remembrance* (2013); *Behind My Eyes* (2008); *Book of My Nights* (2001), which won the 2002 William Carlos Williams Award; *The City in Which I Love You* (1991), which was the 1990 Lamont Poetry Selection; and *Rose* (1986), which won the Delmore Schwartz Memorial Poetry Award.

With regard to Lee's work, the poet Gerald Stern has noted that "what characterizes [his] poetry is a certain humility... a willingness to let the sublime enter his field of concentration and take over, a devotion to language, a belief in its holiness."

He has been the recipient of a Fellowship from the Academy of American Poets, a Lannan Literary Award, a Whiting Writer's Award, the PEN Oakland/Josephine Miles Award, the I. B. Lavan Award, three Pushcart Prizes, and grants from the Illinois Arts Council, the Commonwealth of Pennsylvania, the Pennsylvania Council on the Arts, and the National Endowment for the Arts, as well as a Guggenheim Foundation fellowship. In 1998, he received the honorary degree of Doctor of Humane Letters from State

University of New York at Brockport. He currently lives in Chicago, Illinois, with his wife, Donna, and their two sons.

## Selected Reading

### The Gift

To pull the metal splinter from my palm
my father recited a story in a low voice.
I watched his lovely face and not the blade.
Before the story ended, he'd removed
the iron sliver I thought I'd die from.

I can't remember the tale,
but hear his voice still, a well
of dark water, a prayer.
And I recall his hands,
two measures of tenderness
he laid against my face,
the flames of discipline
he raised above my head.

Had you entered that afternoon
you would have thought you saw a man
planting something in a boy's palm,
a silver tear, a tiny flame.
Had you followed that boy
you would have arrived here,
where I bend over my wife's right hand.

Look how I shave her thumbnail down
so carefully she feels no pain.
Watch as I lift the splinter out.
I was seven when my father
took my hand like this,
and I did not hold that shard
between my fingers and think,
*Metal that will bury me*,

christen it Little Assassin,
Ore Going Deep for My Heart.
And I did not lift up my wound and cry,
*Death visited here*!
I did what a child does
when he's given something to keep.
I kissed my father.

## About the Selection

《礼物》选自李立扬第一本诗集《玫瑰》。诗人从普通生活细节切入，讲述父亲如何从他手掌取出一块铁片，以抒情的笔调，把亲人之间的关爱、对故国的思念与面对死亡的坚强联系起来。诗歌语言纯正、朴实，感情真挚、细腻，从而产生了一种强烈的艺术感染力。

## Research Guide

1. "The Gift" recalls the father's love, and it also makes a connection between the "gift" of care that the father gave to the speaker and the similar "gift" that the speaker bestows on his wife. Although the poem pays tribute to the father's "tenderness," it also includes dark undertones in the father's associations with pain and the "flames of discipline." "The Gift" suggests that love exists despite impediments, and it creates meaning in the shadow of fear and death. Emotional openness combines with an apparently casual but precise, classical style in Lee's work. His poems are influenced by both traditional Chinese poetry and the family studies of poets such as Theodore Roethke, Robert Lowell, and Sylvia Plath. Lee's work reveals the deep resonances to be found in human relationships and ordinary occurrences. (Axelrod, etal. 2012: 507)

2. Li-Young Lee's "The Gift" (1986) offers an unequivocally positive vision of family relations. Lee recalls an incident that occurred when he was seven years old. A metal splinter had pierced his palm, and his father patiently removed it with a blade while diverting Lee's attention from the pain by reciting a story. His father's wise and compassionate action has helped to shape Lee's sense of identity. Paradoxically, it is as if the father had planted something in Lee rather than removed something. Lee then depicts a second, complementary incident—juxtaposing past and present as Merrill and Wilbur had done—in which he carefully removes splinter from his wife's hand. Clearly, Lee's care derives directly from his father's. The poem speaks strongly of the power of role models and of the potential such virtues as care and compassion have, if properly cultivated, of becoming family traditions. Lee implies an entire philosophy of life and family through the actions of father and son. (Burns, 2002: 29-30)

3. As Lee describes in his poem, remembering is closely associated with a deep

experience of vision—the sight and insight. In other words, the insight goes beneath the surface and penetrates the hidden strata of sight. The act of remembrance makes the hidden visible and brings it to light. The poet's recollection develops new principles of intelligibility whereby he is able to understand the unusual relationship between his father's "two measures of tenderness" and "the flames of discipline." Most importantly, poet is now able to perceive in the course of his memory the successive layers of meanings which lie beneath the visible surface of his father's presence. (Zhang, 2008: 83)

## Supplementary Reading

### I Ask My Mother to Sing

She begins, and my grandmother joins her.
Mother and daughter sing like young girls.
If my father were alive, he would play
his accordion and sway like a boat.
I've never been in Peking, or the Summer Palace,
nor stood on the great Stone Boat to watch
the rain begin on Kuen Ming Lake, the picnickers
running away in the grass.
But I love to hear it sung;
how the waterlilies fill with rain until
they overturn, spilling water into water,
then rock back, and fill with more,
Both women have begun to cry.
But neither stops her song.

### Immigrant Blues

*People have been trying to kill me since I was born*,
a man tells his son, trying to explain
the wisdom of learning a second tongue.

It's an old story from the previous century
about my father and me.

The same old story from yesterday morning
about me and my son.

It's called "Survival Strategies
and the Melancholy of Racial Assimilation."

It's called "Psychological Paradigms of Displaced Persons,"

called "The Child Who'd Rather Play than Study."

*Practice until you feel*
*the language inside you*, says the man.

But what does he know about inside and outside,
my father who was spared nothing
in spite of the languages he used?

And me, confused about the flesh and the soul,
who asked once into a telephone,
*Am I inside you*?

*You're always inside me*, a woman answered,
at peace with the body's finitude,
at peace with the soul's disregard
of space and time.

*Am I inside you*? I asked once
lying between her legs, confused
about the body and the heart.

*If you don't believe you're inside me*, *you're not*,
she answered, at peace with the body's greed,
at peace with the heart's bewilderment.

It's an ancient story from yesterday evening

called "Patterns of Love in Peoples of Diaspora,"

called "Loss of the Homeplace
and the Defilement of the Beloved,"

called "I want to Sing but I Don't Know Any Songs."

## References and Further Reading

1. Axelrod, Steven Gould, etal., eds. *The New Anthology of American Poetry: Vol. III: Postmodernisms, 1950-Present*. Piscataway NJ: Rutgers University Press, 2012.
2. Burns, Allan Douglas. *Thematic Guide to American Poetry*. Westport: Greenwood Press, 2002.
3. Xu, Wenying. "Transcendentalism, Ethnicity, and Food in the Work of Li-Young Lee." *Boundary 2* 33.2 (2006): 129-157.
4. Zhang, Benzi. *Asian Diaspora Poetry in North America*. New York: Routledge, 2008.
5. Zhou, Xiaojing. "Inheritance and Invention in Li-Young Lee's Poetry." *MELUS* 21.1 (1996): 113-132.

# Poetics

## 1. Ralph Waldo Emerson

### from "The Poet" (1844)

*"The Poet" was published in Emerson's collection* Essays: Second Series (1844) *and was based on a lecture Emerson gave in* 1842. *In this essay, Emerson describes how the poet is "representative," standing "among partial men for the complete man." The only one capable of articulating the transcendent nature of things, the poet is the one who can identify "symbols" and "emblems" of the world: "The world is a temple, whose walls are covered with emblems, pictures, and commandments of the Deity... there is no fact in nature which does not carry the whole sense of nature." The poet "re-attaches things to nature and the Whole" by "saying" or naming. Emerson writes that the poet has better perceptions than the rest of humanity, "he stands one step nearer to things, and sees the flowing of metamorphosis... his speech flows with the flowing of nature."*

*In "The Poet," Emerson also states that good poetry is not solely a matter of technical prowess: "for it is not metres, but a metre-making argument, that makes a poem,—a thought so passionate and alive, that, like the spirit of a plant or an animal, it has an architecture of its own, and adorns nature with a new thing." The poet speaks most "adequately... when he speaks somewhat wildly... not with the intellect." Emerson observes that a lifestyle "on a key so low and plain" is stimulant enough for poets, our "liberating gods." At the end of the essay, Emerson laments the lack of poets writing about America: "America is a poem in our eyes; its ample geography dazzles the imagination, and it will not wait long for metres."*

A moody child and wildly wise
Pursued the game with joyful eyes,

Which chose, like meteors, their way,
And rived the dark with private ray:
They overleapt the horizon's edge,
Searched with Apollo's privilege;
Through man, and woman, and sea, and star,
Saw the dance of nature forward far;
Through worlds, and races, and terms, and times,
Saw musical order, and pairing rhymes. ①
Olympian bards who sung
Divine ideas below,
Which always find us young,
And always keep us so. ②

Those who are esteemed umpires of taste, are often persons who have acquired some knowledge of admired pictures or sculptures, and have an inclination for whatever is elegant; but if you inquire whether they are beautiful souls, and whether their own acts are like fair pictures, you learn that they are selfish and sensual. Their cultivation is local, as if you should rub a log of dry wood in one spot to produce fire, all the rest remaining cold. Their knowledge of the fine arts is some study of rules and particulars, or some limited judgment of color or form, which is exercised for amusement or for show. It is a proof of the shallowness of the doctrine of beauty, as it lies in the minds of our amateurs, that men seem to have lost the perception of the instant dependence of form upon soul. There is no doctrine of forms in our philosophy. We were put into our bodies, as fire is put into a pan, to be carried about; but there is no accurate adjustment between the spirit and the organ, much less is the latter the germination of the former. So in regard to other forms, the intellectual men do not believe in any essential dependence of the material world on thought and volition. Theologians think it a pretty air-castle to talk of the spiritual meaning of a ship or a cloud, of a city or a contract, but they prefer to come again to the solid ground of historical evidence; and even the poets are contented with a civil and conformed manner of living, and to write poems from the fancy, at a safe distance from their own experience. But the highest minds of the world have never ceased to explore the double meaning, or, shall I say, the quadruple, or the centuple, or much more manifold meaning, of every sensuous fact: Orpheus, Empedocles, Heraclitus, Plato, Plutarch, Dante, Swedenborg③, and the masters of sculpture, picture, and poetry. For we are not pans and barrows, nor even porters of the

① From the poem of "The poet" by Emerson.

② The last four lines come from Emerson's poem "Ode to beauty".

③ Orpheus: the legendary Greek poet; Empedocles, Heraclitus, Plato: three ancient Greek philosophers; Plutarch: an ancient Greek historian, biographer, and essayist; Dante: a major Italian poet of the Middle Ages; Swedenborg: a Swedish scientist, philosopher, theologian, revelator.

fire and torch-bearers, but children of the fire, made of it, and only the same divinity transmuted, and at two or three removes, when we know least about it. And this hidden truth, that the fountains whence all this river of Time, and its creatures, floweth, are intrinsically ideal and beautiful, draws us to the consideration of the nature and functions of the Poet, or the man of Beauty, to the means and materials he uses, and to the general aspect of the art in the present time.

The breadth of the problem is great, for the poet is representative. He stands among partial men for the complete man, and apprises us not of his wealth, but of the commonwealth. The young man reveres men of genius, because, to speak truly, they are more himself than he is. They receive of the soul as he also receives, but they more. Nature enhances her beauty, to the eye of loving men, from their belief that the poet is beholding her shows at the same time. He is isolated among his contemporaries, by truth and by his art, but with this consolation in his pursuits, that they will draw all men sooner or later. For all men live by truth, and stand in need of expression. In love, in art, in avarice, in politics, in labor, in games, we study to utter our painful secret. The man is only half himself, the other half is his expression.

Notwithstanding this necessity to be published, adequate expression is rare. I know not how it is that we need an interpreter: but the great majority of men seem to be minors, who have not yet come into possession of their own, or mutes, who cannot report the conversation they have had with nature. There is no man who does not anticipate a supersensual utility in the sun, and stars, earth, and water. These stand and wait to render him a peculiar service. But there is some obstruction, or some excess of phlegm in our constitution, which does not suffer them to yield the due effect. Too feeble fall the impressions of nature on us to make us artists. Every touch should thrill. Every man should be so much an artist, that he could report in conversation what had befallen him. Yet, in our experience, the rays or appulses have sufficient force to arrive at the senses, but not enough to reach the quick, and compel the reproduction of themselves in speech. The poet is the person in whom these powers are in balance, the man without impediment, who sees and handles that which others dream of, traverses the whole scale of experience, and its representative of man, in virtue of being the largest power to receive and to impart.

For the Universe has three children, born at one time, which reappear, under different names, in every system of thought, whether they be called cause, operation, and effect; or, more poetically, Jove, Pluto, Neptune; or, theologically, the Father, the Spirit, and the Son; but which we will call here, the Knower, the Doer, and the Sayer. These stand respectively for the love of truth, for the love of good, and for the love of beauty. These three are equal. Each is that which he is essentially, so that he cannot be surmounted or analyzed, and each of these three has the power of the others latent in him, and his own patent.

The poet is the sayer, the namer, and represents beauty. He is a sovereign, and stands on the centre. For the world is not painted, or adorned, but is from the beginning beautiful; and God has not made some beautiful things, but Beauty is the creator of the universe. Therefore the poet is not any permissive potentate, but is emperor in his own right. Criticism is infested with a cant of materialism, which assumes that manual skill and activity is the first merit of all men, and disparages such as say and do not, overlooking the fact, that some men, namely, poets, are natural sayers, sent into the world to the end of expression, and confounds them with those whose province is action, but who quit it to imitate the sayers. But Homer's words are as costly and admirable to Homer, as Agamemnon's victories are to Agamemnon. The poet does not wait for the hero or the sage, but, as they act and think primarily, so he writes primarily what will and must be spoken, reckoning the others, though primaries also, yet, in respect to him, secondaries and servants; as sitters or models in the studio of a painter, or as assistants who bring building materials to an architect.

For poetry was all written before time was, and whenever we are so finely organized that we can penetrate into that region where the air is music, we hear those primal warblings, and attempt to write them down, but we lose ever and anon a word, or a verse, and substitute something of our own, and thus miswrite the poem. The men of more delicate ear write down these cadences more faithfully, and these transcripts, though imperfect, become the songs of the nations. For nature is as truly beautiful as it is good, or as it is reasonable, and must as much appear, as it must be done, or be known. Words and deeds are quite indifferent modes of the divine energy. Words are also actions, and actions are a kind of words.

The sign and credentials of the poet are, that he announces that which no man foretold. He is the true and only doctor; he knows and tells; he is the only teller of news, for he was present and privy to the appearance which he describes. He is a beholder of ideas, and an utterer of the necessary and causal. For we do not speak now of men of poetical talents, or of industry and skill in metre, but of the true poet. I took part in a conversation the other day, concerning a recent writer of lyrics, a man of subtle mind, whose head appeared to be a music-box of delicate tunes and rhythms, and whose skill, and command of language, we could not sufficiently praise. But when the question arose, whether he was not only a lyrist, but a poet, we were obliged to confess that he is plainly a contemporary, not an eternal man. He does not stand out of our low limitations, like a Chimborazo① under the line, running up from the torrid base through all the climates of the globe, with belts of the herbage of every latitude on its high and mottled sides; but this genius is the landscape garden of a modern house, adorned with fountains and statues, with well-bred men and women standing and sitting in the walks

① Chimborazo: a 20,560 feet high mountain peak in the Andes in Ecuador.

and terraces. We hear, through all the varied music, the ground-tone of conventional life. Our poets are men of talents who sing, and not the children of music. The argument is secondary, the finish of the verses is primary.

For it is not metres, but a metre-making argument, that makes a poem, —a thought so passionate and alive, that, like the spirit of a plant or an animal, it has an architecture of its own, and adorns nature with a new thing. The thought and the form are equal in the order of time, but in the order of genesis the thought is prior to the form. The poet has a new thought: he has a whole new experience to unfold; he will tell us how it was with him, and all men will be the richer in his fortune. For, the experience of each new age requires a new confession, and the world seems always waiting for its poet, I remember, when I was young, how much I was moved one morning by tidings that genius had appeared in a youth who sat near me at table. He had left his work, and gone rambling none knew whither, and had written hundreds of lines, but could not tell whether that which was in him was therein told: he could tell nothing but that all was changed, — man, beast, heaven, earth, and sea. How gladly we listened! how credulous! Society seemed to be compromised. We sat in the aurora of a sunrise which was to put out all the stars. Boston seemed to be at twice the distance it had the night before, or was much farther than that. Rome, — what was Rome? Plutarch and Shakespeare were in the yellow leaf, and Homer no more should be heard of. It is much to know that poetry has been written this very day, under this very roof by your side. What! that wonderful spirit has not expired! these stony moments are still sparkling and animated! I had fancied that the oracles were all silent, and nature had spent her fires, and behold! all night, from every pore, these fine auroras have been streaming. Every one has some interest in the advent of the poet, and no one knows how much it may concern him. We know that the secret of the world is profound, but who or what shall be our interpreter, we know not. A mountain ramble, a new style of face, a new person, may put the key into our hands. Of course, the value of genius to us is in the veracity of its report. Talent may frolic and juggle; genius realizes and adds. Mankind, in good earnest, have availed so far in understanding themselves and their work, that the foremost watchman on the peak announces his news. It is the truest word ever spoken, and the phrase will be the fittest, most musical, and the unerring voice of the world for that time.

All that we call sacred history attests that the birth of a poet is the principal event in chronology. Man, never so often deceived, still watches for the arrival of a brother who can hold him steady to a truth, until he has made it his own. With what joy I begin to read a poem, which I confide in as an inspiration. And now my chains are to be broken; I shall mount above these clouds and opaque airs in which I live, —opaque, though they seem transparent, — and from the heaven of truth I shall see and comprehend my relations. That will reconcile me to life, and renovate nature, to see trifles animated by a tendency, and to know what I am doing. Life will no more be a noise; now I shall see men and women, and know the signs by which they may be discerned from fools and satans. This day shall be better than my birthday: then I became an animal: now I am invited into the science of the real. Such is the hope, but the fruition is postponed. Oftener it falls, that this winged man, who will carry me into the heaven, whirls me into the clouds, then leaps and frisks about with me from cloud to cloud, still affirming that he is bound heavenward; and I, being myself a novice, and slow in perceiving that he does not know the way into the heavens, and is merely bent that I should admire his skill to rise, like a flow or a flying fish, a little way from the ground or the water; but the all-piercing, all-feeding, and ocular air of heaven, that man shall never inhabit. I tumble down again soon into my old nooks, and lead the life of exaggerations as before, and have lost my faith in the possibility of any guide who can lead me thither where I would be.

But leaving these victims of vanity, let us, with new hope, observe how nature, by worthier impulses, has ensured the poet's fidelity to his office of announcement and affirming, namely, by the beauty of things, which becomes a new, and higher beauty, when expressed. Nature offers all her creatures to him as a picture-language. Being used as a type, a second wonderful value appears in the object, far better than its old value, as the carpenter's stretched cord, if you hold your ear close enough, is musical in the breeze.

"Things more excellent than every image," says Jamblichus[①], "are expressed through images." Things admit of being used as symbols, because nature is a symbol, in the whole, and in every part. Every line we can draw in the sand, has expression; and there is no body without its spirit of genius. All form is an effect of character; all condition, of the quality of life; all harmony, of health; (and for this reason, a perception of beauty should be sympathetic, or proper only to the good). The beautiful rests on the foundations of the necessary. The soul makes the body, as the wise Spenser teaches: —So every spirit, as it is most pure,

And hath in it the more of heavenly light,
So it the fairer body doth procure
To habit in, and it more fairly dight,
With cheerful grace and amiable sight.
For, of the soul, the body form doth take,
For soul is form, and doth the body make.[②]

Here we find ourselves, suddenly, not in a critical speculation, but in a holy place, and should go very warily and reverently. We stand before the secret of the world, there

① Jamblichus: an ancient Syrian Neoplatonist philosopher.

② From "An Hymne in Honour of Beautie" by Edmund Spenser.

where Being passes into Appearance, and Unity into Variety.

The Universe is the externization of the soul. Wherever the life is, *that* bursts into appearance around it. Our science is sensual, and therefore superficial. The earth, and the heavenly bodies, physics, and chemistry, we sensually treat, as if they were self-existent; but these are the retinue of that Being we have. "The mighty heaven," said Proclus①, "exhibits, in its transfigurations, clear images of the splendor of intellectual perceptions; being moved in conjunction with the unapparent periods of intellectual natures." Therefore, science always goes abreast with the just elevation of the man, keeping step with religion and metaphysics; or, the state of science is an index of our self-knowledge. Since every thing in nature answers to a moral power, if any phenomenon remains brute and dark, it is that the corresponding faculty in the observer is not yet active.

No wonder, then, if these waters be so deep, that we hover over them with a religious regard. The beauty of the fable proves the importance of the sense; to the poet, and to all others; or if you please, every man is so far a poet as to be susceptible of these enchantments of nature: for all men have the thoughts whereof the universe is the celebration. I find that the fascination resides in the symbol. Who loves nature? Who does not? Is it only poets, and men of leisure and cultivation, who live with her? No; but also hunters, farmers, grooms, and butchers, though they express their affection in their choice of life, and not in their choice of words. The writer wonders what the coachman or the hunter values in riding, in horses, and dogs. It is not superficial qualities. When you talk with him, he holds these at as slight a rate as you. His worship is sympathetic; he has no definitions, but he is commanded in nature, by the living power which he feels to be there present. No imitation, or playing of these things, would content him; he loves the earnest of the northwind, of rain, of stone, and wood, and iron. A beauty not explicable, is dearer than a beauty which we can see to the end of. It is nature the symbol, nature certifying the supernatural, body overflowed by life, which he worships, with coarse, but sincere rites.

The inwardness and mystery of this attachment, drives men of every class to the use of emblems. The schools of poets, and philosophers, are not more intoxicated with their symbols, than the populace with theirs. In our political parties, compute the power of badges and emblems. See the great ball which they roll from Baltimore to Bunker Hill! In the political processions, Lowell goes in a loom, and Lynn in a shoe, and Salem in a ship. Witness the ciderbarrel, the log cabin, the hickory-stick, the palmetto, and all the cognizances of party. See the power of national emblems. Some stars, lilies, leopards, a crescent, a lion, an eagle, or other figure, which came into credit God knows how, on

① Proclus: Proclus Lycaeus (412 - 485 AD) was a Greek Neoplatonist philosopher, one of the last major Classical philosophers.

an old rag of bunting, blowing in the wind, on a fort, at the ends of the earth, shall make the blood tingle under the rudest, or the most conventional exterior. The people fancy they hate poetry, and they are all poets and mystics!

Beyond this universality of the symbolic language, we are apprised of the divineness of this superior use of things, whereby the world is a temple, whose walls are covered with emblems, pictures, and commandments of the Deity, in this, that there is no fact in nature which does not carry the whole sense of nature; and the distinctions which we make in events, and in affairs, of low and high, honest and base, disappear when nature is used as a symbol. Thought makes every thing fit for use. The vocabulary of an omniscient man would embrace words and images excluded from polite conversation. What would be base, or even obscene, to the obscene, becomes illustrious, spoken in a new connection of thought. The piety of the Hebrew prophets purges their grossness. The circumcision is an example of the power of poetry to raise the low and offensive. Small and mean things serve as well as great symbols. The meaner the type by which a law is expressed, the more pungent it is, and the more lasting in the memories of men: just as we choose the smallest box, or case, in which any needful utensil can be carried. Bare lists of words are found suggestive, to an imaginative and excited mind; as it is related of Lord Chatham, that he was accustomed to read in Bailey's Dictionary, when he was preparing to speak in Parliament. The poorest experience is rich enough for all the purposes of expressing thought. Why covet a knowledge of new facts? Day and night, house and garden, a few books, a few actions, serve us as well as would all trades and all spectacles. We are far from having exhausted the significance of the few symbols we use. We can come to use them yet with a terrible simplicity. It does not need that a poem should be long. Every word was once a poem. Every new relation is a new word. Also, we use defects and deformities to a sacred purpose, so expressing our sense that the evils of the world are such only to the evil eye. In the old mythology, mythologists observe, defects are ascribed to divine natures, as lameness to Vulcan①, blindness to Cupid②, and the like, to signify exuberances.

For, as it is dislocation and detachment from the life of God, that makes things ugly, the poet, who re-attaches things to nature and the Whole, — reattaching even artificial things and violations of nature, to nature, by a deeper insight — disposes very easily of the most disagreeable facts. Readers of poetry see the factory-village, and the railway, and fancy that the poetry of the landscape is broken up by these; for these works of art are not yet consecrated in their readings; but the poet sees them fall within the great Order not less than the bee-hive, or the spider's geometrical web. Nature adopts them very fast into her vital circles, and the gliding train of cars she loves like her

① Vulcan: god of fire and metal working.

② Cupid: god of love.

own. Besides, in a centred mind, it signifies nothing how many mechanical inventions you exhibit. Though you add millions, and never so surprising, the fact of mechanics has not gained a grain's weight. The spiritual fact remains unalterable, by many or by few particulars; as no mountain is of any appreciable height to break the curve of the sphere. As shrewd country-boy goes to the city for the first time, and the complacent citizen is not satisfied with his little wonder. It is not that he does not see all the fine houses, and know that he never saw such before, but he disposes of them as easily as the poet finds place for the railway. The chief value of the new fact, is to enhance the great and constant fact of Life, which can dwarf any and every circumstance, and to which the belt of wampum, and the commerce of America, are alike.

The world being thus put under the mind for verb and noun, the poet is he who can articulate it. For, though life is great, and fascinates, and absorbs, and though all men are intelligent of the symbols through which it is named, yet they cannot originally use them. We are symbols, and inhabit symbols; workman, work, and tools, words and things, birth and death, all are emblems; but we sympathize with the symbols, and, being infatuated with the economical uses of things, we do not know that they are thoughts. The poet, by an ulterior intellectual perception, gives them a power which makes their old use forgotten, and puts eyes, and a tongue into every dumb and inanimate object. He perceives the independence of the thought on the symbol, the stability of the thought, the accidency and fugacity of the symbol. As the eyes of Lyncaeus were said to see through the earth, so the poet turns the world to glass, and shows us all things in their right series and procession. For, through that better perception, he stands one step nearer to things, and sees the flowing or metamorphosis; perceives that thought is multiform; that within the form of every creature is a force impelling it to ascend into a higher form; and, following with his eyes the life, uses the forms which express that life, and so his speech flows with the flowing of nature. All the facts of the animal economy, sex, nutriment, gestation, birth, growth, are symbols of the passage of the world into the soul of man, to suffer there a change, and reappear a new and higher fact. He uses forms according to the life, and not according to the form. This is true science. The poet alone knows astronomy, chemistry, vegetation, and animation, for he does not stop at these facts, but employs them as signs. He knows why the plain, or meadow of space, was strown with these flowers we call suns, and moons, and stars; why the great deep is adorned with animals, with men, and gods; for, in every word he speaks he rides on them as the horses of thought.

By virtue of this science the poet is the Namer, or Language-maker, naming things sometimes after their appearance, sometimes after their essence, and giving to every one its own name and not another's, thereby rejoicing the intellect, which delights in detachment or boundary. The poets made all the words, and therefore language is the archives of history, and, if we must say it, a sort of tomb of the muses. For, though the origin of most of our words is forgotten, each word was at first a stroke of genius, and obtained currency, because for the moment it symbolized the world to the first speaker and to the hearer. The etymologist finds the deadest word to have been once a brilliant picture. Language is fossil poetry. As the limestone of the continent consists of infinite masses of the shells of animalcules, so language is made up of images, or tropes, which now, in their secondary use, have long ceased to remind us of their poetic origin. But the poet names the thing because he sees it, or comes one step nearer to it than any other. This expression or naming, is not art, but a second nature, grown out of the first, as a leaf out of a tree. What we call nature, is a certain self-regulated motion, or change; and nature does all things by her own hands, and does not leave another to baptize her, but baptizes herself; and this through the metamorphosis again. I remember that a certain poet[1] described it to me thus:

Genius is the activity which repairs the decays of things, whether wholly or partly of a material and finite kind. Nature through all her kingdoms, insures herself. Nobody cares for planting the poor fungus: so she shakes down from the gills of one agaric countless spores, any one of which, being preserved, transmits new billions of spores to-morrow or next day. The new agaric of this hour has a chance which the old one had not. This atom of seed is thrown into a new place, not subject to the accidents which destroyed its parent two rods off. She makes a man; and having brought him to ripe age, she will no longer run the risk of losing this wonder at a blow, but she detaches from him a new self, that the kind may be safe from accidents to which the individual is exposed. So when the soul of the poet has come to ripeness of thought she detaches and sends away from it its poems or songs, — a fearless, sleepless, deathless progeny, which is not exposed to the accidents of the weary kingdom of time: a fearless, vivacious offspring, clad with wings (such was the virtue of the soul out of which they came), which carry them fast and far, and infix them irrecoverably into the hearts of men. These wings are the beauty of the poet's soul. The songs, thus flying immortal from their mortal parent, are pursued by clamorous flights of censures, which swarm in far greater numbers, and threaten to devour them; but these last are not winged. At the end of a very short leap they fall plump down, and rot, having received from the souls out of which they came no beautiful wings. But the melodies of the poet ascend, and leap, and pierce into the deeps of infinite time.

So far the bard taught me, using his freer speech. But nature has a higher end, in the production of new individuals, than security, namely, ascension, or the passage of the soul into higher forms. I knew, in my younger days, the sculptor who made the statue of the youth which stands in the public garden. He was, as I remember, unable to tell directly, what made him happy, or unhappy, but by wonderful indirections he could

① A certain poet: referring to Plato.

tell. He rose one day, according to his habit, before the dawn, and saw the morning break, grand as the eternity out of which it came, and, for many days after, he strove to express this tranquillity, and lo! his chisel had fashioned out of marble the form of a beautiful youth, Phosphorus, whose aspect is such, that, it is said, all persons who look on it become silent. The poet also resigns himself to his mood, and that thought which agitated him is expressed, but alter idem① in a manner totally new. The expression is organic, or, the new type which things themselves take when liberated. As, in the sun, objects paint their images on the retina of the eye, so they, sharing the aspiration of the whole universe, tend to paint a far more delicate copy of their essence in his mind. Like the metamorphosis of things into higher organic forms, is their change into melodies. Over every thing stands its daemon, or soul, and, as the form of the thing is reflected by the eye, so the soul of the thing is reflected by a melody. The sea, the mountain-ridge, Niagara, and every flower-bed, pre-exist, or super-exist, in pre-cantations, which sail like odors in the air, and when any man goes by with an ear sufficiently fine, he overhears them, and endeavors to write down the notes, without diluting or depraving them. And herein is the legitimation of criticism, in the mind's faith, that the poems are a corrupt version of some text in nature, with which they ought to be made to tally. A rhyme in one of our sonnets should not be less pleasing than the iterated nodes of a sea-shell, or the resembling difference of a group of flowers. The pairing of the birds is an idyl, not tedious as our idyls are; a tempest is a rough ode, without falsehood or rant: a summer, with its harvest sown, reaped, and stored, is an epic song, subordinating how many admirably executed parts. Why should not the symmetry and truth that modulate these, glide into our spirits, and we participate the invention of nature?

This insight, which expresses itself by what is called Imagination, is a very high sort of seeing, which does not come by study, but by the intellect being where and what it sees, by sharing the path, or circuit of things through forms, and making them translucid to others. The path of things is silent. Will they suffer a speaker to go with them? A spy they will not suffer; a lover, a poet, is the transcendency of their own nature, —him they will suffer. The condition of true naming, on the poet's part, is his resigning himself to the divine aura which breathes through forms, and accompanying that.

It is a secret which every intellectual man quickly learns, that, beyond the energy of his possessed and conscious intellect, he is capable of a new energy (as of an intellect doubled on itself), by abandonment to the nature of things; that, beside his privacy of power as an individual man, there is a great public power, on which he can draw, by unlocking, at all risks, his human doors, and suffering the ethereal tides to roll and circulate through him: then he is caught up into the life of the Universe, his speech is thunder, his thought is law, and his words are universally intelligible as the plants and

① alter idem: another one of the same kind.

animals. The poet knows that he speaks adequately, then, only when he speaks somewhat wildly, or,"with the flower of the mind"; not with the intellect, used as an organ, but with the intellect released from all service, and suffered to take its direction from its celestial life; or, as the ancients were wont to express themselves, not with intellect alone, but with the intellect inebriated by nectar. As the traveller who has lost his way, throws his reins on his horse's neck, and trusts to the instinct of the animal to find his road, so must we do with the divine animal who carries us through this world. For if in any manner we can stimulate this instinct, new passages are opened for us into nature, the mind flows into and through things hardest and highest, and the metamorphosis is possible.

This is the reason why bards love wine, mead, narcotics, coffee, tea, opium, the fumes of sandalwood and tobacco, or whatever other species of animal exhilaration. All men avail themselves of such means as they can, to add this extraordinary power to their normal powers; and to this end they prize conversation, music, pictures, sculpture, dancing, theatres, travelling, war, mobs, fires, gaming, politics, or love, or science, or animal intoxication, which are several coarser or finer quasi-mechanical substitutes for the true nectar, which is the ravishment of the intellect by coming nearer to the fact. These are auxiliaries to the centrifugal tendency of a man, to his passage out into free space, and they help him to escape the custody of that body in which he is pent up, and of that jail-yard of individual relations in which he is enclosed. Hence a great number of such as were professionally expressors of Beauty, as painters, poets, musicians, and actors, have been more than others wont to lead a life of pleasure and indulgence; all but the few who received the true nectar; and, as it was a spurious mode of obtaining freedom, an emancipation not into the heavens, but into the freedom of baser places, they were punished for that advantage they won, by a dissipation and deterioration. But never can any advantage be taken of nature by a trick. The spirit of the world, the great calm presence of the creator, comes not forth to the sorceries of opium or of wine. The sublime vision comes to the pure and simple soul in a clean and chaste body. That is not an inspiration which we owe to narcotics, but some counterfeit excitement and fury. Milton says, that the lyric poet may drink wine and live generously, but the epic poet, he who shall sing of the gods, and their descent unto men, must drink water out of a wooden bowl.

For poetry is not"Devil's wine," but God's wine. It is with this as it is with toys. We fill the hands and nurseries of our children with all manner of dolls, drums, and horses, withdrawing their eyes from the plain face and sufficing object of nature, the sun, and moon, the animals, the water, and stones, which should be their toys. So the poet's habit of living should be set on a key so low and plain, that the common influences should delight him. His cheerfulness should be the gift of the sunlight; the air should suffice for his inspiration, and he should be tipsy with water. That spirit which suffices quiet hearts, which seems to come forth to such from every dry knoll of sere grass, from every pinestump, and half-imbedded stone, on which the dull March sun shines, comes forth to the poor and hungry, and such as are of simple taste. If thou fill thy brain with Boston and New York, with fashion and covetousness, and wilt stimulate thy jaded senses with wine and French coffee, thou shalt find no radiance of wisdom in the lonely waste of the pinewoods.

If the imagination intoxicates the poet, it is not inactive in other men. The metamorphosis excites in the beholder an emotion of joy.

The use of symbols has a certain power of emancipation and exhilaration for all men. We seem to be touched by a wand, which makes us dance and run about happily, like children. We are like persons who come out of a cave or cellar into the open air. This is the effect on us of tropes, fables, oracles, and all poetic forms. Poets are thus liberating gods. Men have really got a new sense, and found within their world, another world or nest of worlds; for the metamorphosis once seen, we divine that it does not stop. I will not now consider how much this makes the charm of algebra and the mathematics, which also, have their tropes, but it is felt in every definition; as, when Aristotle defines space to be an immovable vessel, in which things are contained;—or, when Plato defines a line to be a flowing point; or, figure to be a bound of solid; and many the like. What a joyful sense of freedom we have, when Vitruvius announces the old opinion of artists, that no architect can build any house well, who does not know something of anatomy. When Socrates, in "Charmides", tells us that the soul is cured of its maladies by certain incantations, and that these incantations are beautiful reasons, from which temperance is generated in souls; when Plato calls the world an animal; and Timaeus affirms that the plants also are animals; or affirms a man to be a heavenly tree, growing with his root, which is his head, upward; and, as George Chapman, following him, writes,—

So in our tree of man, whose nervie root
Springs in his top;

when Orpheus speaks of hoariness as "that white flower which marks extreme old age;" when Proclus calls the universe the statue of the intellect; when Chaucer, in his praise of "Gentilesse," compares good blood in mean condition to fire, which, though carried to the darkest house betwixt this and the mount of Caucasus, will yet hold its natural office, and burn as bright as if twenty thousand men did it behold; when John saw, in the apocalypse, the ruin of the world through evil, and the stars fall from heaven, as the figtree casteth her untimely fruit; when Esop reports the whole catalogue of common daily relations through the masquerade of birds and beasts;—we take the cheerful hint of the immortality of our essence, and its versatile habit and escapes, as when the gypsies say, "it is vain to hang them, they cannot die."

The poets are thus liberating gods. The ancient British bards had for the title of their order,"Those who are free throughout the world." They are free, and they make free. An imaginative book renders us much more service at first, by stimulating us through its tropes, than afterward, when we arrive at the precise sense of the author. I think nothing is of any value in books, excepting the transcendental and extraordinary. If a man is inflamed and carried away by his thought, to that degree that he forgets the authors and the public, and heeds only this one dream, which holds him like an insanity, let me read his paper, and you may have all the arguments and histories and criticism. All the value which attaches to Pythagoras, Paracelsus, Cornelius Agrippa, Cardan, Kepler, Swedenborg, Schelling, Oken, or any other who introduces questionable facts into his cosmogony, as angels, devils, magic, astrology, palmistry, mesmerism, and so on, is the certificate we have of departure from routine, and that here is a new witness. That also is the best success in conversation, the magic of liberty, which puts the world like a ball, in our hands. How cheap even the liberty then seems; how mean to study, when an emotion communicates to the intellect the power to sap and upheave nature: how great the perspective! nations, times, systems, enter and disappear like threads in tapestry of large figure and many colors; dream delivers us to dream, and, while the drunkenness lasts, we will sell our bed, our philosophy, our religion, in our opulence.

There is good reason why we should prize this liberation. The fate of the poor shepherd, who, blinded and lost in the snow-storm, perishes in a drift within a few feet of his cottage door, is an emblem of the state of man. On the brink of the waters of life and truth, we are miserably dying. The inaccessibleness of every thought but that we are in, is wonderful. What if you come near to it, — you are as remote, when you are nearest, as when you are farthest. Every thought is also a prison; every heaven is also a prison. Therefore we love the poet, the inventor, who in any form, whether in an ode, or in an action, or in looks and behavior, has yielded us a new thought. He unlocks our chains, and admits us to a new scene.

This emancipation is dear to all men, and the power to impart it, as it must come from greater depth and scope of thought, is a measure of intellect. Therefore all books of the imagination endure, all which ascend to that truth, that the writer sees nature beneath him, and uses it as his exponent. Every verse or sentence, possessing this virtue, will take care of its own immortality. The religions of the world are the ejaculations of a few imaginative men.

But the quality of the imagination is to flow, and not to freeze. The poet did not stop at the color, or the form, but read their meaning; neither may he rest in this meaning; but he makes the same objects exponents of his new thought. Here is the difference betwixt the poet and the mystic, that the last nails a symbol to one sense, which was a true sense for a moment, but soon becomes old and false. For all symbols are fluxional; all language is vehicular and transitive, and is good, as ferries and horses are, for conveyance, not as farms and houses are, for homestead. Mysticism consists in the mistake of an accidental and individual symbol for an universal one. The morning-redness happens to be the favorite meteor to the eyes of Jacob Behman①, and comes to stand to him for truth and faith; and he believes should stand for the same realities to every reader. But the first reader prefers as naturally the symbol of a mother and child, or a gardener and his bulb, or a jeweller polishing a gem. Either of these, or of a myriad more, are equally good to the person to whom they are significant. Only they must be held lightly, and be very willingly translated into the equivalent term which others use. And the mystic must be steadily told, —All that you say is just as true without the tedious use of that symbol as with it. Let us have a little algebra, instead of this trite rhetoric, —universal signs, instead of these village symbols, — and we shall both be gainers. The history of hierarchies seems to show, that all religious error consisted in making the symbol too stark and solid, and, at last, nothing but an excess of the organ of language.

Swedenborg, of all men in the recent ages, stands eminently for the translator of nature into thought. I do not know the man in history to whom things stood so uniformly for words. Before him the metamorphosis continually plays. Every thing on which his eye rests, obeys the impulses of moral nature. The figs become grapes whilst he eats them. When some of his angels affirmed a truth, the laurel twig which they held blossomed in their hands. The noise which, at a distance, appeared like gnashing and thumping, on coming nearer was found to be the voice of disputants. The men, in one of his visions, seen in heavenly light, appeared like dragons, and seemed in darkness: but, to each other, they appeared as men, and, when the light from heaven shone into their cabin, they complained of the darkness, and were compelled to shut the window that they might see.

There was this perception in him, which makes the poet or seer, an object of awe and terror, namely, that the same man, or society of men, may wear one aspect to themselves and their companions, and a different aspect to higher intelligences. Certain priests, whom he describes as conversing very learnedly together, appeared to the children, who were at some distance, like dead horses: and many the like misappearances. And instantly the mind inquires, whether these fishes under the bridge, yonder oxen in the pasture, those dogs in the yard, are immutably fishes, oxen, and dogs, or only so appear to me, and perchance to themselves appear upright men; and whether I appear as a man to all eyes. The Brahmins and Pythagoras propounded the same question, and if any poet has witnessed the transformation, he doubtless found it in harmony with various experiences. We have all seen changes as considerable in wheat and caterpillars. He is the poet, and shall draw us with love and terror, who sees, through the flowing vest, the firm nature, and can declare it.

I look in vain for the poet whom I describe. We do not, with sufficient plainness, or sufficient profoundness, address ourselves to life, nor dare we chant our own times and

① Jacob Behman: probably referring to Jakob Böhme, an ancient German Christian mystic and theologian.

social circumstance. If we filled the day with bravery, we should not shrink from celebrating it. Time and nature yield us many gifts, but not yet the timely man, the new religion, the reconciler, whom all things await. Dante's praise is, that he dared to write his autobiography in colossal cipher, or into universality. We have yet had no genius in America, with tyrannous eye, which knew the value of our incomparable materials, and saw, in the barbarism and materialism of the times, another carnival of the same gods whose picture he so much admires in Homer; then in the middle age; then in Calvinism[①]. Banks and tariffs the newspaper and caucus, methodism and unitarianism, are flat and dull to dull people, but rest on the same foundations of wonder as the town of Troy, and the temple of Delphos, and are as swiftly passing away. Our logrolling, our stumps and their politics, our fisheries, our Negroes, and Indians, our boats, and our repudiations, the wrath of rogues, and the pusillanimity of honest men, the northern trade, the southern planting, the western clearing, Oregon, and Texas, are yet unsung. Yet America is a poem in our eyes; its ample geography dazzles the imagination, and it will not wait long for metres. If I have not found that excellent combination of gifts in my countrymen which I seek, neither could I aid myself to fix the idea of the poet by reading now and then in Chalmers collection of five centuries of English poets. These are wits, more than poets, though there have been poets among them. But when we adhere to the ideal of the poet, we have our difficulties even with Milton and Homer. Milton is too literary, and Homer too literal and historical.

But I am not wise enough for a national criticism, and must see the old largeness a little longer, to discharge my errand from the muse to the poet concerning his art.

Art is the path of the creator to his work. The paths, or methods, are ideal and eternal, though few men ever see them, not the artist himself for years, or for a lifetime, unless he come into the conditions. The painter, the sculptor, the composer, the epic rhapsodist, the orator, all partake one desire, namely, to express themselves symmetrically and abundantly, not dwarfishly and fragmentarily. They found or put themselves in certain conditions, as, the painter and sculptor before some impressive human figures; the orator, into the assembly of the people; and the others, in such scenes as each has found exciting to his intellect; and each presently feels the new desire. He hears a voice, he sees a beckoning. Then he is apprised, with wonder, what herds of daemons hem him in. He can no more rest; he says, with the old painter, "By God, it is in me, and must go forth of me." He pursues a beauty, half seen, which flies before him. The poet pours out verses in every solitude. Most of the things he says are conventional, no doubt; but by and by he says something which is original and beautiful. That charms him. He would say nothing else but such things. In our way of talking, we

① Calvinism: a theological system created by John Calvin which emphasizes the omnipotence of God and salvation by grace alone.

say, "That is yours, this is mine;" but the poet knows well that it is not his; that it is as strange and beautiful to him as to you; he would fain hear the like eloquence at length. Once having tasted this immortal ichor, he cannot have enough of it, and, as an admirable creative power exists in these intellections, it is of the last importance that these things get spoken. What a little of all we know is said! What drops of all the sea of our science are baled up! and by what accident it is that these are exposed, when so many secrets sleep in nature! Hence the necessity of speech and song; hence these throbs and heart-beatings in the orator, at the door of the assembly, to the end, namely, that thought may be ejaculated as Logos, or Word.

Doubt not, O poet, but persist. Say, "It is in me, and shall out." Stand there, balked and dumb, stuttering and stammering, hissed and hooted, stand and strive, until, at last, rage draw out of thee that dream-power which every night shows thee is thine own; a power transcending all limit and privacy, and by virtue of which a man is the conductor of the whole river of electricity. Nothing walks, or creeps, or grows, or exists, which must not in turn arise and walk before him as exponent of his meaning. Comes he to that power, his genius is no longer exhaustible. All the creatures, by pairs and by tribes, pour into his mind as into a Noah's ark, to come forth again to people a new world. This is like the stock of air for our respiration, or for the combustion of our fireplace, not a measure of gallons, but the entire atmosphere if wanted. And therefore the rich poets, as Homer, Chaucer, Shakespeare, and Raphael, have obviously no limits to their works, except the limits of their lifetime, and resemble a mirror carried through the street, ready to render an image of every created thing.

O poet! a new nobility is conferred in groves and pastures, and not in castles, or by the sword-blade, any longer. The conditions are hard, but equal. Thou shalt leave the world, and know the muse only. Thou shalt not know any longer the times, customs, graces, politics, or opinions of men, but shalt take all from the muse. For the time of towns is tolled from the world by funeral chimes, but in nature the universal hours are counted by succeeding tribes of animals and plants, and by growth of joy on joy. God wills also that thou abdicate a manifold and duplex life, and that thou be content that others speak for thee. Others shall be thy gentlemen, and shall represent all courtesy and worldly life for thee; others shall do the great and resounding actions also. Thou shalt lie close hid with nature, and canst not be afforded to the Capitol or the Exchange. The world is full of renunciations and apprenticeships, and this is thine: thou must pass for a fool and a churl for a long season. This is the screen and sheath in which Pan has protected his well-beloved flower, and thou shalt be known only to thine own, and they shall console thee with tenderest love. And thou shalt not be able to rehearse the names of thy friends in thy verse, for an old shame before the holy ideal. And this is the reward: that the ideal shall be real to thee, and the impressions of the actual world shall fall like summer rain, copious, but not troublesome, to thy invulnerable essence. Thou shalt have the whole land for thy park and manor, the sea for thy bath and navigation, without tax and without envy; the woods and the rivers thou shalt own; and thou shalt possess that wherein others are only tenants and boarders. Thou true land-lord! sea-lord! air-lord! Wherever snow falls, or water flows, or birds fly, wherever day and night meet in twilight, wherever the blue heaven is hung by clouds, or sown with stars, wherever are forms with transparent boundaries, wherever are outlets into celestial space, wherever is danger, and awe, and love, there is Beauty, plenteous as rain, shed for thee, and though thou shouldest walk the world over, thou shalt not be able to find a condition inopportune or ignoble.

## 2. Edgar Allan Poe

### The Philosophy of Composition (1846)

*"The Philosophy of Composition" is an 1846 essay written by Edgar Allan Poe that introduces Poe's theories regarding literature. The essay is a methodical account of how he came to write "The Raven." He describes the deliberate choices he made in composing the poem, and the choices reveal his aesthetic. He advises brevity to communicate the essential "effect" of a piece. Beauty is the "province" of his work, and "melancholy... the most legitimate of all the poetical tones." Poe discusses theme, setting, sound, and the merits of refrain. And, in the composition of "The Raven" in particular, he describes how he arrived at the figure of a raven instead of a parrot.*

Charles Dickens, in a note now lying before me①, alluding to an examination I once made of the mechanism of "Barnaby Rudge②," says—"By the way, are you aware that Godwin wrote his 'Caleb Williams' backwards? He first involved his hero in a web of difficulties, forming the second volume, and then, for the first, cast about him for some mode of accounting for what had been done."

I cannot think this the precise mode of procedure on the part of Godwin③—and indeed what he himself acknowledges, is not altogether in accordance with Mr. Dickens' idea—but the author of "Caleb Williams"④ was too good an artist not to perceive the

① a note now lying before me: Poe begins with this essay by referring to a note (or letter) from Dickens, so as to grant his essay's credibility.

② "Barnaby Rudge" is a historical novel by Dickens, published in 1841.

③ Godwin: referring William Godwin (1756—1836), an English journalist, political philosopher and novelist, and also the father of Mary Shelley.

④ Caleb Williams: *The Adventures of Caleb Williams*, is an famous novel of Godwin, it is believed to be a weapon that has attacked aristocratic privilege, and also the first mystery novel.

advantage derivable from at least a somewhat similar process. Nothing is more clear than that every plot, worth the name, must be elaborated to its denouement before anything be attempted with the pen. It is only with the denouement constantly in view that we can give a plot its indispensable air of consequence, or causation, by making the incidents, and especially the tone at all points, tend to the development of the intention.

There is a radical error, I think, in the usual mode of constructing a story. Either history affords a thesis—or one is suggested by an incident of the day—or, at best, the author sets himself to work in the combination of striking events to form merely the basis of his narrative—designing, generally, to fill in with description, dialogue, or autorial comment, whatever crevices of fact, or action, may, from page to page, render themselves apparent.

I prefer commencing with the consideration of an effect. Keeping originality always in view—for he is false to himself who ventures to dispense with so obvious and so easily attainable a source of interest—I say to myself, in the first place, "Of the innumerable effects, or impressions, of which the heart, the intellect, or (more generally) the soul is susceptible, what one shall I, on the present occasion, select?" Having chosen a novel, first, and secondly a vivid effect, I consider whether it can be best wrought by incident or tone — whether by ordinary incidents and peculiar tone, or the converse, or by peculiarity both of incident and tone—afterward looking about me (or rather within) for such combinations of event, or tone, as shall best aid me in the construction of the effect.

I have often thought how interesting a magazine paper might be written by any author who would — that is to say, who could — detail, step by step, the processes by which any one of his compositions attained its ultimate point of completion. Why such a paper has never been given to the world, I am much at a loss to say—but, perhaps, the autorial vanity has had more to do with the omission than any one other cause. Most writers—poets in especial—prefer having it understood that they compose by a species of fine frenzy—an ecstatic intuition—and would positively shudder at letting the public take a peep behind the scenes, at the elaborate and vacillating crudities of thought — at the true purposes seized only at the last moment — at the innumerable glimpses of idea that arrived not at the maturity of full view—at the fully-matured fancies discarded in despair as unmanageable—at the cautious selections and rejections—at the painful erasures and interpolations—in a word, at the wheels and pinions—the tackle for scene-shifting—the step-ladders, and demon-traps—the cock's feathers, the red paint and the black patches, which, in ninety-nine cases out of a hundred, constitute the properties of the literary histrio.

I am aware, on the other hand, that the case is by no means common, in which an author is at all in condition to retrace the steps by which his conclusions have been attained. In general, suggestions, having arisen pell-mell are pursued and forgotten in a similar manner.

For my own part, I have neither sympathy with the repugnance alluded to, nor, at any time, the least difficulty in recalling to mind the progressive steps of any of my compositions, and, since the interest of an analysis or reconstruction, such as I have considered a desideratum, is quite independent of any real or fancied interest in the thing analysed, it will not be regarded as a breach of decorum on my part to show the modus operandi① by which some one of my own works was put together. I select "The Raven"② as most generally known. It is my design to render it manifest that no one point in its composition is referable either to accident or intuition—that the work proceeded step by step, to its completion, with the precision and rigid consequence of a mathematical problem.

Let us dismiss, as irrelevant to the poem, per se③, the circumstance—or say the necessity—which, in the first place, gave rise to the intention of composing a poem that should suit at once the popular and the critical taste.

We commence, then, with this intention.

The initial consideration was that of extent. If any literary work is too long to be read at one sitting, we must be content to dispense with the immensely important effect derivable from unity of impression—for, if two sittings be required, the affairs of the world interfere, and everything like totality is at once destroyed. But since, *ceteris paribus*④, no poet can afford to dispense with anything that may advance his design, it but remains to be seen whether there is, in extent, any advantage to counterbalance the loss of unity which attends it. Here I say no, at once. What we term a long poem is, in fact, merely a succession of brief ones—that is to say, of brief poetical effects. It is needless to demonstrate that a poem is such only inasmuch as it intensely excites, by elevating the soul; and all intense excitements are, through a psychal necessity, brief. For this reason, at least, one-half of the *Paradise Lost*⑤ is essentially prose—a succession of poetical excitements interspersed, inevitably, with corresponding depressions—the whole being deprived, through the extremeness of its length, of the vastly important artistic element, totality, or unity of effect.

It appears evident, then, that there is a distinct limit, as regards length, to all works of literary art—the limit of a single sitting—and that, although in certain classes of prose composition, such as *Robinson Crusoe*⑥(demanding no unity), this limit may be

① modus operandi: an unvarying or habitual method or procedure.

② "The Raven": a narrative poem and one of the most famous poems by Poe. This poem was said to be partly inspired by the raven in the Dickens' novel *Barnaby Rudge*.

③ per se: "by itself" or "in itself," usually referring to its inherent nature.

④ ceteris paribus: Latin, meaning under the condition of all other things being equal.

⑤ *Paradise Lost*: a famous epic poem by the 17th-century English poet John Milton.

⑥ *Robinson Crusoe*: a novel by Daniel Defoe, published in 1719.

advantageously overpassed, it can never properly be overpassed in a poem. Within this limit, the extent of a poem may be made to bear mathematical relation to its merit—in other words, to the excitement or elevation—again, in other words, to the degree of the true poetical effect which it is capable of inducing; for it is clear that the brevity must be in direct ratio of the intensity of the intended effect—this, with one proviso—that a certain degree of duration is absolutely requisite for the production of any effect at all.

Holding in view these considerations, as well as that degree of excitement which I deemed not above the popular, while not below the critical taste, I reached at once what I conceived the proper length for my intended poem—a length of about one hundred lines. It is, in fact, a hundred and eight.

My next thought concerned the choice of an impression, or effect, to be conveyed: and here I may as well observe that throughout the construction, I kept steadily in view the design of rendering the work universally appreciable. I should be carried too far out of my immediate topic were I to demonstrate a point upon which I have repeatedly insisted, and which, with the poetical, stands not in the slightest need of demonstration—the point, I mean, that Beauty is the sole legitimate province of the poem. A few words, however, in elucidation of my real meaning, which some of my friends have evinced a disposition to misrepresent. That pleasure which is at once the most intense, the most elevating, and the most pure is, I believe, found in the contemplation of the beautiful. When, indeed, men speak of Beauty, they mean, precisely, not a quality, as is supposed, but an effect—they refer, in short, just to that intense and pure elevation of soul—not of intellect, or of heart—upon which I have commented, and which is experienced in consequence of contemplating the "beautiful." Now I designate Beauty as the province of the poem, merely because it is an obvious rule of Art that effects should be made to spring from direct causes—that objects should be attained through means best adapted for their attainment—no one as yet having been weak enough to deny that the peculiar elevation alluded to is most readily attained in the poem. Now the object Truth, or the satisfaction of the intellect, and the object Passion, or the excitement of the heart, are, although attainable to a certain extent in poetry, far more readily attainable in prose. Truth, in fact, demands a precision, and Passion, a homeliness (the truly passionate will comprehend me), which are absolutely antagonistic to that Beauty which, I maintain, is the excitement or pleasurable elevation of the soul. It by no means follows, from anything here said, that passion, or even truth, may not be introduced, and even profitably introduced, into a poem for they may serve in elucidation, or aid the general effect, as do discords in music, by contrast—but the true artist will always contrive, first, to tone them into proper subservience to the predominant aim, and, secondly, to enveil them, as far as possible, in that Beauty which is the atmosphere and the essence of the poem.

Regarding, then, Beauty as my province, my next question referred to the tone of its highest manifestation—and all experience has shown that this tone is one of sadness. Beauty of whatever kind in its supreme development invariably excites the sensitive soul to tears. Melancholy is thus the most legitimate of all the poetical tones.

The length, the province, and the tone, being thus determined, I betook myself to ordinary induction, with the view of obtaining some artistic piquancy which might serve me as a key-note in the construction of the poem — some pivot upon which the whole structure might turn. In carefully thinking over all the usual artistic effects — or more properly points, in the theatrical sense — I did not fail to perceive immediately that no one had been so universally employed as that of the refrain. The universality of its employment sufficed to assure me of its intrinsic value, and spared me the necessity of submitting it to analysis. I considered it, however, with regard to its susceptibility of improvement, and soon saw it to be in a primitive condition. As commonly used, the refrain, or burden, not only is limited to lyric verse, but depends for its impression upon the force of monotone—both in sound and thought. The pleasure is deduced solely from the sense of identity—of repetition. I resolved to diversify, and so heighten the effect, by adhering in general to the monotone of sound, while I continually varied that of thought: that is to say, I determined to produce continuously novel effects, by the variation of the application of the refrain — the refrain itself remaining for the most part, unvaried.

These points being settled, I next bethought me of the nature of my refrain. Since its application was to be repeatedly varied it was clear that the refrain itself must be brief, for there would have been an insurmountable difficulty in frequent variations of application in any sentence of length. In proportion to the brevity of the sentence would, of course, be the facility of the variation. This led me at once to a single word as the best refrain.

The question now arose as to the character of the word. Having made up my mind to a refrain, the division of the poem into stanzas was of course a corollary, the refrain forming the close to each stanza. That such a close, to have force, must be sonorous and susceptible of protracted emphasis, admitted no doubt, and these considerations inevitably led me to the long *o* as the most sonorous vowel in connection with *r* as the most producible consonant.

The sound of the refrain being thus determined, it became necessary to select a word embodying this sound, and at the same time in the fullest possible keeping with that melancholy which I had pre-determined as the tone of the poem. In such a search it would have been absolutely impossible to overlook the word "Nevermore." In fact it was the very first which presented itself.

The next desideratum was a pretext for the continuous use of the one word "nevermore." In observing the difficulty which I had at once found in inventing a sufficiently plausible reason for its continuous repetition, I did not fail to perceive that this difficulty arose solely from the preassumption that the word was to be so continuously or monotonously spoken by a human being—I did not fail to perceive, in short, that the difficulty lay in the reconciliation of this monotony with the exercise of reason on the part of the creature repeating the word. Here, then, immediately arose the idea of a non-reasoning creature capable of speech, and very naturally, a parrot, in the first instance, suggested itself, but was superseded forthwith by a Raven as equally capable of speech, and infinitely more in keeping with the intended tone.

I had now gone so far as the conception of a Raven, the bird of ill-omen, monotonously repeating the one word"Nevermore" at the conclusion of each stanza in a poem of melancholy tone, and in length about one hundred lines. Now, never losing sight of the object—supremeness or perfection at all points, I asked myself—"Of all melancholy topics what, according to the universal understanding of mankind, is the most melancholy?" Death, was the obvious reply. "And when," I said, "is this most melancholy of topics most poetical?" From what I have already explained at some length the answer here also is obvious—"When it most closely allies itself to Beauty: the death then of a beautiful woman is unquestionably the most poetical topic in the world, and equally is it beyond doubt that the lips best suited for such topic are those of a bereaved lover."

I had now to combine the two ideas of a lover lamenting his deceased mistress and a Raven continuously repeating the word"Nevermore." I had to combine these, bearing in mind my design of varying at every turn the application of the word repeated, but the only intelligible mode of such combination is that of imagining the Raven employing the word in answer to the queries of the lover. And here it was that I saw at once the opportunity afforded for the effect on which I had been depending, that is to say, the effect of the variation of application. I saw that I could make the first query propounded by the lover—the first query to which the Raven should reply "Nevermore"—that I could make this first query a commonplace one, the second less so, the third still less, and so on, until at length the lover, startled from his original nonchalance by the melancholy character of the word itself, by its frequent repetition, and by a consideration of the ominous reputation of the fowl that uttered it, is at length excited to superstition, and wildly propounds queries of a far different character—queries whose solution he has passionately at heart—propounds them half in superstition and half in that species of despair which delights in self-torture—propounds them not altogether because he believes in the prophetic or demoniac character of the bird (which reason assures him is merely repeating a lesson learned by rote), but because he experiences a frenzied pleasure in so modelling his questions as to receive from the expected "Nevermore" the most delicious because the most intolerable of sorrows. Perceiving the opportunity thus afforded me, or, more strictly, thus forced upon me in the progress of the construction, I first established in my mind the climax or concluding query — that query to which

"Nevermore" should be in the last place an answer—that query in reply to which this word "Nevermore" should involve the utmost conceivable amount of sorrow and despair.

Here then the poem may be said to have had its beginning—at the end where all works of art should begin—for it was here at this point of my preconsiderations that I first put pen to paper in the composition of the stanza:

"Prophet!" said I, "thing of evil! prophet still if bird or devil!
By that Heaven that bends above us—by that God we both adore,
Tell this soul with sorrow laden, if, within the distant Aidenn,
It shall clasp a sainted maiden whom the angels name Lenore—
Clasp a rare and radiant maiden whom the angels name Lenore."
Quoth the Raven—"Nevermore."

I composed this stanza, at this point, first that, by establishing the climax, I might the better vary and graduate, as regards seriousness and importance, the preceding queries of the lover, and secondly, that I might definitely settle the rhythm, the metre, and the length and general arrangement of the stanza, as well as graduate the stanzas which were to precede, so that none of them might surpass this in rhythmical effect. Had I been able in the subsequent composition to construct more vigorous stanzas I should without scruple have purposely enfeebled them so as not to interfere with the climacteric effect.

And here I may as well say a few words of the versification. My first object (as usual) was originality. The extent to which this has been neglected in versification is one of the most unaccountable things in the world. Admitting that there is little possibility of variety in mere rhythm, it is still clear that the possible varieties of metre and stanza are absolutely infinite, and yet, for centuries, no man, in verse, has ever done, or ever seemed to think of doing, an original thing. The fact is that originality (unless in minds of very unusual force) is by no means a matter, as some suppose, of impulse or intuition. In general, to be found, it must be elaborately sought, and although a positive merit of the highest class, demands in its attainment less of invention than negation.

Of course I pretend to no originality in either the rhythm or metre of the "Raven." The former is trochaic—the latter is octametre acatalectic, alternating with heptametre catalectic repeated in the refrain of the fifth verse, and terminating with tetrametre catalectic. Less pedantically the feet employed throughout (trochees) consist of a long syllable followed by a short, the first line of the stanza consists of eight of these feet, the second of seven and a half (in effect two-thirds), the third of eight, the fourth of seven and a half, the fifth the same, the sixth three and a half. Now, each of these lines taken individually has been employed before, and what originality the "Raven" has, is in their combination into stanza; nothing even remotely approaching this has ever been attempted. The effect of this originality of combination is aided by other unusual and some altogether novel effects, arising from an extension of the application of the principles of rhyme and alliteration.

The next point to be considered was the mode of bringing together the lover and the Raven— and the first branch of this consideration was the locale. For this the most natural suggestion might seem to be a forest, or the fields—but it has always appeared to me that a close circumscription of space is absolutely necessary to the effect of insulated incident—it has the force of a frame to a picture. It has an indisputable moral power in keeping concentrated the attention, and, of course, must not be confounded with mere unity of place.

I determined, then, to place the lover in his chamber — in a chamber rendered sacred to him by memories of her who had frequented it. The room is represented as richly furnished— this in mere pursuance of the ideas I have already explained on the subject of Beauty, as the sole true poetical thesis.

The locale being thus determined, I had now to introduce the bird—and the thought of introducing him through the window was inevitable. The idea of making the lover suppose, in the first instance, that the flapping of the wings of the bird against the shutter, is a "tapping" at the door, originated in a wish to increase, by prolonging, the reader's curiosity, and in a desire to admit the incidental effect arising from the lover's throwing open the door, finding all dark, and thence adopting the half-fancy that it was the spirit of his mistress that knocked.

I made the night tempestuous, first to account for the Raven's seeking admission, and secondly, for the effect of contrast with the (physical) serenity within the chamber.

I made the bird alight on the bust of Pallas, also for the effect of contrast between the marble and the plumage—it being understood that the bust was absolutely suggested by the bird — the bust of Pallas being chosen, first, as most in keeping with the scholarship of the lover, and secondly, for the sonorousness of the word, Pallas, itself.

About the middle of the poem, also, I have availed myself of the force of contrast, with a view of deepening the ultimate impression. For example, an air of the fantastic— approaching as nearly to the ludicrous as was admissible — is given to the Raven's entrance. He comes in "with many a flirt and flutter."

Not the least obeisance made he—not a moment stopped or stayed he,
But with mien of lord or lady, perched above my chamber door.

In the two stanzas which follow, the design is more obviously carried out:—

Then this ebony bird, beguiling my sad fancy into smiling
By the grave and stern decorum of the countenance it wore,
"Though thy crest be shorn and shaven, thou," I said, "art sure no craven,
Ghastly grim and ancient Raven wandering from the Nightly shore—
Tell me what thy lordly name is on the Night's Plutonian shore?"①

① Plutonian shore: Coast of the underworld.

Quoth the Raven—"Nevermore."

Much I marvelled this ungainly fowl to hear discourse so plainly,
Though its answer little meaning—little relevancy bore;
For we cannot help agreeing that no living human being
Ever yet was blessed with seeing bird above his chamber door—
Bird or beast upon the sculptured bust above his chamber door,
With such name as "Nevermore."

The effect of the denouement being thus provided for, I immediately drop the fantastic for a tone of the most profound seriousness — this tone commencing in the stanza directly following the one last quoted, with the line,

But the Raven, sitting lonely on that placid bust, spoke only, etc.

From this epoch the lover no longer jests — no longer sees anything even of the fantastic in the Raven's demeanour. He speaks of him as a "grim, ungainly, ghastly, gaunt, and ominous bird of yore," and feels the "fiery eyes" burning into his "bosom's core." This revolution of thought, or fancy, on the lover's part, is intended to induce a similar one on the part of the reader — to bring the mind into a proper frame for the denouement—which is now brought about as rapidly and as directly as possible.

With the denouement proper—with the Raven's reply, "Nevermore," to the lover's final demand if he shall meet his mistress in another world— the poem, in its obvious phase, that of a simple narrative, may be said to have its completion. So far, everything is within the limits of the accountable—of the real. A raven, having learned by rote the single word "Nevermore," and having escaped from the custody of its owner, is driven at midnight, through the violence of a storm, to seek admission at a window from which a light still gleams — the chamber-window of a student, occupied half in poring over a volume, half in dreaming of a beloved mistress deceased. The casement being thrown open at the fluttering of the bird's wings, the bird itself perches on the most convenient seat out of the immediate reach of the student, who amused by the incident and the oddity of the visitor's demeanour, demands of it, in jest and without looking for a reply, its name. The raven addressed, answers with its customary word, "Nevermore"—a word which finds immediate echo in the melancholy heart of the student, who, giving utterance aloud to certain thoughts suggested by the occasion, is again startled by the fowl's repetition of "Nevermore." The student now guesses the state of the case, but is impelled, as I have before explained, by the human thirst for self-torture, and in part by superstition, to propound such queries to the bird as will bring him, the lover, the most of the luxury of sorrow, through the anticipated answer, "Nevermore." With the indulgence, to the extreme, of this self-torture, the narration, in what I have termed its first or obvious phase, has a natural termination, and so far there has been no overstepping of the limits of the real.

But in subjects so handled, however skillfully, or with however vivid an array of incident, there is always a certain hardness or nakedness which repels the artistical eye. Two things are invariably required — first, some amount of complexity, or more properly, adaptation; and, secondly, some amount of suggestiveness — some under-current, however indefinite, of meaning. It is this latter, in especial, which imparts to a work of art so much of that richness (to borrow from colloquy a forcible term), which we are too fond of confounding with the ideal. It is the excess of the suggested meaning—it is the rendering this the upper instead of the under-current of the theme—which turns into prose (and that of the very flattest kind), the so-called poetry of the so-called transcendentalists.

Holding these opinions, I added the two concluding stanzas of the poem — their suggestiveness being thus made to pervade all the narrative which has preceded them. The under-current of meaning is rendered first apparent in the line—

"Take thy beak from out my heart, and take thy form from off my door!"
Quoth the Raven "Nevermore!"

It will be observed that the words, "from out my heart," involve the first metaphorical expression in the poem. They, with the answer, "Nevermore," dispose the mind to seek a moral in all that has been previously narrated. The reader begins now to regard the Raven as emblematical — but it is not until the very last line of the very last stanza that the intention of making him emblematical of Mournful and never ending Remembrance is permitted distinctly to be seen:

And the Raven, never flitting, still is sitting, still is sitting,
On the pallid bust of Pallas just above my chamber door;
And his eyes have all the seeming of a demon that is dreaming,
And the lamplight o'er him streaming throws his shadow on the floor;
And my soul from out that shadow that lies floating on the floor
Shall be lifted—nevermore.

## 3. Walt Whitman

### from Preface to *Leaves of Grass*, first edition (1855)

*In "Preface to* Leaves of Grass, *" Whitman declares that America encloses the past and the future, and that Americans "have probably the fullest poetical nature. The United States themselves are essentially the greatest poem." This is because of the mix of races, of rich and poor, "a teeming nation of nations," where to be a poet is to be "commensurate with a people." In the preface, Whitman is concerned with the qualities of great poets, and their influence over people. To Whitman, there is no better thinker, helper or worker than the poet, who can outrun the swiftest runners, and who can "make every word he speaks draw blood." By his definition, the greatest poets avoid the trivial, instead turning small themes into big themes, connecting reality to the human soul. Among his commandments, Whitman charges his readers to love the earth, give alms to whoever asks it, to go freely, to have patience, "and dismiss whatever insults your own soul, and your very flesh shall be a great poem." The poet's role toward the universe is one of a lover to his beloved, and this dictum informs all of his work: "The proof of a poet is that his country absorbs him as affectionately as he has absorbed it."*

America does not repel the past or what it has produced under its forms or amid other politics or the idea of castes or the old religions... accepts the lesson with calmness... is not so impatient as has been supposed that the slough still sticks to opinions and manners and literature while the life which served its requirements has passed into the new life of the new forms perceives that the corpse is slowly borne from the eating and sleeping rooms of the house... perceives that it waits a little while in the door... that it was fittest for its days... that its action has descended to the stalwart and wellshaped heir who approaches... and that he shall be fittest for his days.

The Americans of all nations at any time upon the earth have probably the fullest poetical nature. The United States themselves are essentially the greatest poem. In the history of the earth hitherto① the largest and most stirring appear tame and orderly to their ampler largeness and stir. Here at last is something in the doings of man that corresponds with the broadcast doings of the day and night. Here is not merely a nation but a teeming nation of nations. Here is action untied from strings necessarily blind to particulars and details magnificently moving in vast masses. Here is the hospitality which forever indicates heroes. ... Here are the roughs and beards and space and ruggedness and nonchalance that the soul loves. Here the performance disdaining the trivial unapproached in the tremendous audacity of its crowds and groupings and the push of its perspective spreads with crampless and flowing breadth and showers its prolific and splendid extravagance. One sees it must indeed own the riches of the summer and winter, and need never be bankrupt while corn grows from the ground or the orchards drop apples or the bays contain fish or men beget children upon women.

Other states indicate themselves in their deputies... but the genius of the United States is not best or most in its executives or legislatures, nor in its ambassadors or authors or colleges or churches or parlors, nor even in its newspapers or inventors... but always most in the common people. Their manners speech dress friendships — the freshness and candor of their physiognomy — the picturesque looseness of their carriage... their deathless attachment to freedom—their aversion to anything indecorous

① hitherto: up to the present time.

or soft or mean—the practical acknowledgment of the citizens of one state by the citizens of all other states — the fierceness of their roused resentment — their Curiosity and welcome of novelty—their self-esteem and wonderful sympathy—their susceptibility to a slight—the air they have of persons who never knew how it felt to stand in the presence of superiors— the fluency of their speech their delight in music, the sure symptom of manly tenderness and native elegance of soul... their good temper and openhandedness— the terrible significance of their elections—the President's taking off his hat to them not they to him—these too are unrhymed poetry. It awaits the gigantic and generous treatment worthy of it.

The largeness of nature or the nation were monstrous without a corresponding largeness and generosity of the spirit of the citizen. Not nature nor swarming states nor streets and steamships nor prosperous business nor farms nor capital nor learning may suffice for the ideal of man... nor suffice the poet. No reminiscences may suffice either. A live nation can always cut a deep mark and can have the best authority the cheapest... namely from its own soul. This is the sum of the profitable uses of individuals or states and of present action and grandeur and of the subjects of poets. —As if it were necessary to trot back generation after generation to the eastern records! As if the beauty and sacredness of the demonstrable must fall behind that of the mythical! As if men do not make their mark out of any times! As if the opening of the western continent by discovery and what has transpired since in North and South America were less than the small theatre of the antique or the aimless sleepwalking of the middle ages! The pride of the United States leaves the wealth and finesse of the cities and all returns of commerce and agriculture and all the magnitude of geography or shows of exterior victory to enjoy the breed of full-sized men or one full-sized man unconquerable and simple.

The American poets are to enclose old and new for America is the race of races. Of them a bard is to be commensurate with a people. To him the other continents arrive as contributions... he gives them reception for their sake and his own sake. His spirit responds to his country's spirit... he incarnates its geography and natural life and rivers and lakes. Mississippi with annual freshets and changing chutes, Missouri and Columbia and Ohio and Saint Lawrence with the falls and beautiful masculine Hudson, do not embouchure where they spend themselves more than they embouchure into him. The blue breadth over the inland sea of Virginia and Maryland and the sea off Massachusetts and Maine and over Manhattan bay and over Champlain and Erie and over Ontario and Huron and Michigan and Superior, and over the Texan and Mexican and Floridian and Cuban seas and over the seas off California and Oregon, is not tallied by the blue breadth of the waters below more than the breadth of above and below is tallied by him. When the long Atlantic coast stretches longer and the Pacific coast stretches longer he easily stretches with them north or south. He spans between them also from east to west and reflects what is between them. On him rise solid growths that offset the growths of pine and cedar and hemlock and liveoak and locust and chestnut and cypress and hickory and limetree and cottonwood and tuliptree and cactus and wildvine and tamarind and persimmon... and tangles as tangled as any canebrake or swamp... and forests coated with transparent ice and icicles hanging from the boughs and crackling in the wind... and sides and peaks of mountains... and pasturage sweet and free as savannah or upland or prairie... with flights and songs and screams that answer those of the wildpigeon and highhold and orchard-oriole and coot and surf-duck and redshouldered-hawk and fish-hawk and white-ibis and indian-hen and cat-owl and water-pheasant and qua-bird and pied-sheldrake and blackbird and mockingbird and buzzard and condor and night-heron and eagle. To him the hereditary countenance descends both mother's and father's. To him enter the essences of the real things and past and present events—of the enormous diversity of temperature and agriculture and mines—the tribes of red aborigines—the weather-beaten vessels entering new ports or making landings on rocky coasts—the first settlements north or south—the rapid stature and muscle—the haughty defiance of '76, and the war and peace and formation of the constitution... the union always surrounded by blatherers and always calm and impregnable—the perpetual coming of immigrants—the wharfhem'd cities and superior marine—the unsurveyed interior—the loghouses and clearings and wild animals and hunters and trappers... the free commerce—the fisheries and whaling and gold-digging—the endless gestation of new states—the convening of Congress every December①, the members duly coming up from all climates and the uttermost parts... the noble character of the young mechanics and of all free American workmen and workwomen... the general ardor and friendliness and enterprise—the perfect equality of the female with the male... the large amativeness—the fluid movement of the population—the factories and mercantile life and laborsaving machinery—the Yankee swap②—the New-York firemen and the target excursion—the southern plantation life—the character of the northeast and of the northwest and south-west—slavery and the tremulous spreading of hands to protect it, and the stern opposition to it which shall never cease till it ceases or the speaking of tongues and the moving of lips cease. For such the expression of the American poet is to be transcendant and new. It is to be indirect and not direct or descriptive or epic. Its quality goes through these to much more. Let the age and wars of other nations be chanted and their eras and characters be illustrated and that finish the verse. Not so the great psalm of the republic. Here the theme is creative and has vista. Here comes one among the wellbeloved stonecutters and plans with decision and science and sees the solid and beautiful forms of the future where there are now no solid forms.

Of all nations the United States with veins full of poetical stuff most need poets and

① Congress every December: before 1933, the new congress convened in December.

② swap: exchange or bargain.

will doubtless have the greatest and use them the greatest. Their Presidents shall not be their common referee so much as their poets shall. Of all mankind the great poet is the equable man. Not in him but off from him things are grotesque or eccentric or fail of their sanity. Nothing out of its place is good and nothing in its place is bad. He bestows on every object or quality its fit proportions neither more nor less. He is the arbiter of the diverse and he is the key. He is the equalizer of his age and land... he supplies what wants supplying and checks what wants checking. If peace is the routine out of him speaks the spirit of peace, large, rich, thrifty, building vast and populous cities, encouraging agriculture and the arts and commerce—lighting the study of man, the soul, immortality— federal, state or municipal government, marriage, health, freetrade, intertravel by land and sea... nothing too close, nothing too far off... the stars not too far off. In war he is the most deadly force of the war. Who recruits him recruits horse and foot... he fetches parks of artillery the best that engineer ever knew. If the time becomes slothful and heavy he knows how to arouse it... he can make every word he speaks draw blood. Whatever stagnates in the flat of custom or obedience or legislation he never stagnates. Obedience does not master him, he masters it. High up out of reach he stands turning a concentrated light... he turns the pivot with his finger... he baffles the swiftest runners as he stands and easily overtakes and envelops them. The time straying toward infidelity and confections and persiflage he withholds by his steady faith... he spreads out his dishes... he offers the sweet firmfibred meat that grows men and women. His brain is the ultimate brain. He is no arguer... he is judgment. He judges not as the judge judges but as the sun falling around a helpless thing. As he sees the farthest he has the most faith. His thoughts are the hymns of the praise of things. In the talk on the soul and eternity and God off of his equal plane he is silent. He sees eternity less like a play with a prologue and denouement... he sees eternity in men and women... he does not see men and women as dreams or dots. Faith is the antiseptic of the soul... it pervades the common people and preserves them... they never give up believing and expecting and trusting. There is that indescribable freshness and unconsciousness about an illiterate person that humbles and mocks the power of the noblest expressive genius. The poet sees for a certainty how one not a great artist may be just as sacred and perfect as the greatest artist. ... The power to destroy or remould is freely used by him but never the power of attack. What is past is past. If he does not expose superior models and prove himself by every step he takes he is not what is wanted. The presence of the greatest poet conquers... not parleying or struggling or any prepared attempts. Now he has passed that way see after him! there is not left any vestige of despair or misanthropy or cunning or exclusiveness or the ignominy of a nativity of color or delusion of hell or the necessity of hell and no man thenceforward shall be degraded for ignorance or weakness or sin.

The greatest poet hardly knows pettiness or triviality. If he breathes into any thing that was before thought small it dilates with the grandeur and life of the universe. He is a seer... he is individual... he is complete in himself... the others are as good as he, only he sees it and they do not. He is not one of the chorus... he does not stop for any regulation... he is the president of regulation. What the eyesight does to the rest he does to the rest. Who knows the curious mystery of the eyesight? The other senses corroborate themselves, but this is removed from any proof but its own and foreruns the identities of the spiritual world. A single glance of it mocks all the investigations of man and all the instruments and books of the earth and all reasoning. What is marvellous? what is unlikely? what is impossible or baseless or vague? after you have once just opened the space of a peachpit and given audience to far and near and to the sunset and had all things enter with electric swiftness softly and duly without confusion or jostling or jam.

The land and sea, the animals, fishes and birds, the sky of heaven and the orbs, the forests mountains and rivers, are not small themes... but folk expect of the poet to indicate more than the beauty and dignity which always attach to dumb real objects... they expect him to indicate the path between reality and their souls. Men and women perceive the beauty well enough... probably as well as he. The passionate tenacity of hunters, woodmen, early risers, cultivators of gardens and orchards and fields, the love of healthy women for the manly form, seafaring persons, drivers of horses, the passion for light and the open air, all is an old varied sign of the unfailing perception of beauty and of a residence of the poetic in outdoor people. They can never be assisted by poets to perceive... some may but they never can. The poetic quality is not marshalled in rhyme or uniformity or abstract addresses to things nor in melancholy complaints or good precepts, but is the life of these and much else and is in the soul. The profit of rhyme is that it drops seeds of a sweeter and more luxuriant rhyme, and of uniformity that it conveys itself into its own roots in the ground out of sight. The rhyme and uniformity of perfect poems show the free growth of metrical laws and bud from them as unerringly and loosely as lilacs or roses on a bush, and take shapes as compact as the shapes of chestnuts and oranges and melons and pears, and shed the perfume impalpable to form. The fluency and ornaments of the finest poems or music or orations or recitations are not independent but dependent. All beauty comes from beautiful blood and a beautiful brain. If the greatnesses are in conjunction in a man or woman it is enough... the fact will prevail through the universe... but the gaggery① and gilt of a million years will not prevail. Who troubles himself about his ornaments or fluency is lost. This is what you shall do: Love the earth and sun and the animals, despise riches, give alms to every one that asks, stand up for the stupid and crazy, devote your income and labor to others, hate tyrants, argue not concerning God, have patience and indulgence toward the people, take off your hat to nothing known or unknown or to any man or number of

① gaggery: kidding, hoaxing.

men, go freely with powerful uneducated persons and with the young and with the mothers of families, read these leaves in the open air every season of every year of your life, re-examine all you have been told at school or church or in any book, dismiss whatever insults your own soul, and your very flesh shall be a great poem and have the richest fluency not only in its words but in the silent lines of its lips and face and between the lashes of your eyes and in every motion and joint of your body. ... The poet shall not spend his time in unneeded work. He shall know that the ground is always ready ploughed and manured... others may not know it but he shall. He shall go directly to the creation. His trust shall master the trust of everything he touches... and shall master all attachment.

The known universe has one complete lover and that is the greatest poet. He consumes an eternal passion and is indifferent which chance happens and which possible contingency of fortune or misfortune and persuades daily and hourly his delicious pay. What balks or breaks others is fuel for his burning progress to contact and amorous joy. Other proportions of the reception of pleasure dwindle to nothing to his proportions. All expected from heaven or from the highest he is rapport with in the sight of the daybreak or a scene of the winter woods or the presence of children playing or with his arm round the neck of a man or woman. His love above all love has leisure and expanse... he leaves room ahead of himself. He is no irresolute or suspicious lover... he is sure... he scorns intervals. His experience and the showers and thrills are not for nothing. Nothing can jar him... suffering and darkness cannot — death and fear cannot. To him complaint and jealousy and envy are corpses buried and rotten in the earth... he saw them buried. The sea is not surer of the shore or the shore of the sea than he is of the fruition of his love and of all perfection and beauty.

The fruition of beauty is no chance of hit or miss... it is inevitable as life... it is exact and plumb as gravitation. From the eyesight proceeds another eyesight and from the hearing proceeds another hearing and from the voice proceeds another voice eternally curious of the harmony of things with man. To these respond perfections not only in the committees that were supposed to stand for the rest but in the rest themselves just the same. These understand the law of perfection in masses and floods... that its finish is to each for itself and onward from itself... that it is profuse and impartial... that there is not a minute of the light or dark nor an acre of the earth or sea without it — nor any direction of the sky nor any trade or employment nor any turn of events. This is the reason that about the proper expression of beauty there is precision and balance... one part does not need to be thrust above the other. The best singer is not the one who has the most lithe and powerful organ... the pleasure of poems is not in them that take the handsomest measure and similes and sound.

Without effort and without exposing in the least how it is done the greatest poet brings the spirit of any or all events and passions and scenes and persons some more and some less to bear on your individual character as you hear or read. To do this well is to compete with the laws that pursue and follow time. What is the purpose must surely be there and the clue of it must be there... and the faintest indication is the indication of the best and then becomes the clearest indication. Past and present and future are not disjoined but joined. The greatest poet forms the consistence of what is to be from what has been and is. He drags the dead out of their coffins and stands them again on their feet... he says to the past, Rise and walk before me that I may realize you. He learns the lesson... he places himself where the future becomes present. The greatest poet does not only dazzle his rays over character and scenes and passions... he finally ascends and finishes all... he exhibits the pinnacles that no man can tell what they are for or what is beyond... he glows a moment on the extremest verge. He is most wonderful in his last half-hidden smile or frown... by that flash of the moment of parting the one that sees it shall be encouraged or terrified afterward for many years. The greatest poet does not moralize or make applications of morals... he knows the soul. The soul has that measureless pride which consists in never acknowledging any lessons but its own. But it has sympathy as measureless as its pride and the one balances the other and neither can stretch too far while it stretches in company with the other. The inmost secrets of art sleep with the twain. The greatest poet has lain close betwixt both and they are vital in his style and thoughts.

The art of art, the glory of expression and the sunshine of the light of letters is simplicity. Nothing is better than simplicity... nothing can make up for excess or for the lack of definiteness. To carry on the heave of impulse and pierce intellectual depths and give all subjects their articulations are powers neither common nor very uncommon. But to speak in literature with the perfect rectitude and insouciance① of the movements of animals and the unimpeachableness of the sentiment of trees in the woods and grass by the roadside is the flawless triumph of art. If you have looked on him who has achieved it you have looked on one of the masters of the artists of all nations and times. You shall not contemplate the flight of the graygull over the bay or the mettlesome action of the blood horse or the tall leaning of sunflowers on their stalk or the appearance of the sun journeying through heaven or the appearance of the moon afterward with any more satisfaction than you shall contemplate him. The greatest poet has less a marked style and is more the channel of thoughts and things without increase or diminution, and is the free channel of himself. He swears to his art, I will not be meddlesome, I will not have in my writing any elegance or effect or originality to hang in the way between me and the rest like curtains. I will have nothing hang in the way, not the richest curtains. What I tell I tell precisely for what it is. Let who may exalt or startle or fascinate or sooth I will have purposes as health or heat or snow has and be as regardless of observation. What I

① insouciance: a cheerful feeling of carefree.

experience or portray shall go from my composition without a shred of my composition. You shall stand by my side and look in the mirror with me.

The old red blood and stainless gentility of great poets will be proved by their unconstraint. A heroic person walks at his ease through and out of that custom or precedent or authority that suits him not. Of the traits of the brotherhood of writers savans musicians inventors and artists nothing is finer than silent defiance advancing from new free forms. In the need of poems philosophy politics mechanism science behaviour, the craft of art, an appropriate native grand-opera, shipcraft, or any craft, he is greatest forever and forever who contributes the greatest original practical example. The cleanest expression is that which finds no sphere worthy of itself and makes one.

The messages of great poets to each man and woman are, Come to us on equal terms, only then can you understand us, We are no better than you, What we enclose you enclose, What we enjoy you may enjoy. Did you suppose there could be only one Supreme? We affirm there can be unnumbered Supremes, and that one does not countervail another any more than one eyesight countervails another... and that men can be good or grand only of the consciousness of their supremacy within them. What do you think is the grandeur of storms and dismemberments and the deadliest battles and wrecks and the wildest fury of the elements and the power of the sea and the motion of nature and of the throes of human desires and dignity and hate and love? It is that something in the soul which says, Rage on, Whirl on, I tread master here and everywhere, Master of the spasms of the sky and of the shatter of the sea, Master of nature and passion and death, And of all terror and all pain.

The American bards shall be marked for generosity and affection and for encouraging competitors... They shall be kosmos[①]... without monopoly or secresy... glad to pass any thing to any one... hungry for equal night and day. They shall not be careful of riches and privilege... they shall be riches and privilege... they shall perceive who the most affluent man is. The most affluent man is he that confronts all the shows he sees by equivalents out of the stronger wealth of himself. The American bard shall delineate no class of persons nor one or two out of the strata of interests nor love most nor truth most nor the soul most nor the body most... and not be for the eastern states more than the western or the northern states more than the southern.

Exact science and its practical movements are no checks on the greatest poets but always his encouragement and support. The outself and remembrance are there... there the arms that lifted him first and brace him best... there he returns after all his goings and comings. The sailor and traveler... the anatomist, chemist, astronomer, geologist, phrenologist, spiritualist, mathematician, historian and lexicographer are not poets, but they are the lawgivers of poets and their construction underlies the structure of every

---

① kosmos: cosmos.

perfect poem. No matter what rises or is uttered they sent the seed of the conception of it... of them and by them stand the visible proofs of souls... always of their fatherstuff must be begotten the sinewy races of bards. If there shall be love and content between the father and the son and if the greatness of the son is the exuding of the greatness of the father there shall be love between the poet and the man of demonstrable science. In the beauty of poems are the tuft and final applause of science.

Great is the faith of the flush of knowledge and of the investigation of the depth of qualities and things. Cleaving and circling here swells the soul of the poet yet is president of itself always. The depths are fathomless and therefore calm. The innocence and nakedness are resumed... they are neither modest nor immodest. The whole theory of the special and supernatural and all that was twined with it or educed out of it departs as a dream. What has ever happened... what happens and whatever may or shall happen, the vital laws enclose all... they are sufficient for any case and for all cases... none to be hurried or retarded... any miracle of affairs or persons inadmissible in the vast clear scheme where every motion and every spear of grass and the frames and spirits of men and women and all that concerns them are unspeakably perfect miracles all referring to all and each distinct and in its place. It is also not consistent with the reality of the soul to admit that there is anything in the known universe more divine than men and women.

Men and women and the earth and all upon it are simply to be taken as they are, and the investigation of their past and present and future shall be unintermitted and shall be done with perfect candor. Upon this basis philosophy speculates ever looking toward the poet, ever regarding the eternal tendencies of all toward happiness never inconsistent with what is clear to the senses and to the soul. For the eternal tendencies of all toward happiness make the only point of sane philosophy. Whatever comprehends less than that... whatever is less than the laws of light and of astronomical motion... or less than the laws that follow the thief the liar the glutton and the drunkard through this life and doubtless afterward... or less than vast stretches of time or the slow formation of density or the patient upheaving of strata—is of no account. Whatever would put God in a poem or system of philosophy as contending against some being or influence is also of no account. Sanity and ensemble characterize the great master... spoilt in one principle all is spoilt. The great master has nothing to do with miracles. He sees health for himself in being one of the mass... he sees the hiatus in singular eminence. To the perfect shape comes common ground. To be under the general law is great for that is to correspond with it. The master knows that he is unspeakably great and that all are unspeakably great... that nothing for instance is greater than to conceive children and bring them up well... that to be is just as great as to perceive or tell.

In the make of the great masters the idea of political liberty is indispensible. Liberty takes the adherence of heroes wherever men and women exist... but never takes any adherence or welcome from the rest more than from poets. They are the voice and exposition of liberty. They out of ages are worthy the grand idea... to them it is confided and they must sustain it. Nothing has precedence of it and nothing can warp or degrade it. The attitude of great poets is to cheer up slaves and horrify despots. The turn of their necks, the sound of their feet, the motions of their wrists, are full of hazard to the one and hope to the other. Come nigh them awhile and though they neither speak or advise you shall learn the faithful American lesson. Liberty is poorly served by men whose good intent is quelled from one failure or two failures or any number of failures, or from the casual indifference or ingratitude of the people, or from the sharp show of the tushes① of power, or the bringing to bear soldiers and cannon or any penal statutes. Liberty relies upon itself, invites no one, promises nothing, sits in calmness and light, is positive and composed, and knows no discouragement. The battle rages with many a loud alarm and frequent advance and retreat... the enemy triumphs... the prison, the handcuffs, the iron necklace and anklet, the scaffold, garrote and leadballs do their work... the cause is asleep... the strong throats are choked with their own blood... the young men drop their eyelashes toward the ground when they pass each other... and is liberty gone out of that place? No never. When liberty goes it is not the first to go nor the second or third to go... it waits for all the rest to go... it is the last.... When the memories of the old martyrs are faded utterly away... when the large names of patriots are laughed at in the public halls from the lips of the orators... when the boys are no more christened after the same but christened after tyrants and traitors instead... when the laws of the free are grudgingly permitted and laws for informers and bloodmoney are sweet to the taste of the people... when I and you walk abroad upon the earth stung with compassion at the sight of numberless brothers answering our equal friendship and caffing no man master—and when we are elated with noble joy at the sight of slaves... when the soul retires in the cool communion of the night and surveys its experience and has much extasy over the word and deed that put back a helpless innocent person into the gripe of the gripers or into any cruel inferiority... when those in all parts of these states who could easier realize the true American character but do not yet—when the swarms of cringers, suckers②, doughfaces③, lice of politics, planners of sly involutions for their own preferment to city offices or state legislatures or the judiciary or congress or the presidency, obtain a response of love and natural deference from the people whether they get the offices or no... when it is better to be a bound booby and rogue in office at a high salary than the poorest free mechanic or farmer with his hat unmoved from his head and firm eyes and a candid and generous heart... and when servility by town or state or the federal government or any oppression on a large scale or small scale can be

① tushes: tusks.

② suckers: blackmailer.

③ doughfaces: north congressmen who did not oppose to the slavery system in civil war time.

tried on without its own punishment following duly after in exact proportion against the smallest chance of escape... or rather when all life and all the souls of men and women are discharged from any part of the earth — then only shall the instinct of liberty be discharged from that part of the earth.

As the attributes of the poets of the kosmos concentre in the real body and soul and in the pleasure of things they possess the superiority of genuineness over all fiction and romance. As they emit themselves facts are showered over with light... the daylight is lit with more volatile light... also the deep between the setting and rising sun goes deeper many fold. Each precise object or condition or combination or process exhibits a beauty... the multiplication table its—old age its—the carpenter's trade its—the grand-opera its... the hugehulled cleanshaped New-York clipper at sea under steam or full sail gleams with unmatched beauty... the American circles and large harmonies of government gleam with theirs... and the commonest definite intentions and actions with theirs. The poets of the kosmos advance through all interpositions and coverings and turmoils and stratagems to first principles. They are of use... they dissolve poverty from its need and riches from its conceit. You large proprietor they say shall not realize or perceive more than any one else. The owner of the library is not he who holds a legal title to it having bought and paid for it. Any one and every one is owner of the library who can read the same through all the varieties of tongues and subjects and styles, and in whom they enter with ease and take residence and force toward paternity and maternity, and make supple and powerful and rich and large.... These American states strong and healthy and accomplished shall receive no pleasure from violations of natural models and must not permit them. In paintings or mouldings or carvings in mineral or wood, or in the illustrations of books or newspapers, or in any comic or tragic prints, or in the patterns of woven stuffs or any thing to beautify rooms or furniture or costumes, or to put upon cornices or monuments or on the prows or sterns of ships, or to put anywhere before the human eye indoors or out, that which distorts honest shapes or which creates unearthly beings or places or contingencies is a nuisance and revolt. Of the human form especially it is so great it must never be made ridiculous. Of ornaments to a work nothing outre can be allowed... but those ornaments can be allowed that conform to the perfect facts of the open air and that flow out of the nature of the work and come irrepressibly from it and are necessary to the completion of the work. Most works are most beautiful without ornament. ... Exaggerations will be revenged in human physiology. Clean and vigorous children are jetted and conceived only in those communities where the models of natural forms are public every day. ... Great genius and the people of these states must never be demeaned to romances. As soon as histories are properly told there is no more need of romances.

The great poets are also to be known by the absence in them of tricks and by the justification of perfect personal candor. Then folks echo a new cheap joy and a divine voice leaping from their brains: How beautiful is candor! All faults may be forgiven of him who has perfect candor. Henceforth let no man of us lie, for we have seen that openness wins the inner and outer world and that there is no single exception, and that never since our earth gathered itself in a mass have deceit or subterfuge or prevarication attracted its smallest particle or the faintest tinge of a shade — and that through the enveloping wealth and rank of a state or the whole republic of states a sneak or sly person shall be discovered and despised... and that the soul has never been once fooled and never can be fooled... and thrift without the loving nod of the soul is only a foetid puff... and there never grew up in any of the continents of the globe nor upon any planet or satellite or star, nor upon the asteroids, nor in any part of ethereal space, nor in the midst of density, nor under the fluid wet of the sea, nor in that condition which precedes the birth of babes, nor at any time during the changes of life, nor in that condition that follows what we term death, nor in any stretch of abeyance or action afterward of vitality, nor in any process of formation or reformation anywhere, a being whose instinct hated the truth.

Extreme caution or prudence, the soundest organic health, large hope and comparison and fondness for women and children, large alimentiveness and destructiveness and causality, with a perfect sense of the oneness of nature and the propriety of the same spirit applied to human affairs... these are called up of the float of the brain of the world to be parts of the greatest poet from his birth out of his mother's womb and from her birth out of her mother's. Caution seldom goes far enough. It has been thought that the prudent citizen was the citizen who applied himself to solid gains and did well for himself and his family and completed a lawful life without debt or crime. The greatest poet sees and admits these economies as he sees the economies of food and sleep, but has higher notions of prudence than to think he gives much when he gives a few slight attentions at the latch of the gate. The premises of the prudence of life are not the hospitality of it or the ripeness and harvest of it. Beyond the independence of a little sum laid aside for burial-money, and of a few clap-boards around and shingles overhead on a lot of American soil owned, and the easy dollars that supply the year's plain clothing and meals, the melancholy prudence of the abandonment of such a great being as a man is to the toss and pallor of years of moneymaking with all their scorching days and icy nights and all their stifling deceits and underhanded dodgings, or infinitesimals of parlors, or shameless stuffing while others starve... and all the loss of the bloom and odor of the earth and of the flowers and atmosphere and of the sea and of the true taste of the women and men you pass or have to do with in youth or middle age, and the issuing sickness and desperate revolt at the close of a life without elevation of naiveté, and the ghastly chatter of a death without serenity or majesty, is the great fraud upon modern civilization and forethought, blotching the surface and system which civilization undeniably drafts, and moistening with tears the immense features it spreads and spreads with such velocity before the reached kisses of the soul. ... Still the right explanation remains to be made about prudence. The prudence of the mere wealth and respectability of the most esteemed life appears too faint for the eye to observe at all when little and large alike drop quietly aside at the thought of the prudence suitable for immortality. What is wisdom that fills the thinness of a year or seventy or eighty years to wisdom spaced out by ages and coming back at a certain time with strong reinforcements and rich presents and the clear faces of wedding-guests as far as you can look in every direction running gaily toward you? Only the soul is of itself... all else has reference to what ensues. All that a person does or thinks is of consequence. Not a move can a man or woman make that affects him or her in a day or a month or any part of the direct lifetime or the hour of death but the same affects him or her onward afterward through the indirect lifetime. The indirect is always as great and real as the direct. The spirit receives from the body just as much as it gives to the body. Not one name of word or deed... not of venereal sores or discolorations... not the privacy of the onanist①... not of the putrid veins of gluttons or rumdrinkers... not peculation or cunning or betrayal or murder... no serpentine poison of those that seduce women... not the foolish yielding of women... not prostitution... not of any depravity of young men... not of the attainment of gain by discreditable means... not any nastiness of appetite not any harshness of officers to men or judges to prisoners or fathers to sons or sons to fathers or of husbands to wives or bosses to their boys... not of greedy looks or malignant wishes... nor any of the wiles practised by people upon themselves... ever is or ever can be stamped on the programme but it is duly realized and returned, and that returned in further performances... and they returned again. Nor can the push of charity or personal force ever be anything else than the profoundest reason, whether it bring arguments to hand or no. No specification is necessary... to add or subtract or divide is in vain. Little or big, learned or unlearned, white or black, legal or illegal, sick or well, from the first inspiration down the wind-pipe to the last expiration out of it, all that a male or female does that is vigorous and benevolent and clean is so much sure profit to him or her in the unshakable order of the universe and through the whole scope of it forever. If the savage or felon is wise it is well... if the greatest poet or savan is wise it is simply the same... if the President or chief justice is wise it is the same... if the young mechanic or farmer is wise it is no more or less... if the prostitute is wise it is no more or less. The interest will come round... all will come round. All the best actions of war and peace... all help given to relatives and strangers and the poor and old and sorrowful and young children and widows and the sick, and to all shunned persons all furtherance of fugitives and of the escape of slaves... all the self-denial that stood ready and aloof on wrecks and saw others take the seats of the boats... all offering of substance or life for

① onanist: a person who practices masturbation.

the good old cause, or for a friend's sake or opinion's sake... all pains of enthusiasts scoffed at by their neighbors... all the vast sweet love and precious suffering of mothers... all honest men baffled in strifes recorded or unrecorded... all the grandeur and good of the few ancient nations whose fragments of animals we inherit... and all the good of the hundreds of far mightier and more ancient nations unknown to us by name or date or location... all that was ever manfully begun, whether it succeeded or no... all that has at any time been well suggested out of the divine heart of man or by the divinity of his mouth or by the shaping of his great hands... and all that is well thought or done this day on any part of the surface of the globe... or on any of the wandering stars or fixed stars by those there as we are here... or that is henceforth to be well thought or done by you whoever you are, or by any one — these singly and wholly inured at their time and inure now and will inure always to the identities from which they sprung or shall spring... Did you guess any of them lived only its moment? The world does not so exist... no parts palpable or impalpable so exist... no result exists now without being from its long antecedent result, and that from its antecedent, and so backward without the farthest mentionable spot coming a bit nearer the beginning than any other spot.... Whatever satisfies the soul is truth. The prudence of the greatest poet answers at last the craving and glut of the soul, is not contemptuous of less ways of prudence if they conform to its ways, puts off nothing, permits no let-up for its own case or any case, has no particular sabbath or judgment-day, divides not the living from the dead or the righteous from the unrighteous, is satisfied with the present, matches every thought or act by its correlative, knows no possible forgiveness or deputed atonement... knows that the young man who composedly periled his life and lost it has done exceeding well for himself, while the man who has not periled his life and retains it to old age in riches and ease has perhaps achieved nothing for himself worth mentioning... and that only that person has no great prudence to learn who has learnt to prefer real longlived things, and favors body and soul the same, and perceives the indirect assuredly following the direct, and what evil or good he does leaping onward and waiting to meet him again — and who in his spirit in any emergency whatever neither hurries or avoids death.

The direct trial of him who would be the greatest poet is today. If he does not flood himself with the immediate age as with vast oceanic tides... and if he does not attract his own land body and soul to himself and hang on its neck with incomparable love and plunge his semitic muscle into its merits and demerits... and if he be not himself the age transfigured... and if to him is not opened the eternity which gives similitude to all periods and locations and processes and animate and inanimate forms, and which is the bond of time, and rises up from its inconceivable vagueness and infiniteness in the swimming shape of today, and is held by the ductile anchors of life, and makes the present spot the passage from what was to what shall be, and commits itself to the representation of this wave of an hour and this one of the sixty beautiful children of the wave—let him merge in the general run and wait his development. . . . Still the final test of poems or any character or work remains. The prescient poet projects himself centuries ahead and judges performer or performance after the changes of time. Does it live through them? Does it still hold on untired? Will the same style and the direction of genius to similar points be satisfactory now? Has no new discovery in science or arrival at superior planes of thought and judgment and behaviour fixed him or his so that either can be looked down upon? Have the marches of tens and hundreds and thousands of years made willing detours to the right hand and the left hand for his sake? Is he beloved long and long after he is buried? Does the young man think often of him? and the young woman think often of him? and do the middle-aged and the old think of him?

A great poem is for ages and ages in common and for all degrees and complexions and all departments and sects and for a woman as much as a man and a man as much as a woman. A great poem is no finish to a man or woman but rather a beginning. Has any one fancied he could sit at last under some due authority and rest satisfied with explanations and realize and be content and full? To no such terminus does the greatest poet bring. . . he brings neither cessation or sheltered fatness and ease. The touch of him tells in action. Whom he takes he takes with firm sure grasp into live regions previously unattained thenceforward is no rest. . . they see the space and ineffable sheen that turn the old spots and lights into dead vacuums. The companion of him beholds the birth and progress of stars and learns one of the meanings. Now there shall be a man cohered out of tumult and chaos. . . the elder encourages the younger and shows him how. . . they two shall launch off fearlessly together till the new world fits an orbit for itself and looks unabashed on the lesser orbits of the stars and sweeps through the ceaseless rings and shall never be quiet again.

There will soon be no more priests. Their work is done. They may wait awhile. . . perhaps a generation or two. . . dropping off by degrees. A superior breed shall take their place. . . the gangs of kosmos and prophets en masse shall take their place. A new order shall arise and they shall be the priests of man, and every man shall be his own priest. The churches built under their umbrage shall be the churches of men and women. Through the divinity of themselves shall the kosmos and the new breed of poets be interpreters of men and women and of all events and things. They shall find their inspiration in real objects today, symptoms of the past and future. . . They shall not deign to defend immortality or God or the perfection of things or liberty or the exquisite beauty and reality of the soul. They shall arise in America and be responded to from the remainder of the earth.

The English language befriends the grand American expression. . . it is brawny enough and limber and full enough. On the tough stock of a race who through all change of circumstance was never without the idea of political liberty, which is the animus of all liberty, it has attracted the terms of daintier and gayer and subtler and more elegant tongues. It is the powerful language of resistance... it is the dialect of common sense. It is the speech of the proud and melancholy races and of all who aspire. It is the chosen tongue to express growth faith self-esteem freedom justice equality friendliness amplitude prudence decision and courage. It is the medium that shall well nigh express the inexpressible.

No great literature nor any like style of behaviour or oratory or social intercourse or household arrangements or public institutions or the treatment by bosses of employed people, nor executive detail or detail of the army or navy, nor spirit of legislation or courts or police or tuition or architecture or songs or amusements or the costumes of young men, can long elude the jealous and passionate instinct of American standards. Whether or no the sign appears from the mouths of the people, it throbs a live interrogation in every freeman's and freewoman's heart after that which passes by or this built to remain. Is it uniform with my country? Are its disposals without ignominous distinctions? Is it for the evergrowing communes of brothers and lovers, large, well-united, proud beyond the old models, generous beyond all models? Is it something grown fresh out of the fields or drawn from the sea for use to me today here? I know that what answers for me an American must answer for any individual or nation that serves for a part of my materials. Does this answer? or is it without reference to universal needs? or sprung of the needs of the less developed society of special ranks? or old needs of pleasure overlaid by modern science and forms? Does this acknowledge liberty with audible and absolute acknowledgement, and set slavery at nought for life and death? Will it help breed one goodshaped and wellhung man, and a woman to be his perfect and independent mate? Does it improve manners? Is it for the nursing of the young of the republic? Does it solve readily with the sweet milk of the nipples of the breasts of the mother of many children? Has it too the old ever-fresh forbearance and impartiality? Does it look with the same love on the last born and on those hardening toward stature, and on the errant, and on those who disdain all strength of assault outside of their own?

The poems distilled from other poems will probably pass away. The coward will surely pass away. The expectation of the vital and great can only be satisfied by the demeanor of the vital and great. The swarms of the polished deprecating and reflectors and the polite float off and leave no remembrance. America prepares with composure and good will for the visitors that have sent word. It is not intellect that is to be their warrant and welcome. The talented, the artist, the ingenious, the editor, the statesman, the erudite... they are not unappreciated... they fall in their place and do their work. The soul of the nation also does its work. No disguise can pass on it... no disguise can conceal from it. It rejects none, it permits all. Only toward as good as itself and toward the like of itself will it advance half-way. An individual is as superb as a nation when he has the qualities which make a superb nation. The soul of the largest and wealthiest and proudest nation may well go half-way to meet that of its poets. The signs are effectual.

There is no fear of mistake. If the one is true the other is true. The proof of a poet is that his country absorbs him as affectionately as he has absorbed it.

## 4. Ezra Pound

### A Retrospect(1918)

*Pound's "A Retrospect," published in* 1918, *is a collection of his essays on poetry. It includes "A Few Don'ts" which was originally published in* Poetry *in* 1913 *as "A Few Don'ts by an Imagiste" and "Prolegomena," which first appeared in the* Poetry Review *in* 1912. *In "A Retrospect" Pound presents his beliefs about what makes good poetry. The essay begins with the three principles of imagism, including "Direct treatment of the 'thing'." Pound defines "image" as "an intellectual and emotional complex in an instant of time." He elaborates on the "rules" of imagism, advising precision, and proclaiming, among other things, "Use either no ornament or good ornament" and "Go in fear of abstraction." Beyond attention to the image, Pound discusses the merits of translation, the rigors of free verse, and poets of the past. The essay is bracing and energetic; after all: "The mastery of any art is the work of a lifetime."*

There has been so much scribbling about a new fashion in poetry, that I may perhaps be pardoned this briefrecapitulation and retrospect.

In the spring or early summer of 1912, "H. D.," Richard Aldington and myself decided that we were agreed upon the three principles following:

1. Direct treatment of the "thing" whether subjective or objective.
2. To use absolutely no word that does not contribute to the presentation.
3. As regarding rhythm: to compose in the sequence of the musical phrase, not in sequence of a metronome.

Upon many points of taste and of predilection we differed, but agreeing upon these three positions we thought we had as much right to a group name, at least as much right, as a number of French "schools" proclaimed by Mr. Flint in the August number of Harold Monro's magazine for 1911.

This school has since been "joined" or "followed" by numerous people who, whatever their merits, do not show any signs of agreeing with the second specification. Indeed *vers libre* has become as prolix and as verbose as any of the flaccid varieties that preceded it. It has brought faults of its own. The actual language and phrasing is often as bad as that of our elders without even the excuse that the words are shoveled in to fill a metric pattern or to complete the noise of a rhyme-sound. Whether or no the phrases followed by the followers are musical must be left to the reader's decision. At times I can find a marked metre in "vers libres," as stale and hackneyed as any pseudo-Swinburnian, at times the writers seem to follow no musical structure whatever. But it is, on the whole, good that the field should be ploughed. Perhaps a few good poems have come from the new method, and if so it is justified.

Criticism is not a circumscription or a set of prohibitions. It provides fixed points of departure. It may startle a dull reader into alertness. That little of it which is good is mostly in stray phrases; or if it be an older artist helping a younger it is in great measure but rules of thumb, cautions gained by experience.

I set together a few phrases on practical working about the time the first remarks on imagisme were published. The first use of the word "Imagiste" was in my note to T. E. Hulme's five poems, printed at the end of my "Ripostes" in the autumn of 1912. I reprint my cautions from *Poetry* for March, 1913.

## A FEW DON'TS

An "Image" is that which presents an intellectual and emotional complex in an instant of time. I use the term "complex" rather in the technical sense employed by the newer psychologists, such as Hart, though we may not agree absolutely in our application.

It is the presentation of such a "complex" instantaneously which gives that sense of sudden liberation; that sense of freedom from time limits and space limits; that sense of sudden growth, which we experience in the presence of the greatest works of art.

It is better to present one Image in a lifetime than to produce voluminous works.

All this, however, some may consider open to debate. The immediate necessity is to tabulate A LIST OF DON'TS for those beginning to write verses. I can not put all of them into Mosaic negative.

To begin with, consider the three propositions (demanding direct treatment, economy of words, and the sequence of the musical phrase), not as dogma — never consider anything as dogma—but as the result of long contemplation, which, even if it is some one else's contemplation, may be worth consideration.

Pay no attention to the criticism of men who have never themselves written a notable work. Consider the discrepancies between the actual writing of the Greek poets and dramatists, and the theories of the Graeco-Roman grammarians, concocted to explain their metres.

## LANGUAGE

Use no superfluous word, no adjective which does not reveal something.

Don't use such an expression as "dim lands of *peace*." It dulls the image. It mixes an abstraction with the concrete. It comes from the writer's not realizing that the natural object is always the *adequate* symbol.

Go in fear of abstractions. Do not retell in mediocre verse what has already been done in good prose. Don't think any intelligent person is going to be deceived when you try to shirk all the difficulties of the unspeakably difficult art of good prose by chopping your composition into line lengths.

What the expert is tired of today the public will be tired of tomorrow.

Don't imagine that the art of poetry is any simpler than the art of music, or that you can please the expert before you have spent at least as much effort on the art of verse as an average piano teacher spends on the art of music.

Be influenced by as many great artists as you can, but have the decency either to acknowledge the debt outright, or to try to conceal it.

Don't allow "influence" to mean merely that you mop up the particular decorative vocabulary of some one or two poets whom you happen to admire. A Turkish war correspondent was recently caught red-handed babbling in his despatches of "dove-grey" hills, or else it was "pearl-pale," I can not remember.

Use either no ornament or good ornament.

## RHYTHM AND RHYME

Let the candidate fill his mind with the finest cadences he can discover, preferably in a foreign language [This is for rhythm, his vocabulary must of course be found in his native tongue], so that the meaning of the words may be less likely to divert his attention from the movement; e.g. Saxon charms, Hebridean Folk Songs, the verse of Dante, and the lyrics of Shakespeare—if he can dissociate the vocabulary from the cadence. Let him dissect the lyrics of Goethe coldly into their component sound values, syllables long and short, stressed and unstressed, into vowels and consonants.

It is not necessary that a poem should rely on its music, but if it does rely on its music that music must be such as will delight the expert.

Let the neophyte[①] know assonance and alliteration, rhyme immediate and delayed, simple and polyphonic, as a musician would expect to know harmony and counterpoint and all the minutiae of his craft. No time is too great to give to these matters or to any one of them, even if the artist seldom have need of them.

Don't imagine that a thing will "go" in verse just because it's too dull to go in prose.

Don't be "viewy"—leave that to the writers of pretty little philosophic essays. Don't be descriptive; remember that the painter can describe a landscape much better than you can, and that he has to know a deal more about it.

When Shakespeare talks of the "Dawn in russet mantle clad" he presents something which the painter does not present. There is in this line of his nothing that one can call description; he presents.

---

① Any new participant in some activity.

Consider the way of the scientists rather than the way of an advertising agent for a new soap.

The scientist does not expect to be acclaimed as a great scientist until he has discovered something. He begins by learning what has been discovered already. He goes from that point onward. He does not bank on being a charming fellow personally. He does not expect his friends to applaud the results of his freshman class work. Freshmen in poetry are unfortunately not confined to a definite and recognizable class room. They are "all over the shop." Is it any wonder "the public is indifferent to poetry"?

Don't chop your stuff into separate *iambs*. Don't make each line stop dead at the end and then begin every next line with a heave.

Let the beginning of the next line catch the rise of the rhythm wave, unless you want a definite longish pause.

In short, behave as a musician, a good musician, when dealing with that phase of your art which has exact parallels in music. The same laws govern, and you are bound by no others.

Naturally, your rhythmic structure should not destroy the shape of your words, or their natural sound, or their meaning. It is improbable that, at the start, you willbe able to get a rhythm-structure strong enough to affect them very much, though you may fall a victim to all sorts of false stopping due to line ends, and caesurae.

The Musician can rely on pitch and the volume of the orchestra. You can not. The term harmony is misapplied in poetry; it refers to simultaneous sounds of different pitch. There is, however, in the best verse a sort of residue of sound which remains in the ear of the hearer and acts more or less as an organ-base.

A rhyme must have in it some slight element of surprise if it is to give pleasure, it need not be bizarre or curious, but it must be well used if used at all.

*Vide* further Vildrac and Duhamel's notes on rhyme in "*Technique Poétique*."

That part of your poetry which strikes upon the imaginative eye of the reader will lose nothing by translation into a foreign tongue; that which appeals to the ear can reach only those who take it in the original.

Consider the definiteness of Dante's presentation, as compared with Milton's rhetoric. Read as much of Wordsworth as does not seem too unutterably dull.

If you want the gist of the matter go to Sappho, Catullus, Villon, Heine when he is in the vein, Gautier when he is not too frigid; or, if you have not the tongues, seek out the leisurely Chaucer. Good prose will do you no harm, and there is good discipline to be had by trying to write it.

Translation is likewise good training, if you find that your original matter "wobbles" when you try to rewrite it. The meaning of the poem to be translated can not "wobble."

If you are using a symmetrical form, don't put in what you want to say and then fill up the remaining vacuums with slush.

Don't mess up the perception of one sense by trying to define it in terms of another. This is usually only the result of being too lazy to find the exact word. To this clause there are possibly exceptions.

The first three simple prescriptions will throw out nine-tenths of all the bad poetry now accepted as standard and classic; and will prevent you from many a crime of production.

"... *Mais d'abord il faut être un poète*①," as MM. Duhamel and Vildrac have said at the end of their little book, "*Notes sur la Technique Poétique*."

Since March 1913, Ford Madox Hueffer has pointed out that Wordsworth was so intent on the ordinary or plain word that he never thought of hunting for *le mot juste*.

John Butler Yeats has handled or man-handled Wordsworth and the Victorians, and his criticism, contained in letters to his son, is now printed and available.

I do not like writing *about* art, my first, at least I think it was my first essay on the subject, was a protest against it.

## PROLEGOMENA

[*Poetry and Drama* (then the *Poetry Review*, edited by Harold Monro), Feb. 1912.] Time was when the poet lay in a green field with his head against a tree and played his diversion on a ha'penny whistle, and, Caesar's predecessors conquered the earth, and the predecessors of golden Crassus embezzled, and fashions had their say, and let him alone. And presumably he was fairly content in this circumstance, for I have small doubt that the occasional passerby, being attracted by curiosity to know why any one should lie under a tree and blow diversion on a ha'penny whistle, came and conversed, with him, and that among these passers-by there was on occasion a person of charm or a young lady who had not read *Man and Superman*; and looking back upon this naïve state of affairs we call it the age of gold.

Metastasio, and he should know if any one, assures us that this age endures—even though the modern poet is expected to holloa his verses down a speaking tube to the editors of cheap magazines—S. S. McClure, or some one of that sort—even though hordes of authors meet in dreariness and drink healths to the "Copyright Bill"; even though these things be, the age of gold pertains. Imperceivably, if you like, but pertains. You meet unkempt Amyclas in a Soho restaurant and chant together of dead and forgotten things—it is a manner of speech among poets to chant of dead, half-forgotten things, there seems no special harm in it, it has always been done—and it's rather better to be a clerk in the Post Office than to look after a lot of stinking, verminous sheep—and at another hour of the day one substitutes the drawing-room for the restaurant and tea is probably more palatable than mead and mare's milk, and little

① But first it was necessary to be a poet.

cakes than honey. And in this fashion one survives the resignation of Mr. Balfour, and the iniquities of the American customs-house, *equel bufera infernal*①, the periodical press. And then in the middle of it, there being apparently no other person at once capable and available one is stopped and asked to explain oneself.

I begin on the chord thus querulous, for I would much rather lie on what is left of Catullus' parlour floor and speculate the azure beneath it and the hills off to Salo and Riva with their forgotten gods moving unhindered amongst them, than discuss any processes and theories of art whatsoever. I would rather play tennis. I shall not argue.

## CREDO

*Rhythm*. —I believe in an"absolute rhythm," a rhythm, that is, in poetry which corresponds exactly to the emotion or shade of emotion to be expressed. A man's rhythm must be interpretative, it will be, therefore, in the end, his own, uncounterfeiting, uncounterfeitable.

*Symbols*. —I believe that the proper and perfect symbol is the natural object, that if a man use "symbols" he must so use them that their symbolic function does not obtrude; so that *a* sense, and the poetic quality of the passage, is not lost to those who do not understand the symbol as such, to whom, for instance, a hawk is a hawk.

*Technique*. —I believe in technique as the test of a man's sincerity; in law when it is ascertainable; in the trampling down of every convention that impedes or obscures the determination of the law, or the precise rendering of the impulse.

*Form*. —I think there is a "fluid" as well as a "solid" content, that some poems may have form as a tree has form, some as water poured into a vase. That most symmetrical forms have certain uses. That a vast number of subjects cannot be precisely, and therefore not properly rendered in symmetrical forms.

"Thinking that alone worthy wherein the whole art is employed" [Dante, *De Vulgari Eloquentia*]. I think the artist should master all known forms and systems of metric, and I have with some persistence set about doing this, searching particularly into those periods wherein the systems came to birth or attained their maturity. It has been complained, with some justice, that I dump my note-books on the public. I think that only after a long struggle will poetry attain such a degree of development, or, if you will, modernity, that it will vitally concern people who are accustomed, in prose, to Henry James and Anatole France, in music to Debussy. I am constantly contending that it took two centuries of Provence and one of Tuscany to develop the media of Dante's masterwork, that it took the Latinists of the Renaissance, Pleiades, and his own age of painted speech to prepare Shakespeare his tools. It is tremendously important that great poetry be written, it makes no jot of difference who writes it. The experimental

① and what an infernal storm.

demonstrations of one man may save the time of many—hence my furore over Arnaut Daniel—if a man's experiments try out one new rime, or dispense conclusively with one iota of currently accepted nonsense, he is merely playing fair with his colleagues when he chalks up his result.

No man ever writes very much poetry that "matters." In bulk, that is, no one produces much that is final, and when a man is not doing this highest thing, this saying the thing once for all and perfectly; [...] [H]e had much better be making the sorts of experiment which may be of use to him in his later work, to his successors.

"The lyf so short, the craft so long to lerne." It is a foolish thing for a man to begin his work on a too narrow foundation, it is a disgraceful thing for a man's work not to show steady growth and increasing fineness from first to last.

As for "adaptations"; one finds that all the old masters of painting recommend to their pupils that they begin by copying masterwork, and proceed to their own composition.

As for "Every man his own poet," the more every man knows about poetry the better. I believe in every one writing poetry who wants to; most do. I believe in every man knowing enough of music to play "God bless our home" on the harmonium, but I do not believe in every man giving concerts and printing his sin.

The mastery of any art is the work of a lifetime. I should not discriminate between the "amateur" and the "professional." Or rather I should discriminate quite often in favor of the amateur, but I should discriminate between the amateur and the expert. It is certain that the present chaos will endure until the Art of poetry has been preached down the amateur gullet, until there is such a general understanding of the fact that poetry is an art and not a pastime; such a knowledge of technique, of technique of surface and technique of content, that the amateurs will cease to try to drown out the masters.

If a certain thing was said once for all in Atlantis or Arcadia, in 450 Before Christ or in 1290 after, it is not for us moderns to go saying it over, or to go obscuring the memory of the dead by saying the same thing with less skill and less conviction.

My pawing over the ancients and semi-ancients has been one struggle to find out what has been done, once for all, better than it can ever be done again, and to find out what remains for us to do, and plenty does remain, for if we still feel the same emotions as those which launched the thousand ships, it is quite certain that we come on these feelings differently, through different nuances, by different intellectual gradations. Each age has its own abounding gifts yet only some ages transmute them into matter of duration. No good poetry is ever written in a manner twenty years old, for to write in such a manner shows conclusively that the writer thinks from books, convention and *cliché*, and not from life, yet a man feeling the divorce of life and his art may naturally try to resurrect a forgotten mode if he finds in that mode some leaven, or if he think he sees in it some element lacking in contemporary art which might unite that art again to its sustenance, life.

In the art of Daniel and Cavalcanti, I have seen that precision which I miss in the Victorians, that explicit rendering, be it of external nature, or of emotion. Their testimony is of the eyewitness, their symptoms are first hand.

As for the nineteenth century, with all respect to its achievements, I think we shall look back upon it as a rather blurry, messy sort of a period, a rathersenti mentalistic, mannerish sort of a period. I say this without any self-righteousness, with no self-satisfaction.

As for there being a "movement" or my being of it, the conception of poetry as a "pure art" in the sense in which I use the term, revived with Swinburne. From the puritanical revolt to Swinburne, poetry had been merely the vehicle—yes, definitely, Arthur Symons's scruples and feelings about the word not withholding—the ox-cart and post-chaise for transmitting thoughts poetic or otherwise. And perhaps the "great Victorians," though it is doubtful, and assuredly the "nineties" continued the development of the art, confining their improvements, however, chiefly to sound and to refinements of manner.

Mr. Yeats has once and for all stripped English poetry of its perdamnable rhetoric. He has boiled away all that is not poetic — and a good deal that is. He has become a classic in his own lifetime and *nel mezzo del cammin*. He has made our poetic idiom a thing pliable, a speech without inversions.

Robert Bridges, Maurice Hewlett and Frederic Manning are [Dec. 1911] in their different ways seriously concerned with overhauling the metric, in testing the language and its adaptability to certain modes. Ford Hueffer is making some sort of experiments in modernity. The Provost of Oriel continues his translation of the *Divina Commedia*.

As to Twentieth century poetry, and the poetry which I expect to see written during the next decade or so, it will, I think, move against poppy-cock, it will be harder and saner, it will be what Mr Hewlett calls "nearer the bone." It will be as much like granite as it can be, its force will lie in its truth, its interpretative power (of course, poetic force does always rest there); I mean it will not try to seem forcible by rhetorical din, and luxurious riot. We will have fewer painted adjectives impeding the shock and stroke of it. At least for myself, I want it so, austere, direct, free from emotional slither.

What is there now, in 1917, to be added?

## RE VERS LIBRE

I think the desire for vers libre is due to the sense of quantity reasserting itself after years of starvation. But I doubt if we can take over, for English, the rules of quantity laid down for Greek and Latin, mostly by Latin grammarians.

I think one should write vers libre only when one "must," that is to say, only when the "thing" builds up a rhythm more beautiful than that of set metres, or more real, more a part of the emotion of the "thing," more germane, intimate, interpretative than the measure of regular accentual verse; a rhythm which discontents one with set iambic or set anapaestic.

Eliot has said the thing very well when he said, "No *vers* is *libre* for the man who wants to do a good job."

As a matter of detail, there is vers libre with accent heavily marked as a drum-beat (as par example my "Dance Figure"), and on the other hand I think I have gone as far as can profitably be gone in the other direction (and perhaps too far). I mean I do not think one can use to any advantage rhythms much more tenuous and imperceptible than some I have used. I think progress lies rather in an attempt to approximate classical quantitative metres (NOT to copy them) than in a carelessness regarding such things. [Let me date this statement 20 Aug. 1917.]

I agree with John Yeats on the relation of beauty to certitude. I prefer satire, which is due to emotion, to any sham of emotion.

I have had to write, or at least I have written a good deal about art, sculpture, painting and poetry. I have seen what seemed to me the best of contemporary work reviled and obstructed. Can any one write prose of permanent or durable interest when he is merely saying for one year what nearly every one will say at the end of three or four years? I have been battistrada for a sculptor, a painter, a novelist, several poets. I wrote also of certain French writers in *The New Age* in nineteen twelve or eleven.

I would much rather that people would look at Brzeska's sculpture and Lewis's drawings, and that they would read Joyce, Jules Romains, Eliot, than that they should read what I have said of these men, or that I should be asked to republish argumentative essays and reviews.

All that the critic can do for the reader or audience or spectator is to focus his gaze or audition. Rightly or wrongly I think my blasts and essays have done their work, and that more people are now likely to go to the sources than are likely to read this book.

Jammes's "Existences" in "*La Triomphe de la Vie*" is available. So are his early poems. I think we need a convenient anthology rather than descriptive criticism. Carl Sandburg wrote me from Chicago, "It's hell when poets can't afford to buy each other's books." Half the people who care, only borrow. In America so few people know each other that the difficulty lies more than half in distribution. Perhaps one should make an anthology: Romains's "Un Etre en Marche" and "Priéres," Vildrac's "Visite." Retrospectively the fine wrought work of Laforgue, the flashes of Rimbaud, the hard-bit lines of Tristan Corbiére, Tailhade's sketches in "Poémes Aristophanesques," the "Litanies" of De Gourmont.

It is difficult at all times to write of the fine arts, it is almost impossible unless one can accompany one's prose with many reproductions. Still I would seize this chance or any chance to reaffirm my belief in Wyndham Lewis's genius, both in his drawings and his writings. And I would name an out of the way prose book, the "*Scenes and Portraits*" of Frederic Manning, as well as James Joyce's short stories and novel, "Dubliners" and the now well known "Portrait of the Artist" as well as Lewis' "Tarr," if, that is, I may treat my strange reader as if he were a new friend come into the room, intent on ransacking my bookshelf.

## ONLY EMOTION ENDURES

"Only emotion endures." Surely it is better for me to name over the few beautiful poems that still ring in my hcad than for me to search my flat for back numbers of periodicals and rearrange all that I have said about friendly and hostile writers.

The first twelve lines of Padraic Colum's "Drover"; his "O Woman shapely as a swan, on your account I shall not die"; Joyce's "I hear an army"; the lines of Yeats that ring in my head and in the heads of all young men of my time who care for poetry: Braseal and the Fisherman, "The fire that stirs about her when she stirs"; the later lines of "The Scholars," the faces of the Magi; William Carlos Williams's "Postlude." Aldington's version of "Atthis," and "H. D. 's" waves like pine tops, and her verse in "Des Imagistes" the first anthology; Hueffer's "How red your lips are" in his translation from Von der Vogelweide, his "Three Ten," the general effect of his "On Heaven"; his sense of the prose values or prose qualities in poetry; his ability to write poems that half-chant and are spoiled by a musician's additions; beyond these a poem by Alice Corbin, "One City Only," and another ending "But sliding water over a stone." These things have worn smooth in my head and I am not through with them, nor with Aldington's "In Via Sestina" nor his other poems in "Des Imagistes," though people have told me their flaws. It may be that their content is too much embedded in me for me to look back at the words.

I am almost a different person when I come to take up the argument for Eliot's poems.

# 5. T. S. Eliot

## Tradition and Individual Talent (1920)

*"Tradition and the Individual Talent" was first published in 1919 and soon after included in* The Sacred Wood: Essays on Poetry and Criticism *(1920). Eliot attempts to do two things in this essay: he first redefines "tradition" by emphasizing the importance of history to writing and understanding poetry, and he then argues that poetry should be essentially "impersonal," that is separate and distinct from the personality of its writer. Eliot's idea of tradition is complex and unusual, involving something he describes as "the*

*historical sense" which is a perception of "the pastness of the past" but also of its "presence." For Eliot, past works of art form an order or "tradition"; however, that order is always being altered by a new work which modifies the "tradition" to make room for itself. This view, in which "the past should be altered by the present as much as the present is directed by the past," requires that a poet be familiar with almost all literary history — not just the immediate past but the distant past and not just the literature of his or her own country but the whole "mind of Europe."*

In English writing we seldom speak of tradition, though we occasionally apply its name in deploring its absence. We cannot refer to "the tradition" or to "a tradition"; at most, we employ the adjective in saying that the poetry of So-and-so is "traditional" or even "too traditional." Seldom, perhaps, does the word appear except in a phrase of censure. If otherwise, it is vaguely approbative, with the implication, as to the work approved, of some pleasing archaeological reconstruction. You can hardly make the word agreeable to English ears without this comfortable reference to the reassuring science of archaeology.

Certainly the word is not likely to appear in our appreciations of living or dead writers. Every nation, every race, has not only its own creative, but its own critical turn of mind; and is even more oblivious of the shortcomings and limitations of its critical habits than of those of its creative genius. We know, or think we know, from the enormous mass of critical writing that has appeared in the French language the critical method or habit of the French; we only conclude (we are such unconscious people) that the French are "more critical" than we, and sometimes even plume ourselves a little with the fact, as if the French were the less spontaneous. Perhaps they are; but we might remind ourselves that criticism is as inevitable as breathing, and that we should be none the worse for articulating what passes in our minds when we read a book and feel an emotion about it, for criticizing our own minds in their work of criticism. One of the facts that might come to light in this process is our tendency to insist, when we praise a poet, upon those aspects of his work in which he least resembles any one else. In these aspects or parts of his work we pretend to find what is individual, what is the peculiar essence of the man. We dwell with satisfaction upon the poet's difference from his predecessors, especially his immediate predecessors; we endeavour to find something that can be isolated in order to be enjoyed. Whereas if we approach a poet without this prejudice we shall often find that not only the best, but the most individual parts of his work may be those in which the dead poets, his ancestors, assert their immortality most vigorously. And I do not mean the impressionable period of adolescence, but the period of full maturity.

Yet if the only form of tradition, of handing down, consisted in following the ways of the immediate generation before us in a blind or timid adherence to its successes, "tradition" should positively be discouraged. We have seen many such simple currents soon lost in the sand; and novelty is better than repetition. Tradition is a matter of much wider significance. It cannot be inherited, and if you want if you must obtain it by great labour. It involves, in the first place, the historical sense, which we may call nearly indispensable to any one who would continue to be a poet beyond his twenty-fifth year; and the historical sense involves a perception, not only of the pastness of the past, but of its presence; the historical sense compels a man to write not merely with his own generation in his bones, but with a feeling that the whole of the literature of Europe from Homer and within it the whole of the literature of his own country has a simultaneous existence and composes a simultaneous order. This historical sense, which is a sense of the timeless as well as of the temporal and of the timeless and of the temporal together, is what makes a writer traditional. And it is at the same time what makes a writer most acutely conscious of his place in time, of his own contemporaneity.

No poet, no artist of any art, has his complete meaning alone. His significance, his appreciation is the appreciation of his relation to the dead poets and artists. You cannot value him alone; you must set him, for contrast and comparison, among the dead. I mean this as a principle of aesthetic, not merely historical, criticism. The necessity that he shall conform, that he shall cohere, is not onesided; what happens when a new work of art is created is something that happens simultaneously to all the works of art which preceded it. The existing monuments form an ideal order among themselves, which is modified by the introduction of the new (the really new) work of art among them. The existing order is complete before the new work arrives; for order to persist after the supervention of novelty, the *whole* existing order must be, if ever so slightly, altered; and so the relations, proportions, values of each work of art toward the whole are readjusted; and this is conformity between the old and the new. Whoever has approved this idea of order, of the form of European, of English literature will not find it preposterous that the past should be altered by the present as much as the present is directed by the past. And the poet who is aware of this will be aware of great difficulties and responsibilities.

In a peculiar sense he will be aware also that he must inevitably be judged by the standards of the past. I say judged, not amputated, by them; not judged to be as good as, or worse or better than, the dead; and certainly not judged by the canons of dead critics. It is a judgment, a comparison, in which two things are measured by each other. To conform merely would be for the new work not really to conform at all; it would not be new, and would therefore not be a work of art. And we do not quite say that the new is more valuable because it fits in; but its fitting in is a test of its value—a test, it is true, which can only be slowly and cautiously applied, for we are none of us infallible judges of conformity. We say: it appears to conform, and is perhaps individual, or it appears individual, and many conform; but we are hardly likely to find that it is one and not the other.

To proceed to a more intelligible exposition of the relation of the poet to the past: he can neither take the past as a lump, an indiscriminate bolus, nor can he form himself wholly on one or two private admirations, nor can he form himself wholly upon one preferred period. The first course is inadmissible, the second is an important experience of youth, and the third is a pleasant and highly desirable supplement. The poet must be very conscious of the main current, which does not at all flow invariably through the most distinguished reputations. He must be quite aware of the obvious fact that art never improves, but that the material of art is never quite the same. He must be aware that the mind of Europe—the mind of his own country—a mind which he learns in time to be much more important than his own private mind—is a mind which changes, and that this change is a development which abandons nothing *en route*, which does not superannuate either Shakespeare, or Homer, or the rock drawing of the Magdalenian draughtsmen. That this development, refinement perhaps, complication certainly, is not, from the point of view of the artist, any improvement. Perhaps not even an improvement from the point of view of the psychologist or not to the extent which we imagine; perhaps only in the end based upon a complication in economics and machinery. But the difference between the present and the past is that the conscious present is an awareness of the past in a way and to an extent which the past's awareness of itself cannot show.

Some one said: "The dead writers are remote from us because we *know* so much more than they did." Precisely, and they are that which we know.

I am alive to a usual objection to what is clearly part of my programme for the *métier* of poetry. The objection is that the doctrine requires a ridiculous amount of erudition (pedantry), a claim which can be rejected by appeal to the lives of poets in any pantheon. It will even be affirmed that much learning deadens or perverts poetic sensibility. While, however, we persist in believing that a poet ought to know as much as will not encroach upon his necessary receptivity and necessary laziness, it is not desirable to confine knowledge to whatever can be put into a useful shape for examinations, drawing-rooms, or the still more pretentious modes of publicity. Some can absorb knowledge, the more tardy must sweat for it. Shakespeare acquired more essential history from Plutarch than most men could from the whole British Museum. What is to be insisted upon is that the poet must develop or procure the consciousness of the past and that he should continue to develop this consciousness throughout his career.

What happens is a continual surrender of himself as he is at the moment to something which is more valuable. The progress of an artist is a continual self-sacrifice, a continual extinction of personality.

There remains to define this process of depersonalization and its relation to the sense of tradition. It is in this depersonalization that art may be said to approach the condition of science. I, therefore, invite you to consider, as a suggestive analogy, the action which takes place when a bit of finely filiated platinum is introduced into a chamber containing oxygen and sulphur dioxide.

II

Honest criticism and sensitive appreciation are directed not upon the poet but upon the poetry. If we attend to the confused cries of the newspaper critics and the *susurrus* of popular repetition that follows, we shall hear the names of poets in great numbers; if we seek not Blue-book knowledge but the enjoyment of poetry, and ask for a poem, we shall seldom find it. I have tried to point out the importance of the relation of the poem to other poems by other authors, and suggested the conception of poetry as a living whole of all the poetry that has ever been written. The other aspect of this Impersonal theory of poetry is the relation of the poem to its author. And I hinted, by an analogy, that the mind of the mature poet differs from that of the immature one not precisely in any valuation of "personality," not being necessarily more interesting, or having "more to say," but rather by being a more finely perfected medium in which special, or very varied, feelings are at liberty to enter into new combinations.

The analogy was that of the catalyst. When the two gases previously mentioned are mixed in the presence of a filament of platinum, they form sulphurous acid. This combination takes place only if the platinum is present; nevertheless the newly formed acid contains no trace of platinum, and the platinum itself is apparently unaffected; has remained inert, neutral, and unchanged. The mind of the poet is the shred of platinum. It may partly or exclusively operate upon the experience of the man himself; but, the more perfect the artist, the more completely separate in him will be the man who suffers and the mind which creates; the more perfectly will the mind digest and transmute the passions which are its material.

The experience, you will notice, the elements which enter the presence of the transforming catalyst, are of two kinds: emotions and feelings. The effect of a work of art upon the person who enjoys it is an experience different in kind from any experience not of art. It may be formed out of one emotion, or may be a combination of several; and various feelings, inhering for the writer in particular words or phrases or images, may be added to compose the final result. Or great poetry may be made without the direct use of any emotion whatever: composed out of feelings solely. Canto XV of the *Inferno* (Brunetto Latini) is a working up of the emotion evident in the situation; but the effect, though single as that of any work of art, is obtained by considerable complexity of detail. The last quatrain gives an image, a feeling attaching to an image, which "came," which did not develop simply out of what precedes, but which was probably in suspension in the poet's mind until the proper combination arrived for it to add itself to. The poet's mind is in fact a receptacle for seizing and storing up numberless feelings, phrases, images, which remain there until all the particles which can unite to form a new compound are present together.

If you compare several representative passages of the greatest poetry you see how great is the variety of types of combination, and also how completely any semi-ethical criterion of"sublimity" misses the mark. For it is not the "greatness," the intensity, of the emotions, the components, but the intensity of the artistic process, the pressure, so to speak, under which the fusion takes place, that counts. The episode of Paolo and Francesca employs a definite emotion, but the intensity of the poetry is something quite different from whatever intensity in the supposed experience it may give the impression of. It is no more intense, furthermore, than Canto XXVI, the voyage of Ulysses, which has not the direct dependence upon an emotion. Great variety is possible in the process of transmutation of emotion: the murder of Agamemnon, or the agony of Othello, gives an artistic effect apparently closer to a possible original than the scenes from Dante. In the *Agamemnon*, the artistic emotion approximates to the emotion of an actual spectator; in *Othello* to the emotion of the protagonist himself. But the difference between art and the event is always absolute; the combination which is the murder of Agamemnon is probably as complex as that which is the voyage of Ulysses. In either case there has been a fusion of elements. The ode of Keats contains a number of feelings which have nothing particular to do with the nightingale, but which the nightingale, partly, perhaps, because of its attractive name, and partly because of its reputation, served to bring together.

The point of view which I am struggling to attack is perhaps related to the metaphysical theory of the substantial unity of the soul: for my meaning is, that the poet has, not a "personality" to express, but a particular medium, which is only a medium and not a personality, in which impressions and experiences combine in peculiar and unexpected ways. Impressions and experiences which are important for the man may take no place in the poetry, and those which become important in the poetry may play quite a negligible part in the man, the personality.

I will quote a passage which is unfamiliar enough to be regarded with fresh attention in the light—or darkness—of these observations:

*And now methinks I could e'en chide myself*
*For doating on her beauty, though her death*
*Shall be revenged after no common action.*
*Does the silkworm expend her yellow labours*
*For thee? For thee does she undo herself?*
*Are lordships sold to maintain ladyships*
*For the poor benefit of a bewildering minute?*
*Why does yon fellow falsify highways,*
*And put his life between the judge's lips,*
*To refine such a thing—keeps horse and men*

*To beat their valours for her?...*

In this passage (as is evident if it is taken in its context) there is a combination of positive and negative emotions: an intensely strong attraction toward beauty and an equally intense fascination by the ugliness which is contrasted with it and which destroys it. This balance of contrasted emotion is in the dramatic situation to which the speech is pertinent, but that situation alone is inadequate to it. This is, so to speak, the structural emotion, provided by the drama. But the whole effect, the dominant tone, is due to the fact that a number of floating feelings, having an affinity to this emotion by no means superficially evident, have combined with it to give us a new art emotion.

It is not in his personal emotions, the emotions provoked by particular events in his life, that the poet is in any way remarkable or interesting. His particular emotions may be simple, or crude, or flat. The emotion in his poetry will be a very complex thing, but not with the complexity of the emotions of people who have very complex or unusual emotions in life. One error, in fact, of eccentricity in poetry is to seek for new human emotions to express; and in this search for novelty in the wrong place it discovers the perverse. The business of the poet is not to find new emotions, but to use the ordinary ones and, in working them up into poetry, to express feelings which are not in actual emotions at all. And emotions which he has never experienced will serve his turn as well as those familiar to him. Consequently, we must believe that "emotion recollected in tranquillity" is an inexact formula. For it is neither emotion, nor recollection, nor, without distortion of meaning, tranquillity. It is a concentration, and a new thing resulting from the concentration, of a very great number of experiences which to the practical and active person would not seem to be experiences at all; it is a concentration which does not happen consciously or of deliberation. These experiences are not "recollected," and they finally unite in an atmosphere which is "tranquil" only in that it is a passive attending upon the event. Of course this is not quite the whole story. There is a great deal, in the writing of poetry, which must be conscious and deliberate. In fact, the bad poet is usually unconscious where he ought to be conscious, and conscious where he ought to be unconscious. Both errors tend to make him "personal." Poetry is not a turning loose of emotion, but an escape from emotion; it is not the expression of personality, but an escape from personality. But, of course, only those who have personality and emotions know what it means to want to escape from these things.

## III

ὁ δενους ισως θειοτερον τι και απαθες εστιν①

This essay proposes to halt at the frontier of metaphysics or mysticism, and confine itself to such practical conclusions as can be applied by the responsible person interested in poetry. To

① Aristotle, "On the Soul": "Surely the mind is divine and not subject to outside impressions."

divert interest from the poet to the poetry is a laudable aim: for it would conduce to a juster estimation of actual poetry, good and bad. There are many people who appreciate the expression of sincere emotion in verse, and there is a smaller number of people who can appreciate technical excellence. But very few know when there is an expression of *significant* emotion, emotion which has its life in the poem and not in the history of the poet. The emotion of art is impersonal. And the poet cannot reach this impersonality without surrendering himself wholly to the work to be done. And he is not likely to know what is to be done unless he lives in what is not merely the present, but the present moment of the past, unless he is conscious, not of what is dead, but of what is already living.

## 6. Langston Hughes

### The Negro Artist and the Racial Mountain (1926)

*"The Negro Artist and the Racial Mountain" was a short essay written by Langston Hughes for* The Nation *magazine in 1926. It became the manifesto of the Harlem Renaissance. In it, Hughes said that black artists in America should stop copying whites, that they will never create anything great that way. Instead they should be proud of who they are, proud to be black, and draw from black culture. Not "white is right" but, as we would now say, "Black is beautiful".*

One of the most promising of the young Negro poets[①] said to me once, "I want to be a poet—not a Negro poet," meaning, I believe, "I want to write like a white poet"; meaning subconsciously, "I would like to be a white poet"; meaning behind that, "I would like to be white." And I was sorry the young man said that, for no great poet has ever been afraid of being himself. And I doubted then that, with his desire to run away spiritually from his race, this boy would ever be a great poet. But this is the mountain standing in the way of any true Negro art in America—this urge within the race toward whiteness, the desire to pour racial individuality into the mold of American standardization, and to be as little Negro and as much American as possible.

But let us look at the immediate background of this young poet. His family is of what I suppose one would call the Negro middle class: people who are by no means rich yet never uncomfortable nor hungry—smug, contented, respectable folk, members of the Baptist church. The father goes to work every morning. He is a chief steward at a large white club. The mother sometimes does fancy sewing or supervises parties for the

① It probably refers to Countee Cullen (1903-1946), an African-American poet who was a leading figure in the Harlem Renaissance.

rich families of the town. The children go to a mixed school. In the home they read white papers and magazines. And the mother often says "Don't be like niggers" when the children are bad. A frequent phrase from the father is, "Look how well a white man does things." And so the word white comes to be unconsciously a symbol of all virtues. It holds for the children beauty, morality, and money. The whisper of "I want to be white" runs silently through their minds. This young poet's home is, I believe, a fairly typical home of the colored middle class. One sees immediately how difficult it would be for an artist born in such a home to interest himself in interpreting the beauty of his own people. He is never taught to see that beauty. He is taught rather not to see it, or if he does, to be ashamed of it when it is not according to Caucasian patterns.

For racial culture the home of a self-styled "high-class" Negro has nothing better to offer. Instead there will perhaps be more aping of things white than in a less cultured or less wealthy home. The father is perhaps a doctor, lawyer, landowner, or politician. The mother may be a social worker, or a teacher, or she may do nothing and have a maid. Father is often dark but he has usually married the lightest woman he could find. The family attend a fashionable church where few really colored faces are to be found. And they themselves draw a color line. In the North they go to white theaters and white movies. And in the South they have at least two cars and house "like white folks." Nordic manners, Nordic faces, Nordic hair, Nordic art (if any), and an Episcopal heaven. A very high mountain indeed for the would-be racial artist to climb in order to discover himself and his people.

But then there are the low-down folks, the so-called common element, and they are the majority — may the Lord be praised! The people who have their nip of gin on Saturday nights and are not too important to themselves or the community, or too well fed, or too learned to watch the lazy world go round. They live on Seventh Street in Washington or State Street in Chicago and they do not particularly care whether they are like white folks or anybody else. Their joy runs, bang! into ecstasy. Their religion soars to a shout. Work maybe a little today, rest a little tomorrow. Play awhile. Sing awhile. O, let's dance! These common people are not afraid of spirituals, as for a long time their more intellectual brethren were, and jazz is their child. They furnish a wealth of colorful, distinctive material for any artist because they still hold their own individuality in the face of American standardizations. And perhaps these common people will give to the world its truly great Negro artist, the one who is not afraid to be himself. Whereas the better-class Negro would tell the artist what to do, the people at least let him alone when he does appear. And they are not ashamed of him—if they know he exists at all. And they accept what beauty is their own without question.

Certainly there is, for the American Negro artist who can escape the restrictions the more advanced among his own group would put upon him, a great field of unused material ready for his art. Without going outside his race, and even among the better classes with their "white" culture and conscious American manners, but still Negro enough to be different, there is sufficient matter to furnish a black artist with a lifetime of creative work. And when he chooses to touch on the relations between Negroes and whites in this country, with their innumerable overtones and undertones, surely, and especially for literature and the drama, there is an inexhaustible supply of themes at hand. To these the Negro artist can give his racial individuality, his heritage of rhythm and warmth, and his incongruous humor that so often, as in the Blues, becomes ironic laughter mixed with tears. But let us look again at the mountain.

A prominent Negro clubwoman in Philadelphia paid eleven dollars to hear Raquel Meller① sing Andalusian popular songs. But she told me a few weeks before she would not think of going to hear "that woman," Clara Smith②, a great black artist, sing Negro folksongs. And many an upper-class Negro church, even now, would not dream of employing a spiritual in its services. The drab melodies in white folks' hymnbooks are much to be preferred. "We want to worship the Lord correctly and quietly. We don't believe in 'shouting.' Let's be dull like the Nordics," they say, in effect.

The road for the serious black artist, then, who would produce a racial art is most certainly rocky and the mountain is high. Until recently he received almost no encouragement for his work from either white or colored people. The fine novels of Chesnutt③ go out of print with neither race noticing their passing. The quaint charm and humor of Dunbar's④ dialect verse brought to him, in his day, largely the same kind of encouragement one would give a sideshow freak (A colored man writing poetry! How odd!) or a clown (How amusing!).

The present vogue⑤ in things Negro, although it may do as much harm as good for the budding colored artist, has at least done this: it has brought him forcibly to the attention of his own people among whom for so long, unless the other race had noticed him beforehand, he was a prophet with little honor. I understand that Charles Gilpin⑥

① Raquel Meller (1888-1962), born as Francisca Romana Marqués López, was a Spanish diseuse, cuplé, and tonadilla singer. She was an international star in the 1920s and 1930s, appearing in several films and touring Europe and the Americas.

② Clara Smith (1895-1935), was an African America classic female blues singer.

③ Charles Waddell Chestnutt (1858-1932), prolific African American writer best known for his conjure tales and his novels of social purpose dealing with the psychological and social costs of the color line.

④ Paul Laurence Dunbar (1872-1906), African American poet, novelist, and short story writer, was both praised and chastised for his dialect poems, which some critics felt reinforced popular stereotypes of a romanticized Old South.

⑤ It refers to what is now known as the Harlem Renaissance, which was considered to be a rebirth of African American arts.

⑥ Charles Sidney Gilpin (1878-1930) was one of the most highly regarded actors of the 1920s. He played in critical debuts in New York: in the 1919 premier of John Drinkwater's *Abraham Lincoln* and played the lead role of Brutus Jones in the 1920 premier of Eugene O'Neill's *The Emperor Jones*, also touring with the play. In 1920 he was the first black American to receive the Drama League of New York's annual award, as one of the ten people who had done the most that year for American theater.

acted for years in Negro theaters without any special acclaim from his own, but when Broadway gave him eight curtain calls, Negroes, too, began to beat a tin pan in his honor. I know a young colored writer, a manual worker by day, who had been writing well for the colored magazines for some years, but it was not until he recently broke into the white publications and his first book was accepted by a prominent New York publisher that the "best" Negroes in his city took the trouble to discover that he lived there. Then almost immediately they decided to give a grand dinner for him. But the society ladies were careful to whisper to his mother that perhaps she'd better not come. They were not sure she would have an evening gown.

The Negro artist works against an undertow of sharp criticism and misunderstanding from his own group and unintentional bribes from the whites. "O, be respectable, write about nice people, show how good we are," say the Negroes. "Be stereotyped, don't go too far, don't shatter our illusions about you, don't amuse us too seriously. We will pay you," say the whites. Both would have told Jean Toomer① not to write "Cane." The colored people did not praise it. The white people did not buy it. Most of the colored people who did read "Cane" hate it. They are afraid of it. Although the critics gave it good reviews the public remained indifferent. Yet (excepting the work of Du Bois) "Cane" contains the finest prose written by a Negro in America. And like the singing of Robeson②, it is truly racial.

But in spite of the Nordicized Negro intelligentsia and the desires of some white editors we have an honest American Negro literature already with us. Now I await the rise of the Negro theater. Our folk music, having achieved world-wide fame, offers itself to the genius of the great individual American Negro composer who is to come. And within the next decade I expect to see the work of a growing school of colored artists who paint and model the beauty of dark faces and create with new technique the expressions of their own soul-world. And the Negro dancers who will dance like flame and the singers who will continue to carry our songs to all who listen — they will be with us in even greater numbers tomorrow.

Most of my own poems are racial in theme and treatment, derived from the life I know. In many of them I try to grasp and hold some of the meanings and rhythms of jazz. I am as sincere as I know how to be in these poems and yet after every reading I answer questions like these from my own people: Do you think Negroes should always write about Negroes? I wish you wouldn't read some of your poems to white folks. How do you find anything interesting in a place like a cabaret? Why do you write about black people? You aren't black. What makes you do so many jazz poems?

---

① Jean Toomer (1894—1967) was an American poet and novelist and an important figure of the Harlem Renaissance and modernism. His first book *Cane*, published in 1923, is considered by many to be his most significant.

② Paul Robeson (1898—1976), renowned African American singer, actor, and advocate for global human rights.

But jazz to me is one of the inherent expressions of Negro life in America: the eternal tom-tom beating in the Negro soul—the tom-tom of revolt against weariness in a white world, a world of subway trains, and work, work, work; the tom-tom of joy and laughter, and pain swallowed in a smile. Yet the Philadelphia clubwoman is ashamed to say that her race created it and she does not like me to write about it, The old subconscious "white is best" runs through her mind. Years of study under white teachers, a lifetime of white books, pictures, and papers, and white manners, morals, and Puritan standards made her dislike the spirituals. And now she turns up her nose at jazz and all its manifestations—likewise almost everything else distinctly racial. She doesn't care for the Winold Reiss① portraits of Negroes because they are "too Negro." She does not want a true picture of herself from anybody. She wants the artist to flatter her, to make the white world believe that all Negroes are as smug and as near white in soul as she wants to be. But, to my mind, it is the duty of the younger Negro artist, if he accepts any duties at all from outsiders, to change through the force of his art that old whispering "I want to be white," hidden in the aspirations of his people, to "Why should I want to be white? I am a Negro—and beautiful"?

So I am ashamed for the black poet who says, "I want to be a poet, not a Negro poet," as though his own racial world were not as interesting as any other world. I am ashamed, too, for the colored artist who runs from the painting of Negro faces to the painting of sunsets after the manner of the academicians because he fears the strange un-whiteness of his own features. An artist must be free to choose what he does, certainly, but he must also never be afraid to do what he might choose.

Let the blare of Negro jazz bands and the bellowing voice of Bessie Smith② singing the Blues penetrate the closed ears of the colored near-intellectuals until they listen and perhaps understand. Let Paul Robeson singing Water Boy, and Rudolph Fisher③ writing about the streets of Harlem, and Jean Toomer holding the heart of Georgia in his hands, and Aaron Douglas④ drawing strange black fantasies cause the smug Negro middle class to turn from their white, respectable, ordinary books and papers to catch a glimmer of their own beauty. We younger Negro artists who create now intend to express our individual dark-skinned selves without fear or shame. If white people are pleased we are glad. If they are not, it doesn't matter. We know we are beautiful. And ugly too. The

① Winold Reiss (1888—1953) was a German-born American artist and graphic designer, whose portraits of African Americans were featured in Alain Locke's Harlem Renaissance anthology, *The New Negro*.

② Bessie Smith (1894—1937) was an American blues singer. Nicknamed the "Empress of the Blues", Smith was the most popular female blues singer of the 1920s and 1930s. She is often regarded as one of the greatest singers of her era and, along with Louis Armstrong, a major influence on other jazz vocalists.

③ Rudolph Fisher (1897—1934) was an African-American physician, radiologist, novelist, short story writer, dramatist, musician, and orator. Fisher was an active participant in the Harlem Renaissance, primarily as a novelist, but also as a musician.

④ Aaron Douglas (1899—1979) was an African-American painter and a major figure in the Harlem Renaissance.

tom-tom cries and the tom-tom laughs. If colored people are pleased we are glad. If they are not, their displeasure doesn't matter either. We build our temples for tomorrow, strong as we know how, and we stand on top of the mountain, free within ourselves.

## 7. William Carlos Williams

### Introduction to *The Wedge* (1944)

*In "Introduction to* The Wedge" *(1944), Williams grounds his poetics in opposition to a view held by critics at the time that poetry would likely become unnecessary once socialism has taken root. Williams sees this view as an extension of the notion that "arts are a resort from frustration." Williams asserts, "a poem is a small (or large) machine made of words." Emphasizing a poem's composition and movement rather than its content, he states, "There is no poetry of distinction without formal invention, for it is in the intimate form that works of art achieve their exact meaning, in which they most resemble the machine, to give language its highest dignity, its illumination in the environment to which it is native."*

The War is the first and only thing in the world today.

The arts generally are not, nor is this writing a diversion from that for relief, a turning away. It is the war or part of it, merely a different sector of the field.

Critics of rather better than average standing have said in recent years that after socialism has been achieved it's likely there will be no further use for poetry, that it will disappear. This comes from nothing else than a faulty definition of poetry—and the arts generally. I don't hear anyone say that mathematics is likely to be outmoded, to disappear shortly. Then why poetry?

It is an error attributable to the Freudian concept of the thing, that the arts are a resort from frustration, a misconception still entertained in many minds.

They speak as though action itself in all its phases were not compatible with frustration. All action the same. But Richard Coeur de Lion wrote at least one of the finest lyrics of his day. Take Don Juan for instance. Who isn't frustrated and does not prove it by his actions — if you want to say so? But through art the psychologically maimed may become the most distinguished man of his age. Take Freud for instance.

The making of poetry is no more an evidence of frustration than is the work of Henry Kaiser or Timoshenko. It's the war, the driving forward of desire to a complex end. And when that shall have been achieved, mathematics and the arts will turn elsewhere — beyond the atom if necessary for their reward and let's all be frustrated together.

A man isn't a block that remains stationary though the psychologists treat him so—and most take an insane pride in believing it. Consistency! He varies; Hamlet today, Caesar tomorrow; here, there, somewhere—if he is to retain his sanity, and why not?

The arts have a complex relation to society. The poet isn't a fixed phenomenon, no more is his work. That might be a note on current affairs, a diagnosis, a plan for procedure, a retrospect—all in its own peculiarly enduring form. There need be nothing limited or frustrated about that. It may be a throw-off from the most violent and successful action or run parallel to it, a saga. It may be the picking out of an essential detail for memory, something to be set aside for further study, a sort of shorthand of emotional significances for later reference.

Let the metaphysical take care of itself, the arts have nothing to do with it. They will concern themselves with it if they please, among other things. To make two bald statements: There's nothing sentimental about a machine, and: A poem is a small (or large) machine made of words. When I say there's nothing sentimental about a poem I mean that there can be no part, as in any other machine, that is redundant.

Prose may carry a load of ill-defined matters like a ship. But poetry is the machine which drives it, pruned to a perfect economy. As in all machines its movement is intrinsic, undulant, a physical more than a literary character. In a poem this movement is distinguished in each case by the character of the speech from which it arises.

Therefore, each speech having its own character, the poetry it engenders will be peculiar to that speech also in its own intrinsic form. The effect is beauty, what in a single object resolves our complex feelings of propriety. One doesn't seek beauty. All that an artist or a Sperry can do is to drive toward his purpose, in the nature of his materials; not to take gold where Babbitt metal is called for; to make: make clear the complexity of his perceptions in the medium given to him by inheritance, chance, accident or whatever it may be to work with according to his talents and the will that drives them. Don't talk about frustration fathering the arts. The bastardization of words is too widespread for that today.

My own interest in the arts has been extracurricular. Up from the gutter, so to speak. Of necessity. Each age and place to its own. But in the U.S. the necessity for recognizing this intrinsic character has been largely ignored by the various English Departments of the academies.

When a man makes a poem, makes it, mind you, he takes words as he finds them interrelated about him and composes them—without distortion which would mar their exact significances—into an intense expression of his perceptions and ardors that they may constitute a revelation in the speech that he uses. It isn't what he says that counts as a work of art, it's what he makes, with such intensity of perception that it lives with an intrinsic movement of its own to verify its authenticity. Your attention is called now and then to some beautiful line or sonnet-sequence because of what is said there. So be it. To me all sonnets say the same thing of no importance. What does it matter what the line "says"?

There is no poetry of distinction without formal invention, for it is in the intimate form that works of art achieve their exact meaning, in which they most resemble the machine, to give language its highest dignity, its illumination in the environment to which it is native. Such war, as the arts live and breathe by, is continuous.

It may be that my interests as expressed here are pre-art. If so I look for a development along these lines and will be satisfied with nothing else.

## 8. Charles Olson

### Projective Verse (1950)

*As Olson's most influential essay, "Projective Verse," was written and rewritten correspondence with Fances Bolderoff and Robert Creeley, and printed in* Poetry New York, *no. 3, 1950. The essay introduces his ideas of "composition by field" through projective or open verse. In brief, it reorients meter to the breathing of the poet in the act of composition and places sound before sense in the construction of the phrase. The projective poem took on a sprawling appearance on the page as it attempted to transpose (project) the flow and mingling of words in the poet's mind onto paper. Olson praised the typewriter as a tool for registering the process by which language formed in the imagination. In conclusion, Olson suggests a movement he calls "objectism," which he defines as "the getting rid of the lyrical interference of the individual as ego, of the "subject" and his soul [...] For man is himself an object."*

(projectile (percussive (prospective

*vs.*

The NON-Projective

*(or what a French critic*[①] *calls "closed" verse, that verse which print bred and which is pretty much what we have had, in English & American, and have still got, despite the work of Pound & Williams: it led Keats, already a hundred years ago, to see it (Wordsworth's, Milton's) in the light of "the Egotistical Sublime"; and it persists, at this latter day, as what you might call the private-*

① Identified by Ralph Maud as René Nelli, who asks "But is there a poetry open on the real and a poetry closed on the words?"

*soul-at-any-public-wall*)

Verse now, 1950, if it is to go ahead, if it is to be of *essential* use, must, I take it, catch up and put into itself certain laws and possibilities of the breath, of the breathing of the man who writes as well as of his listenings. (The revolution of the ear, 1910, the trochee's heave, asks it of the younger poets.)

I want to do two things: first, try to show what projective or OPEN verse is, what it involves, in its act of composition, how, in distinction from the non-projective, it is accomplished; and II, suggest a few ideas about what stance toward reality brings such verse into being, what the stance does, both to the poet and to his reader. (The stance involves, for example, a change beyond, and larger than, the technical, and may, the way things look, lead to a new poetics and to new concepts from which some sort of drama, say, or of epic, perhaps, may emerge.)

I

First, some simplicities that a man learns, if he works in OPEN, or what can also be called COMPOSITION BY FIELD, as opposed to inherited line, stanza, over-all form, what is the "old" base of the non-projective.

(1) the *kinetics* of the thing. A poem is energy transferred from where the poet got it (he will have some several causations), by way of the poem itself to, all the way over to, the reader. Okay. Then the poem itself must, at all points, be a high-energy construct and, at all points, an energy-discharge. So: how is the poet to accomplish same energy, how is he, what is the process by which a poet gets in, at all points energy at least the equivalent of the energy which propelled him in the first place, yet an energy which is peculiar to verse alone and which will be, obviously, also different from the energy which the reader, because he is the third term, will take away?

This is the problem which any poet who departs from closed form is specially confronted by. And it involves a whole series of new recognitions. From the moment he ventures into FIELD COMPOSITION—puts himself in the open—he can go by no track other than the one the poem under hand declares, for itself. Thus he has to behave, and be, instant by instant, aware of some several forces just now beginning to be examined. (It is much more, for example, this push, than simply such a one as Pound put, so wisely, to get us started: "the musical phrase," go by it, boys, rather than by, the metronome.)

(2) is the *principle*, the law which presides conspicuously over such composition, and, when obeyed, is the reason why a projective poem can come into being. It is this: FORM IS NEVER MORE THAN AN EXTENSION OF CONTENT. (Or so it got phrased by one, R. Creeley, and it makes absolute sense to me, with this possible corollary, that right form, in any given poem, is the only and exclusively possible extension of content under hand.) There it is, brothers, sitting there, for USE.

Now (3) the *process* of the thing, how the principle can be made so to shape the energies that the form is accomplished. And I think it can be boiled down to one statement (first pounded into my head by Edward Dahlberg): ONE PERCEPTION MUST IMMEDIATELY AND DIRECTLY LEAD TO A FURTHER PERCEPTION. It means exactly what it says, is a matter of, at *all* points (even, I should say, of our management of daily reality as of the daily work) get on with it, keep moving, keep in, speed, the nerves, their speed, the perceptions, theirs, the acts, the split second acts, the whole business, keep it moving as fast as you can, citizen. And if you also set up as a poet, USE USE USE the process at all points, in any given poem always, always one perception must must must MOVE, INSTANTER, ON ANOTHER!

So there we are, fast, there's the dogma. And its excuse, its usableness, in practice. Which gets us, it ought to get us, inside the machinery, now, 1950, of how projective verse is made.

If I hammer, if I recall in, and keep calling in, the breath, the breathing as distinguished from the hearing, it is for cause, it is to insist upon a part that breath plays in verse which has not (due, I think, to the smothering of the power of the line by too set a concept of foot) has not been sufficiently observed or practiced, but which has to be if verse is to advance to its proper force and place in the day, now, and ahead. I take it that PROJECTIVE VERSE teaches, is, this lesson, that that verse will only do in which a poet manages to register both the acquisitions of his ear *and* the pressure of his breath.

Let's start from the smallest particle of all, the syllable. It is the king and pin of versification, what rules and holds together the lines, the larger forms, of a poem. I would suggest that verse here and in England dropped this secret from the late Elizabethans to Ezra Pound, lost it, in the sweetness of meter and rime, in a honey-head. (The syllable is one way to distinguish the original success of blank verse, and its falling off, with Milton.)

It is by their syllables that words juxtapose in beauty, by these particles of sound as clearly as by the sense of the words which they compose. In any given instance, because there is a choice of words, the choice, if a man is in there, will be, spontaneously, the obedience of his ear to the syllables. The fineness, and the practice, lie here, at the minimum and source of speech.

O western wynd, when wilt thou blow①
And the small rain down shall rain
O Christ that my love were in my arms
And I in my bed again

It would do no harm, as an act of correction to both prose and verse as now written, if both rime and meter, and, in the quantity words, both sense and sound, were less in

① Anonymous poem from the sixteenth century.

the forefront of the mind than the syllable, if the syllable, that fine creature, were more allowed to lead the harmony on. With this warning, to those who would try: to step back here to this place of the elements and minims of language, is to engage speech where it is least careless—and least logical. Listening for the syllables must be so constant and so scrupulous, the exaction must be so complete, that the assurance of the ear is purchased at the highest—40 hours a day—price. For from the root out, from all over the place, the syllable comes, the figures of, the dance:

> "Is" comes from the Aryan root, *as*, to breathe. The English "not" equals the Sanscrit *na*, which may come from the root *na*, to be lost, to perish. "Be" is from *bhu*, to grow.

I say the syllable, king, and that it is spontaneous, this way: the ear, the ear which has collected, which has listened, the ear, which is so close to the mind that it is the mind's, that it has the mind's speed...

it is close, another way: the mind is brother to this sister and is, because it is so close, is the drying force, the incest, the sharpener...

it is from the union of the mind and the ear that the syllable is born.

But the syllable is only the first child of the incest of verse (always, that Egyptian thing, it produces twins!). The other child is the LINE. And together, these two, the syllable *and* the line, they make a poem, they make that thing, the—what shall we call it, the Boss of all, the "Single Intelligence." And the line comes (I swear it) from the breath, from the breathing of the man who writes, at the moment that he writes, and thus is, it is here that, the daily work, the WORK, gets in, for only he, the man who writes, can declare, at every moment, the line its metric and its ending— where its breathing, shall come to, termination.

The trouble with most work, to my taking, since the breaking away from traditional lines and stanzas, and from such wholes as, say, Chaucer's *Troilus* or S's *Lear*, is: contemporary workers go lazy RIGHT HERE WHERE THE LINE IS BORN.

Let me put it baldly. The two halves are:

the HEAD, by way of the EAR, to the SYLLABLE

the HEART, by way of the BREATH, to the LINE

And the joker? that it is in the 1st half of the proposition that, in composing, one lets-it-rip; and that it is in the 2nd half, surprise, it is the LINE that's the baby that gets, as the poem is getting made, the attention, the control, that it is right here, in the line, that the shaping takes place, each moment of the going.

I am dogmatic, that the head shows in the syllable. The dance of the intellect is there, among them, prose or verse. Consider the best minds you know in this here business: where does the head show, is it not, precise, here, in the swift currents of the syllable? Can't you tell a brain when you see what it does, just there? It is true, what the master says he picked up from Confusion: all the thots men are capable of can be entered on the back of a postage stamp. So, is it not the PLAY of a mind we are after, is not that that shows whether a mind is there at all?

And the threshing floor for the dance? Is it anything but the LINE? And when the line has, is, a deadness, is it not a heart which has gone lazy, is it not, suddenly, slow things, similes, say, adjectives, or such, that we are bored by?

For there is a whole flock of rhetorical devices which have now to be brought under a new bead, now that we sight within the line. Simile is only one bird who comes down, too easily. The descriptive functions generally have to be watched, every second, in projective verse, because of their easiness, and thus their drain on the energy which composition by field allows into a poem. *Any* slackness takes off attention, that crucial thing, from the job in hand, from the *push* of the line under hand at the moment, under the reader's eye, in his moment. Observation of any kind is, like argument in prose, properly previous to the act of the poem, and, if allowed in, must be so juxtaposed, apposed, set in, that it does not, for an instant, sap the going energy of the content toward its form.

It comes to this, this whole aspect of the newer problems. (We now enter, actually, the large area of the whole poem, into the FIELD, if you like, where all the syllables and all the lines must be managed in their relations to each other.) It is a matter, finally, of OBJECTS, what they are, what they are inside a poem, how they got there, and, once there, how they are to be used. This is something I want to get to in another way in Part II, but, for the moment, let me indicate this, that every element in an open poem (the syllable, the line, as well as the image, the sound, the sense) must be taken up as participants in the kinetic of the poem just as solidly as we are accustomed to take what we call the objects of reality; and that these elements are to be seen as creating the tensions of a poem just as totally as do those other objects create what we know as the world.

The objects which occur at every given moment of composition (of recognition, we can call it) are, can be, must be treated exactly as they do occur therein and not by any ideas or preconceptions from outside the poem, must be handled as a series of objects in field in such a way that a series of tensions (which they also are) are made to *hold*, and to hold exactly inside the content and the context of the poem which has forced itself, through the poet and them, into being.

Because breath allows *all* the speech-force of language back in (speech is the "solid" of verse, is the secret of a poem's energy), because, now, a poem has, by speech, solidity, everything in it can now be treated as solids, objects, things; and, though insisting upon the absolute difference of the reality of verse from that other dispersed and distributed thing, yet each of these elements of a poem can be allowed to have the play of their separate energies and can be allowed, once the poem is well composed, to keep, as those other objects do, their proper confusions.

Which brings us up, immediately, bang, against tenses, in fact against syntax, in fact against grammar generally, that is, as we have inherited it. Do not tenses, must they not also be kicked around anew, in order that time, that other governing absolute may be kept, as must the space-tensions of a poem, immediate, contemporary to the acting-on-you of the poem? I would argue that here, too, the LAW OF THE LINE, which projective verse creates, must be hewn to, obeyed, and that the conventions which logic has forced on syntax must be broken open as quietly as must the too set feet of the old line. But an analysis of how far a new poet can stretch the very conventions on which communication by language rests, is too big for these notes, which are meant, I hope it is obvious, merely to get things started.

Let me just throw in this. It is my impression that *all* parts of speech suddenly, in composition by field, are fresh for both sound and percussive use, spring up like unknown, unnamed vegetables in the patch, when you work it, come spring. Now take Hart Crane. What strikes me in him is the singleness of the push to the nominative, his push along that one arc of freshness, the attempt to get back to word as handle. (If logos is word as thought, what is word as noun, as, pass me that, as Newman Shea used to ask, at the galley table, put a jib on the blood, will ya.) But there is a loss in Crane of what Fenollosa is so right about, in syntax, the sentence as first act of nature, as lightning, as passage of force from subject to object, quick, in this case, from Hart to me, in every case, from me to you, the VERB, between two nouns. Does not Hart miss the advantages, by such an isolated push, miss the point of the whole front of syllable, line, field, and what happened to all language, and the poem, as a result?

I return you now to London, to beginnings, to the syllable, for the pleasures of it, to intermit;

If music be the food of love, play on,
give me excess of it, that, surfeiting,
the appetite may sicken, and so die.
That strain again. It had a dying fall,
o, it came over my ear like the sweet sound
that breathes upon a bank of violets,
stealing and giving odour. ①

What we have suffered from, is manuscript, press, the removal of verse from its producer and its reproducer, the voice, a removal by one, by two removes from its place of origin *and* its destination. For the breath has a double meaning which Latin had not yet lost②.

The irony is, from the machine has come one gain not yet sufficiently observed or used, but which leads directly on toward projective verse and its consequences. It is the advantage of the typewriter that, due to its rigidity and its space precisions, it can, for a

① Shakespeare's *Twelfth Night* 1. 1. 1-17.
② "Spiritus" —both breath and spirit.

poet, indicate exactly the breath, the pauses, the suspensions even of syllables, the juxtapositions even of parts of phrases, which he intends. For the first time the poet has the stave and the bar a musician has had. For the first time he can, without the convention of rime and meter, record the listening he has done to his own speech and by that one act indicate how he would want any reader, silently or otherwise, to voice his work.

It is time we picked the fruits of the experiments of Cummings, Pound, Williams, each of whom has, after his way, already used the machine as a scoring to his composing, as a script to its vocalization. It is now only a matter of the recognition of the conventions of composition by field for us to bring into being an open verse as formal as the closed, with all its traditional advantages.

If a contemporary poet leaves a space as long as the phrase before it, he means that space to be held, by the breath, an equal length of time. If he suspends a word or syllable at the end of a line (this was most Cummings' addition) he means that time to pass that it takes the eye—that hair of time suspended—to pick up the next line. If he wishes a pause so light it hardly separates the words, yet does not want a comma—which is an interruption of the meaning rather than the sounding of the line—follow him when he uses a symbol the typewriter has ready to hand:

What does not change / is the will to change①

Observe him, when he takes advantage of the machine's multiple margins, to juxtapose:

Sd he:
    to dream takes no effort
        to think is easy
            to act is more difficult
        but for a man to act after he has taken thought, this!
is the most difficult of all②

Each of these lines is a progressing of both the meaning and the breathing forward, and then a backing up, without a progress or any kind of movement outside the unit of time local to the idea.

There is more to be said in order that is convention be recognized, especially in order that the revolution out of which it came may be so forwarded that work will get published to offset the reaction now afoot to return verse to inherited forms of cadence and rime. But what I want to emphasize here, by this emphasis on the typewriter as the personal and instantaneous recorder of the poet's work, is the already projective nature of verse as the sons of Pound and Williams are practicing it. Already they are composing as though verse was to have the reading its writing involved, as though not the eye but

① Opening line of Olson's poem "The Kingfishers".

② From Olson's "The Praises".

the ear was to be its measurer, as though the intervals of its composition could be so carefully put down as to be precisely the intervals of its registration. For the ear, which once had the burden of memory to quicken it (rime & regular cadence were its aids and have merely lived on in print after the oral necessities were ended) can now again, that the poet has his means, be the threshold of projective verse.

II

Which gets us to what I promised, the degree to which the projective involves a stance toward reality outside a poem as well as a new stance towards the reality of a poem itself. It is a matter of content, the content of Homer or of Euripides or of Seami[①] as distinct from that which I might call the more "literary" masters. From the moment the projective purpose of the act of verse is recognized, the content does—it will—change. If the beginning and the end is breath, voice in its largest sense, then the material of verse shifts. It has to. It starts with the composer. The dimension of his line itself changes, not to speak of the change in his conceiving, of the matter he will turn to, of the scale in which he imagines that matter's use. I myself would pose the difference by a physical image. It is no accident that Pound and Williams both were involved variously in a movement which got called "objectivism." But that word was then used in some sort of a necessary quarrel, I take it, with "subjectivism." It is now too late to be bothered with the latter. It has excellently done itself to death, even though we are all caught in its dying. What seems to me a more valid formulation for present use is "objectism," a word to be taken to stand for the kind of relation of man to experience which a poet might state as the necessity of a line or a work to be as wood is, to be as clean as wood is as it issues from the hand of nature, to be as shaped as wood can be when a man has had his hand to it. Objectism is the getting ride of the lyrical interference of the individual as ego, of the "subject" and his soul, that peculiar presumption by which western man has interposed himself between what he is as a creature of nature (with certain instructions to carry out) and those other creations of nature which we may, with no derogation, call objects. For a man is himself an object, whatever he may take to be his advantages, the more likely to recognize himself as such the greater his advantages, particularly at that moment that he achieves an humilitas sufficient to make him of use.

It comes to this: the use of a man, by himself and thus by others, lies in how he conceives his relation to nature, that force to which he owes his somewhat small existence. If he sprawl, he shall find little to sing but himself, and shall sing, nature has such paradoxical ways, by way of artificial forms outside himself. But if he stays inside himself, if he is contained within his nature as he is participant in the larger force, he will be able to listen, and his hearing through himself will give him secrets objects share. And by an inverse law his shapes will make their own way. It is in this sense that the

① A Japanese writer of the late fourteenth and early fifteenth centuries, also known as Motekiyo.

projective act, which is the artist's act in the larger field of objects, leads to dimensions larger than the man. For a man's problem, the moment he takes speed up in all its fullness, is to give his work his seriousness, a seriousness sufficient to cause the thing he makes to try to take its place alongside the things of nature. This is not easy. Nature works from reverence, even in her destruction (species go down with a crash). But breath is man's special qualification as animal. Sound is a dimension he has extended. Language is one of his proudest acts. And when a poet rests in these as they are in himself (in his physiology, if you like, but the life in him, for all that) then he, if he chooses to speak from these roots, works in that area where nature has given him size, projective size.

It is projective size that the play, *The Trojan Women*①, possesses, for it is able to stand, is it not, as its people do, beside the Aegean—and neither Andromache or the sea suffer diminution. In a less "heroic" but equally "natural" dimension Seami causes the Fisherman and the Angel to stand clear in *Hagoromo*②. And Homer, who is such an unexamined cliché that I do not think I need to press home in what scale Nausicaa's girls wash their clothes.

Such works, I should argue—and I use them simply because their equivalents are yet to be done—could not issue from men who conceived verse without the full relevance of human voice, without reference to where lines come from, in the individual who writes. Nor do I think it accident at that, at this end point of the argument, I should use, for examples, two dramatists and an epic poet. For I would hazard the guess that, if projective verse is practiced long enough, is drive ahead hard enough along the course I think it dictates, verse again can carry much larger material than it has carried in our language since the Elizabethans. But it can't be jumped. We are only at hits beginnings, and if I think that the *Cantos* make more "dramatic" sense than do the plays of Mr. Eliot, it is not because I think they have solved the problem but because the methodology of the verse in them points a way by which, one day, the problem of larger content and of larger forms may be solved. Eliot is, in fact, a proof of a present danger, of "too easy" a going on the practice of verse as it has been, rather than as it must be, practiced. There is no question, for example, that Eliot's line, from "Prufrock"③ on down, has speech-force, is "dramatic," is, in fact, one of the most notable lines since Dryden. I suppose it stemmed immediately to him from Browning, as did so many of Pound's early things. In any case Eliot's line has obvious relations backward to the Elizabethans, especially to the soliloquy. Yet O. M. Eliot is *not* projective. It could even be argued

---

① *The Trojan Women* by Euripides.

② One of the Noh plays translated by Pound, whose introductory note declares, "The play shows the relation of the early Noh to the God-dance".

③ T. S. Eliot's poem "The Love Song of J. Alfred Prufrock."

(and I say this carefully, as I have said all things about the non-projective, having considered how each of us must save himself after his own fashion and how much, for that matter, each of us owes to the non-projective, and will continue to owe, as both go alongside each other) but it could be argued that it is because Eliot has stayed inside the non-projective that he fails as a dramatist — that his root is the mind alone, and a scholastic mind at that (no high *intelletto* despite his apparent clarities) — and that, in his listenings he has stayed there where the ear and the mind are, has only gone from his fine ear outward rather than, as I say a projective poet will, down through the workings of his own throat to that place where breath comes from, where breath has its beginnings, where drama, has to come from, where, the coincidence is, all acts spring.

## 9. Allen Ginsberg

### What Way I Write (1960)

*"What Way I Write" was first published in Writer's Digest in October, 1960. In this essay, Ginsberg talks about how to write a poem to the general public. A note added by the author to explain the writing of this essay helps to better understand this essay. It says, "Some intelligent editor of middlebrow digest, impressed by my transitory notoriety of late '50s, invited me to contribute a statement of 'How I Write.' I enjoyed the opportunity to explain the startling (?) freedom possible in really professional writing to this commercial trade journal. I had to talk down and explain myself from my high horse, and thus assumed a relative modesty and moderation in explanation to presumably junior high school teachers in a class of scriveners. Explaining to multitudes was the focus."*

Once, chancing to read Blake and dwelling on the word of "Ah! Sunflower," I heard his voice and looked out of the window, realizing that this universe was the sunflower seeking eternity. The experience led me to know art as a time-machine to carry the secret revelation and transmit it unbroken from mind to mind.

Cézanne speaks of his "petit sensation," a feeling he derived from the observation of nature, and at the end of his life refers to it in his letters as none other than "Pater Omnipotens Aeterna Deus." His art became an attempt to "reconstitute" on canvas an abstract (by means of planes, cubes, etc.) of the spacetime data fed to his senses by Mount St. Victoire.

Pound turned to the Chinese written character as a medium for poetry seeing that data can be juxtapoed (like planes, cubes, etc.) in clear word-pictures (visual images) on the page. Elliptical flashes of "sensation" in the reader's mind connect these polar images.

With this as the basic form of the poem, certain practical effects develop. There can be no interruption of the poem for mechanical measure, outside of the data presented. The images by their very nature are the design of the poem as in William Carlos Williams or the later American School of Haiku. The purest shape of the image on the page is the true measure.

This seems to work out in practice, since, when the natural-tongue words that compose these images are pronouced aloud, many curious rhythms are heard. These are rhythms heard in day-to-day speech, hitherto unnoticed. Practically speaking, classical systems of prosody are not workable in dealing with these natural rhythms.

It's premature to expect classification of sounds only recently noticed, but as they become familiar they will become subject to stereotype and classification perhaps.

Some methods of handling these rhythms consciously have become evident in the practice of various poets. Short lines in William Carlos Williams are balanced mainly by relative weight of phrasing — speechsize, special emphasis, weight as mental imagery, silences indicated, etc. in Olson the lines may be said to bear equal weight in that each is a unitary particle of energy in spontaneous composition. In Creeley, discrete short rhythmic entities are separated by breathstop to form new type couplets.

However, the mind is more than the tongue, as many writers have noticed recently. We are aware of events in other parts of the psyche besides that part which thinks in words. At certain times all diverse simultaneous impressions and events focus together to make a new, almost a mutant, consciousness.

It is necessary to resort to some very crude and rapid method of notation to sketch some fleeting sensory detail of this process of myriad sensations running thru the being.

I have adapted, for myself, the single breath-unit as the measure of how much material I can handle-notate-compose at one continuous stroke. I learned much from Kerouac.

The rhythm of this transcription becomes in this case the guiding rhythm of the poem when read aloud.

This means that I generally compose in long lines, depending on how falls my attempt to become conscious of my thought, look aside and notate it. I focus on the verbal transaction level, then my mind goes blank and I'm left only with words. So I must go on with the next thought. I do not know what I do. On what multitudes of levels do I operate? I get lost. I tell lies. I follow what comes in my mind next. Often short lines come in because I'm afraid I'll miss notating some particularly striking recurrent realization flashed thru the mind. The tricks of notation are many and varied. Just how do we think? And how can we watch ourselves think and notate? I'm not sure what happens; generally I pause at the beginning of a new line, having short circuited my visual processes by the constant stop to notate. Unless the impulse-rhythm of the last speeds me forward; then I may stop in midline to invent a continuation of what I had forgotten after I began writing it down— or move on with a dash. I get some very strangely unexpected verbal and imagual connections this way, illogical recognitions that I cry as they are poetry. In the course of this notation I finally get out beyond what I'd anticipated and discover what it is that's underlying my whole mind and soul at the moment—and find the course of that discovery now transcribed in the composition just finished. So that it is going to write, if the writing is to become anywhere near sublime. That's that.

## 10. Robert Lowell

### On"Skunk Hour" (1964)

*"On 'Skunk Hour'" was a response in a symposium to the criticisms on "Skunk Hour" written by three poet-critics (John Berryman, John Federick Nims and Richard Wilbur). In this essay, Lowell declares that "The author of a poem is not necessarily the ideal person to explain its meaning. He is as liable as anyone else to muddle, dishonesty, and reticence." Then, he explains how the poem was written and his response to the comments of the three critics. On the one hand, he admits that their criticisms are to the point; but on the other hand, he is unwilling to agree with them completely.*

#### I / The Meaning

The author of a poem is not necessarily the ideal person to explain its meaning. He is liable as anyone else to muddle, dishonest, and reticence. Nor is it his purpose to provide a peg for a prose essay. Meaning varies in importance from poem to poem, and from style to style, but always it is only a strand and an element in the brute flow of composition. Other elements are pictures that please or thrill for themselves, phrases that ring for their music or carry some buried suggestion. For all this the author is an opportunist, throwing whatever comes to hand into his feeling for start, continuity, contrast, climax, and completion. It is imbecile for him not to know his intentions, and unsophisticated for him to know too explicitly and fully.

Three papers by three poets [John Berryman[1], John Frederick Nims, Richard Wilbur] on another's poem! Perhaps they should be considered as short stories and variant on my original. I shall comment on them later; here, I only want to say that I learned much from them. Very little of what I had in mind is untouched on; much that never occurred to me has been granted me. What I didn't intend often seems now at least

① John Allyn Berryman (1914—1972) was an American poet and scholar, a key figure in the Confessional school of poetry. His best-known work is *The Dream Songs*.

as valid as what I did. My complaint is not that I am misunderstood but that I am overunderstood. I am seen through.

I am not sure whether I can distinguish between intention and interpretation. I think this is what I more or less intended. The first four stanzas are meant to give a dawdling more or less amiable picture of a declining Maine sea town. I move from the ocean inland. Sterility howls through the scenery, but I try to give a tone of tolerance, humor, and randomness to the sad prospect. The composition drifts, its direction sinks out of sight into the casual, chancy arrangements of nature and decay. Then all comes alive in stanzas V and VI. This is the dark night. I hoped my readers would remember John of the Cross's poem. My night is not gracious, but secular, puritan, and agnostic. An existentialist night. Somewhere in my mind was a passage from Satre or Camus about reaching some point of final darkness where the one free act is suicide. Out of this comes the march and affirmation, an ambiguous one, of my skunks in the last two stanzas. The skunks are both quixotic and barbarously absurd, hence the tone of amusement and defiance. "Skunk Hour" is not entirely independent, but the anchor poem in its sequence.

## II / How the Poem Was Written

What I can describe and what no one else can describe are the circumstances of my poem's composition. I shan't reveal private secrets. John Berryman's pathological chart comes frighteningly close to the actual event. When I first read his paper, I kept saying to myself, "Why, he is naming the very things I wanted to keep out of my poem." In the end, I had to admit that Berryman had hit a bull's-eye, and often illuminated matters more searchingly and boldly than I could have wished. Is his account true? I cannot decide, the truth here depends on what psychologists and philosophers one accepts. Berryman comes too close for comfort.

"Skunk Hour" was begun in mid-August 1957 and finished about a month later. In March of the same year, I had been giving reading on the West Coast, often reading six days a week and sometimes twice on a single day. I was in San Francisco, the era and setting of Allen Ginsberg and all about, very modest poets were waking up prophets[1]. I became sorely aware of how few poems I had written, and that these few had been finished at the latest three or four years earlier. Their style seemed distant, symbol-ridden, and wilfully difficult. I began to paraphrase my Latin quotations, and to add extra syllables to a line to make it clearer and more colloquial. I felt my old poems hid what they were really about, and many times offered a stiff, humourless, and even

[1] This experience in San Francisco greatly influenced Lowell; he began to reflect on his own poems, and developed a new style.

impenetrable surface. I am not convert to the "beats." I know well, that the best poems are not necessarily poems that read aloud. Many of the greatest poems can only be read to one's self, for inspiration is no substitute for humor, shock, narrative, and a hypnotic voice, the four musts for oral performance. Still, my own poems seemed like prehistoric monsters dragged down into the bog and death by their ponderous armor. I was reciting that I no longer felt. What influenced me more than San Francisco and reading aloud was that for some time I had been writing prose. I felt that the best style for poetry was none of the many poetic styles in English, but something like the prose of Chekhov and Flaubert.

When I returned to my home, I began writing lines in a new style. No poem, however, got finished and soon I left off and tried to forget the whole headache. Suddenly, in August, I was struck by the sadness of writing nothing, and having nothing to write, of having, at least, no language. When I began writing"Skunk Hour," I felt that most of what I knew about writing was a hindrance.

The dedication is to Elizabeth Bishop, because rereading her suggested a way of breaking through the shell of my old manner. Her rhythms, idiom, images, and stanza structure seems to belong to a later century. "Skunk Hour" is modeled on Miss Bishop's "The Armadillo," a much better poem and one I had heard her read and had later carried around with me. Both "Skunk Hour" and Bishop's "The Armadillo" use short line stanzas, start with drifting description, and end with a single animal.

This was the main source. My others were Hölderlin's "*Brod und Wein*," particularly the moon lines:

*Sieh! Und das Schattenbild unserer Erde, der Mond,*
*kommet geheim unu auch; die Schwärmerische, die Macht kommt*
"*vou*" *mit Sternen und* "*wohl*" *wenig bekümmert um uns,*

and so forth. I put this in long straggling lines and then added touches of Maine scenery, till I saw I was getting nowhere. Another source, probably undetectable now, was Annette von Droste-Hülshoff's "Amletzten Tage des Jahres."She, too, uses a sic-line stanza with short lines. Her second stanza is as follows:

*'s ist tiefe Nacht!*
*Ob wohl ein Auge offen noch?*
*In diesen Mauern rüttelt dein*
*Verrinnen, Zeit! Mir schaudert; doch*
*Es will die letzte Stunde sein*
*Einsam durchwacht.*

*Gesehen all...*

Here and elsewhere, my poem and the German poem have the same shudders and situation.

"Skunk Hour" was written backward, first the last two stanzas, I think, and then the next-to-last two. Anyway, there was a time when I had the last four stanzas much as they now are and nothing before them. I found the bleak personal violence repellent. All was too close, though watching the lovers was not mine, but from an anecdote about Walt Whitman in his old age. I began to feel that real poetry came, not from fierce confessions, but from something almost meaningless but imagined. I was haunted by an image of a blue china doorknob, I never used the doorknob, or knew what it meant, yet somehow it started the current of images in my opening stanzas. They were written in reverse order, and at last gave my poem an earth to stand on, and space to breather.

## III / The Critics

I don't think I intended either the Spartan boy holding the fox or Satan's feeling of sexual deprivation while he watched Adam and Eve in the Garden. I may have, but I don't remember. The red fox stain was merely meant to describe the rusty reddish color of autumn on Blue Hill, a Maine mountain near where we were living. I had seen foxes playing on the road one night, and I think the words have sinister and askew suggestion.

I can't imagine anything more thorough than Nim's stanza-by-stanza exposition. Almost all of it is to the point. I get a feeling of going on a familiar journey, but with another author and another sensibility. This feeling is still stronger when I read Wilbur's essay. Sometimes he and I are named as belonging to the same school, what *Time* magazine calls "the couth poets." Sometimes we are set in battle against one another. I have no idea which, if either, is true. Certainly, we both in different way owe much to the teaching and practice of John Crowe Ransom. Certainly, his essay embodies and enhances my poem. With Berryman, too, I go on a strange journey! Thank God, we both come out clinging to spars, enough floating matter to save us, though faithless.

# 11. Gary Snyder

## Unnatural Writing (1992)

*"Unnatural Writing" is Gary Snyder's most clear statement on ecopoetics. The original version of this essay was given as a keynote lecture at the opening of the first "Art of the Wild" Squaw Valley Nature Writing Conference in July 1992. In this essay, he rejects the term "nature writing" and replaces it with a concept he himself calls "unnatural writing". In the end of the essay, he puts forward the definition of "new*

*nature poetics". These nine points summarize much of the major poetic statements Snyder made from the mid-1960s to the mid-*1990*s*.

"Nature writing" has become a matter of increased literary interest in the last few years. The subject matter "nature," and the concern for it (and us humans in it), have come-it is gratifying to note-to engage artists and writers. This interest may be another strand of postmodernism, since the modernist avant-garde was strikingly urban-centered. Many would-be writers approach this territory in a mode of curiosity, respect, and concern, without necessarily seeking personal gain or literary reputation. They are doing it for love—and the eco-warrior's passion, not money. (There is still a wide range of views and notions about what nature writing ought to be. There is an older sort of nature writing that might be seen as largely essays and writing from a human perspective, middle-class, middlebrow Euro-American. It has a rhetoric of beauty, harmony, and sublimity. What makes us uncomfortable sometimes with John Muir's writing is an excess of this. He had contemporaries, now forgotten, who were far worse.)

Natural history writing is another branch. Semiscientific, objective, in the descriptive mode. Both these sorts are "naively realistic" in that they unquestioningly accept the front-mounted bifocal human eye, the poor human sense of smell, and other characteristics of our species, plus the assumption that the mind can, without much self-examination, directly and objectively "know" whatever it looks at. There has also always been a literature of heroic journals and adventure. And there is an old mix of science, nature appreciation, and conservation politics that has been a potent part of the evolution of the conservation movement in the United States. The best of this would be seen in the work of Rachel Carson and Aldo Leopold. All of these writings might be seen by some as mildly anthropocentric, but the work is worthy and good-hearted. We are in its debt.

Nature writing has been a class of literature held in less than full regard by the literary establishment, because it is focused on something other than the major subject matter of mainstream occidental writing, the moral quandaries, heroics, affairs of the heart, and soul searchings of highly gifted and often powerful people, usually male. Tales of the elites. In fact, up until a decade ago nature writing was relegated pretty much to a status like that of nineteenth-century women's writing — it was seen as a writing of sensibility and empathy and observation, but off to the side, not really serious, not important.

But if we look at the larger context of occidental history, educated elites, and literary culture, we see that the natural world is profoundly present in and an inescapable part of the great works of art. The human experience over the larger part of its history has been played out in intimate relationship to the natural world. This is too obvious even to say, yet it is often oddly forgotten. History, philosophy, and literature naturally foreground human affairs, social dynamics, dilemmas of faith, intellectual constructs. But a critical subtheme that runs through it all has to do with defining the human relationship to the rest of nature. In literature, nature not only provides the background, the scene, but also many of the characters. The "classical" world of myth is a world in which animal beings, supernatural figures, and humans are actors and interacters. Bears, bulls, and swans were not abstractions to the people of earlier times but real creatures in very real landscapes. The aurochs—the giant wild cow, *Bos primigenius*, who became Zeus to Europa—survived in pockets of the European forests until medieval times.

In *The Practice of the Wild* (San Francisco: North Point Press, 1990), I point out that through most of human history

> *populations were relatively small and travel took place on foot, by horse, or by sail. Whether Greece, Germania, or Han China, there were always nearby areas of forest, and wild animals, migratory waterfowl, seas full of fish and whales, and these were part of the experience of every active person. Animals as characters in literature and as universal presences in the imagination and in the archetypes of religion are there because they were there. Ideas and images of wastelands, tempests, wildernesses, and mountains are born not of abstraction but of experience: cisalpine, hyperboreal, circumpolar, transpacific, or beyond the pale. [This is the world people lived in up until the late nineteenth century. Plentiful wildlife, open space, small human population, trails instead of roads—and human lives of individual responsibility and existential intensity. It is not "frontier" that we're considering, but the Holocene era, our present era, in all its glory of salmon, bear, elk, deer, and moose.] Where do the sacred salmon of the Celts, the Bjorns and Brauns and Brun-(hilde)-s [bher = bear] of northern European literature, the dolphins of the Mediterranean, the Bear dances of Artemis, the Lion skin of Herakles come from but the wild systems the humans lived near?*
>
> *Those images that yet*
> *Fresh images beget*
> *That dolphin-torn, that gong-tormented sea.*

Many figures in the literary field, the critical establishment, and the academy are not enthralled with the natural world, and indeed some positively doubt its worth when compared to human achievement. Take this quote from Howard Nemerov, a good poet and a decent man:

> *Civilization, mirrored in language, is the garden where relations grow; outside the garden is the wild abyss.*

The unexamined assumptions here are fascinating. They are, at worst, crystallizations of the erroneous views that enable the developed world to displace Third and Fourth World peoples and overexploit nature globally. Nemerov here proposes that language is somehow implicitly civilized or civilizing, that civilization is orderly, that intrahuman relations are the pinnacle of experience (as though all of us, and all life on the planet, were not interrelated), and that "wild" means "abyssal," disorderly, and chaotic.

First take language. Some theorists have latched onto "language" as that which somehow makes us different. They have the same enthusiasm for the "Logos" as the old Summer Institute of Linguistics had for Bible translation into unwritten languages. In fact, every recent writer who doesn't know what else to say about his or her work—when asked to give a sound bite—has declared, "Well, I'm just fascinated with language." The truth is language is part and parcel of consciousness, and we know virtually nothing about either one. Our study and respect should extend to them both.

On another tack, the European deconstructionists assume, because of their monotheistic background, that the Logos died along with God. Those who wish to decenter occidental metaphysics have begun to try to devalue both language and nature and declare them to be further tools of ruling-class mythology. In the past, the idea that the external world was our own invention came out of some variety of idealist thought. But *this* version leads to a totally weird philosophical position that, since the proponents are academic "meta-Marxists," might be called "materialist solipsism." But they are just talk.

There is some truly dangerous language in a term heard in some business and government circles: "sustainable development." Development is not compatible with sustainability and biodiversity. We must drop talking about development and concentrate on how to achieve a steady state condition of real sustainability. Much of what passes for economic development is simply the further extension of the destabilizing, entropic, and disorderly functions of industrial civilization.

So I will argue that consciousness, mind, imagination, and language are fundamentally wild. "Wild" as in wild ecosystems — richly interconnected, interdependent, and incredibly complex. Diverse, ancient, and full of information. At root the real question is how we understand the concepts of order, freedom, and chaos. Is art an imposition of order on chaotic nature, or is art (also read "language") a matter of discovering the grain of things, of uncovering the measured chaos that structures the natural world? Observation, reflection, and practice show artistic process to be the latter.

Our school-in-the-mountains here at Squaw Valley is called "art of the wild." (I was wondering just what edible root might have been growing so profusely in this wet mountain bottomland to have caused it to be called "Squaw Valley." Any place with the word *squaw* in the name is usually where some early trappers saw numerous Native American women at work gathering wild food; here it might have been *Brodiaea* bulbs.

This naming practice is as though some native women coming on a Euro-American farming community had called it White Boy Flats.)

The"art of the wild" is to see art in the context of the process of nature—nature as process rather than as product or commodity—because "wild" is a name for the way that phenomena continually actualize themselves. Seeing this also serves to acknowledge the autonomy and integrity of the nonhuman part of the world, an "Other" that we are barely beginning to be able to know. In disclosing, discovering, the wild world with our kind of writing, we may find ourselves breaking into unfamiliar territories that do not seem anything like what was called "nature writing" in the past. The work of the art of the wild can well be irreverent, inharmonious, ugly, frazzled, unpredictable, simple, and clear-or virtually inaccessible. Who will write of the odd barbed, hooked, bent, splayed, and crooked penises of nonhuman male creatures? Of sexism among spiders? Someone will yet come to write with the eye of an insect, write from the undersea world, and in other ways that step outside the human.

In *Practice* it says:

*Life in the wild is not just eating berries in the sunlight. I like to imagine a "depth ecology" that would go to the dark side of nature — the ball of crunched bones in a scat, the feathers in the snow, the tales of insatiable appetite. Wild systems are in one elevated sense above criticism, but they can also be seen as irrational, moldy, cruel, parasitic. Jim Dodge told me how he had watched — with fascinated horror — orcas methodically batter a gray whale to death in the Chukchi Sea. Life is not just diurnal and a property of large interesting vertebrates, it is also nocturnal, anaerobic, cannibalistic, microscopic, digestive, fermentative: cooking away in the warm dark. Life is well maintained at a four mile ocean depth, is waiting and sustained on a frozen rock wall, and clinging and nourished in hundred-degree desert temperatures. And there is a world of nature on the decay side, a world of beings who do rot and decay in the shade. Human beings have made much of purity, and are repelled by blood, pollution, putrefaction. The other side of the "sacred" is the sight of your beloved in the underworld, dripping with maggots. Coyote, Orpheus, and Izanagi cannot help but look, and they lose her. Shame, grief, embarrassment, and fear are the anaerobic fuels of the dark imagination. The less familiar energies of the wild world, and their analogs in the imagination, have given us ecologies of the imagination. ...*

*Narratives are one sort of trace that we leave in the world. All our literatures are leavings, of the same order as the myths of wilderness peoples who leave behind only stories and a few stone tools. Other orders of beings have their own literatures. Narrative in the deer world is a track of scents that is passed on from deer to deer, with an art of interpretation which is instinctive. A literature of bloodstains, a bit of piss, a whiff of estrus, a hit of rut, a scrape on a sapling, and long gone. And there might be a "narrative theory" among these other beings—they might ruminate on "intersexuality," or "decomposition criticism."*

I propose this to turn us loose to think about "wild writing" without preconception or inhibition, but at the same time with craft. The craft could be seen as the swoop of a hawk, the intricate galleries of burrowing and tunneling under the bark done by western pine bark bettles, the lurking at the bottom by a big old trout—or the kamikaze sting of a yellow jacket, the insouciant waddle of a porcupine, the constant steadiness of a flow of water over a boulder, the chatter of a squirrel, hyenas moaning and excavating the bowels of a dead giraffe under a serene moon. Images of our art. Nature's writing has the potential of becoming the most vital, radical, fluid, transgressive, pansexual, subductive, and morally challenging kind of writing on the scene. In becoming so, it may serve to help halt one of the most terrible things of our time—the destruction of species and their habitats, the elimination of some living beings forever.

Finally, let us not get drawn too far into dichotomous views and arguments about civilization versus nature, the domesticated versus the wild, the garden versus the wild abyss. Creativity draws on wildness, and wildness confers freedom, which is (at bottom) the ability to live in the real physical daily world at each moment, totally and completely.

## SOME POINTS FOR A "NEW NATURE POETICS"

- That it be literature—that is, nature literate. Know who's who and what's what in the ecosystem, even if this aspect is barely visible in the writing.
- That it be grounded in a place—thus, place literate: informed about local specifics on both ecological-biotic and sociopolitical levels. And informed about history (social history and environmental history), even if this is not obvious in the poem.
- That is use Coyote as a totem—the Trickster, always open, shape shifting, providing the eye of other beings going in and out of death, laughing with the dark side.
- That is use Bear as a totem — omnivorous, fearless, without anxiety, steady, generous, contemplative, and relentlessly protective of the wild.
- That it find further totems — this is the world of nature, myth, archetype, and ecosystem that we must each investigate. "Depth ecology."
- That it fear not science. Go beyond nature literacy into the emergent new territories in science: landscape ecology, conservation biology, charming chaos, complicated

systems theory.

- That it go further with science — into awareness of the problematic and contingent aspects of so-called objectivity.
- That it study mind and language — language as wild system, mind as wild habitat, world as a "making" (poem), poem as a creature of the wild mind.
- That it be crafty and get the work *done*.

## 12. Charles Bernstein

### Introjective Verse (1999)[①]

*Charles Bernstein is closely related to language poetry, a literary trend of avant-garde poetry in the United States. Language poetry offers an extreme poetical experimentation characteristic of postmodern poetry. Important language poets include Susan Howe, Ron Silliman, Lyn Hejinian, Hannah Weiner, Michael Palmer, Bob Perelman, Barrett Watten, Bruce Andrews, and many others, while Bernstein is a leading theorist and poet of this trend. Bernstein's poetics best illustrate the philosophy of language poetry. His "Introjective Verse" is an anti-projective manifesto that parodies Charles Olson's programmatic article "Projective Verse."*

)introversive )implosive )introspeculative

*incorporating*

The Rejected

Verse, what? if it is to trip and flail and fall , if it is to be *inessential*, useless, maybe could consider, losing it, forgetting laws and breadth: the breathlessness of the person who refuses to be a man when she listens.

I won't do two things: first, I won't show what introjective or CENTRIPETAL verse is, how it recoils, in its fate as decomposition, how, in distinction to the projective, it is dismayed, and 2, I'll hold back from suggesting a few contradictions about how the ebullient denial of reality takes such a verse out of believing, what that aversion does, both to the poet and her nonreaders. (Such aversion involves, for example, a return to the technical, and may, the way things hokey-poke around, lead away from drama and

① From *My Way: Speeches and Poems*, 1999.

epic and toward the materials of poems, their sounds and shapes.)

I

First, some complexities that a person learns, if she works INTROJECTIVELY, or what can be called MISCOMPOSITION BY EAR.

(1) the *pataphysics* of the thing. A poem is energy absconded by the poet from where she got it (she will have several stashes), by way of the nonreaders themselves, all the way over to, the poem. Oy!

This is the problem which any poet who departs from adenoidal forms is specially coddled by. And it involves a whole series of blunders. From the moment she jumps back into CENTRIPETAL MISCOMPOSITION—puts herself in the bin—she can aver by no tack other than the one the poem refuses.

(It is much more, for example, this backward somersaulting, than simply such a one as Wilde put, so giddily, to get us startled: life imitates art, not the other way round. Come on, girls & boys, think complex, act to redistribute the wealth!)

(2) is the *abandonment of principle*, the ludicrousness that presides so conspicuously over such dysraphisms, and, when averred, is the reason why an introjective poem refuses belief. It is this: FORM IS NEVER MORE THAN AN EXTENSION OF MALCONTENT. There it went, flapping, more USELESSNESS.

Now (3) the clumsiness of the thing, how the awkwardness of the thing can be made to dishevel the energies that the form thought it accomplished. It can never be boiled down to a statement: ONE PERCEPTION MUST NEVER LEAD DIRECTLY TO ANOTHER PERCEPTION. It means something very different than what it says, is never a matter of, at *no* points, (even—I shouldn't say—of our injuring reality as our weekly bliss) get off it, invoke arrestation, keep out of it, slow down, the perceptions, ours, the evasions, the long-term evasions, none of it, stop it as much as you can, citizen. And if you also slouch as a poet, REFUSE REFUSE REFUSE the process at some points, in some poems, once in a blue while: one perception STOPPED, SLOWED, BY ANOTHER!

So there we were, looping, where there's no dogma. And its inexcusableness, its uselessness, in theory. Which doesn't get us, ought not to get us, outside the cyberfactory, then, or 1995, where centripetal verse is made.

If I sing tunelessly—if I forget, and keep crying wolf, out of breath—of the sound as distinguished from the voice, it is for no cause except to loosen the part that breath plays in verse, which has been observed and practiced too well, so that verse may retreat to its proper immobility and placelessness in the mouths that are already lost. I take it that INTROJECTIVE VERSE teaches nothing, that that verse will never do what the poet intends either by the tones of her voice or theater of her breath...

Because the centripetal questions the speech-force of language (speech is the "red herring" of verse, the secret of the poem's delusions), because, then, a poem has, by language, evanescence, nothing that can he mistreated as solid, objectified, thinged.

## II

Which makes no promises, no realities outside the poem; no stances only dances. It is the matter of content, this discontent. The content of Clease, of Bruce, of Ball, as distinct from what I might call more "literary" ministers. There is no moment in which the introjective evasion of verse is finished , the form fuels blame. If the beginning and end is the breathlessness of words, sound in that material sense, then the domain of poetry blurs and blurts.

It's hardly this: the uselessness of a baby, by itself and thus by others, crying in its misconception of its relation to culture, that semiotic fluidlessness to which it owes its gigantic existence. If it squall, it shall find much to squall about, and shall squirm too, culture has such flummoxing ways of terrorizing all that is outside. But if it stays inside itself, if it is contained in its infancy as if it is a participant in the life immediately surrounding, it will be able to babble and in its babbling hear what is shared. It is in this sense that the introjective ache, which is the artist's artlessness in the intimate streets of enfoldment, leads to scales more intimate than the child's. It's all so easy. Culture works from irreverence, even in its constructions. Irreverence is the human's special qualification as vegetable, as mineral, as *animalady*. Language is our profanest act. And when a poet squalls about what is outside herself (in "the material world", if you object, but also the materiality in her, for that matter), then she, if she chooses to reflect on this restlessness, pays in the street where culture has given her scale, centripetal scale.

Such works, though it's no argument, could not issue from persons who conceive verse without the full resonance of human voicelessness. The introjective poet staggers from the failings of her own boasts to that syntaxophony where language digs in, where sound echoes, where utterances concatenate, where, inevitably, all acts stall.